Praise for
The Journal of Mortifying Moments

"Harding is a skillful writer who is able to transcend and even
exploit cliché. . . . *The Journal of Mortifying Moments* is
light fiction executed by a writer who knows her craft."
—*The Boston Globe*

"Brilliantly conceived . . . This is a laugh-out-loud
funny book . . . a big, big winner."
—*The Kingston Observer*

"What's truly original is the central character—a wonderfully
and fully developed thirty-one-year-old woman who deliberately
writes a journal of her life to discover how she might improve the
present. . . . Just go and get a copy as soon as you can."
—*Statesman Journal*

The JOURNAL of Mortifying Moments

A NOVEL

Robyn Harding

BALLANTINE BOOKS • NEW YORK

2005 Ballantine Books Trade Paperback Edition

Copyright © 2004 by Robyn Harding
Excerpt from *The Secret Desires of a Soccer Mom*
copyright © 2005 by Robyn Harding

Published in the United States by Ballantine Books, an imprint
of The Random House Publishing Group, a division of
Random House, Inc., New York.

BALLANTINE and colophon are registered trademarks of Random House, Inc.

Originally published in hardcover in the United States by Ballantine Books,
an imprint of The Random House Publishing Group, a division
of Random House, Inc., in 2004.

This book contains an excerpt from the forthcoming hardcover edition of
The Secret Desires of a Soccer Mom. This excerpt has been set for this edition
only and may not reflect the final content of the forthcoming edition.

ISBN 0-345-47627-1

Printed in the United States of America

www.ballantinebooks.com

2   4   6   8   9   7   5   3   1

Text design by Susan Turner

For my kids

ACKNOWLEDGMENTS

First off, I must thank my wonderful agent Joe Veltre of Carlisle & Company for plucking my query letter from a sea of online submissions and making all this happen. His support, guidance, and encouragement have been invaluable. Also thank you to his assistant Pilar Queen for her help and advice when I came to New York. To Linda Marrow, Charlotte Herscher, and Arielle Zibrak, my editorial team at Ballantine Books: Thank you for your enthusiasm, expertise, and guidance, and for being so nice to work with. Your input made the book better without sacrificing any of the funny parts . . . okay, maybe one funny part.

Thank you to Justin Young (M.W.), whose friendship inspired the character of Trevor; to Pam Dueck for letting me share our ski hill misadventures from high school; to Jenn Ramsey for making me believe I could do it. To all my friends and family: Thank you for laughing at my jokes all these years and making me feel like I was funny enough to write a book like this. And to John, for doing your best to keep the kids out of my office when I was trying to write, and for always believing in me.

The Journal of Mortifying Moments

Mortifying Moment #1

We were in a secluded thicket of trees, the ground a carpet of bright yellow leaves. There were six of us, all twelve years old, except James, who was eleven. He was in our grade, though; he came from Scotland, where kids started school a year earlier.

"So . . . ," Lisa, the unelected ringleader began. She was the prettiest—blond and petite—also the meanest. Not like she was mean all the time, but she was capable of great meanness, which made her powerful in the teenybopper community. This gathering was her idea: She was brave enough to phone the boys and invite them; she made up the story of a neighborhood game of kick-the-can to tell our parents. "Who wants to go first?"

No one volunteered; we all looked at each other, giggling shyly. I looked at James specifically. His cheeks were glowing red, and if I had been brave enough to reach out and touch them, they would have been hot. I'd often thought about touching his face. Sitting across the aisle and slightly behind him at school had given me ample opportunity to study his smooth, pale, Celtic skin and the childish down that still covered his jawline. James didn't return my look. He was staring at the ground ahead of him.

"Okay," said Lisa, taking charge. "Heather can go first."

"No!" Heather gasped, covering her face. But I could tell she was secretly pleased—I would have been pleased if I'd been picked.

"Truth or dare?" Lisa asked wickedly.

"Hmmmm . . . ," Heather said, as if she were really contemplating her choice. "Dare."

"I dare you—" Lisa looked around the circle, pausing for dramatic effect. She would have made a great game-show host. "—to kiss Sean for five minutes!"

Everyone squealed. . . . Well, the boys didn't really squeal; they laughed and threw leaves at Sean, who was almost as red as James.

"You have to do it!" Lisa called over us. "If you chicken out, you have to tell the truth about something really embarrassing!"

Finally, after putting on an adequate show of reluctance, Heather and Sean got up and went behind a saskatoon berry bush—the kissing bush. We talked nervously among ourselves until Lisa called out, "Okay! Five minutes is up!"

They reappeared, none too quickly, smiling self-consciously. Every-one clapped, and Heather curtsied. She looked over at Sean. He smiled at her, and I was filled with envy for the special bond they now shared after five minutes of kissing behind a bush.

"Okay, so one of you gets to pick next," Lisa said.

"I'll go," Sean volunteered. "James."

James's head snapped up; his eyes filled with panic. He looked unbe-lievably sweet and cute and scared. "Truth or dare?" Sean continued.

"Ummm—" His eyes darted nervously around the circle. "—ummm . . . dare, I guess," he said in his adorable accent.

"Okay." Sean smiled. "I dare you to kiss—" He looked at each of us girls. Heather leaned over and whispered in his ear. My heart leapt! My stomach flipped! Heather knew that I was secretly in love with James! I had told her, on many occasions, that I thought he was really cute and nice and his accent was totally ace!

She would tell Sean to dare James to kiss me! We would go behind the kissing bush, and when we emerged, we would exchange special looks that only those who have touched tongues can share! I played with the yellow leaves, trying to act nonchalant—though I was freaking out inside.

"I dare you to kiss . . . Kerry."

I jumped a little with surprise (very convincingly) and then covered my face—the obligatory shocked and dismayed response. Everyone woo-wooed, and I laughed, embarrassed. It took me a few moments to realize that James was sitting stock-still, completely silent.

"Go on, then," Sean urged.

James looked at me, his eyes wide and filled with terror. He blinked and swallowed loudly.

Awww . . . he was so nervous! And so cute! I tried to make him feel more comfortable by looking at him with an expression of understanding. "It's okay," my look said. "I'm nervous, too, but it will be fun. We have to do it sometime. . . ."

This look was a challenge as I was simultaneously trying to convey to the rest of the group that I wasn't actually that keen on kissing James. It seemed to be confusing him. He blinked and swallowed some more, then said a long, drawn out, "Ummmm . . . ummmm."

"*Get going, you guys,*" Lisa said, a hint of impatience in her voice. I started to rise, still smiling encouragingly at James while trying to look indifferent to everyone else. I was on one knee when he said, "*I pick truth.*"

I froze in my awkward position and then pretended to be stretching out a kink in my hamstring. "*Ooooh,*" I said, massaging the back of my thigh. "*Kink in my hamstring.*"

"*Really? You want truth?*" Sean said, laughing incredulously.

"*Yes, please,*" James replied. His accent actually sounded a bit snotty and annoying.

"*You asked for it!*" Sean said, and called the other boys over for a conference. They laughed cruelly, then dispersed. "*Okay . . . ,*" Sean continued. "*You have to tell the truth, James.*"

"*Yes.*" Blink. Swallow.

"*How many times a day do you—*" Pause for dramatic effect in manner of a game-show host or Lisa. "*—touch your willy?*"

Everyone squealed—boys included. James's face turned various shades of red: pink, then scarlet, then fuchsia.

"*Okay!*" Lisa called, calming everyone down. "*There's your choice James. Kiss Kerry or tell us how many times a day you touch your willy.*"

Gee Lisa, thanks for laying it out like that, just in case anyone couldn't figure it out on their own. That was the mean side of her I mentioned.

James looked at me and seemed to be on the verge of tears. God. I didn't really want him to kiss me if it was that painful for him. But it was obviously a better choice than telling everyone—

"*Thirteen,*" James said.

Chapter 1

IT WAS MY THERAPIST'S IDEA—THE JOURNAL OF MORTIFYING MOMENTS. Of course, she called it "a diary of past encounters with men that may be contributing to your current negative and dysfunctional quasi-relationship." Go back as far as you can remember, she encouraged me; the more painful and humiliating, the better. Easy for her to say. My therapist is this strong, independent, rather intimidating woman who has probably never even had a bad relationship, let alone kept a diary of all of them! The fact that she is large and masculine with an unflattering "helmet" hairstyle may also help keep her man troubles to a minimum.

But it is worth a try. Since my boyfriend, Sam, suggested we take a break to "explore our feelings as individuals," my self-esteem has been in the toilet. Of course, "exploring our feelings as individuals" does not preclude us having casual sex whenever Sam wants it. And since he is so ridiculously good-looking and successful and sexy, and I am, well . . . not, I can't seem to say no. Probably because I realize that I will never find anyone even remotely as wonderful as he is and will end up a morbidly obese, housebound spinster or, alternatively, married to some puny dweeb with back acne and nervous tics. My therapist says we need to get to the bottom of all these negative, self-defeating feelings. So, if writing down every devastating encounter I've had with the male species in painstaking detail will help me do that, then I'm game.

With a heavy sigh, I snap the small lilac notebook closed and bury it in the bottom of my desk drawer. I place a couple of outdated magazines and a stapler on top of it, just in case there is an office snoop.

I know it was supposed to be therapeutic, but I feel rather drained now. I could really use a glass of wine, but since it is only 8:45 AM, I'll have to settle for a chai latte. I sift through my wallet and find four dollars, just enough for a latte and a gingersnap at Starbucks. I am just swiveling in my chair to leave my tiny office when Sonja appears in the doorway. I gasp involuntarily at her pale, ice-queen presence.

"Where are you off to?" she says pointedly, indicating the purse slung over my shoulder. "You just got here!"

"Ummm . . . ," I stammer, blushing like she's just caught me reading porn in the office. "I—uh—I'm just off to the bathroom." I tap my purse. "That time of the month, you know."

She gapes at me, apparently repulsed by the thought. "Too much information, Kerry," she says, holding up her hand lest I go on. "Don't forget we've got a nine o'clock." She leaves.

"Nope! I won't forget!" I call after her. "I'll just take care of . . . you know . . . *things*." I tap my purse again. "And meet you in the boardroom!"

As I stride through the spare and modern lobby of Ferris & Shannon Advertising, I mentally berate myself. Why do I let her get to me like that? Sonja has this uncanny ability to make me feel awkward and embarrassed about the smallest, most inconsequential things—for example, having my period. I mean, I'm not even having my period! Not that there's anything wrong with having it—it's the most normal, natural thing in the world. Why does Sonja make me feel like having my period is some embarrassing secret? I mean, we all have it! Except probably Sonja—I would imagine she is too thin to menstruate.

No time for my chai latte now. I must go change my imaginary tampon and get to the boardroom.

I am scheduled to present a communications plan for our client Prism Communications, the second-largest Internet service provider in the country and one of the largest companies in Seattle. It's an internal presentation only, which is actually more nerve-racking than presenting to the client. Sonja is very, very difficult to please.

As I approach the boardroom, I become aware of a buzz of conversation emanating from within. I walk inside to see thirty people gathered around an enormous slab-concrete table. Okay, not really thirty, but ten—which is five times the number I was expecting. Sonja reads the surprise and chagrin on my face.

"Kerry, I've invited the team in to hear your communications plan and provide feedback. This is an important campaign, and it is essential that we have internal consensus."

"Okay," I say as cheerfully as I can muster. "I'll just run and make seven more copies."

I return and distribute the document around the table. In attendance are

✔ Dave, creative director—an obnoxious, arrogant A-hole
   so devoid of humanity that many of us suspect he is a
   serial killer

✔ Tanya, art director—a goth chick, sleeping with Dave,
   so therefore, also an obnoxious, arrogant A-hole

✔ Dennis, production manager—short nerd who will
   emphatically support whatever Dave says because
   (*a*) he is afraid of being murdered by him, or (*b*) he is
   just a major butt-smooch

✔ Terry, media director—dog-loving spinster—or possibly lesbian, given short, spiky haircut

✔ Louise, media planner—chubby, permed, cat-loving spinster—probably not lesbian, given Richard Gere collage on office wall

✔ Fiona, account planner—a small, nervous Chihuahua of a woman who's extremely passionate about her job, although none of us really understand what she does

✔ Claire, online manager—sweet and soft-spoken, completely wrong for this business

✔ Maya, manager of direct marketing—tall stylish brunette who is nice but very keen on her job; given my attitude, this precludes our being friends

✔ Gavin, account executive—a skinny wiener who is basically Sonja's foster child and will soon be promoted to take over my job even though he is only nine

✔ And Sonja, the queen of Norway

"All right, everyone," Sonja begins, tucking her immaculate blond bob behind one ear. "Kerry is going to take us through her initial attempt at a communications plan. Feel free to jump in with any comments or criticisms that come to mind."

"Thanks," I say, and then begin to address my document. "Given that back-to-school is a very busy time for new Internet sign-ups—"

"The market is totally cluttered at that time of year," interjects Louise, the media planner/Richard Gere fan. "The creative will have to be breakthrough if we want to have any impact."

"Why don't you let the creative team worry about that?" Dave mutters.

"Dave, I don't think that attitude is really conducive to getting the most out of this meeting," account planner Fiona says nervously. "We need to take a team approach if we're going to move Prism into the number-one position. Now, my research bears out the fact that students twelve to eighteen crave a high-speed connection. Their parents, however, often feel that a dial-up connection is sufficient."

"That's a joke!" says Gavin, who is practically in the twelve- to eighteen-demographic.

Sonja laughs and smiles at him adoringly. "Isn't it?"

"Anyway . . . ," I continue. "Given that September is traditionally the strongest month for sales, I felt we should launch our media plan in late August—"

"August?" Terry, the lesbian media director croaks. (She is a heavy smoker.) "No one watches TV in August!"

"Well, TV isn't actually in the plan. We didn't really have the budget."

"*What!*" Dave explodes. "If they're not going to do TV, they may as well close their fucking doors!"

"There are media that are just as effective on the younger demographic!" Fiona screams back. "My research shows that transit shelters and cinema advertising resonate with young people!"

"Perhaps an online component?" Claire asks hopefully, but no one listens.

"You can shove your research!" Dave says to Fiona. "I've been in this business for fifteen years, and I know that clients who don't put their money where their mouth is don't survive."

"That's it!" Fiona stands up. Her hands are shaking as she gathers her papers into a neat leather folder. "Obviously my input isn't appreciated here." She storms out.

The meeting progresses in this antagonistic manner for seventeen hours until the receptionist knocks on the door and says that the room is booked for a client presentation. As I pack up my belongings, I realize that I have read exactly three sentences of my communications plan. Sonja follows me to my office.

"Thanks, Kerry," she says. "Now if you'll just address the issues brought up today and integrate the suggestions from media and DM, I'd like the finished plan on my desk by nine tomorrow." She smiles tightly.

I feel like crying. I lost interest in all the bickering and conflicting opinions shortly after Fiona left, and sat thinking about where I'm going to go for drinks with the girls this weekend. I have no idea what the issues or suggestions were! I hate my job.

An hour later my best work-friend, Trevor, appears in my office. "Are we going for sushi?"

"I can't," I say dejectedly. "Sonja needs this revised plan by tomorrow morning, and I don't even know what I'm doing."

"I'll help you over lunch," Trevor offers, and I stifle a guffaw. Trevor is an account manager, too, but it is the general opinion of the agency that he charmed his way into the position. He is tall and stylish, with the chiseled jaw, slender physique, and lazy gait of a male model. His dark hair falls sexily into his stunning blue eyes, their beauty undiminished by small, wire-rim glasses that I am convinced have nothing to do with correcting his vision and are worn only to give the impression that he has actually read enough to damage his eyesight. As we all know, anyone that gorgeous has to be gay, and Trevor is. And as if his appearance weren't enough, he also has an uncanny ability to enchant people into thinking he knows exactly what he's talking about when he is actually completely clueless! He uses a lot of catchphrases and buzzwords like, "This campaign really pushes the envelope," or "We're totally shifting the paradigm."

"Thanks," I say as sincerely as possible. "But I'd better just grab a sandwich and keep working."

"But I really need to talk to you about this fucking Rory situation," he pleads.

Fucking Rory is the guy Trevor has been dating for three weeks. Last week (or was it the week before?) Trevor was concerned that they were getting too serious too fast. "It sounds crazy," he said. "But somehow we just know that this is it . . . that we're meant to be together. Am I crazy?"

"A bit," I said.

"Why am I even asking you?" he snapped, annoyed. "Like *you're* one to judge relationships."

The tables have turned this week, and fucking Rory is thinking that he should give his ex, Ken, another chance. "I really need to talk Kerr Bear," Trevor whines. "Pleeeeze? I'll treat?"

I sigh. "Okay." My already tight office walls seem to be closing in on me, and I feel the possibility of a claustrophobic fit coming on. Besides, there's not much I can do about this plan anyway until I can accost someone who was paying attention in the meeting and get them to tell me what was said—without, of course, letting on that I was daydreaming through the whole thing.

At the restaurant, we sit cross-legged on dingy satin cushions while our shoes perch on the ledge beside us. Given this position, I am thankful that I didn't wear a skirt today—not that Trevor would notice anyway. We each order the "B Box." Then Trevor closes the sliding rice-paper screen for privacy before launching into the details.

"He says he loves me and he knows I'm the one, but he needs closure on the Ken thing before he can move on. He thinks that if he doesn't give his relationship with Ken another chance—with one hundred percent effort—he'll never be able to feel positive about moving on with me."

"That's bullshit," I say, sipping my green tea. "If he knows you're the one, why does he need to go back to Ken unless he thinks there's a chance that *he's* the one?"

"I know!" Trevor says, banging his hand on the table and sloshing our tiny cups of tea. "That's what I said! Fucking Rory. He's got to go."

"I'm afraid so," I agree.

"I can really pick 'em," Trevor says morosely.

"I hear ya, sister."

"So what's going on with gorgeous Sam, then?"

Ugh. Sam. At the mention of his name, I feel the familiar churning of my stomach, the involuntary reddening of my face. It does not help that Trevor insists on referring to Sam as "gorgeous Sam" as if the fact may have escaped me. Not to mention that, in contrast, he calls me just plain Kerry—I mean, not like he calls me "just plain Kerry," but he might as well. Anyway, I refuse to fall apart at the mere mention of Sam like some pathetic lovesick loser! I can be cool. I can be calm. I can be "I don't really care that much about him anyway so, like, whatever . . ."

I shrug, feigning indifference. "We're having dinner on Thursday, I think."

"And where do you guys stand on the moving back in together issue?" Trevor asks.

"On the fence." I blush a deeper hue despite my cool facade. The fact is . . . since I moved out of Sam's apartment last spring, we haven't even discussed moving back in together. But I have sort of led everyone to believe that it is inevitable.

I clear my throat nervously. "Can I have some of your wasabi?" He passes me the green paste. "Thanks," I mutter, sighing heavily as I dab the end of my chopstick in my tiny dish of soy sauce. "I'm just so stressed about this communications plan." I am, of course, but I am mostly trying to change the subject away from Sam. "I mean, I don't even remember what went on in the meeting, and I supposedly chaired it."

"I'm going to help you," Trevor says magnanimously. "I'll ask Gavin for you."

"That's a great idea!" Gavin is guaranteed to have paid attention and to know every syllable that was uttered and by whom, as he is some kind of advertising wunderkind.

"Besides," Trevor says. "I think Gavin might be gay—or at least not completely decided either way. I might be able to persuade him to join our team," he says suggestively.

"Ewww. Why would you want to? He's a gross little wiener."

"He's cute. He's just very slight."

"Slight? He's the same size as my cousin Mandy's daughter. She's six."

"Well, not everyone can be built like you, Kerry! What do you call that build again—'big-boned'?"

"Oh, fuck off."

Chapter 2

LATER THAT NIGHT, I AM SITTING AT THE TINY PINE KITCHEN TABLE I RE-cently purchased from IKEA, trying to transpose the notes I took from Trevor's debriefing. I tap away at the office laptop, attempting to turn this gibberish into some sort of comprehensive document. Apparently, Gavin was very forthcoming with Trevor. Maybe he *is* gay?

It was nice of Trevor to gather this information for me, but now I am left trying to decipher all his catchy advertising phrases and turn them into plain English. As a matter of principle, I never use catchy advertising phrases. If they turned up in my document, Sonja would know at once that I hadn't been paying attention in the meeting and had sent Trevor to get all the details and report back to me. Okay . . .

Move the needle. = Increase sales.

Think outside the box. = Be creative.

Take it offline. = Discuss further at a later date.

I get up and take three steps until I am at the counter in my galley kitchen. My apartment is bright, sunny, and about the size of the average refrigerator. Since I moved out of Sam's place, I could afford only a tiny suite on my pathetic advertising wage. Thankfully, I didn't have to resort to living in one of Seattle's distant suburbs and enduring a two-hour commute every day. I found this one-bedroom apartment in a heritage building settled steeply on Queen Anne Hill. Several years ago, the Historical Preservation Society or some such group rallied to keep developers from demolishing it and replacing it with trendy new condos. Of course, I appreciate their efforts, but there are times when I think that a structure built in the 1880s isn't entirely appropriate for modern life.

For example, there are two electrical outlets in the kitchen, but they cannot be used simultaneously without blowing a fuse and plunging the entire east side of the building into darkness. This means that you cannot pop popcorn and microwave butter at the same time. The same applies for making toast and coffee. I guess residents of such old buildings are not meant to own a lot of kitchen appliances. Unfortunately, I amassed a ridiculous number of them when I lived in Sam's spacious high-rise.

With a sigh, I reach for a bottle of wine that is wedged between the toaster and microwave, careful not to knock over the food processor or coffeemaker. I pour myself another glass of Shiraz. I prefer to work at home where there are no distractions and there is wine.

Okay, focus. So then Dave said, "They can lick my crack if they think I'm going to do some corny back-to-school campaign with apples and pencils—" Oh, phone is ringing.

"Hello?"

"Hi, babe."

Sam! I feel giddy, relieved—he is phoning me; he still loves me! At the same time, I feel nauseated and tense—he's drawing me back in and will eventually stomp my heart into a bloody pancake.

I force a casual tone. "How's it going?"

"Good. Good. What are you up to?"

"Working, actually. I've got to have a communications plan for Prism on Sonja's desk by nine."

"Well, don't kill yourself," he laughs. "You know it'll never be *up to her standards.*" Without having met her, he manages a very accurate impersonation of Sonja. It is so nice how he mocks my boss to make me feel better.

"True," I say. "What are you doing?"

"Well . . . Ed and the guys want me to go out for a beer. . . ."

My stomach drops. In the span of three milliseconds, I have visualized Sam at the bar: a beautiful blonde approaches, she joins him for a drink, they flirt and giggle, then leave to have the best sex of their lives. "What a toned body you have," he says, admiring her nakedness. "My last girlfriend was rather—"

"But . . . ," he says, interrupting my disturbing fantasy. "I was kind of hoping to see you tonight?"

"Really?"

"Yeah. I've been thinking about you all day . . . about us. But if you're working—"

"Give me an hour!"

The communications plan is slapped together at best, but obviously this is far more important. Sam has been thinking about me all day! About us! With ten minutes to spare, I have applied makeup and changed into a black push-up bra and matching thong. Unfortunately, since our relationship fell apart, I have sought comfort in cream-cheese icing, wine, and endless hours of TV. As I stare in the full-length mirror, I can't help but notice that my butt is bearing a disturbing resemblance to my grandmother's. (I had the unfortunate opportunity of viewing hers this summer when my mom and I took her swimming at the community pool.) This is not at all a good sign. It took my grandmother eighty-three years to develop that ass: I am well on my way at thirty-one.

I finish dressing and return to my laptop (purposely left open to give the impression that I have been working the entire time and not rushing around putting on makeup and sexy underwear). The intercom rings, and I pause before answering, not to seem too anxious. I buzz Sam in and then give myself the once-over. I'm wearing casual yet flattering jeans, a red V-neck sweater, and quite a bit of makeup (but in very subtle colors, not to be too obvious). My hair looks a little too "done," so I muss it up for a devil-may-care look. That's better. He won't think I've gone to any extra effort for him—until he discovers the lacy, black underthings. I mean *if* he discovers them. He may just want to talk about our future.

When he knocks on my door, I wait six seconds (one Mississippi . . .) before answering it. This is probably overkill, as I could run around the apartment thirty-five times in six seconds, but it is meant to convey the message, "Oh! You're here already? I was so immersed in my work that I actually forgot you were coming!"

"Hey," I say, opening the door.

"Hey," he says as he enters, kissing me quickly on the lips. He is wearing faded jeans and a black sweater with a rugged, outdoorsy, fleece jacket over top. Sam is tall and muscular, with ridiculously thick, soft, wavy dark hair, smoldering gray eyes, and dimples a la Jeff Bridges. He is far, far too good-looking for me.

And this is the problem. Even though we've been seeing each other off and on for two and a half years, I still melt at the very sight of him! Despite the fact that I lived with him for a year and witnessed him plucking his nose hairs and turning the bathroom into a toxic fume zone, it seems to have had no ill effects. I still turn into a fluttering schoolgirl in his presence! Apparently, I am so shallow and superficial that I will put up with all sorts of shabby treatment from a guy if he is gorgeous enough. Sam is definitely gorgeous enough *and* he drives a Mercedes . . . hence, the therapy.

"How did you make out?" He points to the open laptop on the kitchen table.

I wave my hand dismissively. "It's crap."

"I'm sure it's good," he says.

"No. I can't seem to get into work these days." I give him a meaningful look to let him know I've been preoccupied with thoughts about the tenuous state of our relationship, but he doesn't seem to notice. "How's work for you?"

"Busy," he says. "Big project coming up in SoDo." Sam is an executive with Kazzerkoff Developments, Seattle's largest property development firm. "He's done very well for himself," my mother incessantly points out. (He is also far too successful for me.)

"Cool. Do you want a beer?" I ask. I keep beer in the fridge just for him.

"Sure." He follows me into the kitchen.

"So," I say, squeezing into the fridge. (The door cannot open all the way because of my water cooler.) "What were you thinking about today?" I pass him a beer.

"Thanks." He takes it and twists off the cap. "Sorry?"

"Umm, you said you were thinking about me today. . . . About us . . ." I refill my wineglass. This will be my third, or is it fourth? I'm feeling a bit tipsy. "So . . . I was wondering, you know, what you were thinking?"

He takes a long pull of his beer and then looks at me intently. "I *was* thinking about you today," he says in his deep husky voice. "I was thinking about how sexy you are . . . and how hot you make me. . . ."

Oh, no. Not this again! He doesn't want to talk about our relationship. He is only here for a roll in the hay. Well, not this time, buddy. I want to talk, and until we do, there will be no hanky-panky!

But then he is behind me, his hands running up and down my body, his lips on my neck. The proximity of him makes my knees go weak—actually more than just my knees, my resolve, too. Weak, weak, weak, that's what I am. He steers me to the kitchen table and lays me down on it. All my work papers flutter to the floor; the laptop is somewhere under my left thigh. Yes, very, very weak.

Later, we are cuddling on the couch, watching *Law & Order.*

"I knew the son did it," Sam says, clapping his hand onto my leg. "I'd better hit the road. I've got an early start tomorrow."

"Okay," I say wanly. I want him to stay, but I have my dignity . . . at least a little dignity. Besides, we're having dinner on Thursday.

"Oh, and about dinner on Thursday . . . I'm going to have to pass. We've got clients in from out of town."

"Sure," I respond. "I'll see you later, then?"

"Later." He kisses me and is gone.

Isn't that just fucking typical of fucking, bloody bastard Sam!

When will I learn? This is how he treated me the whole time we were living together—and now? More of the same bloody crap! I shuffle to my bedroom to change into my flannel pajamas. This stupid thong is practically cutting me in two lengthwise. I know—I'll make a bowl of cream-cheese icing. May as well add a few more lumps to this ass since I am unlovable anyway.

The next morning I am late for work. I seem to have a sugar hangover from the bowl of icing and couldn't get moving until I'd had three Tylenol and two cups of coffee. As soon as I reach my desk, I boot up the laptop. I will print the communications plan and put it on Sonja's desk. I hope she's tied up in a meeting or giving Gavin a foot massage or something. If she's there, I'll say, "Sorry I'm a bit late, but an old lady was hit by a car at Westlake and Olive. I felt I had to stop to help." Make that a blind old lady.

File. Open. Prismcommplan.doc. What the—? Close. Try this again. File. Open. Prismcommplan.doc. *What?* It's blank! The whole document is blank. And then it comes to me—the laptop somewhere under my left thigh. That vaguely annoying pressure on my left butt cheek appears to have been the backspace key. Shit, shit, shit!

This is all Sam's fault! Actually, it's my fault for being such a slut every time I get around Sam! This is bad—very, very bad. Before, my relationship with Sam was damaging only to my self-esteem and self-worth. But now, it could ruin my career. I'm cracking up. I'm truly cracking up. I need some help—this is an emergency! I pick up the phone to call my therapist.

"Oh, there you are," Sonja says behind me.

I drop the receiver, and it clatters loudly against the phone. "Oh, hi!" I jump. "Sorry I'm late, but there was a blind dead woman at Westlake. . . ."

"Mmm-hmm," she murmurs. "Have you got the Prism plan done?"

I swallow loudly. "There's a problem."

"What kind of problem?" Her eyes are like a rattlesnake's before it strikes and kills you.

"Well . . . ," I begin. "It's a funny story, actually. I had sex on the kitchen table with my ex-boyfriend, who keeps stringing me along, and apparently, the laptop was under us and my left butt-cheek was pressing the backspace key the whole time!"

Of course I don't say that—although, a joke about doing a half-assed job springs to mind. "There's something wrong with the laptop," I say instead.

"What do you mean?" Her rattlesnake eyes narrow as she asks.

"My document . . . It's blank." I look at her with my saddest, most emotionally devastated expression. How could this happen, my face says, how?

"I'll call IT and get them to look into it," she says coolly. "In the meantime, I suggest you start working on another document on your PC. I'll buy us some time with the client. You have until tomorrow morning."

"Okay." I gulp.

"Kerry . . ." Shit! I thought she was gone. She comes into my office and sits in the chair across from me. "Is everything . . . all right?"

The rattlesnake expression is gone, and now she looks like . . . like . . . Julie Andrews in *The Sound of Music*. Oh, she is a clever chameleon!

"Of course!" I say with a loud, joyful laugh. "Why?"

"You just seem . . . a little out of sorts lately. A little . . . tense."

I smile brightly. "Nope. Fine."

"Well, I just want you to know that if you ever feel like you're having trouble coping . . . or you need to talk to someone . . . a professional . . . the company has a great mental health plan."

She seems so bloody sincere that for a moment, I consider confessing my biweekly therapist visits. There's no shame in it, really. But then I get a mental picture of Gavin smirking at me in every meeting and thinking, She's crazy, nuts, bound to fall apart at any moment, and then her wonderful job will be mine! Allllll miiiiiiiiiiiine!

"Thanks, Sonja," I say. "I'll keep that in mind in case I ever need it in the future."

"Great," she says, instantly cold-blooded and reptilian again.

Mortifying Moment #2

I was lying semiconscious in the dentist's "recovery" area. The room used to be a coat closet, but with the addition of a cot and some cheerful pictures of kittens and flowers, it was now perfect for convalescence. "My bofren ith coming to get me," I mumbled through the cotton packing my jaw. "My boyfren ith thooo nithe. I freally, freally love him. . . ."

"Yes. I'm sure you do, hon," the pretty dental assistant said, squeezing my hand patronizingly. I found out later that this kind of babbling is very normal when one is coming out from under anesthesia.

"We've had thum tough timeth," I continue, on and on and on. "But thingth are tho good now. I freally love him . . . an' he freally loveth me, too."

Sam showed up sometime into my speech about how, like an enormous elastic band, our relationship had stretched to the breaking point, only to snap back, bringing us closer together than ever. Our bond was so special that it was almost like we had known each other in a past life.

"Hi, chipmunk," he said, smiling kindly into my swollen face. "Did everything go okay?"

I started to cry. This, too, is apparently very normal when coming out from under anesthesia.

"It went fine—Sam, is it?" The dental assistant had sprung to life. "She's going to be a little sore and swollen for a while, but the wisdom teeth came out smoothly. If you have any questions about her condition . . . or whatever . . . feel free to call." She handed him a card.

"Thanks," Sam said. "I'll take good care of her."

I'm tho lucky.

AS WE DROVE HOME, I BEGAN TO FEEL CLOSE TO NORMAL AGAIN. I STOPPED sniveling and babbling and sat vacantly watching the scenery go by, still a bit dopey from the painkillers.

Sam helped me out of the car and escorted me into our high-rise apartment building, holding my arm as we went up the elevator like I was his elderly grandmother. "Here we are," he said when we were inside. He deposited me on the couch and covered me with a flannel blanket.

"Do I look like Marlon Brando?" I mumbled.

"A bit." He leaned down and kissed my forehead. "Do you want some tea?"

"Not right now. You don't haff to go to work, do you?"

"No."

"Thankth. Thit here with me."

He did, stroking my hair absently as he stared out the plate glass window at the fifteenth-story view of the city and Mount Rainier in the distance. The sky was gray and dark; it was starting to rain. I began to doze off, comforted by his presence, the warmth of his hand on my hair. It was like when I was sick as a little girl and my mom would feed me ginger ale and stroke my hair. My eyes flickered open to give him a smile of gratitude. He was staring at me, a strange look on his face.

I fought my way through the drug-induced fog. "What?" I asked.

"Nothing. Go back to sleep."

"What'th wrong?"

Sam sighed heavily, very heavily. "Kerry . . ." He sat up, turning his body away from me. "There's something I've been meaning to tell you, and well . . . it's probably not the best time but . . . I can't keep this to myself any longer."

"What ith it?" All sorts of horrifying thoughts were flooding my brain: He's got cancer, a brain tumor, only two months to live, HIV or syphilis—and he's afraid he's passed it on to me!

"It's just not working anymore."

"What!" I screeched, wads of bloody cotton flying out of my mouth.

"I'm moving out."

This was worse than a brain tumor or syphilis! "When?"

"Tonight."

"Why!"

"I'm sorry, hon," he began. "It's not you; it's me. Well, actually it is you, in a way. I need to be concentrating on my career right now, and I can't be with someone so . . ."

"So what?"

"Needy."

"Needy!"

"I can't be stuck in your idea of domestic bliss, Kerry. I need to be able to put in the time and effort required for me to succeed at Kazzerkoff." [Blah blah blahblahblah blahblahblah.] "Look, if you want me to stay the night because of your teeth . . ."

"What is this really about, Sam?"

"I told you. I need to focus on work. . . ."

"You're lying," I said. My voice sounded surprisingly cool and detached, masking my inner turmoil. "There's someone else, isn't there?"

"No! This is about us, not someone else."

"Who is she?" I said quietly. There was a long silence. "Who is she?"

"Her name's Jasmine. She's a consultant we've been working with on the Collingwood development. But this isn't about her. We haven't even slept together—"

"Get out, you bastard!" I shrieked, on the verge of hysteria—actually, well past the verge. "I hope you and Jasmine and your fucking career will be very happy together!"

The next morning, when he came back to collect his stuff, I was contrite. I wasn't ready to throw away the years we'd spent together over some consultant he hadn't even slept with. Surely by discussing the issues, we could work things out.

"I'm sorry," I said. "I think it was the medication making me act so psycho. Let's talk about this."

"There's really nothing to talk about, Kerry."

"But . . . things were going so well, Sam. We were like an elastic band, stretched to the breaking point but then snapping back together. We can work this out."

"I don't think so, Kerry."

"You can spend more time at work, Sam. I don't need to spend every weekend with you. You don't have to come home for dinner . . . ever. I want this to work. We can make it work!" I was aware that I was begging but was powerless to stop. The fact that I looked like Winston Churchill did nothing to help my self-esteem.

"Sorry, Kerr . . . I just need some time. Maybe . . . with a little dis-

tance and perspective [blah blahblahblah blah.]" He began to place his belongings in boxes.

"Stop," I said quietly.

"Kerry, it's no use."

"You stay here," I said. My voice was cold and emotionless. "I'll leave."

Chapter 3

THAT LAST ENTRY WAS MY THERAPIST'S IDEA. (I MANAGED TO SQUEEZE IN an emergency session after rewriting the communications plan from memory.) After I confessed my weakness on the kitchen table the other night, she instructed me to jump ahead several mortifying moments and deal with this Sam issue head-on.

"I want you to move forward in your diary and write about Sam," she said in her calming monotone.

"Okay," I mumbled. Despite my intense chagrin, I couldn't help but take in her appearance as she sat rigidly in her leather-upholstered chair. Her outfit, a gray-blue pantsuit, was so . . . I don't know . . . cheap looking. I mean, where did she shop? Kmart? Surely with the money she made off me and the other crazies, she could buy some current and stylish clothes?

"Find a comfortable seat," she continued. "Have a glass of wine. Burn a soothing candle, and write about the most painful moment you experienced in your relationship with him."

"Do I have to?" I snuffled.

"Yes," she commanded. "Perhaps then, when you see the words staring back at you in black-and-white, you'll be able to gain some clarity on your relationship."

I had followed her advice to the letter. With a glass of wine before me and a vanilla-scented candle burning at my side, I'd poured my angst onto the page.

So now here they are: the words staring back at me in black-and-white. Unfortunately, a crystal vase burgeoning with a dozen red roses is also staring back at me from the coffee table. The tiny card is just visible through the thick foliage: *Sorry about cancelling dinner. Thinking of you. Sam.* The bottom corner also features an adorable little teddy bear clutching a large red heart.

How am I supposed to get clarity on the situation when I am faced with two such opposing forces—the horrific entry in my journal and these beautiful, velvety red roses that say Sam really wishes we could have had dinner last Thursday and is currently thinking of me? And wouldn't the teddy bear clutching the heart on the card indicate that he still loves me? You'd hardly choose a teddy-bear-clutching-a-heart card for a coworker or great aunt or someone, would you? Unless Sam didn't choose the card at all . . . Come to think of it, he could have phoned in that order and had nothing to do with selecting the teddy-bear-clutching-a-heart card. Or worse—he could have gotten his secretary to place the order!

With that, I jump up and carry the heavy vase to the kitchen. I shove the bouquet into a back corner on the counter, teddy-bear-with-heart card facing the wall. Returning to the living room, I pick up the journal. Maybe now I will be able to gain some clarity on this relationship? Maybe this entry will make me see that I deserve better, that Sam is just using me and no matter how hard I try, no matter what I do, I have always been second in his life and always will be.

Yes! Yes, I do see it. Who cheats on his live-in girlfriend with someone named *Jasmine*? I mean, what is she—a stripper or a Disney character? And what kind of guy breaks up with someone right after she's had her wisdom teeth out? The same type of guy who would show up at your apartment, make love to you on the laptop housing your communications plan, and then leave without so much as a "See you for dinner on Thursday."

I was gone only a month when he called and asked if we could talk. Things hadn't worked out with Jasmine, he really missed me, and he felt he could probably squeeze me into his busy work schedule.

"I don't know . . . ," I said, enjoying my new position of power. "I don't think our living together is such a good idea."

"Oh, I don't think we should live together either," Sam pronounced. "But I thought maybe we could see each other casually? You know . . . while we explore our feelings as individuals?"

I know what I should have said—what I should *still* say. I should move on and find someone who puts me first, someone who is true and loving and kind. But Sam has some kind of power over me! When I hear his voice, or worse—see him—I'm done for. I had suggested my therapist employ hypnotherapy to make Sam look like . . . I don't know . . . Keith Richards or Danny DeVito or someone. That would make things much easier. But my therapist says that hypnosis can't actually do that. I think she might be wrong. I've been meaning to do some research on the Web.

So instead, we've come up with another plan: avoidance. I will not talk to or see Sam until I feel strong enough to cut all ties. Although common courtesy would dictate that I call and thank him for the roses, I am going to resist my natural civility. I am going to go down to the Verizon store and buy a caller-ID box. That way, if he calls, I will not answer, but won't miss any calls from any true and loving and kind guys who might want to ask me out.

Anyway, I'm sure Sam won't be calling this week, as he has clients in from out of town—or more likely, he has told me he has clients in from out of town so that he's not obligated to spend an evening eating dinner with me. Either way, he won't be calling.

Speaking of dinner, I'm meeting my mom and Darrel at The Living Room tonight. That should be an enjoyable and uplifting experience that will take my mind off my troubles. (Note sarcastic tone.)

I arrive at The Living Room forty minutes late. I waffled back and forth on whether I should take my car or a cab, and finally decided on the cab since my mother often drives me to drink and The Living Room makes wonderful martinis. So I called the cab company, and they said "That'll be half an hour to forty-five minutes, ma'am."

I scan the dim restaurant and spot a couple ensconced in a paisley booth at the back, necking furiously. That would be them. This is reinforcing my decision to take a cab. I flag the bartender as I walk by and ask him to send a Flaming Walter martini to the back table.

"Ahem." I clear my throat. "Get a room, why don't ya?" I am only half joking.

"Oh, hi, sweetie!" my mom says, pulling her lips from Darrel's with a loud suction noise. Gawd! Despite the fact that my mom is in her mid-fifties, she never fails to tell me—or in this case, show me—that she is in her sexual prime. "I'm a late bloomer, I guess!" she always says. "All those years in a loveless marriage to your father must have set my clock back!"

"Hi, Kerry," Darrel says.

"Hi, Darrel." Darrel is forty-two but looks twenty (not in a good way—in a chubby, baby-faced-but-with-a-beard kind of way). Darrel and my mother have been living together for three years. He is always pleasant and friendly enough, but something about him gives me the heebie-jeebies. For one, why would he be living with a fifty-four-year-old woman unless there is something seriously wrong with him that prevents him from dating women his own age? My mother is an attractive woman in her aging hippie way, but come on! She's practically sixty! For two, I just witnessed him necking with my mother . . . *necking*, not kissing or smooching or canoodling. I'm talking seriously going at it. In public! I'm not exaggerating.

I sit down, and my martini arrives just in the nick of time. I take a huge gulp as my mother looks on, her expression a combination of judgment and concern. "How are you dear?" she says. "You look like you could use some fresh air. Have you been cooped up in your office all summer?"

"Pretty much."

"I'm sure the company wouldn't fall apart if you took twenty minutes out for a brisk walk outside. You're in a lovely part of town. You should take advantage of being so close to the waterfront."

"You look good, Mom." It is a wise change of subject. The only thing my mother would rather talk about than how bad I look is how good she does.

"Thanks, sweetie." She smiles at me. "It's the yoga. I'm doing Ashtanga twice a week—that's the fast yoga that Madonna does. And I'm doing Bikram on Saturdays. That's the yoga in the hot room. It's amazing! Very cleansing. I read recently that yoga can actually *stop* the aging process!"

"Well, it certainly has in your case." Darrel brings my mother's fingers to his lips in the manner of an Italian lothario. Their eyes meet, and I'm afraid they're going to start French-kissing again.

"Waiter!" I shriek somewhat hysterically. He comes. "I'll have another Flaming Walter, please."

"I'll have a Perrier," my mother orders, but pronounces it: *Peh—* I've got a ball of phlegm in my throat that I must expel—*ee-ay*. I recall that she has been taking French lessons.

"I'll have a Heineken," Darrel says.

"You naughty boy!" My mom leans over and nibbles his ear. "Are you going to make me drive home?"

"I'll be fine. It's just a beer, Gwen."

"I don't want you all silly, now," she giggles. "Don't forget you have to work tomorrow!"

"Honey, it's one beer. You act as if I'm doing tequila shots!"

"Don't give me any ideas! I've done a few tequila shots in my day."

I consider lighting my hair on fire to get some attention.

The banter between them continues throughout the evening, interspersed with updates on my aunts and uncles and cousins. "Have you heard from your brother lately?" she asks me.

"Yeah, we e-mail every now and then."

"Then you know that he's having a fabulous time in Sydney? Oh, if I could do it all over again, I'd never have gotten married and tied down with responsibilities so young."

"Sorry," I say, shoveling risotto into my mouth. Since I am one of the responsibilities of which she speaks, I feel I should apologize.

"What? Oh, please! I loved being a mother. I just think Greg is wise to go out into the world and really live life!"

Somehow my brother, who flunked out of university after one semester, slept on my mom's couch for a year and a half, and then borrowed money to fly to Australia, where he now works at a bar, is the golden child. I guess absence makes the heart grow fonder.

"Hmmm . . . What else do I know?" She muses over bites of poached salmon (*sans* sauce *avec une petite* sprinkle of lemon juice). "Well, your cousin Julie just got a very high-level job with the Bank of America in New York," my mom says, beaming like Julie is her own daughter and not her sister's. "We could not be more proud of her. She's always been a bright light, that one."

"Great," I mumble, my lips immersed in my martini. I am convinced that my mother doesn't know what I do for a living. She sort of asked once, but when I started to explain, she lost interest and began sucking on Darrel's neck.

"Oh! And Mandy and Kevin are expecting their fourth baby," she says gleefully. "It's so wonderful to see! No one has big families anymore."

"That's because everyone knows it's crazy to have more than two kids."

Darrel sniggers, but my mom looks like I just threw my drink in her face. "Why do you say that? Children are a joy!"

Easy for her to say, now that Greg and I are in our thirties. I don't remember her being so full of joy when she was chasing us with the wooden spoon for drawing on the walls or stuffing raisins up our noses.

"I know . . . ," I agree, trying to placate her. "I just think kids are a lot of work . . . and expensive. I think two's enough. Just my opinion."

"Well . . ." She is obviously still annoyed. "Perhaps such judgments should be reserved for those who know something about raising a family?"

"Fine. Sorry for making a joke." Why do I feel like I'm thirteen again? I order a third martini.

"Speaking of having families . . . ," my mom says, grabbing the saltshaker and preparing to sprinkle it in my open wound. "What's going on with you and Sam? Have you sorted things out yet?"

My mom is the unofficial president of Sam's fan club, which has never been very helpful, given the volatile nature of my relationship with him. I suspect she realizes, much as I do, that he is way out of my league and I will never find anyone even remotely as successful and attractive as he is. (Of course, she doesn't know about the *Jasmine* incident. I thought it best to keep that to myself in case we do work things out.)

I take a deep breath. "Actually . . ." I clear my throat. I can say this now, bolstered by the vodka. "Actually, I've decided not to see him anymore."

My mom snorts. "*You've* decided?"

"What is that supposed to mean?"

"Kerry, you know as well as I do that Sam calls the shots in your relationship. If he wants to be with you, you're there like an eager puppy. If he doesn't, you mope around and eat too much and drink too much—" She shoots a look at the drink just placed before me.

"I'm quite capable of ending my relationship with Sam, thank you very much! And I'd also like you to know how much I appreciate your support and faith in me. It's so nice when a girl can always count on her mom."

"Kerry . . . ," she starts, but I am already standing, guzzling my Flaming Walter.

"I've got to go. . . . Big day at the ad agency tomorrow. That's where I work, by the way."

"What?" They are looking at me like I am drunk and crazy—which I guess I am.

I throw a couple of twenties on the table. "See you later." I march (in a fairly straight line) to the door and out into the night.

That was awful. Maybe I should take a tip from my brother and move to the other side of the planet? Then perhaps she'd have a change of heart and brag about me to my cousins and aunts. But I refuse to let her drive me from my home, from the city that I love.

It is not easy having it out with my mother, but I feel better for having said my piece. This should give her something to mull over while she's baking vegan brownies or doing upward-facing dog at yoga class.

Unfortunately, my big exit is somewhat destroyed when I can't catch a cab and am still standing on the sidewalk when my mom and Darrel leave the restaurant. I quickly duck behind a mailbox but then realize that my larger-than-usual ass is poking out and reveal-ing my position. It doesn't matter anyway; they'd already seen me.

"Come on, Kerry," my mom says in a resigned voice that clearly says "Where did I go wrong? Where?" "We'll run you home."

Chapter 4

WHAT A SHITTY WEEK—BUT ON THE BRIGHT SIDE, IT IS FRIDAY AND I will have some good stories to tell the girls over drinks. The communications plan being erased by my left buttock will be a good laugh, and then my decision to end things with Sam will provide a serious discussion topic. . . . They may not take it all that seriously, since this is far from the first time they've heard it. But I will tell them about the avoidance plan and the caller-ID box. I will also ask them if they know anything about using hypnosis to make someone really gorgeous look like Danny DeVito.

Sneaking out of work just before five, I race home to shower, change, and apply makeup. Since I'm a free agent, it is imperative that I look my best every time I go out in public. (Note to self: Must stop eating bowls of cream-cheese icing before bed.) While trying on several stylishly sexy outfits, I dance around the apartment to some very upbeat and boppy Kylie Minogue. I am a happy-go-lucky, free-spirited kind of gal! I am a fun-loving and carefree woman who is perfectly capable of getting another boyfriend as gorgeous and sexy as Sam. Not that I need one.

I am meeting the girls at the Lizard Lounge, a trendy Capitol Hill bar that has slushie machines with alcohol in them. Needless to say, this is a very popular spot for girls who are barely of legal drinking age, so it may not be the best choice for a bunch of cougars like us. But we are all still attractive and youthful women who—

Ouch! Damn! My bopping to Kylie Minogue has caused me to stab myself in the eyeball with the mascara wand. There is a bunch of black goop stuck to my contact lens, and my right eye is watering like crazy.

Despite my best efforts to clean it, the lens is destroyed, and I am forced to wear my glasses. This may not sound like a major disaster, but then, you haven't seen my glasses. They are out of style, to say the least. In fact, they are the same large, tortoiseshell-frame-with-dropped-arm pair that I have had since 1986.

I can handle this. My vision is not really that bad—at worst, negative five or six diopters. I will take off my glasses as soon as I am safely inside the cab. Once inside the vehicle, I begin to feel a little carsick looking out at the blurry scenery, and I have to lean over the front seat so my nose is four inches from the meter in order to read what it says. But I'm here now.

I stumble into the Lizard Lounge and scan the large industrial-style space. It is a sea of gray—concrete floors and walls, and black and charcoal furnishings. Shit. I haven't had my vision checked in years, and it has obviously worsened. Maybe I am legally blind now? I am about to resort to surreptitiously putting on the fifty-eight-year-old-bank-teller glasses when I notice an arm waving. I am going to take a chance and hope it is waving at me.

As I get closer, I begin to make out the familiar forms. When I am about a foot away, I realize the arm belongs to Sandra.

"Hi!" I say, relief sweeping over me as I fumble blindly for the chair. God! I feel like Stevie Wonder. "Sorry I'm late. I had a mascara accident."

"Poor thing," Sandra says. "How are you?"

"God! What a week. I need a drink."

"This is a squashed strawberry cannonball," Michelle says. "It's really good."

"What's that?" I point to the glowing orange concoction in front of Sandra.

"Mango tango madness."

"And that?"

"Vodka soda," Val says. "I'm on a diet."

I know I should go the vodka soda route, too, but after the week I've had, I opt for a wacky melon-baller.

"So tell us what's been going on?" Sandra asks. Sandra and I have known each other since college. She is pretty in a plump, blond, rosy-cheeked kind of way (like Nancy Drew's friend Bess). Sandra has been involved with a married man for three years and is therefore the only one of my close friends who is more screwed up than I am. And she's not even in therapy. She seems to think that sleeping with your boss who is almost sixty and married with three kids is an absolutely fabulous life for any single, thirty-something gal. It is all very strange and mysterious. She never admits that their relationship is more than a boss–assistant kind of thing, until Christmas rolls around, and we all have to take turns talking her out of slitting her wrists.

"Well . . . ," I say, and then I tell the deleted-document story and that I've ended my relationship with Sam.

"Great," Michelle says. "I hope you mean it this time." Michelle, on the other hand, *is* Nancy Drew (except that she's director of marketing for a software company and not a girl detective). She is so close to perfect that I can barely be friends with her. She is thin, gorgeous, and single by choice—for real! Her focus is her career, and she doesn't want a man to get in the way of her climb up the corporate ladder. She has a date now and again, but they never turn into anything serious. She certainly never gets drunk and sleeps with the guys on the first date, or gets obsessed or freaked out if they don't call. And half the time, when a man does call, she says, "Thanks, but no thanks," because his earning potential wasn't quite in line with what she had in mind, or he had back hair or feminine hands. She spends at least one weekend a month at a spa retreat so she can get "centered." She and my mother get along fabulously.

"I do mean it this time." I address Michelle directly. "But I'll really need the help and support of my friends."

"We support you, Kerry," Michelle says, patting my hand in what could be a sincere gesture, but in my current state of mind comes across as completely condescending. God. Sometimes I think she is in my life only to provide a benchmark to ensure that I will never feel adequate.

"Thanks, then." I smile falsely and order another drink.

"I think you'll do it this time," Val jumps in. She is a few years older than the rest of us, and half Chinese. She is twice divorced, so hypothetically, that should put her ahead of me on the screwed-up scale. But, her first marriage was to her high school sweetheart back in Walla Walla, so it doesn't really count. And everyone is allowed one failed marriage, right? Val really has her act together now. She has to, because she has a daughter. She can come out with us only when Taylor spends the weekends with her dad. Taylor is seven and really sweet.

"I will do it this time," I say, slurping the last of my wacky melon-baller. I turn to Michelle. "I know it's not going to be easy. Not everyone can be as independent as you are." I wanted to say "cold and emotionless," but I don't want this evening to end up like the one with my mother. There's no way I could storm out of here without my glasses on.

"It's true," Val agrees. "You are the only woman I know who doesn't feel the need to have a man in her life."

"Well, *you* don't," Michelle counters.

"That's because I have Taylor. I barely have time for you guys, let alone a man."

"Then stay away from men," I say, giving her hand a squeeze. "We don't want to lose you."

Val smiles, and I can tell it means a lot to her. "You'll do it this time," she says, giving my hand a squeeze, too.

"The reason I don't need a man is because I don't want children," Michelle says. "So there's no pressure. I've got my whole life to find someone."

I ponder this for a moment. Sure, I'd like to have a couple of kids one day, but not for ages. The thought of gaining forty pounds, swearing off cocktails and caffeine, and doing Kegel exercises every waking moment is not particularly appealing. Neither are the poopy diapers, chapped nipples, sleepless nights. . . . I've heard all the horror stories from Val and cousin Mandy.

"Well . . . I don't think any of us are ready to get out the turkey-baster just yet," I joke.

"Admit it, Kerry," Michelle says. "Your biological clock must have played some part in your staying with Sam for so long."

"Oh . . . you would have had such beautiful babies!" Sandra gushes.

"Thanks. That's helpful," I snap.

"If I ever change my mind about children," Michelle says. "I'll adopt. So I still wouldn't need a man. Anyway . . . for now I want to focus on my career. It's a man's world, and taking time out for a family is going to set you back at least seven years. Even if you go straight back to work after, you're not going to be able to put in the hours required to play with the big boys." She drones on about how she is the youngest director in the company and is sure to make VP before she's forty.

I am feeling blue now, which is obviously the opposite effect I wanted from a night out with my girlfriends. Girlfriends are supposed to lift you up, not put you down further. I slurp my grape-a-licious. Thanks to Sandra's comment, I can't stop thinking about the beautiful dark-haired children with dimples like their father that I will probably never have. No fixed-up old house with shutters and a flower garden. No cries of "Daddy, Daddy" as Sam comes home from work and the gorgeous children run out to greet him.

And it's not like I'll have a fabulous career to replace all I am missing out on. Unlike Michelle, I am definitely not on the fast track at my company. At the rate I'm going, Gavin will be my boss in a year or two.

Well, hello! What's this? It seems there is a very handsome guy sitting up at the bar, and he's looking right at me. I squint to get a clearer picture and then realize squinting isn't very attractive or subtle. It also causes crow's-feet and frown lines. But this dark-haired stranger is definitely looking this way. Oh, my god! He waved! I wave back—just a little wave.

"Hey . . ." I tap Michelle beside me, who is still talking about her type-A personality. "See the dark-haired guy up at the bar?"

"Mmm-hmm," she says appreciatively.

"Not bad, eh?"

"Not bad at all," she says.

That's all the affirmation I need. I'm going to go talk to him. This could mark a new beginning for me. There's still hope for those beautiful dark-haired children! I'm not sure about the dimples—I'm still too far away to tell—but there is still a chance that I won't end up an overweight spinster with a boss nine years my junior.

"Excuse me for a second." I get up and feel my way toward the bar, careful not to knock over any chairs or waiters. I can feel the eyes of my friends on my back. "What is she doing?" they are wondering. "Is she going to talk to that handsome fellow at the bar? How brave! *Carpe diem*, Kerry!"

I will show them how over Sam I am. That Sam I am, that Sam I am, I do not like green eggs and ham. Oooh, that grape-a-licious went right to my head.

"Hi," I say to the dark-haired guy, who waved. I walk up very close in order to get a good look at him. Definitely handsome.

"Hi," he says with a smile.

"I'm Kerry." I hold out my hand, and he takes it briefly.

"Glen."

"So, Glen . . ." I smile flirtatiously.

"So, Kerry . . ." He smiles back.

"So . . ."

"So . . ."

Jeez, for all his staring and waving, he's not exactly making this conversation easy. "So umm . . . do you come here often?" I can't believe I said that! How lame! I may as well ask him his astrological sign.

"I do, actually," Glen says. "My fiancée is the hostess." He points to said fiancée, who is standing at her post, directly behind the table my friends and I occupy. She is bare midriffed, with long copper hair and a nose ring. She looks about twenty-two. She waves.

"Great! Great!" I enthuse. "You know, Glen, I actually thought that you were someone that I had met before at a party at my boyfriend's house. Did I say *boyfriend?*"—hysterical giggle—"I meant fiancé. The man I love so so much. He's at home waiting for me. Anyway, obviously I am mistaken, so I think I'll just head home to be with my wonderful fiancé." With another hysterical laugh, I turn and stumble blindly away. When I arrive at the table, my face is burning with shame.

"What was that?" Sandra asks.

"I thought I'd met that guy before at a party with Sam because he looks exactly like this guy that Sam went to school with, but apparently he only looks *almost* exactly like this guy that I met before with Sam. Anyway, I'm gonna go."

"But it's still early," Val says.

"Don't go," Michelle adds. The three of them are looking at me, their eyes full of pity.

"Thanks, guys," I say through the lump in my throat. "But I'm in the mood for an early night." I turn and walk toward the blurry shape that is the exit door.

Chapter 5

I HAVE SUCCESSFULLY AVOIDED SAM FOR NINE DAYS. THE CALLER-ID BOX is a godsend! Now, I can still talk to all the people I want to, but can also see when Sam is calling and refuse to answer. It's amazing!

There does seems to be something wrong with the box, though. It appears that Sam has called me only twice over the last nine days, and that can't possibly be right. I mean . . . *he* doesn't know I've decided not to see him anymore. For all he knows, we are currently broken up but seeing each other casually while we explore our feelings as individuals. There's no way he could have called me only twice! I will exchange the box for a new one when I get around to it. On the bright side, it has ID'd twenty-seven calls from my mother, most of which I have avoided. She now thinks I have an actual social life and have been getting tons of fresh air.

The journal of mortifying moments has not been opened since the entry on Sam. With the way I feel lately, dredging up one more painful interaction with the male species would have me hanging from the ceiling fan. My therapist is mad at me for not following through on her great idea. Although, therapists don't really get mad, do they? They say, "So . . . you've chosen not to utilize the useful tool I recommended that may get to the bottom of all your dysfunction. Would you like to tell me why? Mmm-hmm. Mmm-hmm. How does that make you feel?" Anyway, I am concentrating on work.

Today is the internal creative presentation for the Prism campaign. After all the stress over my hapless communications plan, Sonja basically rewrote the thing anyway. With one phone call to the VP of Marketing, she managed to get an extra forty grand so that we can afford to do a TV campaign after all. Sonja has no soul, and antifreeze courses through her veins, but she is very good at her job. Dave is happy, too—or as happy as a serial killer ever gets when he is stuck in an office and not out murdering people.

We convene in the boardroom. For some reason, Sonja doesn't feel it necessary to invite half the company to critique Dave's creative presentation as she did with my communications plan. In attendance are Sonja, Gavin, myself, Pam (broadcast producer), Tanya (art director who is Dave's creative partner–lover), and Dave . . . who, by the way, has three ex-wives, which absolutely baffles me. How can there be three women in the world who would marry him? Dave is not a bad-looking guy, but to compensate for *that* personality he'd have to be Brad Pitt.

"Thanks for coming, everyone," Sonja begins, as formal as ever. "As you are aware, I managed to come up with some extra funds to make a TV campaign possible, so we hope you're going to blow us all away with the creative today." She smiles at the creative side of the table. "Prism needs an amazing campaign to raise its market share. We need to turn the dial up to eleven on this one!" She giggles a little.

What the heck was that? Was that a *Spinal Tap* reference from Sonja? How out of place . . . and out of character! She's a weird one, all right. I look over at Gavin, and he is shaking with laughter and muttering "Eleven!" gleefully under his breath. God, I wish Dave would drop his creative director facade and murder the two of them right here and now.

"Okay," Dave says, oblivious of Sonja's attempt at humor, as are his cohorts. "We've got some tissues today. . . ." Tanya pulls a stack of loose papers from her portfolio. "We spent a lot of hours on this, and we've come up with something we feel strongly about. We will present just the one concept, take it or leave it." He looks around challengingly. Of course, none of us is about to speak up.

"Okay . . ." Dave lays a few rough drawings out on the table in a loose storyboard fashion. "First scene . . . ," he begins.

I listen in shocked silence, my mouth gaping open in horror. The script is . . . It's just . . . I can't . . . I'm not sure how . . . I'll lay it out for you as simply as possible.

SCENE 1

Visual: Two teenyboppers are heading into school on the first day back after summer vacation. One is a fourteen-year-old girl in a plaid skirt, a sweater, and braids. The other is a disheveled thirteen-year-old boy with a faded jeans jacket sporting a Marilyn Manson logo on the back.

Suzie: So, Gary . . . did you have a good summer vacation?

Gary: It rocked, man.

Suzie: But isn't it nice to be back at Central High?

Gary: Whatever, dude.

Suzie: I can't wait to get back into my studies! My parents bought me a great new computer to help me with my homework. They even got me a super, dial-up Internet connection!

Gary: You gotta be kidding, man? Dial-up is so yesterday. I've got a high-speed connection from Prism Communications. I'll be able to kick *bleep* in the homework department.

SCENE 2

Visual: A dirty and disheveled woman sits in an alley with a shopping cart full of her belongings. She is holding a crack pipe, obviously a junkie about to get high. A man in a pin-striped suit is kneeling down, talking to her, a look of concern on his face.

Suzie: Spare some change, mister?

Gary: No, sorry. I'm late for a very important meeting with the president of Microsoft. . . . Wait a minute! Suzie? Suzie Walton, is that you?

Suzie: How'd you know my name?

Gary: It's me, Gary! God, I haven't seen you since Central High. What . . . what happened?

Suzie: (to camera) My parents should have gotten me a high-speed Internet connection from Prism Communications. That's what happened.

"Bravo!" Gavin and Sonja are clapping. "Hits the nail on the head, Dave! Nice work, Tanya!"

I am stunned, silent.

"That's the basic premise," Dave says, smiling despite himself. "We have two more executions that we didn't mock up. One has the guy who got high-speed growing up to be a lawyer, and he's called to help a death-row inmate with his appeal. And of course, the inmate is . . ."

"The one who had a dial-up connection!" Sonja and Gavin say in unison, their voices loud with joy.

"Then the other one," Tanya says, speaking in her usual monotone. "Is about two high school girls. The one without high-speed gets pregnant when she's, like, fourteen, and has six kids living in a trailer before she's thirty. Her friend who got high-speed is the social-services worker sent to remove them from the squalor of their home."

"Excellent!" Sonja says. "I'm very pleased. Gavin?"

"Lovin' it, guys," he says, obviously kissing their asses.

"And Kerry?" I can tell by her voice that she doesn't really want to hear from me. Part of my brain is telling me to smile and go along, say "great work," and leave it at that, but I don't know if I can do it.

"Ummm . . . well . . ." Gulp. Apparently, I can't do it. "I think it's horrifying," I say bluntly.

Sonja whirls on me. "What?"

"Horrifying?" Dave is smirking at me like I am the most inept, unsophisticated person he has ever met.

"Threatening parents that their children will grow up to be junkies or murderers if they don't have a high-speed Internet connection? That's not a bit sick?"

"It's a joke." Dave glowers at me.

"It's a sick joke!" I retort.

"Well, you're entitled to your opinion." Sonja is smiling tightly at me. "But obviously, you're outnumbered here."

"Janet will never go for it." Janet is the Prism client. She is also a mother of three. "It's too mean."

Dave blows up. "Well, she can just lick my crack if she thinks—"

"No one's saying you have to do creative with chalkboards and apples!" I scream. "Just not with children turning into junkies and murderers!" Uh-oh. I am going to start crying now. I have a very embarrassing habit of bursting into tears whenever I get riled up about something. I must make a hasty exit. "Whatever." I wave my hand at them. "I'm outnumbered anyway." I run to my office.

A few deep breaths and a quick call to Trevor to tell him I have a great story to share over lunch, and I have regained my composure. It is a good thing, because Gavin suddenly appears in my doorway.

"Yes, Gavin?" I say with the enthusiasm of someone who is about to have a wart removed.

"Umm, yeah . . . Can I talk to you for a sec?"

"Sure."

He comes in and shuts the door. "I just felt that I should tell you—since you obviously haven't figured it out for yourself—that it's really career-limiting to go against Dave like that." He's smiling at me smugly.

"What are you talking about?"

"Dave is the golden boy, Kerry. He was a big shot in Toronto and New York, and the agency is lucky he wanted to mellow out on the West Coast for a while. He's won awards all over the continent, and management is looking to him to single-handedly build the agency's creative reputation. We need to support his ideas and take chances."

If you put a blond wig on him, he could be Sonja's Mini-Me. "Gavin, what did you think about the Prism creative?" I ask, point blank.

"Well . . . I definitely think it's pushing the boundaries—"

"—of good taste," I finish for him. "Let me give you a tip," I say, remembering for the first time that I have more seniority and am nine years older than he is. "Sometimes you have to follow your gut and do what you think is right for the client. Advertising's not all about whose ass you kiss."

He actually seems to be pondering what I've said, for just the briefest moment. Then the smug smile returns, and he says, "Consider yourself warned." And he leaves.

Chapter 6

MY MOM IS TAKING ME TO HAVE MY TAROT CARDS READ AND THEN FOR lunch. "It is simply amazing what the spirit world can tell us about ourselves," she says. "We just need to open our minds and our hearts, and the guidance we seek is ours."

Sounds a bit wacky, but I could really use some guidance on this whole Sam issue. I have still not spoken to him, but I must admit I'm on the verge of calling. My therapist says that would be a grave mistake. But she also told me that writing down all the horrible, painful incidents in my life would make me feel better . . . eventually, of course.

My mother and I approach a seedy-looking apartment building, and she presses the buzzer on the intercom. "Hello?" a staticky, female voice says.

"Hello, Ramona? It's Gwen Hunter here with my daughter, Kerry. She has an appointment at eleven?"

"Come on up," Ramona says, and buzzes us in. I think when you name your child Ramona, you are seriously increasing the likelihood that she will be psychic.

"I'm so excited!" My mom squeezes my hand in the small and musty elevator. She is wearing a kelly-green caftan of sorts, and chunky African jewelry. This outfit seems far more suited for gaining guidance from the spirit world than my sweatpants and jeans jacket. "Make sure you ask about future children and a husband, of course," she instructs me. She is more keen to know my future than I am.

I, on the other hand, am suddenly paralyzed with dread. Open my mind. . . . Open my heart. . . . I repeat this mantra to myself. But I can't shake this very ominous feeling that Ramona will tell me I have two months to live, or that I will never get married and will spend the rest of my life working for a man named Gavin.

We reach Ramona's apartment, and my mom knocks on the door. She then tucks my hair behind my ears and straightens the collar of my jacket. Does she think that if I impress the psychic, I will have a better future? If that is the case, I should have worn one of my work outfits instead of these sweatpants.

The door swings open, and Ramona stands before us. God, she looks really normal. She is a few years older than me, with funky black glasses and a stylish haircut. I think I was expecting Stevie Nicks. "Hi," she says casually. "Come on in."

My mom has a seat in the waiting room (aka the living room), and Ramona takes me into the, uh, psychic room (aka the spare bedroom). "Have a seat." She motions to a folding chair opposite hers at a tiny table. There is incense burning on the shelf beside us, and in one corner a small fountain trickles soothingly. I take a deep breath.

"Are you nervous?" Ramona asks.

"Yeah," I admit. "I just don't want to hear anything bad."

"I like to be very honest about what I see," she says. "But I'm not going to tell you that you're going to die or anything like that."

"Okay," I say, somewhat relieved. Although, if she's any good at all, she'll tell me I'm in love with a heartless cad who has tried calling me only four times in two weeks.

"When's your birthday?" she asks.

"October seventh."

"Libra . . . sensitive, creative, indecisive, fickle."

Wow! It's like she's known me forever.

"Librans are great lovers of beauty. . . ."

That explains my infatuation with Sam.

"You crave harmony. . . ."

And that explains why I hate my job and spend so much time trying not to burst into tears at the office.

"Okay . . . ," Ramona says, handing me a large plaid deck of cards. "Shuffle these." I do, with an open mind and an open heart. I cut the deck in three and then restack the cards from right to left.

Ramona begins to lay them out in a complicated pattern. As each card is turned faceup, my horror increases. Oh, my God! Death. The Devil. A burning tower. People impaled on swords, weeping into their hands. Surely this must mean the end of the world as we know it? How did I let my mom talk me into this?

Ramona, however, is calm. "I see a man in your life." She taps one of the cards. "He's very good-looking . . . very charming. And you have very strong feelings for him, and he cares for you but . . ."

But? But?

"You're not his number-one priority. He will always put himself and his career before you. I don't think he really knows you as a person . . . or cares to know you. You need to cut him loose."

"Already done," I say confidently.

"I'm not so sure," she says. "I think you have more to deal with where he's concerned."

Apparently, you can't bluff a psychic.

"There's another man here, too," she says. "He is very kind, with an open, giving heart. His feelings for you are much more genuine."

"Really?" I am excited by the prospect. "Who is he?"

"I don't think you've met him yet . . . or you may know him casually."

"Where will I meet him? When? What does he look like? Will we get married?"

Ramona chuckles. "The tarot cards are not a crystal ball. Fate is still in your hands. Let's see. . . ." She touches the card, closes her eyes, and breathes deeply. "He's in a creative field—an artist, or a photographer . . . maybe a writer, but it's more likely to be a visual art. You'll meet him at a social gathering, but there's a work connection. Where do you work?"

"At Ferris and Shannon Advertising."

"Yeah, it's got something to do with work . . . some kind of work-related function."

"Okay."

"He's nice looking, with sandy-colored hair, and he has a wonderful, caring soul. There's a *D* here, like Darren or Daniel or something. There will be obstacles to you two getting together, but if you follow your heart and go with him, he'll make you very happy."

"Great." I feel peaceful and hopeful.

On the next spread of cards, Ramona addresses my career. "You're not happy in your job."

She's good.

"You're eventually going to have to decide what you want to do. I'm not saying you're in the wrong career necessarily, but there are all sorts of negative vibrations here. There's a woman. . . . She doesn't like you."

Really? I wonder who that could be?

"She's jealous of you, even though she's your superior at work. She will always try to keep you down. Your career will go nowhere as long as you're working for her."

"Thank you," I say sincerely as I pay her sixty bucks. "That was really helpful."

"The cards are just a tool to help us read what our intuition already knows," Ramona says. She seems very wise and centered—not at all spooky and weird like I had expected.

"So?" My mom jumps up as I exit the psychic room. "How'd it go?"

"Good," I say, feeling a bit funny. "It was very interesting."

As soon as we are alone in the elevator she asks, "Am I going to be a grandma anytime soon? What about a husband—is there a husband in your future? Are you going to be able to work things out with Sam?"

"We mostly talked about work stuff," I say.

"Oh . . ." She is clearly disappointed, having no interest in my career whatsoever. "Where shall we go for lunch?"

Mortifying Moment #3

Lisa and I were at the ski hill. It was a brisk winter day, but the sun was shining and conditions were perfect. Lisa had on a baby blue ski suit that looked great with her pale blond hair. I was wearing black—a black ski jacket, black ski pants, black hat, black gloves. There were darts of color across my chest and down my thighs, elongated triangles of fuchsia and turquoise. The effect was supposed to make me look smaller.

"Oh, my god! There they are!" Lisa whispered to me as we lined up for the chairlift. She was pointing to the ski hill. The two boys were cruising at frightening speed down the face, both of them expert skiers. They skidded to a snowy stop at the bottom and skated themselves over to the line. Lisa looked back, none too subtly, then turned and giggled. It had the desired effect: they noticed us.

The boys were four chairlifts behind, but we were quite sure they could see us as we rode up the mountain. "Totally!" We shrieked with laughter. "That's so true, isn't it? God!"

"Such a loser!"

"Like, totally from Loserville!"

Laugh, laugh, laugh. They would think we were very cool . . . assuming they could hear us. They were still quite a ways down the mountain.

At the top, we glided off the lift, stopping to ponder which run. "Hmmm? Which run should we take? I don't know? What are you in the mood for—easy or hard or in between? Hmm . . . which run? Which run?"

Soon, they skied up to us. "Hey," the best-looking one said to Lisa. "You guys want to ski with us?"

"I guess," she said indifferently, masking her inner euphoria. We followed them down an intermediate run. I was not a great skier, but I did my best to keep up. But I still lagged behind, as even less cool than not keeping up would be having an embarrassing wipeout. Not far down, the really good-looking boy pulled into a secluded stand of evergreens. The rest of us followed.

"I'm Kyle, by the way," he said to Lisa.

"Lisa." She pulled off her hat and shook her shiny blond hair. "And this is Kerry."

"Todd," the other guy said, looking at me. He was kind of cute too, but really skinny. He was an excellent skier, though, which was cool and sexy, *and his eyes were very blue and sparkly. I smiled at him flirtatiously. At least I hoped it was flirtatiously. At fifteen, this was all quite new to me.*

"Wanna smoke a joint?" Kyle asked, pulling one from his pocket. I looked with panic-filled eyes to Lisa for a cue. What did we do now? Would they think we were immature little girls if we said no? Would they ski off and leave us, destroying any possibility of budding romance? But if we said yes, would we be able to get safely down the mountain? We had never smoked pot before, so who knew the effect it would have on our coordination.

"Sure," Lisa said casually, showing no sign of the anxiety that was gripping me.

Kyle lit up, inhaled deeply, and passed the joint to Lisa. She took a little puff and then passed it to me. I followed her lead but ended up coughing and hacking uncontrollably. Soon Lisa had joined me, and we were both doubled over, our lungs fighting for air.

"Virgins," Kyle said to Todd with a laugh.

I righted myself, turning fifteen shades of purple with embarrassment until I realized he meant that we'd never smoked pot before. Phew!

I passed the joint to Todd, who took a huge drag, held it in for an impossibly long time, and then blew it into the air. He was really very manly—must be seventeen at least. A few more tokes for the boys, and we were on our way again.

Todd stayed behind with me, darting back and forth across the hill, banking off the sides, and doing little jumps and tricks. I tried to watch him, but I was concentrating heavily on not falling. I didn't think the marijuana had any effect, since I had coughed all the smoke out, but it may have subtly messed with my equilibrium. I had to stay focused on getting down the hill safely. Todd was very impressive, though. I quite liked him.

When we reached the bottom, Kyle and Lisa were already lined up for the chairlift. Todd and I sidled in behind them. I was feeling excited, nervous, and self-conscious at the prospect of sitting beside him for the seven-minute ride up the mountain. He was not really that skinny—more wiry. And those blue eyes. Sigh.

"What school do you go to?" he asked when we were seated, our skis floating against the blue backdrop of the sky.

"Maple Grove," I said. "You?"

"West Seattle, but I'm graduating in June."

Oooh! An older man! "You're so lucky," I said. "I can't wait to graduate and move out."

"Yeah." He smiled at me. He was still smiling at me, and I was still smiling back. Our eyes were locked, and his head was slowly moving toward mine. Oh, my God! He was going to kiss me right there on the chairlift. How romantic! A soft gentle kiss as we soared above the glistening white slopes. It was like a movie.

The kiss wasn't exactly soft and gentle. Todd seemed to be trying to dislodge something stuck in my back teeth with his tongue, but I guessed that was the way older boys kissed. It didn't last too long. He pulled away and smiled at me, his eyes glassy from the passion—or was it from the pot?

"Thanks," I said. Why did I say thanks? What a loser! You don't thank a guy for kissing you!

"You're welcome," he said sexily.

We stared straight ahead in silence for a while. I felt colder when we stopped skiing, but the sun was warming our faces. My nose was beginning to run, so I sniffed quietly. I reached into my pocket for a tissue and dabbed daintily at my nose, keeping my head down so I wouldn't gross him out. When I pulled the tissue away, it was bright red.

"Oh, no!" I shrieked, destroying any hope of keeping this disaster from Todd.

"What?"

"My nose is sort of bleeding a bit," I said with a lame giggle. I pinched my nostrils with the tissue as I'd seen my dad do. He was very prone to nosebleeds. The flow seemed to have stopped by the time we reached the top of the hill, and we unloaded, gliding to where Lisa and Kyle were waiting for us.

"Let's go down the face this time," Kyle said. Without waiting for a response, he was off. My new, sort of, possibly boyfriend stayed behind with me again, impressing me with his Nordic abilities. About halfway down the hill, Lisa and Kyle stopped and waited for us.

"Hey!" I called, skiing up to them.

"Oh, god!" Lisa said, looking at me in horror. "What's wrong? You've got blood all over your face!"

"What?" I touched my upper lip, and my mitten came away red. "I've got a fucking nosebleed." I hoped the swearing would make me sound cool and possibly compensate for the uncoolness of a bleeding nose. "Do you have any Kleenex?"

Lisa handed me a wadded-up ball, and I pressed it to my face. It will be fine, I told myself. I will pinch the nostrils to stop the flow, wash the dried blood off with some snow, and hopefully have another kissing session with Todd on the chair. It will all be fine.

"Kerry . . ." Lisa still looked on the verge of barfing. "The Kleenex . . . it's soaked through."

The ball of tissues was now a soggy red mess in my hand. I fished in my own pocket and found a few spare sheets. I pressed them frantically to my nose. Please stop bleeding, I willed it. Please. Not today. You can bleed all day tomorrow if you want.

"Do you guys have any tissues?" Lisa asked Kyle and Todd, who were standing by awkwardly.

"Just some rolling papers," Kyle said.

"Kerry, you're going to have to use these." She handed me a small pack of rolling papers.

"What? How?" I sank down into the snow, dropping my second soaked ball of tissue. I withdrew a few of the flimsy papers, crumpled them up, and stuffed them in my nostrils. That should as least stop the drip. Shit! I could feel it still trickling down my face. I pulled the rolling paper out of my left nostril, and behind it trailed a long, snakelike blood clot.

"Ahhh!" Lisa, Kyle, and Todd screamed.

"Oh, no! Oh, no!" I started to cry. I stuck more rolling papers to my bloody nose and lay back in the snow.

"What's going on here?" It was a ski patrol guy. He sounded very serious. I suppose the scene was cause for concern. I was lying prostrate in a circle of bloodstained snow with several rolling papers stuck to my face.

"She's got a nosebleed!" Lisa said, pointing at me like I was a cat run over on the street.

"What's your name?" the ski patrolman asked me.

"Kerry," I moaned.

"Are you feeling light-headed, Kerry? Dizzy?"

"A bit, I guess."

He pulled out a walkie-talkie and called down to someone at first aid. "We've got a girl on the north face in danger of bleeding to death. We need a stretcher up here on the ASAP and lots of gauze. It's a nosebleed, but it's a bad one. Yep . . . clots and everything."

In what seemed like six hours, the first-aid team arrived. They packed gauze around my nose and secured it with white medical tape stuck to my cheeks. Then they zipped me into what was probably a body bag and buckled me onto a stretcher on skis. One of the first-aid guys was wearing a harness that they clipped the stretcher to. He would tow me down the hill.

"You kids can follow her down," he told Kyle, Todd, and Lisa, who were still looking horrified.

And then we were zooming down the hill. I was beginning to feel a little dizzy, so I closed my eyes. Occasionally, I opened them to catch glimpses of Lisa and the boys skiing behind me. I couldn't read their expressions from my body bag, but I was sure they were ones of disgust.

I was taken to the first-aid shack, where I was placed on a rickety metal cot and given Tang to drink. Lisa sat beside me. The boys stood awkwardly at the door.

"So umm . . . ," Kyle said. "We're gonna take off."

"Okay," Lisa said.

"Can I, uh . . . get your number?" he asked her.

"Sure." She wrote it on a paper towel from the dispenser by the sink.

"Okay, then," Kyle said. This was obviously the cue for Todd to ask me for my number. I looked over at him. I just hoped he could remember the girl he'd kissed on the chairlift instead of this blood-soaked monster with her nostrils packed with gauze.

"So, uh, Kerry . . . ," he said.

"Yes?" I responded encouragingly.

"Uh . . . good luck with the nose problem." And he was gone.

Chapter 7

RAMONA HAS GIVEN ME RENEWED HOPE FOR THE FUTURE. I AM NOW strong enough to resume entries in the journal of mortifying moments. My therapist was thrilled. "I'm so glad you've decided to continue with your journal, Kerry. Now . . . you do realize that the nosebleed was probably due to the cold and elevation, and therefore nothing you could have prevented?"

"I do!" I said brightly, marveling at the fact that she has such a bad haircut despite being so well educated and having so much money.

Anyway, my numerous therapy visits have not had nearly the impact that my one session with Ramona did. I am walking on air! In addition to the prediction of true love with one sandy-haired and creative Douglas or Dean or Dale, there is another factor in my new positive attitude. Sam has been leaving me messages. Make that one message—but still. He had previously called but hung up when I didn't answer—as evidenced by the call log on my caller-ID box:

294-6062 (Mom)
294-6062 (Mom)
294-6062 (Mom)
294-6062 (Mom)
294-6062 (Mom)
294-6062 (Mom)
620-3579 (Sam)
294-6062 (Mom)
294-6062 (Mom)
619-4135 (Val)
620-3579 (Sam)
294-6062 (Mom)
294-6062 (Mom)

But yesterday, he left a message!

"Hey, Kerry, it's me . . . Sam. I haven't heard from you, and I was just wondering how you're doing. I hope everything's okay." Pause. "Call me."

I played it over a few times last night . . . twenty-three times last night. I had to ensure I wasn't missing any subtle innuendo in his tone or word choice. From my analysis, I deduced that he sounded concerned . . . like the fact that I haven't called him must mean I am dead or in a coma at the very least. Because why else would an averagely pretty, rather bottom-heavy woman of thirty-one *not* phone the gorgeous sexy man she has been involved with for two and a half years?

Unless . . . his concern is that I've moved on. Maybe met someone else who is more on my level in the looks department? Maybe now he is regretting letting me go?

Whatever the reason, he sounded a bit bummed, which has lifted my spirits immensely. Whether he is mourning my death (or coma) or my new, more equal relationship, the fact that he may feel an ounce of the pain and confusion I have been living with is extremely satisfying. I have called home four times today to listen to the message . . . just to keep my spirits bolstered.

Wouldn't it be fabulous if he called again tonight? Tonight I will be out drinking, dancing and flirting with kind, open, and giving Don or Dennis or Damon. Because tonight there is a fund-raiser for the National Advertising Philanthropic Institute (NAPI), which is an organization that helps people in the advertising industry who suffer a personal tragedy or crack-up and need hospitalization (which happens surprisingly often). This would certainly constitute a work-related function, would it not?

Sam will wonder why I haven't returned his call and may even be alarmed if he phones and I am not home again. He might just call my mom to find out what hospital I'm in or when the funeral service will be held. I can almost hear my mom's reply: "She's as fit as a fiddle as far as I know, Sam. But she's been impossible to get a hold of lately. I can only assume she's dating someone—if not several men. You know she never tells me anything."

I am in such a good mood, I will see if Trevor can sneak away for a chai latte.

"Fucking Rory," Trevor says when we are seated at a corner table in Starbucks. "He called last night."

"I thought you told him it was over."

"I haven't really had a chance to."

"Trevor . . . ," I begin in a voice disturbingly like my mother's.

"Look, Kerry. *I* know it's over. The fact that I haven't conveyed that to fucking Rory doesn't make it any less true."

I nod. That actually makes a lot of sense to me.

"Anyway," Trevor continues. "He called and said he's more sure than ever that I'm the one, but he's just waiting for the right time to tell Ken."

"Oh. And when might that be?"

"They're spending a week in Cancún in December. He thought he'd probably have an opportunity after that."

I bite into my blueberry white chocolate scone to keep from commenting. "Anyway," I say, through the mouthful of muffin. "Let's forget about our depressing love lives and party it up at the NAPI event tonight."

"What?" Trevor gapes at me. "We hate those parties!"

"No, we don't."

"We do! We always say we can barely stand spending time with advertising people when we're being paid for it, let alone on our own time."

"I've never said that. I love work-related functions!"

"Since when?"

"Since . . . umm . . . okay," I confess. "My mom took me to a psychic, and she told me I'd meet the sandy-haired, creative love of my life at a work-related function."

"Wow."

"And his name starts with *D.*"

"Very specific."

"She was really good, Trevor. She told me I had been involved with a gorgeous man who didn't even know the real me."

"Obviously gorgeous Sam."

"Obviously. And she said that there was a negative woman at work who would always hold me back."

Trevor gasps loudly. "Sonja!"

"Yes!"

"Oh, my god! Maybe I should go see your psychic? She could tell me if I should wait for fucking Rory to come back from Cancún."

"I'm sure she could tell you that."

"Cool!" he says, oblivious of the tone in my voice. "Okay. Let's go tonight, and if we find your soul mate, I'm definitely making an appointment with her."

Back in my office, the message light on my phone is blinking furiously. I dial in and find a message from Sandra.

"Hi, Kerry. Look . . . I'm sorry to bother you at work but . . . Oh shit, here I go again." I can hear her sniffling on the message. "I . . . I really need someone to talk to. Call me if you have a chance."

I don't bother checking the other four messages waiting, and I dial Sandra directly.

"Hi!" her cheerful voice says. "You've reached the desk of Sandra Conner. I can't take your call right now. . . ." I hang up and dial her cell phone.

"Hello?" Her voice is weak and shaky.

"It's me. Where are you?"

"On the bus. I'm going home."

"What's wrong?"

"It's . . . it's . . ." She is falling apart again.

"Is it George?" I volunteer. He is her married boss/lover.

"Y-yes. Sort of."

"What do you mean?" I coax.

She begins to wail. "It's his wife!"

"Oh, no! Did she find out about you two?" Despite my reaction, I am not surprised. George's wife must be the stupidest person alive if she believes George needs to have emergency meetings with his legal secretary on Saturday nights. He is in wills and probates, after all.

"Nooo . . . ," Sandra says. "She's pregnant."

"What? Is that even possible? Isn't he like, sixty-five?"

"He's fifty-eight, and yes, it's possible." Sandra sounds a bit annoyed through her tears.

"Sorry. I just thought that at his age, the chances of getting someone pregnant would be pretty slim. I mean, I think you'd have to try and t—" Oops.

There is silence on the other end of the line. Then, "He says they hadn't been intimate in years. It was just one time. . . ."

Maybe George's wife isn't the stupidest person alive.

"Anyway," Sandra continues, "I had to get out of the office. People have been sending him pink and blue balloons and boxes of cigars all day. It was horrible!"

"Okay, listen, I don't think you should be alone."

"I'm f-f-fine!" She is bawling again.

"I'll meet you at your place."

I grab my coat and briefcase and hustle out of the office. "Off to a meeting at Prism," I tell the receptionist, stabbing the elevator DOWN button frantically. Once downstairs, I race to my car and peel out of the parking lot. I am sunk low in my seat in case Sonja happens to be walking by. At the same time, I am dialing my cell phone. I realize it's not a very safe driving method, but this is an emergency situation.

Michelle answers on the first ring. "Michelle Dueck," she says aggressively.

"Hey, it's me." I sit up as I gain distance from the office building. "We've got a problem."

"What is it?"

"Sandra's falling apart. George's wife is pregnant."

"Oh, Christ," Michelle mutters. She has never been very sympathetic to Sandra's plight. She can't understand how a woman could have such low self-esteem that she'd put her life on hold to be at a man's beck and call. I, on the other hand, can kind of relate to that situation.

"I'm on my way over there to make sure she's okay," I say as I weave through traffic. "But someone needs to be with her tonight."

"I have a Pilates class."

"Sandra's a wreck! I'm sure you can miss one Pilates class."

"Okay," she says reluctantly. "What have you got on tonight that's so important?"

"A work-related function."

"I thought you hated work-related functions."

"No, I don't! Anyway . . . I have to go to this one," I say. "It's mandatory."

Michelle acquiesces. "All right. Tell Sandra I'll be over around seven. We can order in some dinner."

"Thanks, Michelle. You're a good friend."

I pull into Safeway and scurry into the store. I race through the aisles, loading my red plastic basket with cookies, chips and dip, herbal tea, and a tub of ready-made frosting. Everyone has a different way of coping with heartache. I, myself, am partial to the sweet-and-creamy group of foods, but I have known others who prefer to go the salty-and-crunchy route. I also pop into the liquor store next door for a bottle of chardonnay and a pack of cigarettes. You never know.

Sandra answers her door, and I resist cringing at the sight of her. It's a good thing she decided to come home! Her eyes are almost swollen shut with thick rings of mascara beneath them. Her nose is red and shiny and running. Her lips look chapped and puffy. Oh, dear. "There, there," I say, taking her into my embrace.

"I—can't—be-be-be-lieve he—did this—to—to me!" She sobs into my shoulder. After a few moments, I can feel the dampness soaking through my collar. I extricate myself and lead her to the couch. I don't want to meet the love of my life this evening with a snot stain on my shoulder.

"You're going to be okay," I tell her, holding both her hands in mine. "Maybe this is for the best?"

"If you're here to—to—g-give me a lecture," Sandra screams. "You c-can just leave!"

Yikes! She's really freaking out. "I brought supplies," I say, sheepishly changing the subject. I begin to unload the bag. "Chips, icing, cookies . . ." She grabs the chips and tears open the bag.

"That's a girl," I say, patting her knee. "It's all going to be okay. Time heals all wounds. That which does not kill us makes us stronger. There's dip in the bag."

"I know I've been stupid," Sandra says after she's inhaled half a package of potato chips. She's now smoking a cigarette—who knew? "But he's played a huge role in my life for so long—professionally and personally. He was a father figure"—Sandra's father passed away when she was twelve—"a lover, a mentor. . . ." She is starting to get upset again.

"I've got icing? Do you want some icing?" I try to distract her.

"No." She waves her hand. "I like salty and crunchy."

"Okay."

"I'm going to have to quit my job."

"Yeah. But it'll be a fresh start for you."

"Oh, God! I'm going to have to start all over . . . ," she moans. "I'm thirty-three, and I have to start all over!"

I take my friend in my arms again, deciding to ignore any mess on my shoulder. I should have time to change before tonight's work-related function. I glance at my watch. *Gak!* It's quarter to four!

Sandra feels my panic. "What?"

"I didn't realize it was so late," I say. "I, umm . . . I have a really important meeting this evening . . . a work-related function that I can't miss."

"I'll be fine," Sandra says, flopping back on the couch in a pout.

"Michelle's going to come over tonight. She thought you guys could order some dinner?"

"Michelle?" Sandra jumps up. "Michelle! Why would I want Michelle over here? So she can tell me I'm an idiot? That something like this was bound to happen sooner or later? That I'm weak and pathetic because I need a man in my life?"

"She's not going to say that," I say, while making a mental note to call Michelle with instructions not to say that. "She cares about you. She wants to support you."

"Thanks a lot, Kerry. I think I'd rather be alone." She flops down on the plush sofa and curls into the fetal position.

I feel like the worst friend in the world, but I can't miss the chance to meet the ideal man intended for me by the spirit world. "Here," I say. "Have another cigarette. I'll open you a bottle of wine. You'll feel better in no time."

And that's how I leave her: curled up on the couch, a bottle of chardonnay clutched in her hand, and a pack of cigarettes on the coffee table in front of her. It's okay, I tell myself. Michelle will be there in a couple of hours. But I still feel awful—though, obviously not awful enough to keep me from the NAPI party tonight.

Chapter 8

BY FIVE THIRTY, TREVOR AND I HAVE SQUEEZED INTO THE BACK OF A CAB with our friend Shelley, an account exec who is very negative and bitter and whom we find hilarious. In the front seat, barely visible because of the headrest, is Gavin.

"Gavin's going to catch a ride with us," Trevor had announced. I started to object and then noticed that Gavin was standing directly behind him. Of course, I could not see him as he is so minuscule.

"Great," I muttered instead. It seemed Trevor was still trying to persuade Gavin to join the gay brotherhood.

We arrive at the Silver Unicorn, a seedily trendy club in Pioneer Square and show the thick-necked bouncer our tickets. Once inside, we climb the musty stairwell into the club and head directly to the bar. Unfortunately, we do not manage to lose Gavin in transit through the crowded club. He seems to be clinging to Trevor like a baby chimpanzee to its mother.

Ordering three crantinis and a Budweiser for Gavin (which causes Trevor to furrow his brow with concern), we park ourselves at a centrally located table and begin to scour the scene for my future husband. Trevor has taken the liberty of filling Shelley in on Ramona's predictions. I was able to stop him—upon penalty of severe physical abuse—from telling Gavin. I could just hear Gavin in the next Prism meeting: "How do you think sales will do this fall, Kerry? Or shall we wait while you read your tea leaves?"

"So . . . any candidates?" Trevor whispers to me. I scan the crowd in the dim, nightclub lighting.

"Not yet, but it's still early."

We order another round as the president of NAPI steps up to a microphone positioned in the middle of the dance floor. "Test, test!" he says, the mic popping loudly with each consonant. The crowd settles, and he begins to expound on all the good works the organization is doing. "Stan Worobey, an art director in Portland, was recently hospitalized for exhaustion. The NAPI fund helped Stan and his wife get some help with household duties while he was incapacitated."

Everyone claps uproariously. I lean over to Trevor. "I could use some help with household duties. My shower grout is disgusting. How do I get in on this?"

"It seems you have to be exhausted," he whispers back.

"I am exhausted."

"No, like Mariah Carey exhausted. I can give you some tips later."

The president continues. "And the NAPI fund helped Brenda Johnstone, a production coordinator in Spokane, get a new motorized wheelchair."

More applause. I join in enthusiastically. I find myself more supportive of using funds to pay for wheelchairs than housekeepers.

"I wonder if the NAPI fund would pay Dave's legal bills if he ever gets arrested for being a serial killer?" I whisper to Trevor.

"I doubt it. But Ferris and Shannon would. They'd hire O. J.'s dream team to get him off. How could the agency possibly go on without his incredible creative expertise?"

"And if he didn't get off, we'd have to have all the creative presentations during visiting hours at the McNeil Island Corrections Center."

We are launching into uncontrollable giggles when we notice several people shooting us pointed looks. The NAPI president is still going on about all the emotionally disturbed advertising people the fund has provided nannies and housekeepers for. It is inappropriate for us to be laughing, which makes it even harder to stop.

Finally, he instructs us all to have a great time and leaves the stage. Phew! We collect ourselves enough to approach the buffet table set up at one end of the dance floor. As we load our plates with food, we continue our repartee. "Dave would be like Hannibal Lecter. . . . He'd have to give creative presentations with one of those goalie masks on so he didn't bite anyone's face off."

I am in hysterics, barely able to stand up. I reach for the tongs to grab a spring roll when my hand collides with a larger, much hairier hand.

"Sorry," I say, pulling back.

"No, I'm sorry. Go ahead."

"Thanks." I take the proffered tongs and look up at the owner of the hand. He is a nice-looking guy, tall with amused blue eyes and brown hair. On closer inspection, I would have to say his hair is actually sandyish. On first sight, one might call it brown, but I would have to say it is definitely on the sandy side. Could this be him?

"So . . ." I smile flirtatiously. "Are you in advertising?" I grab a spring roll and then pass the tongs to him.

"No." He kind of laughs. "My buddy dragged me—sorry, *brought* me along."

"I know what you mean. I don't usually come to these work-related functions either."

"No?"

"No! I hate them normally."

"What's different about this one?" His eyes are twinkling at me.

"Oh . . . umm . . . my friend really wanted me to come with him."

Trevor pops his head around. "Hi. I'm Trevor. And you are?"

"Nick."

"Ohhhh," he says, his voice relaying grave disappointment. "Well, nice to meet you, Nick. This is my friend, Kerry. We've got to get back to our drinks."

"In a second," I growl at him. God. Does he really think I will walk away from a cute, sandyish-haired guy who might very well have a wonderful and caring soul and be in the visual arts, just because his name doesn't start with *D*? Ramona can't be infallible. "So, Nick . . ."

And in that moment, it happens. All the bad karma for ditching Sandra with a bottle of wine and a pack of cigarettes in her time of need, for giggling cruelly during the speech about all the suffering advertising people, it all comes back to make me pay. Gavin, who is scurrying after Trevor, passes by me just as I reach up to flick my hair in a sexy and attractive manner. My hand hits Gavin's burgeoning plate (so much food for such a minute person) and knocks the end of it, sending it sailing from his grip. It flies from his hand, the contents arcing through the air, only to fall, in an edible hailstorm, on my right shoulder and breast.

"Gavin!" I screech at him.

"What?" He wails back. "You hit my plate!"

I am tempted to smash *my* plate on the edge of the buffet table and stab him in the jugular with a pointed shard. "God, look at this mess!"

It's disgusting. Leave it to Gavin to be eating deviled eggs, hot wings, chicken satay with peanut sauce, and Caesar salad. Not only do I look gross, but I smell it, too!

"Watch out, people!" A waiter with a mop has approached. "Be careful. We don't want anyone to slip in this huge mess of food. And there's broken glass here, too! Watch your step, people! Don't want anyone to get cut."

Why is he yelling like that? The attention of everyone in the bar is now on our "accident." And on me standing here with Caesar salad and deviled eggs dripping off my boob.

"Thanks a lot, Gavin," I hiss as I storm to the rest room. I forgot to even acknowledge Nick. Good thing he is not "the one."

I clean myself up as best I can with paper towels dampened in the sink, but there is no denying I will have to leave. Thanks to Gavin, I've been humiliated in front of the whole advertising community. Not to mention the fact that I will never meet the love of my life smelling like anchovies and eggs. Keeping a low profile, I scurry to the coat check near the exit.

Relief washes over me when I have covered my ruined blouse with my raincoat. I just hope this smell won't be transferred to my coat. I will hurry home and throw the whole outfit into the washer.

I am in the refuge of the dim stairwell when I hear my name.

"Kerry!"

I turn, expecting to see Trevor, but no! It's Dave! Creepy, serial-killer, creative-director Dave. Surely the universe is treating me rather harshly. I admit it wasn't very kind of me to leave Sandra alone and to laugh through the speech about less fortunate ad people, but I don't think I deserve to have my face bitten off.

"Dave . . . ," I say weakly. I glance nervously around. We are all alone on the secluded and darkened stairway. This is like a movie . . . a very scary movie where you just know that the character is going to get killed off because she wasn't a very nice person in the beginning.

"Listen . . ." He comes up close to me. "I've been meaning to talk to you."

"Okay." I swallow loudly. Maybe the anchovy smell will scare him away before he does anything painful to me. Like the way garlic works on vampires.

"It's about the Prism campaign."

I feel a glimmer of hope. Perhaps this is just a harmless work conversation in a spooky darkened stairwell?

"I want you to know that I respected you stating your opinion. You were wrong, but I still respect you standing up to me. Sometimes I think—" He takes a pull from the beer bottle in his hand. "—that people are afraid to tell me the truth. Everyone's always agreeing with me and supporting my ideas."

"That must suck."

He looks at me. "It does, actually. That's why it was so refreshing the other day . . . when you . . . you know . . . stood up to me."

He is leaning in close to me, and I realize he's very drunk. Otherwise he'd be repulsed by my smell.

"I think you've got a lot of spirit, Kerry," he says as he leans in farther. "You're really feisty and . . . beautiful. . . ."

God! What is he doing? He is leaning in toward me like he's going to—oh, good God! He wants to kiss me.

"Look, Dave . . ." I step down another step. "I really have to get going. I've got Caesar salad all over my shirt and—"

"One little kiss, Kerry," he whines.

"It would make things awkward at work," I say.

"Nothing would change. I can keep my personal life separate from my professional life."

"You're already dating someone in the office!"

"Yeah, but it's not working out. It's over be—"

"Dave?" It is Tanya, all pierced and ominous, standing at the top of the stairs. "What's going on here?"

"Nothing," Dave slurs. "We were just talking about Prism."

"Yeah. Thanks for that very helpful and useful comment. I must run and change out of these stinky clothes! *À bientôt!*"

I fly down the stairs and out into the night.

Chapter 9

I WAS MORTIFIED TO COME TO WORK THIS MORNING AFTER LAST NIGHT'S disaster, but since I'd spent yesterday afternoon at Sandra's, I have a lot of work to catch up on. I would also look like the biggest baby in the universe if I didn't show up just because I'd had a plate of appetizers tipped all over me. Besides, I must tell Trevor about what happened (or didn't happen) with Dave.

"What do you mean, you can't go for coffee?" I whisper angrily into the phone.

"Lunch okay?" Trevor says. "I've got a brain-dump session." He practically hangs up on me.

I'm a bit annoyed with Trevor for not coming to my rescue last night, but I know what he's like. He's very gay (if there are degrees of gayness), in that the sight and smell of me covered with food would probably have turned his stomach and we'd have had an even bigger mess to deal with. And now I'm a bit annoyed that he can't meet me for coffee. I'm absolutely bursting to tell someone about Dave coming on to me last night. I know! I'll call Shelley.

"Good morning."

Oh, shit. Sonja.

"Good morning." I smile. "How are you?"

"Fine. I was looking for you yesterday afternoon."

"You were? I was at Prism . . . meeting with Janet."

"She called looking for you."

Oh, this is just great. Now I will be fired! The way things are going, I don't know why I'm surprised.

"Look . . . ," I say, gazing forlornly into Sonja's face. I am hoping to force a return of the tender, Julie Andrews expression I'd glimpsed the other day. "I know I shouldn't have lied, but a friend of mine was in crisis. I had to go to her."

"Oh?" There is a hint of understanding there.

"She's in an awful state. I was worried she might—" Pause for dramatic effect. "—harm herself."

"Oh, God!" Sonja is suitably shocked. "What's wrong?"

"Her boss's wife is pregnant."

"Uh . . . so?"

"Oh, sorry." I laugh a little. "He's also her lover . . . and her father figure and mentor." I look at her then, nodding my head in an "obviously you can understand why I had to be there for her" way.

"Kerry, I'm sorry to hear that your friend is having some issues with her married lover, but I don't consider that an adequate excuse to be lying about your whereabouts. Janet needed to talk to you."

"She has my cell number," I counter. "I was still available."

"She told me she tried your cell several times and kept getting a busy signal."

"That's strange," I say, feeling myself blush despite my best efforts. "I rarely use my cell for personal calls."

Sonja prepares to leave. "I know this isn't the first time we've had this conversation, Kerry, but I strongly urge you to take care of any personal problems you have that may be affecting your work."

"Yeeeesssss, Sonja," I sigh heavily. Ooops, that came out a little more sardonic than I'd planned.

"Perhaps I should put it another way: You're not irreplaceable. You'd better shape up, or you'll be out of a job."

Bitch! She's just jealous of me and will always hold me back, just like Ramona said. Don't let her get to you—breathe deeply, calmly. But I can feel the emotion welling up in my throat. Don't start crying, don't start crying. . . . God, what is wrong with me? I don't even like this stupid job! I swivel in my chair and stare at the computer screen. There is nothing to be upset about. I will buckle down. . . . I will focus on the job at hand. . . . But what I need now is a distraction. I click on my e-mail inbox.

There are several work-related missives and one from my brother in Australia.

Name: Greg Spence
Subject: Hey Big Sis!!

I open it.

How r u? How's Sam? Work? Have you seen mom lately? Are she and Darrel still pawing each other like horny teenagers? Have you heard from Dad? I got an email the other day. He said he wants us to come to London next Christmas.

Things in Sydney are so rad man! I'm talking, totally fucking insane! I can't tell you how awesome my life is now! I get up around eleven, have a coffee on the beach, go for a surf, then hang out till my shift starts at three. Then I party all night with these great people: Aussies, Kiwis, Canadians, Americans, Germans, tons of Brits. I'm meeting so many rad dudes and gorgeous birds. I don't think I'll ever come home!!

Anyway sis . . . hope things are just as awesome back in Seattle at the ad agency.
Love your lil bro',
Greg

I hit REPLY.

Dear Greg,
    FUCK YEWWWWWWWWWWWWW you spoiled, self-absorbed little "wanker"!
Love your big sis,
Kerry

Of course I don't really send it. If I did, he'd be on the phone to my mom within seconds saying, "Mommy! Mommy! Kerry sent me an abusive e-mail! She was swearing and everything! What is going on in her life that is so terrible that she feels the need to take it out on me—her innocent, surfing, bartender brother?"

Anyway, time to deal with reality. I click on the e-mail from Janet at Prism.

Name: Janet Morrow
Subject: Back to School brochure

Hi Kerry,
    I've tried to call you at the office and on your cell but it seems you are MIA. I've got some last-minute changes to the brochure that need to be incorporated. There is an error in the pricing of the multi-connection package and we can't print the brochure without correcting it. I hope it has not gone to press, because we're not paying for another run. Please call me at your earliest convenience.
J.

I call production first. "Hey, Dennis. What's the status on the back-to-school brochure for Prism?"

"Just waiting for the ink to dry—then it can be scored and folded."

I put my head down on my desk. "Great," I moan into the receiver.

"What's wrong?" Dennis senses my pain.

"There's a mistake in the brochure. It's going to have to be reprinted."

"What!" He completely spazzes out. "Why wasn't the mistake caught on the proofs? Who's fault is this? Who's going to pay for another print run?"

"Calm down!" I say, surprised by my forcefulness. "I'll take care of it, okay?"

He simmers a bit. "Fine."

"One more thing, Dennis . . . What time did the brochure go on the press last night?"

"The late shift. Around five."

And that seals it. It is my fault. If I had been at work to take Janet's call and make the changes she wanted, none of this would have happened. Instead, I was plying my distraught friend with wine and junk food in a half-assed attempt to make her feel better. The agency is going to have to pay for another run of brochures. That will not make them happy. On the bright side, perhaps now they won't fire me. They'll probably want to keep me on so they can garnishee my wages.

How did everything get so messed up? Tears are stinging my eyes, and I want nothing more than to crawl under my desk, curl up in a ball, and cry for three hours. But it is not to be.

"Ohmigawd! There you are!"

"Hi, Trevor," I say glumly as he takes a seat in my office.

"I'm so sorry about what happened to you last night! You must be mortified."

"Yes, I am."

"I tried to come into the ladies' room to help you, but one of the bouncers saw me and wouldn't let me through. I was all, like, 'Trust me, honey. There's nothing in there that interests me,' but he wasn't budging. So I went back to the bar and had a few more cocktails, and I met the most amazing guy who works at LPM. So gorgeous, smart, and sexy! He makes fucking Rory look . . . fat and boring!"

"Great."

Silence.

"So . . . obviously, you made it home all right?"

"Yeah . . ." Despite my somber mood, I am filled with glee to finally be able to share my Dave story. "But . . . I was almost murdered."

"What?"

"Dave accosted me in the stairwell."

"Oh, God! Kerry, how horrifying! What did he do?"

"He tried"—I lower my voice to a dramatic whisper—"to kiss me!"

"*No!* Oh, my God!" Trevor screams at the top of his lungs.

"Shhhhhhhhh! I've practically been fired already this morning. I don't want to draw attention to myself."

"Sorry," Trevor whispers, and scoots his chair closer to me. We pretend to be poring over a creative brief while I quietly give him the details of last night's stairwell encounter.

When I am finished, Trevor sits back and looks at me. "You know what?"

"What?"

"I hate to say this, but I think Dave's 'the one.' "

"The one what?"

"The 'one,' the 'one' Ramona was talking about."

"Yuck! Shut up! Don't be gross."

"Think about it," he says. "He's got sandy hair, his name starts with *D*, he's in a creative field."

"It's not him, Trevor. He's been married three times! He has a girlfriend!"

"She said there would be obstacles to you two getting together."

"Those are pretty major obstacles." My voice is getting louder. "It's not him! It's not him, okay?"

"Okay . . . but maybe you should have more of an open mind? You don't want to let true love walk out the door just because he's a serial killer with a girlfriend."

Just then Sonja walks by with Bob Copley, the managing director. Trevor is quick on his feet. "The brief looks great, Kerr," he says. "Nice point of difference. Way to push the envelope!"

Chapter 10

THIS WEEKEND MARKS THE BEGINNING OF THE NEW KERRY SPENCE. I AM
turning over a new leaf. I will be a kinder, gentler, more spiritual and
true person, and in return, the universe will reward me with abun-
dance. It's all outlined in this book I picked up after work on Friday.
It is called *You Get What You Give*, by Dr. Rainbow Hashwarma, and
it's helped me enormously already. I've read only the first two chap-
ters, but I've managed to glean the central theme of the book. Basically, it purports that the life you have is the life you deserve. So, if
you are lonely, hate your job, and the man you are meant to be with
is a two-timing murderer, that is because you are a shitty person and
you deserve it. I have decided to make some major changes in my life
and attitudes. I have created a short list of ways to become a better
human being.

✔ Be a better friend. (I will never again desert a friend in
her time of need to go off to a stupid work-related
function—or even to a really good party.)

✔ Deal with Sam in an honest and straightforward manner. (This avoidance thing is getting rude. He left another message this morning.)

✔ Never giggle and make jokes when someone is talking about a person who is emotionally exhausted or getting a new wheelchair.

✔ Develop a strong, loving, and uncritical relationship with my mother. (This is more of a long-term goal.)

✔ Write and phone my dad more. (Just because he is a workaholic who lives on another continent doesn't mean he doesn't love and miss his children.)

✔ Write frequently in the journal of mortifying moments in order to analyze these situations with my therapist, absolve myself of blame, and learn to love men with an open, unguarded heart.

✔ Start going to yoga.

✔ Volunteer for something. (Hopefully something that is kind of fun where I can meet single men who are also kind, gentle, spiritual, and true.)

✔ Stop joking about Dave being a serial killer. This is unkind to the victims of real serial killers, and if it does (God forbid) turn out that he is the "one" I am meant to be with, I'd like the joke to just go away.

My first step is taking Sandra out for brunch. Thankfully, she doesn't seem angry at me about the other night. When she hears how that event turned out, she will realize I have already been punished enough.

I pick her up, and we head to a tiny diner we frequent near the waterfront. Sandra looks quite a bit better, but I'm a little worried that she's on something. She seems glassy eyed and lethargic, but otherwise, in fine spirits.

We find a seat by the window and order coffees and French toast for me, an omelette for her.

"It's a beautiful view, isn't it?" I say, gazing out the window. "The ocean looks so haunting when it's gray and rainy out."

"Mmm-hmm," she agrees distractedly.

"So . . . how are you, anyway?" I ask, taking her hand across the table. "I'm sorry I couldn't stay with you the other night."

"I'm fine." She smiles vacantly.

"Really? You're okay?" Something is not right about this.

"Yeah . . . I mean, the situation is less than ideal, but we can work through it."

"Pardon me?" I sputter on my ice water. "What are you saying?"

"I'm saying George and I have worked things out."

"Worked things out?" I scream. All eyes in the restaurant turn to our table. I lean forward and hiss the rest of my discourse. "Sandra, please tell me you are not going to continue your relationship with him."

"Kerry . . . I've thought a lot about this, and it's my decision to make. He told me you guys would try to talk me out of it."

"Are you high?" Oops. The volume level has crept up again. "Seriously, are you on something?" I whisper.

"I've taken a little something to help me relax," she says. "It's no big deal."

"What is it?" I demand, although I don't know anything about hard drugs, and unless she says crack or heroin, I'm not going to know whether I should be concerned.

"A little Valium."

At least I have heard of Valium—but should I be concerned? Didn't all the housewives in the fifties take Valium, like every day? But didn't many of them also end up dead inside? I don't know what to do! "I don't think you should be taking Valium, Sandra," I say in a strong voice that conceals all doubt. "You need to keep a clear head."

"It's clear," she says, pouring cream into her coffee. "I know what I want, and that's George in my life."

We sit in silence for a while, each staring at the ocean, immersed in our own thoughts. At least I am immersed in my own thoughts; Sandra is probably floating on a fluffy pink cloud. Given my recent commitment to being a better friend, I must carefully consider the tack I take with her. On the one hand, maybe her relationship with George is enough for her. Maybe she doesn't want a man who loves only her and will give her a home and children and stability and security. In that case, I should just butt out. But on the other hand, I've known Sandra since college, and I can't forget the dreams she'd shared with me. She *did* want a family and a home and a man to love her! It's not like she'd fantasized about a relationship with her old geezer boss who evidently still screws his wife!

"Listen," I say, pouring syrup on my French toast. "As your friend, I need to tell you how I feel."

"I know how you feel," Sandra says casually, taking a bite of her omelette. "But no one understands the situation like I do."

Is there a computer chip planted in her brain? Has George replaced her with a Stepford mistress? "Sandra . . . I know it's hard to end things with him, but you deserve more than this. You deserve a man who loves only you! You deserve to have a home. And children."

She smiles. "I am going to have children."

"Oh, come on!" I say, frustrated by her Zen-like acceptance. "By the time George's latest child grows up, he'll be ninety."

"Seventy-six."

"Okay, seventy-six. Do you really want your child to have a father who's almost eighty? Too old to play catch, too blind to play video games, too incontinent to—"

"No, I don't," she says calmly. "George and I have discussed it, and we're not going to wait. We're going to try for a baby later this year."

"*What?*" I cannot believe I'm hearing this. Again, I grasp frantically for the right way to handle the situation. I wish I'd read more of *You Get What You Give*. Surely Dr. Rainbow Hashwarma must have a chapter on how to support your friend but make her see sense, as well. I decide I must take a hard line. It's for Sandra's own good.

"I'm sorry, Sandra, but that's the stupidest thing I've ever heard. Who does George think he is, François Mitterrand?"

"Who?"

"The president of France who had—look, it doesn't matter. The point is . . . I don't think you should settle for this. You deserve to have a proper family, not a part-time husband and father for your child."

"You're entitled to your opinion, Kerry."

"Seriously, Sandra," I continue in a firm yet gentle tone. "I think you need to make a clean break from George. Maybe you should see my therapist? She's really helped me move beyond my relationship with Sam."

"Really?" She smirks at me. "You call screening your calls and avoiding him moving beyond him?"

"I'm going to talk to him very soon," I say, blushing. "Anyway . . . this isn't about me. This is about you."

"My mind is made up," she says with a shrug. "I'm happy and at peace."

"That's the Valium talking! You can't do this. If you have a baby with George, I'll—"

"You'll what?" Her eyes narrow, and there is a glimpse of the real Sandra through the fog of contentment.

"I . . . I'm not going to support you in this," I say firmly. "I will not stand by and watch you throw your life away."

"Thanks, Kerry. You're a real friend."

"It's called tough love."

"It's called being a judgmental bitch," she says. She throws a ten-dollar bill on the table. "Nice seeing you." She storms out.

I drive home on autopilot, my tears camouflaged by the pouring rain. When I am inside my apartment, I rush to pick up *You Get What You Give.* I flip through it frantically, eager for some reinforcement that my tough-love approach was the right one. I find the section I am looking for on page 112.

When you are truly at one with the universe, you must let those you love find their way to true enlightenment by making their own mistakes. One must not force his or her opinions or beliefs on a friend or loved one, no matter how clear the answer may seem. Only by allowing the people you care about to come to their own conclusions can your relationships endure.

Shit, shit, shit!

Mortifying Moment #4

"You look amazing!" my best friend Rhonda squealed as she opened her front door for me.

"You do!" Maureen, my other best friend, chorused. "A mermaid-style dress is perfect for you!"

"Thanks, you guys! You look so beautiful, too," I gushed. And they did. Rhonda was radiant with her blond, feathered hair and lacy pink gown. Maureen's cheeks glowed with happiness, framed by curling-ironed tendrils of dark hair. Soon, we had all three dissolved into tears and were clinging to each other, the taffeta of our prom dresses rustling with each sob.

"Look at the princesses!" Rhonda's dad said, circling us and snapping photos.

"You look like angels," said Rhonda's mom. "Pink, mauve, and peach angels."

"I have a little gift for you guys," Maureen said through the lump of emotion in her throat. She broke away from the circle.

"I do, too."

"Me, too."

We retrieved the wrapped boxes from their plastic bags and sat in the living room for the gift exchange. Rhonda didn't sit, though. Her pink dress was formfitting; it did not allow sitting.

"Open mine first," I said, presenting them each with a small box.

They both gasped, removing the small gold pendants from their green velvet nests. "Oh!"

"Turn them over," I said excitedly. Engraved on the back of each tiny heart was

THE TRANSISTERS 4 EVER!
1989.

"Oh, my god!" We all started to cry again. The Transisters (pronounced Transistors) was the name of the rock band we were going to form after graduation.

"Now mine," Maureen said. Rhonda and I tore off the wrapping to find pewter goblets, each engraved with

THE TRANSISTERS.
CLASS OF '89.

More tears.
Rhonda passed out the last gift. "It's beautiful!" we bawled when we saw the bronzed plaques reading

LIVE LOVE LAUGH.
THE TRANSISTERS ALWAYS AND FOREVER.
CLASS OF '89 ROCKS!

"You girls better freshen up," Rhonda's mom said, wiping a tear from her eye. "The boys will be here in a few minutes."

We all giggled and scurried (as fast as one can scurry in skintight taffeta) to Rhonda's room. We passed around the Mary Kay plum eye shadow trio, the cherry blush, the pink pearl lip gloss. Then we stood side by side and took in our reflection in the mirror.

"We made it," I said.

"Yep," Rhonda agreed. "This is the beginning of the next chapter."

"Yeah," said Maureen. "Just think . . . next time this year we'll be traveling the country as the Transisters."

"It's going to be so awesome!" We'd been planning our rock band since tenth grade. Maureen would play drums (she had been practicing on her cousin's drum set), and Rhonda would be lead guitar (she planned to start taking lessons soon). I would be the lead singer. I knew this was not because I had the best voice necessarily, but since I was the tallest, we felt I'd have the most stage presence. We would begin our search for a bass player in the summer.

"It's a big night for us."

"In more ways than one," Maureen giggled.

"Are you guys still in?" Rhonda turned from the mirror and looked at us each gravely.

"I'm in," I said, my stomach turning over with nerves.

"Me, too," Maureen said. "Just think . . . tomorrow we'll be real women."

"Yeah," I said nervously. "It's really cool that tonight will be the first time for all of us."

"Yeah," Maureen said. "It's very cool."

Rhonda was conspicuously silent.

"Why are you so quiet?" Maureen asked. "Are you chickening out?"

"No!" Rhonda's face was red. "No . . . it's just that . . . umm . . ."

"What?" I asked, secretly hoping that she would chicken out, thus letting me off the hook.

"It's just that Wes and I kind of . . . already . . ."

"What?" Maureen and I shrieked. "When?"

"Last month." Rhonda shrugged.

"That's just great," Maureen sniped. "We've promised each other since tenth grade that we'd all lose our virginity on prom night."

"Yeah," I said to support Maureen's indignation, although I was only slightly perturbed that Rhonda broke our pact.

"Look, you guys," Rhonda said, normal color returning to her face. "It just sort of happened, okay? The point is, we will all have sex tonight, and tomorrow, all three of us will be nonvirgins."

"True," I said to smooth things over. "That's really the point."

Maureen gave in grudgingly. "Okay."

"Besides," Rhonda said to me. "You and Brent are such a great couple. You are so totally meant to be."

"Thanks," I said shyly.

She addressed Maureen. "And you and Eddie, too. You're so lucky to have found your soul mate at such a young age."

Maureen smiled. "Yes, I am."

"Okay . . ." Rhonda lowered her voice. "Here's the plan. You know how I'm looking after my Auntie Shirley's cat while she's in Reno?"

"Yeah," Maureen and I said in unison.

"I got two extra keys cut." She reached into her jewelry box and presented us each with a silver key. "There's a bedroom downstairs, and two upstairs. If the door is shut, that means the room is occupied, okay?"

"Okay." We heard the doorbell ring downstairs.

"*Good luck tonight, girls,*" Rhonda said. We all hugged and then checked our makeup one more time. As we headed down the stairs, I had to ask. "*So, Rhonda? Was it . . . you know . . . fun?*"

"*Pretty fun,*" she whispered back.

BRENT AND I HAD BEEN DATING SINCE ELEVENTH GRADE. I'D HAD A CRUSH on him since the ninth, but I was four inches taller than he was then, so he hadn't really been interested. The year we turned seventeen, he shot up to almost six feet and finally noticed me. He had shiny, dark feathered hair, deep brown eyes, and was the strong and silent type. He was also a really good basketball player. Some people thought he could make it to the NBA. That would be cool, I guess, except that with my career as lead singer in a rock band, we'd hardly ever see each other.

I held his hand as we sat in the back of the limo with our friends. I looked up at him and smiled adoringly; he glanced over and gave me a quick grin. He seemed tense. Maybe the pressure of tonight's events was weighing on him, too? I had always thought that boys just wanted to "do it" all the time, but I suppose there would be some anxiety attached to the whole affair for them, as well. Tonight would not be Brent's first time, though. He told me he had slept with a girl the summer before we got together. She was his cousin's neighbor in Olympia. I was actually quite relieved that he would know what he was doing.

The dance was magical! The gymnasium had been transformed into a splendid ballroom. As Brent and I grooved to "*She Drives Me Crazy*" by the Fine Young Cannibals, I succumbed to the enchantment of this special evening. I was so immersed in the festivities that I didn't even sneer at the crepe paper streamers, the plastic pompoms, the silk flowers adorning our tables. The surroundings all seemed perfect, celebrating our passage into adulthood. Maureen, Rhonda, and I periodically gave each other the thumbs-up or a suggestive up-and-down movement of our eyebrows.

Wes had sneaked in a bottle of white rum that we furtively sipped under the tablecloth. We were all getting quite drunk, laughing and falling all over each other. The adult chaperons eyed us suspiciously but didn't take any action. They would be lenient because it was the most important night of our lives.

As the evening wound down, the butterflies in my stomach reactivated. They were somewhat calmed by the effect of the rum, but as the moment of devirgining drew closer, the more nervous I got. I pressed my body against Brent's as we swayed to "Wicked Game" by Chris Isaak.

I crooned the lyrics in his ear. " 'Oh IIIIIIIIIIIIIIIIIIIIIIIII don't wanna fall in love. . . .' " Yes, I was doing the right thing. Brent was so cute and cool. He might make it to the NBA one day, and even if we didn't get married, I could say I lost my flower to a big basketball star. I whispered in his ear. "Tonight has been so wonderful, Brent. I'm so glad you're my date. So . . . what do you want to do now?"

"There's a party at Jason Mannering's," he responded. "Why don't we go for a while?"

"Okay." I shrugged. Obviously, Brent was a bit nervous about what was to come. That made me feel even more connected to him. We would spend a few hours unwinding with our friends and then head over to Rhonda's aunt's house. I knew our moment would be magical when it happened.

"Hey!" I called to Maureen and Rhonda. "Are you guys going to Jason Mannering's party?"

"We're gonna skip it," Maureen giggled as Eddie came up behind her and wrapped his arms around her waist. She flashed the silver key in her palm. "We're going to take off now." She gave me the thumbs-up signal.

"Have fun!" I said, giving an enthusiastic yet subtle thumbs-up. I couldn't help but feel a twinge of jealousy. It would have been nice if Brent were as keen to get to Auntie Shirley's place as Eddie was. But I felt fairly confident that his hesitation was due to nerves, and not to lack of enthusiasm.

"We'll go for a little while," Rhonda said. Of course, Rhonda was already a real woman, so going to the party was fine for her.

The limo took us to Jason's, where a large number of teenagers were swilling champagne, pouring it in each other's hair, down their tops or their pants. A bottle passed by, and Brent took a long pull. He passed it to me, and I followed suit. Then I smiled up at him, hoping to turn this into a special intimacy shared between us. Unfortunately, the bubbles in the champagne caused me to cough and sputter. Brent hit me hard on the back several times. He seemed to think the champagne cork was lodged in my throat.

"Thanks," I said, regaining my composure and wiping tears from my eyes.

"No prob," he said, taking a beer proffered by a guy on his basketball team.

"It's really special being here with you," I whispered. No response. "It's really special being here with you!" I bellowed over Janet Jackson's "Miss You Much."

"Yeah," he said without looking at me. "You, too."

"I have to tell you that I'm really glad that . . . you know . . . that later . . . we're, umm . . . you and I—"

"Hey, Dirk!" Brent screamed across the room. "Get over here, you dweeb!" He launched himself at Dirk, and they wrestled like five-year-olds with ADD.

Everyone laughed. I laughed, too, catching the eye of Stephanie Miller and some of her girlfriends, who were enjoying the guys' antics. "Boys will be boys," I said with a dismissive wave of my hand. I was feeling very sage and mature. I would soon be a real woman after all.

The night progressed in much the same manner until, at 2 AM, Rhonda approached. "What are you guys waiting for?"

"I think Brent's a bit nervous," I said lamely. "And he's having fun with his buddies."

"What—is he gay? Tell him you want to go and do it! He'll go with you."

"You're right," I said, and guzzled the remains of my beer. "I'm taking him to Auntie Shirley's."

I marched up to him. He had Jason Mannering in a headlock and was giving him a noogie. Stephanie Miller and her friends were cheering them on. "I need to talk to you," I said, positioning my body between him and the group of spectators. He was my boyfriend, this was my prom night, and I needed some devirgining.

"Okay." He let Jason go and followed me into the hall.

I pressed myself against him and whispered in his ear. "I've got a key to an empty house, and I want to take you there and ravage you, and we can even . . . you know . . . go all the way."

He was quiet for a long moment.

"I said—"

"Yeah, I heard you. Let's go."

We made out in the back of a taxi, and I could tell that Brent's nerves (*and other parts of him*) *had steeled for the event. He seemed really into it, kissing me and pawing at my mermaid dress.*

"You kids take it easy," the Pakistani cabdriver said. "This is not a porno."

I let us into Auntie Shirley's house, still kissing him as we stumbled through the unfamiliar rooms. We found an empty bedroom; the door opposite was closed, indicating that Maureen and Eddie were in there. We left the light off, but the moon through the window illuminated the bed. It had a floral bedspread, and propped against the pillows were several teddy bears seated on a lace doily. With a sweep of his arm, Brent knocked them to the floor.

"Thanks," I said, giggling. Then I slowly and seductively unzipped the back of my mauve mermaid dress. Brent was watching intently as the taffeta began to slide to the floor. Unfortunately, a dress of this style required some serious undergarments. I was wearing a corset of sorts, with industrial strength whalebone to hold up my breasts in the strapless gown. I was also wearing control-top pantyhose, which were really hideous, but if I could pull them off quickly enough, I did have some cute lacy panties on underneath.

"Wow," Brent murmured, seemingly unfazed by the matronly underwear. He began to unbutton his shirt as I walked slowly toward him.

" 'Close your eyes,' " I sang. " 'Lend me your hand. . . .' " I affected a sweet, girlish tone, much like Susanna Hoffs from the Bangles. My hands gripped the waistband of my pantyhose. " 'Is this burning . . . an eternal flaaaaaaaaaaaaaame?' "

There was a loud and angry banging at the back door.

"Oh, my God!" I shrieked, pulling my pantyhose back up. "Oh, my God! What is that?" My first thought was that it was the police. Surely a houseful of teenagers having sex must be breaking several laws? Or worse—it was a guy in a hockey mask with a butcher knife who couldn't get laid on prom night and finally snapped!

Brent looked terrified, as well. His hands fumbled with the buttons of his shirt but had no success. "I'm going out there," he said.

God, he's brave. It would have been wonderful to lose my virginity to someone so courageous, but now he was sure to be arrested or stabbed. I considered struggling back into my mermaid dress, but there was no time. I wrapped the taffeta around my hips and followed Brent into the kitchen.

Eddie and Maureen were already there, their naked bodies wrapped in sheets. I would have given her the thumbs-up if we weren't in such a dire situation. "What the fuck is going on?" *Eddie demanded of Brent.*

Brent was marching toward the door.

"Grab a knife!" *I called after him.* "Just in case."

He paid me no mind and opened the door. "What are you doing here?"

Stephanie Miller stumbled into the room. "You prick!" *She screamed at Brent.* "Did you sleep with her?! Did you? Did you have sex with her!" *She was crying, black rivulets of mascara running down her cheeks.*

"What are you doing here, Stephanie?" *I demanded, going over to stand by Brent.*

"You were supposed to tell her after the dance," *she continued to scream at Brent.* "You were going to tell her it's over!"

"What are you talking about?" *I was filled with panic. Stephanie had obviously gone mad, and we could all be in serious danger.*

"Tell her now, Brent!" *she screeched.* "Tell her nooooooooooooooooo-oowwww!" *She collapsed on the floor in a sobbing heap of sea foam satin.*

To my surprise, Brent dropped to his knees and cradled her in his arms. "It's okay," *he murmured.* "It's all going to be okay." *He looked up at me then.* "I'm sorry, Kerry. I should have told you before. Steph and I . . . we've been seeing each other for a while."

"What?" *I was in shock. How could this be happening? Two minutes ago I was singing* "Eternal Flame" *and getting naked with him. This couldn't be real!*

"I'm sorry but . . . it's true. Steph and I are together." *He picked her up off the floor, and the two of them headed out the back door. Just before he closed it behind him, Brent turned to me.* "I hope I didn't ruin your prom night."

Maureen approached me with an afghan and wrapped me in the multicolored yarn. It was only then that I realized Brent's last vision of me would be standing in the kitchen, wearing a corset and control tops.

Chapter 11

I PLACE THE JOURNAL IN THE JUNK DRAWER IN MY KITCHEN. THAT WAS A hard entry to write, but I am sticking to my commitment to deal with these issues and eventually resolve them. I feel a sense of melancholy whenever I reflect on that night. It seems everyone has some romantic memory of their prom night, of their deflowering. And I have that fiasco. I think about Maureen and Rhonda for a moment. We speak only about twice a year now, although they live in a suburb less than an hour away from me. Maureen stays home with her three kids. (The first child is Eddie's.) She's married to a salesman. Rhonda is living with a guy who owns a bar in Kent. I met him once—he was overweight and sweaty but apparently has quite a lot of money. I should call them one day. Perhaps reconnecting with the the Transisters should go on my self-improvement list?

Today though, I am tackling a major item on that list. I am facing Sam in person. In my last therapy session, I told my therapist that I felt the need to meet with Sam face-to-face.

"Are you sure you can handle that, Kerry?" she said, her heavy eyebrows knitting together with concern. A little waxing would really lighten up her face and improve her looks immensely.

"I'm quite sure," I replied, sounding more confident than I actually felt.

"Well, if you're sure that you're ready for this major step, then we'll proceed." Her man hands were clasped together, fingers entwined. "But this meeting must take place in a public place, with absolutely no alcohol involved."

"Okay," I agreed, feeling rather sheepish that she knew how easy I am after a couple of cocktails.

So I'm meeting him for coffee at Pike Place Market at 10:30 AM.

Yes, it is time to deal with Sam openly and honestly. Since my disastrous brunch with Sandra, I am more committed than ever to the principles outlined in *You Get What You Give.* I even left her an apologetic message:

"Sandra? It's me, Kerry. I just wanted to say that I'm really sorry about the way I acted at brunch. I have realized that the only way you can find your way to true enlightenment is by making your own mistakes. It was wrong of me to force my beliefs on you, no matter how clear it is to me that you're going to regret this decision for the rest of your life. Only by allowing you to come to your own conclusions can our relationship endure."

She hasn't called back.

I've been up since seven. I did a few sun salutations in my living room, called my mom to wish her a happy Saturday, and then began grooming to meet Sam. The grooming is not to impress Sam and make him want to get back together with me; it is to make him realize that I am an attractive, confident woman who can live without him and will likely be able to find someone creative and sandy-haired to love me in the foreseeable future.

It is a beautiful fall day as I head to the bus stop. There is a nip in the air, but the sun is shining. The leaves are vivid shades of red and yellow, and the city feels clean and fresh. I am wearing a chunky orange turtleneck sweater and a chocolate down-filled vest. My outfit and my mood fit the beautiful autumn weather perfectly: cheerful, upbeat, confident.

A quick trip down the hill, and I am at the market. As I hop off the bus, I check my watch and see that I am ten minutes early for our date—I mean, meeting. That will not do. Sam cannot see me sitting there, waiting for him like an anxious, love-starved spinster. I plan to be six minutes late, thus sending the message that my life is full and busy and he is such a low priority that it was hard for me to get there on time.

I stroll around the market, immersing myself in the energy and diversity of Pike Place. Absorbing the plethora of colors and smells, I cheer on the fish-tossers, say good morning to vendors, and smile at passersby, even helping an elderly lady load her groceries into the basket of her motorized wheelchair. I am bound and determined to be positive and helpful in my everyday life, thus ensuring the smooth, karmic flow of good fortune back to me (page 78). And my good deeds keep me from dwelling on the upcoming encounter with Sam.

When I arrive at Sally's Café on Pike, I am only two minutes late. I prepare to walk on by and go around the block for another four minutes when I notice Sam seated inside. He is reading the paper with a mug of steaming coffee sitting in front of him. I may as well get this over with. Taking a deep breath, I enter the coffee shop.

His head pops up at the sound of the door, and he smiles at me. Oh, those dimples . . . No, I am strong, positive, confident. . . . Remember what Ramona said: Sam doesn't even know the real me, or care to get to know the real me. Although . . . she didn't exactly say it was Sam, did she? She just said it was someone really good-looking whom I was completely crazy about. What am I saying? Of course it was Sam! Who else could it be?

"Hi." I smile coolly, giving no indication of the manic internal dialogue proceeding in my head.

"Hey . . ." He stands up and kisses my cheek. "It's good to see you. You look great."

"Thanks. So do you," I say formally without looking at him. He pulls out my chair, and I sit.

"How have you been?" he asks.

"Excellent. And you?"

"Pretty good. Busy with work."

"Me, too. Really busy with work. Absolutely swamped, in fact."

"That's going well, then?"

"Great!" I give a false smile. I look at him and realize he's not buying it. "Well . . . it's going okay," I admit. "At least I haven't been fired yet."

He seems to find this incredibly funny and throws his head back with laughter. "How could they ever fire you?" he says, looking at me fondly.

"Yeah . . . well . . . Look, Sam—"

"Let me get you a coffee. Americano?"

"Okay, but I can pay for it." I dig in my purse for my wallet.

"It's just a cup of coffee," he says with a wink, and goes to the counter to order. He is back within minutes, presenting me with a tall mug. "Two sugars, right?" He passes me two sugar packets.

"Right," I say, feeling the resolve drain out of me like air from a leaky balloon. He remembers that I take two sugars? How could someone who doesn't care to know the real me remember such a minor yet important detail? I clear my throat and steel myself for what's ahead.

"Look, Sam . . . I think we need to talk."

"I agree."

"You do?"

"Of course I do. I haven't seen you in almost a month. You don't return my calls. There's obviously something going on with you."

"Well, yes . . ." I stop to consider what to say next. I want to tell him that it is time for me to move on, to find someone who wants to have a future with me, not just a quickie on the kitchen table, but the words are harder to summon than I imagined.

He interrupts my reverie. "I may as well just ask you point-blank. Are you seeing someone else?"

"Yes," I say quickly, sensing a solution to all my problems. "Yes, I am seeing someone else, so obviously it wouldn't be right for me to go on seeing you and calling you and stuff."

He heaves a heavy sigh. "I guess I knew this was coming," he says. "But it's still hard." He looks up at me with those beautiful, intense gray eyes, and I feel like I might cry.

"It is," I say mistily.

Suddenly, we are interrupted. "Excuse me?" a twentyish, skinny blond thing is saying to Sam. "Sorry to interrupt, but my friends and I are having a debate. Are you Patrick Dempsey?"

"No," he chuckles. "I'm not Patrick Dempsey."

"He's not Patrick Dempsey!" She calls to her friends. "Okay . . . sorry about that."

"No problem. I get that quite a lot."

"I bet you do," she says flirtatiously as she backs away. "You're actually better looking than Patrick Dempsey . . . more like JFK Jr."

"Okay, run along now!" I wave her away with my hand. God. This is not helping things.

Sam turns his attention back to me. "Sorry."

"Oh, don't worry," I snap. "You can't help it that you look like Patrick Dempsey except even better."

"So who's the guy?"

"What?"

"The guy you're seeing?"

"Oh . . . I met him at a work function. He's in the visual arts . . . Sandy-hair, wonderful and caring soul."

"You deserve him," he says sincerely.

"Thanks," I mumble. "Yeah . . . I do."

He leans forward and takes my hand gently. "I'm sorry about everything, Kerry. I've been a selfish bastard in this relationship, and now I've lost you. I know it's too late for excuses, but I let myself get so wrapped up in my career and my lifestyle." He shakes his head sadly. "I don't mean to be one of those New Agey self-analyzers, but I was trying so hard to prove to my father that I could really make a name for myself in this city that it kind of took over my life."

I recall that Sam's father, whom I have never met, is a potato farmer in Idaho. He'd always looked down on Sam for deciding to escape to the city instead of helping out with the family business. I'd heard the story several times over our years together: As Sam packed up to move West, his father had dismissed him with the words, "You'll never make it, kid. That city will eat you alive."

Sam continues. "And now I've proved to him that I can make it here. I've achieved everything I wanted to . . . more, even." He looks at me, and his eyes are so warm and caring. "But in the process, I lost you. And it's going to take me a long time to forgive myself. I guess it's true what they say—you don't know what you've got till it's gone."

I know he is just quoting Joni Mitchell lyrics to me, but it is working. What is wrong with me? I came here wanting to end things cleanly, and now I want to throw myself into his arms, inhale the scent of his cologne, and bury my hands in his thick, dark, Patrick Dempsey–ish hair. "You haven't lost me!" I want to scream. "Your dad is an ignorant jerk for ever doubting you! You are a wonderful, amazing man, and I am yours forever!" But I don't.

"I'd better go, Sam," I say through the thickness in my throat. "Busy day."

"Okay . . ." He releases my hand. "But, Kerr . . . would it be okay if I called you once in a while? Just to see how you're doing?"

I know what I should say here, but I am made of flesh and blood and not cold hard steel. "Sure," I say. "Give me a call sometime."

Chapter 12

VAL HAS CALLED AN EMERGENCY MEETING TO DISCUSS THE SANDRA situation. I was very relieved when she phoned. My new enlightened position of butting out and letting people make their own mistakes is very unnatural for me. In fact, it's downright painful. I have reread Dr. Rainbow Hashwarma's chapter on friendships several times to keep myself focused.

We are drinking red wine at a cozy bar on Pine Street. It is a cold and rainy night, but we are toasty and warm, seated by a large rock fireplace. Val dips a chip into her watercress dip and launches the topic of the evening.

"What are we going to do about Sandra? She can't go ahead with this plan to have a baby with George."

"I agree," Michelle says. "We need to take a hard-line approach with her. We've looked the other way on her pathetic excuse for a relationship for long enough. If she goes through with it, it will be the biggest mistake of her life."

"I know what it's like to have a child," Val continues. "It'll be so difficult for her without a proper father in the picture. At least I had Jay around until Taylor was four."

"And Sandra's so fragile," Michelle adds. "How will she handle all the sleepless nights, the shitty diapers, the sore breasts? . . . Ugh!" She shudders at the thought.

"As much as I agree with your opinions," I say, "I don't believe we can force her into our way of thinking. It is only by making her own mistakes that she can find the path to true enlightenment."

They gape at me in silence for a long moment. Then Michelle says, "What the fuck are you talking about?"

"I'm reading this book called *You Get What You Give,* and it says that you can't control your friends' lives and—"

"Oh, for Christ's sake!" Michelle interrupts. "We don't have time for this New Age shit, Kerry. Sandra's considering getting pregnant by a married man!"

"New Age shit?" I fire back. "Who's the one who takes off for yoga retreats every month to get *centered?* Who are you to call Dr. Rainbow Hashwarma's book 'New Age shit'?"

"Calm down, both of you," Val admonishes. "We need to focus on Sandra and her situation, okay?"

"Okay," we both mumble like scolded children.

"I propose an intervention," Val says. "We need to invite her for dinner, then sit her down and tell her that we won't stand by while she ruins her life."

"I tried that," I said. "She stormed out of the restaurant, and now she won't return my calls."

"You can't storm out of an intervention," Val continues. "You're locked in. It's very intense. My aunt did one because my cousin was smoking too much pot. The person has to sit there until they've heard you out and agree to deal with their problem."

"Okay," Michelle says. "It has to be done."

"Ummm . . . okay," I say hesitantly. It is difficult for me to con-tradict my newfound values of noninterference, but I can see the logic in an intervention. Learning from your mistakes is one thing, but when that mistake is a baby with a married man, that's quite another.

"Good," Val says. "Michelle, can we do it at your place? She won't come over to Kerry's, and I'd rather not do it at my place because of Taylor. This thing could go on all night, and I don't want her coming back from her dad's and witnessing it." She sounds very ominous.

"Okay . . . ," Michelle says unenthusiastically. Her apartment is spare, modern, and expensively decorated. I'm sure she is having visions of us tackling Sandra to the ground to get her to listen to sense, and breaking some expensive knickknacks or lamps in the process. I know I am.

"Okay . . . I'll bring the wine, and I'll make an artichoke dip," I volunteer.

"Kerry, you don't bring wine and artichoke dip to an intervention!" Val sounds exasperated.

"This is serious," Michelle adds. "We're not going to sit around and have cocktails while we talk about her becoming a single mother."

"Sorry!" I retort. "What do I know about interventions? I don't have any cousins who smoked too much pot. I just thought that it would be comforting for her to have a glass of wine and a snack while we discuss things."

"No wine or snacks," Val says authoritatively. "We'll have water and some protein bars to keep our energy up, but that's it."

I have visions of us in a damp room with a bare lightbulb hanging from the ceiling. Sandra is tied to her chair while we take turns alternately screaming at her and offering her cigarettes and coffee.

Michelle pulls out her Palm. "How's the third Saturday of next month for everyone?"

"She could practically have had the baby by then!" I scream.

"She'll have ovulated at least twice," Val says. "We have to do it sooner. This Saturday."

"But that's the Women of Influence dinner!" Michelle whines.

"I've had my ticket for months. All the female VPs in my industry will be there, and it'll look bad if I . . ." She trails off, noticing our disapproving looks. "Okay," she gives in. "This Saturday at my place."

With that unpleasantness out of the way, we drink more wine and discuss our respective weeks. They are impressed that I met with Sam and didn't offer to blow him under the table in order to start things up again. "It was difficult, of course," I say, sipping my merlot, "but I have a much more positive outlook now. I know that someone will come along who's genuine and kind and cares about the real me."

"Of course he will," Val says. "Don't give up hope."

"Mr. Right is bound to be just around the corner," Michelle says, with just a hint of condescension in her tone.

I change the subject. "And how's work?"

"Boring," Val says.

"Great!" Michelle enthuses. "There's a possibility that Pinnacle Tech could buy a majority share in our company, which would mean [blah blah blah]."

Val and I exchange subtle looks as Michelle goes on about the value of her shares in relation to other tech stocks. Thankfully, we are interrupted by a visitor to our table.

"Val? I thought that was you."

"Matt! Hello!" Val rises out of her chair to embrace him. "How are you?"

"Good, good. And you?"

"Really good, thanks. These are my friends Michelle and Kerry."

"Hi," Matt says to each of us. He has dark hair, golden skin, and a strong jawline. He looks to be Spanish or Argentinean or something equally Latin and exotic.

"Matt used to work with me," Val explains. "Until he was headhunted by one of the big banks. How's it going there, anyway?"

"It's good," he says. "Really busy. I work a lot more hours than I did at the credit union, but I guess that goes with the territory."

"That's the price you pay for being a rising star!" Val teases. "Can you join us for a drink?"

Do . . . Do . . . , I mentally will him. Sit down and join us for a drink . . . and maybe some sex afterward?

"I'd love to," he says, looking directly at me. All the blood in my body rushes to my groin area. "But I'm here with some friends, so I'd better get back."

"Okay," Val says. "Give me a call sometime. You know where I work."

"I will." He smiles at her. "Nice to meet you," he says, fixing me again with his intense Latin gaze. "You, too," he says to Michelle before leaving.

"Oh, my God!" I squeal when he is safely out of earshot. "He is gorgeous!"

"Yum, yum," Michelle says.

"Isn't he?" Val gushes. "All the girls in the office just loved him! We were devastated when he left. He was by far the best scenery we had, and he's really sweet and nice, too."

"He seems it," I say.

"And he's going to go far. He's a very bright guy. He's only twenty-four, and he's already heading up customer service at the Bank of America on Pike."

"Twenty-four!" I gasp.

"Yeah. He's a baby."

Michelle laughs. "Maybe Sandra could adopt him, and that would solve all her problems?"

"Twenty-four?" I say again. "Am I allowed to date twenty-four-year-olds?"

"The rule is," Val says knowledgably, "divide your age in half, and add seven. So . . . you're thirty-one, divided by two is fifteen and a half plus seven is . . . twenty-two and a half."

"I can date twenty-two-and-a-half-year-olds?" I ask, shocked.

"The rule?" Michelle interjects. "What rule is this?"

"It was in *Cosmo*," Val continues. "Divide by two and add seven—that's the youngest man you are allowed to date."

"Wow. Twenty-two and a half," I say. "I had no idea. Maybe I should start hanging out at skateboard parks and arcades?"

"Or the Bank of America on Pike?" Val asks with raised eyebrows.

"I must definitely set up an account there." I wink. "And I will have many, many problems with customer service, and I will demand to see the manager!" I bang my fist on the table for emphasis.

"Yes!" Michelle adds. "I need some servicing, young man!"

We carry on with our jokes about "putting the customer first" and "the customer is always right" until the bottle of wine is gone and it's time to go home.

"If you're ever talking to young Matt," I say to Val as we pile into a taxi. "Ask him if he'd like to go out with a woman who is—what is it?—two times half his age plus what?"

"Older! A woman who's older," Michelle yells.

"Okay," I say. "Ask him that."

Chapter 13

THE INTERVENTION WAS A DISASTER! IN MY WILDEST, MOST NEGATIVE fantasies, it could not have gone any worse.

It had all started smoothly. Sandra was successfully lured to Michelle's apartment, where I was sequestered in her Asian-inspired bedroom until Sandra was safely inside with the door locked. They didn't want her to lay eyes on me and turn around and leave in a huff.

Sandra was suspicious right off the bat. She glanced at the bare dining room table, noted the lack of cooking smells, the bottle of water in Michelle's hand, and the protein bar Val was munching on. "What's for dinner?" she asked hesitantly.

That's when I emerged. I was pained by the look of chagrin on Sandra's face when she saw me. "What is *she* doing here?" she snarled.

"We're all here for the same reason," Val said. "Because we need to talk to you about the mistake you're about to make."

"I know what you're going to say, and I don't want to hear it."

"Well, you're going to hear it," Michelle said forcefully. "Have a seat. Would you like a protein bar?"

Sandra acquiesced, and we all took turns ranting about her dismal future if she had a baby with George. We each had assigned topics:

- ✔ Val would talk about the difficulties of raising a child alone, using her firsthand experience with Taylor for impact.

- ✔ Michelle would discuss how George would never be there for Christmas, for summer holidays, for the baby's birthday. Eventually, the child would start to wonder why she was such a low priority in her father's life, which would have a devastating impact on her self-esteem.

- ✔ My role was to give Sandra hope for a normal, happy future that would involve children and a husband. "Look at me," I would say. "I'm still hopeful that I'll find someone."

Of course, all these points were to be followed up with, "We love you and care about you and want you to be happy."

Sandra listened, her face impassive, for more than two hours. Finally, she downed the remains of her water bottle and stood up. "I can see your point," she said. "I guess there were a lot of things I didn't factor into my decision when I decided to continue on with George. You've really given me a lot to think about."

"Well . . . ," Val said, taken off guard by the change in attitude this early in the process. "I'm glad you're starting to see things our way."

"I am," Sandra said. "Would it be all right if I left now? I'm really exhausted."

A quick conference determined that her leaving at this stage would be a bit premature, but we offered to make her some tea and toast and let her lie on the couch. "Okay," she said. "I just need to use the bathroom."

We were busying ourselves in the kitchen, whispering about how persuasive we were and wondering if we should start a business as professional "interventionists." Really, we were quite good at it. Val's cousin had taken fourteen hours to convince to stop smoking so much pot, and we'd made Sandra reevaluate her relationship in less than three. Our self-congratulations were interrupted by a pounding at the apartment door.

"Open up. Seattle Police Department."

"Oh, my God!" we all shrieked. "What are the police doing here?" Michelle rushed to open the door.

"We had a 911 call from someone who is being kept here against her will?" the burly officer said. At that moment, Sandra emerged from the bathroom, tucking her cell phone into her purse.

"It was me, Officer. I called."

"Are you all right, ma'am?" he asked. "Have you been hurt or abused?"

"Just mentally and emotionally," Sandra sniffed, going to stand between the big cop and his female partner. "They kept me here against my will." She shot us a triumphant look.

"Are you ladies aware that forcibly restraining someone from leaving the premises is tantamount to kidnapping?"

"Oh, pleeeeeeeeeeeze!" Michelle erupted. "Kidnapping? We're her friends!"

"This is an intervention, Officer," Val said calmly. "We need Sandra to stay here and listen to us until we can convince her not to destroy her life."

"Are you a drug user, ma'am?" the female officer asked Sandra.

"No!" she shrieked.

"Alcoholic?"

"No!"

"Exactly what kind of intervention was this?" the policeman asked.

"She's considering having a baby with a married man," I piped in, looking directly at the female officer. Surely she would understand the magnitude of the situation.

"Pardon me?" the big guy asked, like I'd just said Sandra's been chewing too much gum.

"Officer—" Michelle stepped up. "—we were trying to get our friend to listen to reason. Yes, we locked the door—yes, we told her she couldn't leave—yes, we didn't give her anything to eat but protein bars and water—but our intentions were the best."

"We were going to make her toast," I added lamely.

Suddenly, Sandra erupted in tears. "I was terrified," she wailed. "I told them I'd consider what they said, but they still told me I couldn't leave. They said I had to sleep here. I couldn't even go home to feed my cat!"

"Why didn't you feed your cat before you left?" Michelle screamed back. "Any normal person would feed her cat before she went out, not after she came home!"

"When I feed my cat is my own goddamn business and not yours!" Sandra was on the verge of hysteria.

"You can't even take care of your cat, let alone a baby!" Michelle hurled at her.

Sandra started to launch herself at Michelle, but she was restrained by the two police officers. "Violence is not the answer, ma'am," the first officer soothed her. "Do you want to press charges against these ladies? They could be charged with unlawful confinement."

"Yes, I do!"

"Sandra!" Val and I were shocked. "You can't be serious? We were only trying to help!"

"You—you—kidnapped me!" She collapsed into the arms of the female officer. "You unlawfully confined me!"

The three of us were taken "downtown" in the back of the police car while Sandra was given a ride in a separate vehicle to make her statement. The police station was horrific—full of junkies and hookers and generally smelly people. We were separated and asked a bunch of questions. The only saving grace of the evening was that the cop interrogating me was kind of sexy in an Andy Sipowicz kind of way. (Weird, I know, but I've always kind of had a thing for him.)

"What now?" I asked when he had taken down my particulars and my statement about the events of the night.

"Now, you can go home," he said.

"Really?" I was thrilled. "How come?" I leaned in conspiratorially. "Did you pull some strings for me or something?" My subtle flirtation with him must have really done its job.

"Nope. The charges were dropped. Your friend's husband came in and talked her out of going through with it. They just left a few minutes ago."

"He's not her husband," I mumbled as I gathered my purse and coat, preparing to leave.

"Hey, lady." He stopped me. "I know you and your friends meant well, but you can't force people into your way of thinking. They have to make their own mistakes and learn for themselves."

"Are you reading *You Get What You Give* by Dr. Rainbow Hashwarma?" I think I may have found my soul mate.

"Huh? It's just common sense, lady."

"Uh, yeah . . . good night."

Chapter 14

THE DISASTROUS INTERVENTION IS ALL THE PROOF I NEED THAT THE PRIN-
ciples outlined in *You Get What You Give* should be followed to the letter. I had completely contradicted Dr. Rainbow Hashwarma's advice,
and where did it get me? Hauled down to the police station, that's
where!

Michelle doesn't think she will ever be able to forgive Sandra.
Not only did she miss her Women of Influence dinner, but she also
thinks several of the guests may have spotted her in the back of the
squad car as we sped past the Grand Hyatt Hotel. Val is confused and
torn. She is angry and disappointed that Sandra would try to have us
arrested, but thinks maybe her rash actions could be blamed on her
high stress level with George's wife's baby and everything.

I—being more enlightened than my other two friends—have already left Sandra a voice message telling her that I forgive her, and
will support her in whatever decision she makes, no matter how
wrong I think it is. She hasn't called back yet, but I'm confident she
will.

Instead of dwelling on the sad outcome of the intervention, I have decided to devote myself to my self-improvement list. My karmic flow needs a big boost, so I'm going to undertake one of the major items. I'm going to make a generous, selfless contribution to society. I'm going to volunteer.

After much online research, I have come up with an organization that seems like a mutual fit. It is called the Shooting Star program, and volunteers act as mentors to *teenagers* who are "high- to medium-risk" kids or who have "high-risk tendencies." I'm not exactly sure what that means, but I have always been hip and cutting edge despite my age, so I think I would make a very positive yet still cool role model to an adolescent. I've made the call to Shooting Star, and I have an interview set up this afternoon.

But now, I have to go to a preproduction meeting for the Prism TV campaign. Not surprisingly, the clients were persuaded to approve Dave and Tanya's scripts featuring young children growing up to be crack whores and murderers without a Prism high-speed Internet connection. Despite my objections to the concept, I will be managing the production of the campaign. Sonja says I need to take Gavin under my wing on this one, as he needs the television experience.

Dave has basically ignored me since the attempted kiss on the stairwell. He either does not remember, or is pretending he does not remember. I suspect he *does* remember and is too embarrassed to acknowledge it because he is treating me with even more disdain than he does the other account people. On the few occasions when he has conceded my presence, it has only been to mock my ideas or sneer at my contributions. That is fairly normal behavior for a creative director, but something in his tone indicates that I have bruised his ego.

Gavin pops his head into my office. "Ready?"

"Yep," I say, grabbing my file and notebook. I am trying to keep a positive outlook and not let Gavin annoy me. Deep down, I suspect he is a decent, if somewhat insecure person masquerading as a brownnosing weasel. As my new bible suggests, I'm going to look beyond the facade that society has dictated, to find the true person within.

Gavin is positively bubbling at the prospect of going on a TV shoot. "I was talking to Pam, and she says we need to start shooting by the end of the month."

"Well—" I chuckle sagely. "—I don't think we can scout locations and get casting done by the end of the month."

"But the air date is October twenty-second!" Gavin continues. "I put together a work-back schedule, and if we scout locations and do auditions over the weekend, we could start shooting by Friday the thirtieth." He hands me a copy of the schedule.

"Uh, great . . . but that means working over two weekends."

"Yeah?"

I want to say that I'm trying to improve myself through yoga, volunteering, and developing a better relationship with my parents, which means I can't afford to give up two weekends, but I decide not to respond. He'd probably run back to Sonja and tell her we were going to miss our air date because Kerry was too lazy to do what it took to get the job done. Instead I say, "Let's just see how this meeting goes before we hand out the schedule, okay, Gavin? I really appreciate your initiative, though."

"What's wrong with this fucking coffeepot?" Dave is growling as we enter the room. He is trying to pour himself a cup from the upright urn, but it is sputtering black liquid all over his hand and sleeve.

"It's empty," I say, indicating the clear line that shows the level of the coffee.

"It's the suit's job to make sure we've got fucking coffee, Kerry . . . or is that beneath you?"

Oh, yeah. He definitely remembers trying to kiss me. "I'll ask Jennifer to bring some in, Dave." I smile pleasantly. Although I am being abused and sworn at, I feel I have the upper hand.

I sit at the boardroom table across from Tanya and Pam. Tanya is tapping her pencil on the table and glowering at me. Apparently she, too, knows that Dave tried to kiss me. Tanya can be very intimidating—with her jet-black hair and pierced eyebrow and lip—but I am calm and at peace with myself and the universe. I cannot help it if her lover finds me very attractive and feisty.

"Okay . . ." I start the meeting. "Pam, let's talk about production dates. Have you had a chance to select a production house?"

Before Pam can speak, Dave interjects. "Why are you asking her about dates? You should be giving her a schedule to stick to in order to reach the air date. Is this your first TV campaign or something?"

"No," I say, breathing deeply to remain calm. "This isn't my first TV campaign, Dave. When I've managed them in the past, we have had a preliminary meeting to discuss everyone's needs and time frames, and then we'll put together a work-back schedule."

"We don't have time to dick around discussing everyone's needs and time frames! We need to be on air on October twenty-second!" He is screaming.

"Fine!" I retort. "Gavin, hand out the work-back. We just thought it would be considerate to get your feedback before we presented a schedule."

"Considerate," Tanya scoffs, and Pam sniggers.

"Gavin," I say, ignoring them. "Would you like to walk us through it?"

"Sure," he says, trying to conceal his glee at my shabby treatment. "I'd be happy to."

The creatives listen impassively until we reach the shoot date. "You expect us to work two weekends in a row?" Dave grumbles, looking directly at me. "That might be fine for some of you who have no life outside this place, but I'm not gonna spend two fucking weekends in a row at work. I have kids to visit!"

I notice Tanya shifting uncomfortably in her seat. "I don't particularly want to work two weekends in a row either, Dave." I speak slowly, though my face is burning with anger and frustration. "That's why we thought we'd ask Pam if any of the dates can be shifted so that—"

"Oh, so now Pam has to move her schedule around to suit you!"

"*What are you doing?*" I explode. "You're trying so hard to contradict me that you're not even making sense anymore!"

"If you can't handle this shoot effectively," he rages back, "then I'll tell Sonja to pull you off the job and get someone else to run it!"

"Fine by me!" I scream, gathering my papers. "And don't think I don't know what this is all about," I hiss as I prepare to leave.

He is strangely silent, and for a moment I think I may be able to exit unchallenged.

"Why don't you tell us what this is all about, Kerry?" Tanya says, her eyes narrowed dangerously.

I stall, looking to Dave for a hint about what to do here. He is staring at the table, seemingly in some kind of trance. "Nothing," I say. "It doesn't matter. It was a disagreement between Dave and me."

"On the stairwell after the NAPI party, perhaps?" Tanya says. She stands up and begins to slowly and purposefully circle the table. She reminds me of one of the female prosecutors on *Law & Order*—except for the ripped sweater and multiple piercings. "Could it have been a disagreement about, say—you wanting to sleep with Dave and him turning you down?"

"What?"

"He told me all about it, Kerry," she continues. "Pam knows about it, too."

"I can't believe this!" I say directly to Dave. "You are such a liar! You tried to kiss *me*! You told me it was over with Tanya."

"No, I didn't," he says calmly.

"You did! You said you liked how I stood up to you at the creative presentation! You said I was feisty and beautiful!"

Tanya rolls her eyes. "Pleeeeeeeeeze!"

"This is unbelievable," I say, tears springing to my eyes. Shit! I can't give them the satisfaction of seeing me cry. I've got to get out of here. "I'll tell Sonja to get someone else on this project—in fact, on any project where I have to work with you!"

As I storm out, I hear Dave say, "Hell hath no fury . . ."

The rest of the room erupts in laughter.

Chapter 15

"DON'T THINK ABOUT IT," I TELL MYSELF AS I DRIVE TO THE SHOOTING Star office. "I know the truth. I am honest and kind and contributing to society. Dave is superficial, immoral, and a flat-out liar. Tanya is stupid, insecure, and possessed by the devil." I know the book says to keep negative energy out of your calming mantra, but the words keep circulating in my brain. And I can't seem to stop the visions of Tanya with a serious lip-ring infection that she passes on to Dave, resulting in the amputation of most of his face.

I am so glad I have this interview today. It will counteract all the dark forces from the meeting and should get my karma back on track. I am honest and kind and contributing to society.

I walk through the double doors and am instantly greeted by a young woman with jet-black hair, gothic makeup, and spiked collars around the wrists.

"Hi, Kerry!" she says, extending her hand and beaming up at me. "My name's Theresa. I'm one of the coordinators here at Shooting Star."

"Nice to meet you." I smile back. God, she is like a younger, happier version of Tanya! Her T-shirt reads THE HIVES.

"It's so great that you're interested in mentoring with us," Theresa says as she leads me into a tiny makeshift boardroom. "Would you like some coffee or anything?"

"I'm fine, thanks," I say politely. "I'd like to get right down to business. I'm very excited about becoming involved in your program."

"Great." She smiles again. "Let me tell you what the process is. I'll interview you using standardized questions developed for us by the department of child welfare and social services. If I feel confident from the interview that you can move on to the next phase, we'll set up a psychiatric interview for you to ensure that you don't pose any sort of risk to the teenagers. If that goes well, we'll proceed to a police record check, and once cleared, you'll be ready to begin changing the life of a troubled teen." Again, she smiles genuinely at me.

I am suddenly gripped by fear. I had no idea it would be so intensive. I'm sure to fail at least one of these tests. The interview today might be fine, but the psychiatric evaluation will undoubtedly expose me as a borderline sociopath. And the police record check—well after the other night, who knows what the police could say about me? *She was picked up for kidnapping but never charged.* I may as well leave right now.

"So . . . what made you decide to become a mentor?" Theresa continues.

I answer all her questions with ease, and I feel fairly confident that I have at least passed phase one. It's phases two and three that will cause problems! But I don't let on that I'm a reject as I thank her for her time.

"We really look forward to matching you up with a girl in need," Theresa says at the door. "I think you'll be a great friend to a high- to medium-risk teen."

She must have noticed how hip and cutting edge I am despite my age.

I fight my way through 3 PM traffic back to the office. I know what will be waiting for me when I get there: a pink slip and a lecture from Sonja. The pink slip I can handle, but having to listen to Sonja harp on about my many weaknesses and fallibilities fills me with dread. What happened to the good old days when people yelled, *"You're fired!"* And you were free to pack up your belongings and go? Now they want to talk about it: "What's wrong, Kerry? Are you having troubles in your personal life that are affecting your job? Did your gorgeous boyfriend dumping you impact your self-esteem so much that you find it hard to concentrate? Did the fact that Dave didn't want to have sex with you keep you from creating a proper work-back schedule?"

As expected, Jennifer, our receptionist, has a message for me. "Sonja wants to see you," she says with a grimace. Jennifer hates Sonja, too, who is even more condescending to clerical staff than she is to the account people below her.

"Great," I mutter. "Where is she?"

"Probably in her office. But if she's not, she told me to tell you to find her and interrupt her."

"Will do."

I don't even have a chance to hang up my coat when she approaches. "Can we talk?" She is with the managing director, Bob Copley. I'm being fired for sure.

I follow them into a boardroom, and Bob closes the door. I'm not sure how I feel about this; I've never been fired before. Well . . . not for a really long time, anyway. I was fired from the gas station I worked at in ninth grade. I had called in sick for a shift, and then my boss saw me at Dairy Queen with my friends. She'd marched right up to me and said, *"You're fired!"* It wasn't so bad. I hated the job, anyway. But when my mom found out, all hell broke loose. God, my mom's not going to be very impressed with this firing either.

"Dave came to us," Sonja says sternly. "He says you two are having problems working together."

"We are," I say.

"He says you ran out of the Prism meeting and told them to find someone else to manage the account," Bob Copley adds. He is short and pudgy, with graying hair and the personality of a dishrag.

"Well . . . technically that's true," I begin. "But—"

"How do you expect to contribute to this agency if you can't work with the creative director?" Bob says.

"Well, I thought I could be more behind the scenes. I could do planning and strategy—"

It is Sonja's turn to interrupt. "Account people are generalists, not specialists. You can't pick the things you want to work on, Kerry. A manager who refuses to see a project through to fruition is of no value to us."

" . . . Okay."

"We suggest you think seriously about how you can overcome this . . . *issue* you have with Dave," Bob says. "If you think it's insurmountable, then we will seriously need to reevaluate whether this is the right job for you."

"Thanks," I say, standing. "You've given me a lot to think about."

"Well . . . ," Sonja says. "I guess we're done here."

"Yes. If you don't mind, I'd like to go home and get thinking on this," I say. Without waiting for a response, I turn on my heel and march out.

I am absolutely furious. It is ridiculous that I am about to lose my job after being sexually harassed. Dave is the one who should be fired, not me! He needs to learn that he can't go around trying to kiss people and then pout and throw tantrums when they turn him down. I should really show him that his behavior is not acceptable, that he can't get away with it! But I already know how my allegations would play out. Ferris and Shannon have made it abundantly clear who is the more valuable employee.

As I walk into my office, the phone is ringing. The caller-ID display indicates that it's Trevor.

"Oh, my God!" he says. "Are you okay?"

"Just great," I say, my voice dripping with sarcasm.

"I heard all about it from Pam," he says. "Let's go have a drink somewhere and talk."

"I don't know, Trevor," I say. "I don't think I'd be very good company."

"Come on, Kerry. It'll make you feel better to get it off your chest."

"I guess."

"Okay. Meet me at that sports bar at Fourth and Virginia in twenty minutes."

"Why don't we walk up together?"

"I've got some stuff to take care of first. And it'll look bad if they see us walking out together at four o'clock."

"You're embarrassed to be seen with me!" I hiss. "You don't want anyone to associate you with the office pariah!"

He laughs. "You're crazy! I'll see you at Corky's in twenty."

Corky's is dark, seedy, and a bit smelly. It suits my mood perfectly. I order a pint of lager, since I would feel out of place sipping a glass of merlot while surrounded by TVs blaring hockey, football, and horse racing. I look at my watch. Trevor should be here any second. He'd better not be late and leave me sitting alone in this dive.

"Hello."

I look up. Jesus Christ! It's Dave. "What are you doing here?"

"I wanted to talk to you . . . to clear this all up."

"I'm not interested in anything you have to say. And I'm meeting Trevor here in five minutes."

"No, you're not." He sits down across from me.

"What are you talking about?"

"Trevor set this up so we could talk."

He is dead to me.

"Kerry, this isn't worth losing your job over. We need to figure this out."

"What is there to figure out?" I snap. "You tried to kiss me. I turned you down. Now you're trying to ruin my career."

"It's not that simple, and you know it."

"It is that simple! It's sexual harassment."

"Come on . . . there's always been this sexual tension between us, and I thought it was about time one of us acted on it."

I gape at him, speechless.

"I'm sorry that I told Tanya that you came on to me, but what could I do? If she knew what really happened between us, she'd quit, and she's a valuable art director."

"And I'm a completely dispensable account manager?"

"Well . . . no, but . . ." The waitress interrupts us. "You want something?" she asks. Dave orders a beer. "Do you want another one?" she asks me.

I look down and realize my glass is practically empty. "Sure," I say. "Bring me another."

Three pints later, I am very drunk and embroiled in a deep discussion with Dave about the future of the agency, the negative side of a career in advertising, and the end of his three marriages. "People who aren't in the industry just don't understand," he explains about his first and second wife. "The hours it takes to build a career and the social side of it."

"I guess." I shrug. "My ex, Sam, never cared about me working late or socializing with clients or coworkers. But that was actually the problem. He didn't seem to care much about me, period."

"He was crazy," Dave says, looking at me intently. I shift uncomfortably in my seat.

"We're getting off topic here," I say formally (although the pints of beer have made my speech a little slurry). "I want you to tell Tanya that I didn't come on to you at that NAPI party."

"Tanya . . ." He sighs heavily and signals the waitress to bring us a couple more pints. "I've got to find a way to end it while still salvaging our working relationship."

"Well, Dave, I'm afraid that's your problem. I'd appreciate you leaving me out of it."

"But I can't leave you out of it, Kerry," he says seriously. "You're a big part of the reason I've got to dump her."

Oh, shit. I look at Dave through the beer-induced fog in my brain. He is not a bad-looking guy really, now that the arrogant sneer is gone and his permanent scowl has lifted somewhat. And he's not nearly so rude and obnoxious in a one-on-one conversation. And I would have to say that our serial-killer suspicions were largely unfounded. If anything, Dave is like a lost puppy, looking for the comfort and solace of a home, but not finding it, so he's throwing himself into his career and putting up walls and . . .

What am I saying? I hate Dave! He embarrassed me in front of my peers and almost got me fired today! He is sooooooooooo not the one Ramona was talking about in my reading. "Dave . . . there's nothing between us, okay? I'm sorry that I am so irresistibly feisty and good-looking, but it's never going to happen."

"Even if Tanya was out of the picture?"

"Even if Tanya was out of the picture . . . What do you mean *out of the picture?*"

"If she left the agency . . . would you go out with me then?"

"What?" I start to stand up with indignation, but I am drunk and clumsy and hit the table with my thigh, sloshing beer all over it. I sit down again and pass Dave a napkin. "Are you saying you'd get rid of Tanya if I said I'd go out with you?"

"Would you?"

Well . . . I do hate Tanya, but no! I can't stoop to that level. And I don't like Dave that way, I don't! "And then when you were tired of me, you'd have me fired so you could date some other coworker! No thanks."

"It wouldn't be that way with us."

"Dave . . ." I pause. "I'll tell you what. You get me back in Sonja and Bob's good books, and maybe we can talk about this further at some later date?"

"Deal," he says. We clink mugs.

I take several large swallows. "I'd better go," I say, digging in my purse.

"I've got this," he says throwing some money on the table. "Can I drive you home?"

"Drive? You've got to be kidding? Neither one of us can drive. I'll catch a cab."

He follows me out to the street. It has grown dark while we were ensconced in the dingy bar. I manage to hail a taxi almost immediately.

"I'm really glad we talked," Dave says as he opens the door for me.

"Me, too. You're going to take care of things with Sonja and Bob?" I ask.

"I will." He leans in to kiss me, and I proffer my cheek.

"Take care of this issue, Dave, and there might be more where that came from." Did I really say that? God, I'm really learning how to play the game. I hop in the cab and take off.

Mortifying Moment #5

"Oh, my God," I whispered to Sandra. "He is, like, totally the sexiest guy ever!"

"He totally is," she agreed, sipping her beer. We were seated at a sticky table in The Den, the campus bar in the basement of the Student Union building. Our seats were close to the stage, where a shaggy-haired musician was singing Cat Stevens. The air was filled with a haze of smoke and the aroma of draft beer. The stage lights illuminated him in the darkened space, making him ethereal . . . surreal. (I'd had quite a bit to drink.)

" 'Climb on the peace train!' " I sang along joyfully, my eyes interlocked with his. I was sweating, trembling, almost high with the excitement of this flirtation. I had always had a thing for musicians. (I was almost the lead singer of a band, after all.) But as yet, my "thing" had consisted of erotic fantasies about Bono and Eddie Vedder.

"Thank you very much, everyone," the singer said as the song finished.

"Woo-hoo!" Sandra and I screamed and applauded.

"I'll be back after I take a pee break and grab a beer." The shaggy-haired sex god exited.

"Did you see that?" I asked Sandra when he had left the stage.

"What?"

"The eye contact! He was totally eye-contacting me!"

"I saw it," she said. "You are so lucky."

"I know!" I giggled despite myself. "Do you want another beer?"

"I should probably get going. I've got an exam—"

"No!" I screamed. "No, Sandra. You can't go yet. Let's just stay for the rest of his set!"

"But it's a statistics exam, and I'm doing really badly already. . . ."

"Pleeeeeeeeze," I begged her. "Just one more beer? I'm buying."

As I leaned on the bar, waiting for the bartender's acknowledgment, I was suddenly aware of a presence at my left shoulder. I glanced over, and there he was.

"Hi." He smiled at me sexily.

"Hi." I smiled back. "You were great."

"Thanks. You seemed to be enjoying yourself."

"I was. I love music. I used to be a singer . . . sort of."

"What do you mean, sort of?" His eyes were dancing with amusement.

The bartender interrupted our banter. "What can I get you?"

"Two beers," I said. "Make that three beers." I turned to him. "You are drinking beer, aren't you?"

"Yeah. Thanks a lot. I'm Chris."

"Hi, Chris. I'm Kerry."

By the end of his set, I'd practically had an orgasm in my chair. He'd been singing to me all night, looking directly into my eyes, both of us oblivious of our surroundings. In fact, I was so oblivious that I didn't even realize Sandra had gone home some time ago. It was better this way, though. Chris was coming to join me.

"That was awesome," I said. "Really amazing." I hoped I wasn't overdoing it with my enthusiasm, but he was so talented . . . and so good-looking. "You should be playing much bigger venues."

"One day . . . I hope."

"I'm sure you will," I flattered. "You were so awesome! Really amazing!"

"So . . . do you go to U Dub?"

"Yeah. It's my first year."

"Whatcha taking?" He lit up a cigarette.

"I'm thinking about majoring in communications."

"Lucky you."

"Yeah, right!" I squealed. "It's really boring, actually."

"I just mean you're lucky you can afford to go to school. I have to scrape for every penny."

"But you're a musician," I said. "College would be a waste of time for you. You've got bigger and better things ahead."

"Maybe. It's a tough row to hoe," he said, taking a long and stoic drag on his cigarette.

"Have faith in yourself," I said, leaning in close to him. "You are really talented . . . really special."

He leaned in and kissed me, and I soared to the highest heavens on a wave of euphoria. His lips were soft and tasted like cigarettes (which I have never really minded). He had a bit of manly and bohemian stubble, which scratched my cheek and chin. When he pulled away, he touched my cheek and stared at me with smoldering eyes. Oh, my God! I was already head-over-heels.

"Do you want to come to my place for a drink?" I said hoarsely.

I had never had a one-night stand before—in fact, at nineteen, my sexual experience was extremely limited—but something about this felt so right. Chris was so sexy and charismatic and talented. He was sure to become a huge success, and I would be by his side, the woman who saw something special in him and supported him while he struggled to the top. When he won his first Grammy award, he'd say, "I dedicate this to the woman who always believed in me. To Kerry! My love, my muse, my raison d'être!"

I let us into the darkened apartment that I shared with Sandra. Her door was closed, and the light was off. I was relieved that she wasn't still up studying for her calculus exam . . . or whatever exam she was supposed to be studying for. I held my finger to my lips and led Chris to my bedroom. We didn't need the facade of a nightcap; we both knew why we were there.

"Chris," I murmured between kisses. "I don't usually do this kind of thing. . . ."

"What kind of thing?" He whispered huskily.

"Bring guys home that I've just met . . ."

He stopped midkiss and looked at me. "It doesn't feel like we've just met," he said. "I don't know what it is, but . . . I feel like I know you . . . like I've always known you."

"Me, too!" I said, kissing him passionately. I couldn't believe he felt the same way I did! It was the most magical moment of my life.

We made love, hungrily, passionately, and yet, somehow, still tenderly. It felt incredibly right. I wasn't worried about tomorrow, when the effects of the beer had worn off and we were facing each other with sticking-up hair and hangovers. I knew it wouldn't be awkward and uncomfortable; it would be the start of something wonderful.

We fell asleep in each other's arms. Normally, I could not sleep with a stranger's shoulder under my head, but with him, it felt natural, comfortable. It was also close to 2 AM, and I had four pints of beer in me—I could probably have slept with a cactus for a pillow.

He stirred a few hours later. I wasn't sure what time it was, but the sky was still dark. "Shhhh . . . ," he said as I rolled over to face him. "Go back to sleep. I've got to go now, but I'll call you tomorrow."

"Okay . . . ," I said sleepily. "You don't have my number, though."

"I'll write it down off your phone," he said with a smile. "I'll call you, okay? What time will you be up?"

"Around nine," I whispered, smiling up at him. "I had a great time last night, Chris."

"Me, too," he said, kissing me tenderly on the forehead. "Talk to you soon."

I fell back to sleep.

I was awakened several hours later by Sandra's shrieking. "Oh, my God! Kerry! Get out here!"

"What? What?" I stumbled blearily into the living room.

"We've been robbed! Someone broke in and stole our TV."

I glanced at the overturned milk crate that served as our TV stand. Sure enough, it was now vacant. "Oh, no!" I said, running frantically around the apartment. "Is anything else missing?"

"I don't think so," Sandra said. She rushed to the door. "It's unlocked! You left the door unlocked when you came home!"

"Oh, shit." I sank down onto the couch. "I didn't leave it unlocked, Sandra."

"Well, how do you explain the fact that it is unlocked, Kerry?" She sounded angry.

"It was Chris," I said.

"Who?"

"Chris . . . the singer. He, uh . . . came over here last night. And when he left . . . well, he couldn't lock the door without a key."

"Jesus, Kerry! What's wrong with you? You can't bring a strange guy into our apartment like that. It was probably him that stole the TV!"

"It wasn't him!" I screamed at her. "He would never do that to me. We have something special."

"Special?" she snorted. "You picked him up in a bar, and you think you have something special?"

"We do!" I cried. "It's like we've known each other forever!"

"Whatever." Sandra turned her back to me and stalked to her room. "I've got a statistics exam in ten minutes."

I would prove Sandra wrong. When Chris called, I would ask him if he saw any suspicious characters loitering in the hallway. I would suggest he get his own key cut so he could lock the door behind him when he had to leave early. I didn't worry about seeming too forward with Chris. We both knew this was real.

But he didn't phone all day. I rushed home between classes to check the answering machine. Nothing. I decided to visit The Den.

"I'm looking for Chris, the musician who played here last night?" I asked the bartender.

"He's done," the burly guy said while drying beer mugs. "Last night was his last night."

"Oh . . ." I could not start crying in front of this man. If I ever wanted to be able to show my face in here again, I could not start crying in front of this man. "Any chance you have a phone number for him?" I said, playing it cool. "He's got some stuff that belongs to me, and I need to get it back."

"Sorry, hon," he said. "Chris was a bit of a drifter. He didn't leave a number."

"No big deal," I said with a phony laugh. "Catchya later."

I hurried through the Student Union building to the nearest bathroom, where I dissolved into tears.

Chapter 16

I CLOSE THE LILAC JOURNAL AND BLOW OUT THE VANILLA CANDLE. GOD, I am such a loser. I can't believe that the first guy I have a one-night stand with most likely robbed me. And the worst part is, it didn't even scare me off one-night stands. I had several others, a few of which will likely make their way into the journal of mortifying moments, as well. Apparently, I am too stupid to learn from my own mistakes. The journal is backfiring. I am supposed to absolve myself of blame and learn to love with an open, unguarded heart—not beat myself up further.

Okay, deep breath. I close my eyes and envision myself in my therapist's wood-paneled office. I am seated in the dark brown leather chair. She is opposite me, wearing an ill-fitting, beige polyester suit. I can hear her soothing voice: "You were young and naïve, Kerry. At that age, you were unable to discern a grifter from the love of your life. It's okay. It's a common mistake." Ahhhh . . . I feel so much better. Maybe I could subsist on these imaginary therapy visits and save myself some money?

The rest of the week is a grand improvement, thanks to the positive karma generated by my good intentions. Dave was true to his word, and I have been reinstated as the project manager for the Prism TV campaign. It is a bittersweet development, as I am less than eager to work on this project and am considering reevaluating my career in general. On the other hand, I'm relieved that I am not being fired, because I can't afford to lose my job.

I even got an "apology" from Sonja (inasmuch as Sonja is capable of apologizing). She walked into my office the morning after my night out with Dave, just as I was taking a couple of Tylenols to combat the draft-beer-induced headache. "Dave explained the situation to us, Kerry."

"Explained?" Oh, God. What did he tell her?

"I'm pleased to hear that you two have been able to put aside your differences and can work together to create an award-winning campaign for Prism." She flashed a phony smile. "Sometimes it's good to just sit down and hash things out over a beer." She kind of punched the air to emphasize her point. God, she's weird.

I also passed the psychiatric exam for the Shooting Star program with flying colors. Well . . . there was one "area of concern." Dr. Shleminger called me into his spacious office to discuss it with me in person.

"Your test results indicate a very stable and secure individual, Kerry."

"Thank you." I nod, as though I would have been shocked if they had indicated otherwise.

"There was one area of concern, though." He puts on his reading glasses, his gray brows furrowing as he scans my multiple-choice exam. "You seem to feel that people are out to get you, that your destiny is not in your own hands but in the hands of those around you. Do you ever suffer from panic attacks?"

"No." Although I feel I could have one right now.

"Do you have any explanation for these feelings? Is there anything going on in your personal or professional life that has made you feel powerless and at the mercy of others?"

Only everything. I decide that would be the wrong answer. "I have had some relationship issues recently that could be at the root of this," I say. "But I'm in therapy and feel very confident that I'll be able to overcome these hurdles."

"Okay . . . ," he says hesitantly, still perusing my test results.

"I was also almost fired last week"—nervous giggling—"so that may have impacted things, too."

"Mmm-hmm."

"I'm not crazy, Doctor. I'm not! I want to make a difference in a high- to medium-risk teen's life. Please don't keep me from being a mentor just because I've been going through a rough time person-ally and professionally."

He snaps the folder housing my exam closed and looks up at me. "I won't. I think you'll be a fine mentor."

It turns out my police record check came through clear, as well. Perhaps my *NYPD Blue* pal had something to do with keeping the kidnapping issue under wraps?

Theresa calls me at the office on a Thursday. "I've got some great news!"

"Really?"

"We've found a girl who needs a mentor, and we think you'd be perfect!"

"Wow," I say, my stomach filling with butterflies. I suddenly feel completely inadequate to be a role model to anyone.

"We'd like you to meet with her school counselor first—then you can meet your protégée right after."

"Okay," I say. My voice has gone hoarse.

"I can give you a bit of background. Her name is Tiffany. She's fifteen and in ninth grade. She's bright but doesn't put any effort into school. She also has a very strained relationship with her mother and recently moved out to live with an aunt. Her father lives in Canada, so she doesn't see him much. Tiffany was recently caught smoking pot at school, and her truant record is dangerously high."

"Oh, my God," I mumble. I think I am in way over my head.

"She has been dating a twenty-year-old who is unemployed and appears to have a drinking problem. Tiffany also smokes."

"Oh, my God!" I scream. "I'm sorry, Theresa, but she sounds like she needs a psychiatrist or a . . . warden, not a mentor."

Thankfully, Theresa laughs. "I know it sounds daunting, but you'd be surprised how much of a difference you can make just by being there. No one's asking you to turn her into Madeleine Albright."

"Okay." I swallow audibly. "I'll go to her school on Friday." I take down the address and hang up.

CONNIE WALLACE IS TIFFANY'S SCHOOL COUNSELOR. SHE IS FRIENDLY AND genuine as she ushers me into her windowless office, despite looking exhausted and somewhat haggard. "Let me just say, right off the bat, how much we appreciate people like you."

"Thanks." I feel like crying.

"Tiffany is a great girl who has lost her way, but we're all very hopeful that another positive adult role model will help her get back on track."

"Well, I'm hopeful, too, Ms. Wallace—"

"Call me Connie."

"Okay, Connie. But I have to tell you I'm a little nervous. I haven't really had anything to do with teenagers since I was one— which was about eight years ago."

She doesn't let on if she catches my exaggeration. "That's understandable. All we ask is that you spend some time with her—we suggest an hour a week—and be there if she needs someone to talk to. Don't judge her or scold her. Let her know if you don't agree with her actions, but in a gently supportive manner. We're not asking you to turn her into Janet Reno."

"Okay . . ."

"I'll go get her."

I am tense and on edge as I wait to meet Tiffany. My heart is thudding loudly in my chest. There doesn't seem to be any rational explanation, but I feel like I'm waiting to be interviewed for a job I really want but am hopelessly underqualified for.

The door swings open, and Tiffany steps into the room, followed by Connie.

"Hi," I say, jumping up and extending my hand.

"Hi," she says disinterestedly. Oh, right—teenagers don't really shake hands. I hold my hand up in the high-five position, but she chooses to ignore that, too.

"Tiffany," Connie Wallace says kindly. "This is Kerry Spence, and she'll be your new mentor."

"It's really great to meet you, Tiffany," I say, my hands safely at my sides.

"Yeah." She shrugs indifferently.

"Why don't I leave you two alone to get to know each other better?" Ms. Wallace says. I want to cling to her legs to keep her from leaving, but I am the adult here. I must set a good example, while still being hip.

"Sounds cool, Con." I smile at Tiffany.

She looks at the floor.

Connie says, "I'll be back in a few minutes."

And we are alone.

There is a long awkward silence. "So . . . ," I say, frightened that she can hear my heart beating. "What made you want to join the Shooting Star program?"

"I didn't." She looks up at me then. Her eyes are icy blue, ringed in heavy black liner. Her skin is coated in a thick layer of makeup, which does a poor job of camouflaging her acne problem. She has shoulder-length, lank, blond hair—at least the bottom two-thirds are blond; the roots are jet-black. "They made me sign up for Shooting Star," she finishes.

"Oh . . ." I am momentarily speechless. "I didn't realize that. Well . . . I hope that we'll be able to do some fun things together anyway."

"Whatever."

"What kind of things do you like to do, Tiffany?"

She shrugs.

"Because . . . well . . . I thought maybe we could go to a movie or a play sometime? Or we could go out for dinner?"

"Do you like wrestling?"

"Sorry?"

"Wrestling," she says. "I love WWF and RAW. If they ever do a live show here, I totally want to go."

"Uh . . . okay, I'll keep my eyes open, and if I see that they're coming, I'll get us some tickets. What was it called again?"

She rolls her eyes like I am the stupidest adult she's ever met. "You've never heard of WWF?"

"I have . . . but the other one. What was it?"

"RAW. It's the best one. It has Booker T and Triple H. My boyfriend says they are the toughest dudes in the sport."

"Oh, right!" I say. "Booker T is so cool. In the meantime, why don't I see if I can get us tickets for something else? You know, just while we're waiting for WWF or RAW to come to town."

"Whatever."

"So . . . ," I say resisting the urge to look at my watch. Where the hell is Connie Wallace? How could she leave me here for so long with this hostile teenager? What do I say? What do I ask her?

"So . . . you're fifteen?"

"Yeah . . ."

"Uh . . . do you like school?"

"No!" she snorts. "It sucks."

"Yeah . . . I didn't really like school either."

"You didn't?" She sounds somewhat interested.

"Well . . . I liked some things about it, but I always felt that we had to learn so much useless information."

"Totally," she agrees.

"Like, I've never had to dissect a frog in my adult life," I say.

She is laughing!

"Or a sheep's eyeball."

"Gross!" she says gleefully.

"And it's not like I read tons of Shakespeare in my free time."

"Shakespeare bites," she says.

We continue on like this until Connie Wallace returns.

"And the value of x," I am saying as she enters. "No one has ever asked me to calculate the value of x! What a waste of time! And how about those exponents?"

"Sorry to interrupt," Connie says. I blush a little at being caught bashing the curriculum, but the point was for us to bond, wasn't it? "Tiffany, you'd better get back to class."

"It was great to meet you," I say as she gets up to leave.

"Yeah," she says, in a tone that is quite a bit warmer than when she first entered.

"So . . . we'll have coffee next week, okay? I'll pick you up."

" 'Kay!" she calls over her shoulder.

I think the meeting was a success.

Chapter 17

Val calls me at the office on Thursday. "We have to meet for dinner. Jay's taking Taylor out for pizza, so I'm free after work."

"Is this about Sandra?" Surprisingly, I have still not heard from her.

"Well . . . we *should* talk about Sandra, but there's something else," she says cryptically.

"Really? What?" I am intrigued.

"It has to do with you."

"With me?" I panic. "What? Is it good or bad? Oh, no. It's bad, isn't it?"

"It's good, it's good, you spaz!" Val is laughing. "It's about a certain twenty-four-year-old who called me and asked for your number."

"*Get out!*" I shriek. Oops. I lower my voice to a whisper. "That Matt guy? He asked for my number?"

"Yep. I'll fill you in tonight. Let's meet at The Palomino on Second at six."

"I'll be there."

Wow. Life is really good right now. I don't know what Dave told Sonja and Tanya, but they have both been basically leaving me alone. And when they do have to acknowledge my existence, they are borderline pleasant. I think my first meeting with Tiffany went really well, all things considered, and now cute young Matt wants my number! This is further proof that *You Get What You Give* really works (although, I sort of lost interest after chapter 6 and have decided to use it as more of a reference book).

When I finally meet Val in the swanky yet casual second-floor restaurant, I have worked myself into a frenzy. All day I've been dwelling on Matt: his smooth golden skin and the exotic air about him, his taut young body with its chiseled pectorals clearly visible through his sweater. At first, it was getting me excited (and a bit hot and flustered) but as I thought about it more, I began to feel insecure. I am in my thirties. I have a deep frown wrinkle between my eyebrows and the butt of an eighty-three-year-old. I have crows'-feet when I smile and an ugly spider vein on my right thigh. He will undoubtedly find me repulsive.

"You're being too hard on yourself," Val says. "You're barely thirty."

"Barely thirty? I'm thirty-one!" I inform her.

"So? Look at Jennifer Lopez. She's thirty-two or something like that."

"What does that have to do with anything?" I snap. "You're supposed to be making me feel better! Comparing me to J. Lo is not making me feel better!"

"I'm just saying that woman are sexy and desirable well into their thirties, forties, even fifties. Look at Sophia Loren."

"She is a freak of nature. She'll be sexy and beautiful when she's ninety."

"True. But it's no big deal, Kerry. Everyone's dating younger men these days. It's like a trend or something."

"What about you?" I ask Val, who is thirty-six. "Would you go out with Matt?"

"Well . . . Matt's always seen me as more of a maternal figure, I think. But if I'd just met him, then yeah, definitely."

"And would you get naked with him?" I spread some chèvre rolled in poppy seeds onto a cracker and pop it in my mouth.

"In the dark, yes," she says, sipping her Bellini. "But I'm older than you, and I've had a baby. I think you're worrying too much."

"Val . . . ," I say, pausing to swallow my cracker. "When Sam and I were going through our problems, I ate a bowl of cream cheese icing every night. You can't do that and not have some lasting effects."

"Well . . . ," she says.

"And this wrinkle!" I point to the deep indentation by my right eyebrow.

"What wrinkle?" She squints her eyes to see.

"Come on! You can totally see it. It's from frowning so much. . . . I blame my mother."

"Look, Kerry," she says, spreading cheese on a cracker. "If you're feeling that insecure, you've got lots of time to do something about it. He hasn't even called you yet."

"Great idea. I'll book myself in for some emergency Botox and liposuction."

"You don't have to be so extreme," Val says, sounding very motherly. "Drink more water, eat salads for a few days, tape up the wrinkle . . ."

"I guess." I shrug. " . . . What do you mean, tape up the wrinkle?"

"Lots of stars do it," she says. "I read about it in some magazine. When you go to bed at night or when you're puttering around the house, you apply tape to the wrinkle to pull it smooth. When you remove it, it's less noticeable."

"Really? I've never heard about that."

"Rene Russo does it."

"What kind of tape do you use?"

"Anything sticky," she says. "And if you do it enough, the wrinkle may even disappear."

"Really?" This is great. I know I'll never be able to save enough for Botox, and I don't like needles.

"Well . . . theoretically anyway."

It's worth a try. I immediately begin my new regime to make me look good enough to seduce a twenty-four-year-old. I bring a liter container to work, fill it with water, and drink four of them throughout the day. For lunch, I eat salad with only a few sesame seeds on top and a low-fat yogurt-based dressing. As soon as I get home from work, I apply tape to my deep frown line. It makes me look a bit like a creature off *Star Trek*, but that is the beauty of living alone—it doesn't matter! For dinner, I eat one and a half Lean Cuisines (because one is just ridiculously small).

The phone rings on Sunday evening. My caller-ID box shows an unrecognized number, and my stomach fills with butterflies. "Hello?" I say, sounding as youthful as possible.

"Hi. Is this Kerry?"

"Yes, it is."

"This is Matt Torres calling." He sounds shy. "I don't know if you remember me. . . . I used to work with Val Campbell."

"I remember you, Matt," I say, in a very deep and seductive Lauren Bacall–ish voice. Then I remember that Lauren Bacall is about eighty, so probably not the best celebrity impersonation to choose when trying to entice a younger man. So I say, "Like . . . totally, dude!"

"I was just wondering if you'd like to go out sometime? With me?"

"That would be great, Matt. I'd love to."

We settle on the following Thursday. He suggested Tuesday or Wednesday, but I told him I was busy until Thursday. This way, I will have had a full week to work on my cellulite and frown wrinkle, and I will also appear to have a very busy and active social life.

When the day arrives, I make an excuse and sneak out of the office at four thirty. He is taking me for dinner and drinks at seven. I want to take my time getting ready—have a glass of wine, do some calming breathing exercises, maybe meditate a bit. Tonight is going to be great. I don't need to feel intimidated just because he is twenty-four with a body like Enrique Iglesias. I have a lot to offer such a young stud.

I shower, dry my hair while scrunching for tousled, carefree waves, and apply my makeup. When I am done, it is only five thirty. I decide to tape my wrinkle, pour a glass of Shiraz, and listen to some calming Enya on my stereo. I sit cross-legged on the floor in my flannel pajamas, breathing deeply while the melodies wash over me. "I am sexy. I am youthful. I have a lot to offer a hot young man." I repeat this mantra until it is time to get dressed.

"HI," I SAY BRIGHTLY, OPENING THE DOOR TO MATT. GOD, HE IS GOOD looking. He looks just showered fresh; his skin is all dewy and soft and twenty-four.

"Hi," he says, his eyes darting around anxiously. Awwww . . . He's nervous. It must be intimidating dating someone with so much . . . experience. I must put him at ease.

"I'm really glad you called, Matt," I say sincerely. "I think we're going to have a great time tonight."

"Uh . . . yeah," he says. "So . . . uh . . . are you ready?"

"Yeah. I'm like, totally psyched!" I say, employing some of the youthful lingo I've picked up from hanging out with Tiffany.

Matt drives us to a dark and intimate bistro in his red Acura Integra. I am relieved to see that he's made a reservation. I thought maybe guys his age didn't make reservations (much like teenagers don't shake hands). But Matt is mature beyond his years. He has direction and purpose and a very bright future. I must remember that and stop thinking of him as someone Tiffany could hang out with.

"Would you like a cocktail, or should we order some wine?" he asks when we are seated in our candlelit booth.

"Wine would be great," I say. He really is very debonair for his age.

"Uh . . . okay. What, uh . . . kind do you like?"

I select a cabernet sauvignon from the wine list, and he orders it from our sleeveless waitress. Did I just see him checking out her toned arms? No, my own insecurities are planting ideas in my head. I hope I've chosen an appropriate outfit. I'm wearing a black rayon blouse that wraps at the waist, revealing just the right amount of cleavage. I have on black slacks with a subtle white pinstripe for a slimming effect. My hair is tousled and carefree. My makeup is understated and elegant. *I am sexy. I am youthful. I have a lot to offer a hot young man.*

Our conversation is stilted over dinner. He seems somewhat unfocused, like there's somewhere else he needs to be—or would rather be. I use my excellent skills as a conversationalist to draw him into an interesting exchange, but his eyes and thoughts seem to wander. As attractive as Matt is, perhaps guys his age just don't have anything very interesting to say. The term "eye candy" floats through my brain.

When the waitress asks if we'd like dessert or an after-dinner drink, Matt says, "Not for me, thanks. I've got an early morning."

"I'm fine, too," I say with a forced smile. "Big day tomorrow at the ad agency. We're casting for a commercial we're shooting next week."

"Cool," Matt says uninterestedly. "Just the bill, please."

On the ride home, I can't help but feel disappointed. Matt really was quite dull . . . and hard to talk to. Maybe we should have done something more appropriate to his age—like gone to a sports bar where we drank beer and watched baseball. Or a video arcade? But I am still hopeful that this evening won't be a total loss. I am dying to kiss him and run my hands over his hard, youthful physique.

We pull up in front of my building, and I turn to him. "Thanks so much for dinner. It was wonderful."

"No problem." He nods.

"So . . ." I lean toward him, prompting him to at least put the bloody car into park. "I had a really great time tonight."

"Me, too. Good night."

"Good night." I hop out of the car before he speeds off into the night.

What a disaster. I let myself into the solace of my apartment, glad to be alone and out of that awkward and uncomfortable situation. I kick off my shoes and wander dejectedly to the bathroom. No flirtatious banter over drinks, no eye contact over dinner, no goodnight kiss . . .

I stare in shock at my reflection in the mirror. "Noooooooooooooo-ooo," I screach. "Noooooooooooo!" I sink dramatically to the floor, my head in my hands. I can't believe this! I really can't. This is just fucking perfect. I wallow in self-pity for a few moments; then I pull myself together. I stand up, look in the mirror, and peel the Scotch tape from my forehead.

Mortifying Moment #6

(See Previous Chapter)

Chapter 18

"WHAT DID HE SAY?" I ASK VAL WHEN SHE CALLS ME AT THE OFFICE FRI-
day afternoon. I know full well what he said, but there is always a
slim chance that he didn't notice.

"He said you had Scotch tape on your head."

"It was for the wrinkle!" I cry. "I forgot to take it off."

"I know that, but poor Matt was totally confused."

"Did you tell him what it was for?" I'm not sure if I want him to
know or not.

"No . . . I played dumb."

"Hmmm. I wonder if I could tell him it was on for some medical
reason. Like . . . I had a skull fracture or something?"

"He's twenty-four—he's not an imbecile," Val says. "He's not
going to buy that you were holding your skull together with Scotch
tape."

"True. Well, it's too bad. He's really gorgeous. But . . . he's not
the 'one' anyway."

"The one what?"

I realize I haven't told Val about Ramona's predictions for my future soul mate. That's because I don't want Michelle to know. She's so pragmatic and skeptical that she'd undoubtedly scoff and laugh at my gullibility. "Oh, nothing," I say. "It's just that Matt was too young for me anyway. And I'd be so insecure dating someone that good looking."

"Sam was that good looking."

"Yeah, and I was so insecure dating him!"

Val laughs. "Well, hopefully you'll find yourself someone old and ugly soon."

"Hopefully," I say. "I'd better get back to work."

I have two new messages in my e-mail inbox. One is from my brother, asking me to pick up a Christmas present for Mom from him. "Spend about fifty bucks," he says. "I'll send you a check to cover it."

Sure he will. I know I'll never see a dime from him, and I also know that I'll hustle out and buy a really nice gift on his behalf. My mother will love it more than anything else she's received until she finds out that I selected it, and then she'll complain that it's a bit too small, or the scent gives her a headache, or it doesn't quite go with the color scheme in the condo, but it was a lovely gesture.

There is also a message from Theresa at Shooting Star.

Dear Shooting Star Mentors:

I've got free tickets to the hockey game on Monday between the Seattle Indians and the visiting Canadian team the Kamloops Ice Dogs. This is senior men's amateur hockey, and promises to be a fun filled and exciting night! If you and your protégée would be interested in going, please send me an e-mail to reserve your tickets.

Thanks for your time and commitment to helping a high- to medium-risk teen.

Theresa

Hockey! Fighting, swearing, poking each other with sticks! Hockey is sure to appeal to Tiffany's pugilistic appetites. I e-mail Theresa and request two tickets.

I pick Tiffany up at her aunt's apartment. Julie, her aunt, is about my age. She answers the door in her bathrobe with a cigarette dangling from her mouth. "Hi," she says in a gravelly voice that was probably once Demi Moore–ish but now sounds more like one of Marge Simpson's sisters. "Tiffany'll be right out." Then she leaves.

I wait in the hall until Tiffany appears.

"Heeeeeeeeyyy! 'S'up girlfriend?"

Tiffany gawks at me. Her nose is turned up slightly, like she's just discovered me in her hallway wearing only Saran Wrap.

Perhaps it is best not to try to speak her language. "How have you been?"

"Fine."

"Don't be too late!" Julie calls over the blare of *Wheel of Fortune.* "It's a school night."

"Yeah, yeah . . . ," Tiffany says, closing the door behind her. "She thinks she's, like, my mom now."

"Well, I'm sure it's just because she cares about you."

"Whatever."

The drive to the arena is awkward. I babble a constant stream of small talk—about the traffic, the buildings we pass, the rain, the game we're about to see . . . "Do you watch much hockey on TV?" I ask.

"My dad used to watch it, but he took off eight years ago, so not really. . . ."

"Oh. That's too bad."

Long awkward silence . . .

"My dad took off, too," I continue. "He's British, and he moved back to London for a job." I don't mention that my dad relocated when I was twenty and that his leaving had very little negative impact on me.

But in the interest of bonding with Tiffany, I sigh heavily and say, "It's been tough."

Silence.

"So I guess we have that in common, eh? Our dads taking off?"

This revelation does not have the bonding impact I had antici-pated. "I guess." She shrugs.

The Shooting Star program has a block of seats right behind the goal donated by Raincoast, Inc., a large and philanthropic shipping corporation. An employee from Shooting Star is there, handing out T-shirts and baseball caps for us to wear. Unfortunately, the T-shirts are fluorescent green, and the hats are tomato red.

Tiffany turns her nose up. "I'm not wearing that."

"Ugh. Could they have picked uglier colors?" I whisper.

She smiles.

"Here are your hats and shirts," the bubbly brunette from Shooting Star says. "Please wear them. We might be on TV later."

"I'm not wearing that on TV!" Tiffany screeches.

"Don't worry," I say, my voice hushed. "I'll cover for you." I don the hideous garments and shield Tiffany from the prying eyes of the Shooting Star girl.

The game begins with an impressive light show and dramatic music as the Seattle Indians take to the ice. Hockey was an excellent choice; with all the theatrics, it is quite similar to WWF or . . . that other one.

The first two periods are uneventful. Tiffany seems vaguely in-terested. I buy her a Coke and a bag of popcorn at the second inter-mission, which elicits a small smile of appreciation. Our group is featured briefly on the Jumbotron screen high above the ice.

"Ladies and gentlemen!" a booming voice says. "Please give a round of applause for the Shooting Star program! Providing men-tors for high- to medium-risk teens." Some of the kids wave to the camera. Tiffany practically crawls beneath her seat.

In the third and final period, the game becomes exciting. The score is two–all as the few remaining minutes are played out. The crowd is on the edge of their seats, cheering loudly for Seattle's vic-tory. Even Tiffany, who has previously been ambivalent to the outcome, is getting into it. When two players begin to tussle in the corner, she springs to life.

"Kill him! Kill him!" She screams, flecks of foam flying from her mouth. *"Smash his face in Roberts! Don't be such a wimp!"*

Oh, my! All eyes in the Shooting Star section turn to us, as do several in the neighboring seats. *"Murder him, number nineteen! He doesn't deserve to live! You suck! You suck!"*

She is standing now, leaning over the mentor and protégé seated in front of us as she hurls insults at the players. The mentor, a tallish guy in fluorescent green and tomato red turns to me. His eyes plead with mine: Do something, please. Make her stop. We're frightened.

"Hi," I say to the fruit-and-vegetable-hued mentor. "We've met before."

After a moment, recognition shows on his features. "Right! At the Silver Unicorn. How are you?"

"Good, thanks. And you?"

"Rip his head off, you big baby! Fight! Fight! Fight!"

We are unable to chat until Seattle scores with two minutes remaining and everyone starts to leave. *"You bite, Kamloops!"* Tiffany yells. *"Losers!"* I am now actually glad to be wearing this ridiculous red hat. It is providing camouflage in case I know anyone here—which I'm really hoping I do not. Except, of course, this brownish-sandy-haired guy I met at the work-related function.

When the final buzzer sounds, the crowd moves slowly toward the exit. I find myself standing directly in front of him as we inch our way out of the stadium.

"So . . . how long have you been a mentor?" he asks.

"Just a few weeks," I say. "You?"

"Two years. I met Brian when he was just twelve." He gives Brian a friendly punch in the arm. Brian is an overweight, acne-prone teen who beams up at his mentor with a look of adoration. I hope someday Tiffany will look at me that way. "I'm Nick, by the way."

"Right! Nick!" I say as I recall our previous meeting. "I'm—"

"Kerry. I remember."

"You have a good memory," I say, a bit flirtatiously (but not overly so—I don't want to send the wrong message to Tiffany and Brian).

"It's not hard to remember a girl covered in Caesar salad and chicken satay."

"I guess not." I smirk sheepishly.

We make pleasant small talk until we reach the doors and part ways. "It was nice to see you again, Kerry." He smiles sincerely. He really does have a very nice face: square jaw, twinkling blue eyes, and a hint of sexiness in his smile. In fact, he must be really quite good looking, considering I am finding him attractive despite his tomato hat and lime-green T-shirt.

"You, too, Nick." I smile back. "I'm sure our paths will cross again at another Shooting Star event."

"I hope so," he says.

"Bye, Tiffany," Brian says. "See you at school."

"Whatever." Tiffany turns away from him dismissively. As we walk into the drizzly night, she says, "What a loser."

"Who? Brian?"

"Yeah, Brian. Who else?"

"He goes to your school?"

"Yeah."

"Is he in your grade?"

"Some classes. But he's in a bunch of idiot classes, too."

"You mean remedial classes?"

"Whatever. We call them idiot classes."

I know I'm supposed to show support and not scold; I know I'm supposed to be a big sister, not a mother figure, but I can't let this pass. "You know Tiffany, a lot of people who became very successful started out as overweight kids in remedial classes."

"Sure." She snorts in disbelief. "Like who?"

"Albert Einstein, for one."

She scoffs, uninterested.

"Tom Cruise," I say.

She stops snorting and seems to absorb it a little.

"Brett 'the Hitman' Hart and Hulk Hogan."

"Really?"

"Really," I say, though I am totally making this up as I go along. "They were both fat and pimply and in special classes for math and science. And look at them now!"

"Yeah." She nods.

"So who knows? Brian could end up becoming a really famous wrestler. You wouldn't want him to remember you as the girl who was mean to him at school, would you?"

"No."

I am pretty good at this mentoring thing.

Chapter 19

I AM DUE AT THE TELEVISION SHOOT AT ELEVEN. I WILL GO INTO THE OF-
fice first to check e-mails, follow up on a few other projects, and generally show my face around, so as to look very zealous. (I could
probably have gotten away with sleeping in and going straight to the
shoot.) I also had a frantic call from Trevor last night, requesting an
emergency chai latte session this morning. It seems he is having
some issues with the amazing guy he met at the Silver Unicorn.

I have barely taken my coat off when Trevor appears in my doorway.

"Can we go now?" he says. "I've been waiting all morning."

"It's only eight thirty!"

"Yeah . . . let's go."

I will at least turn my computer on to give the impression that I
have already been in . . . which I have. If Sonja happens by, she may
wonder "Where is Kerry?" but a glance at my computer will tell her
that I have obviously been in to catch up on e-mails and other proj-

ects. I'm not sure why I am still trying to impress Sonja. I know it's a hopeless situation—the spirit world knows it, too! Sucking up to her must be force of habit.

At Starbucks, we order our beverages then find our usual secluded back table. I was very angry with Trevor after he tricked me into meeting with Dave at Corky's; I wasn't sure it was possible to be friends with someone so deceitful. And I told him so.

"But, Kerry," Trevor responded. "I had the best intentions, and you have to admit, things did turn out well."

"I guess they did, but how would you feel if I asked you to go for a drink and instead, fucking Rory showed up?"

"I see your point." He acquiesced. "I'm sorry." He gave me a quick hug. "But I can't help it! I still think Dave is the one the psychic was talking about!"

"He's not! How many times do I have to tell you? It's not him."

"I think she doth protest too much."

"I doth nothing, Trevor. And if you care at all about our friendship, you'll stop talking about Dave right now."

He did.

So . . . now we are ensconced in the most private corner of the busy Pine Street Starbucks, and Trevor is about to spill the details of his latest drama. "I don't know why I have such shitty luck with men," he says, taking a sip of his latte.

"Well, if you'd like to borrow *You Get What You Give* by Dr. Rainbow—"

He silences me with a look.

"What's wrong?" I ask sympathetically.

"I told you about Joseph, right?"

"Not much. Just that you met him that night at the NAPI party and that he works at LPM. *And* that he's amazing."

"He was amazing," Trevor says morosely. "*Is* amazing, I guess. I mean . . . he is amazing, but . . ."

"But what?"

"I'm starting to think he might be a bit . . . old."

"Old? He's old?"

"He's not old!" Trevor snaps. "He's old*er*. You know . . . older than me."

"How older is he?"

"Forty."

"That's not so old."

"Okay . . . he's forty-four, but he doesn't look it. Except—"

"Except?"

"Naked. He looks older when he's naked."

"Oh."

"Yeah, I know it sounds shallow, but there are other things, too."

"Like what?"

"His taste in music."

"Uh-oh." I know Trevor takes his music very seriously. He is really into house.

"He likes show tunes. Especially Rodgers and Hammerstein. He has the same taste as my mom!"

"Well . . . ," I say, taking a sip of my frothy drink. "I am a huge fan of *The Sound of Music.*"

"How nice," Trevor retorts. "Perhaps we should invite you over for a duet? You and Joseph can be Lisa and Ralph."

"*Leisel* and *Rolf,*" I say. Like, duh?

"Whatever." He waves his hand dismissively. "I can't stand it."

"Can't stand it? Are you crazy?" I begin to sing in my sweetest Leisel voice. " '*I am sixteen, going on seventeen, I know that I'm naïve.*' "

"Stop!"

"Okay . . . How about this one? *'High on a hill was a lonely goatherd—*' "

"If you yodel, I will scald you with this latte!"

We are holding our sides with laughter when suddenly—

"You two look like you're having an awfully good time."

Shit. Sonja.

"I thought you'd be at the shoot, Kerry."

"I will be," I say quickly. "I just came in to check my e-mails and follow up on some other projects. I think you'll notice that my computer is already on in my office."

Trevor shoots me a look. I guess that wasn't very subtle.

Sonja ignores my comments anyway and looks at her watch. "It's nearly ten. You should get going. Janet said she'd be there before eleven, and I wouldn't want the client to show up before you."

"Yes, I was just about to leave. I'll just go back to the office and grab Gavin and give him a ride out there."

"Oh, Gavin's already there," Trevor interjects. "I saw him earlier this morning. He said he came in to the office at seven to catch up on some things and left for the shoot around eight."

Gee, thanks, Trevor. Remind me to serenade you with "Edelweiss" at every given opportunity.

"Well," Sonja says. "I suggest you join him. Please call in with a progress report this afternoon."

As I drive to the Tacoma set, I realize that I didn't have a chance to check my e-mails or follow up on any other projects. No doubt, Dennis the production manager will see Sonja in the hall and ask, "Have you seen Kerry? She was supposed to follow up on several projects, and I haven't heard from her." If this sparks her curiosity, she may open my e-mail program to find a row of unopened messages, dated this morning. She will know I came into the office, turned on my PC, then promptly walked out to drink chai lattes with Trevor. It is definitely time to dust off my résumé.

I enter the cavernous building that was once actually a high school but is now used primarily for AA meetings and television shoots. Paper signs with red arrows drawn on them point me to the set. I walk down the echoing hallway until I become aware of the din of the crew just ahead. Turning the corner, I am affronted by a throng of people milling between massive lights, a number of large cameras, and a craft services table (danger zone). In the midst of it all, I see Gavin chatting amiably with Janet.

"It's true, Janet. Kerry is completely replaceable. In fact, I am actu-

ally a better account manager but with a lower charge-out rate. If you asked Sonja to fire her and give me her job, you would be saving yourself a lot of time and money."

"Hi," I say, rushing over to them. "Sorry I'm late. I had a couple of things I had to do in the office."

"Me, too." Gavin smiles. "I went in at seven so I could get here early."

I ignore him. "How are you, Janet? Do you like the set? Is it how you visualized it?"

"It's fine," Janet says tartly. I used to really like Janet, but given some of our recent run-ins, I am starting to find her annoying. She is really rather serious about her stupid company.

I glance around and see Dave and Tanya chatting with the director. Dave looks up and waves. I wave back—a little too seductively perhaps, because Tanya's eyes shoot daggers across the room. I'm not trying to encourage Dave or anything, but I can't help feeling a little . . . I don't know . . . *special* because the creative director has such a huge crush on me.

I grab Janet and me a plate of snacks from craft services, and we sit back to watch the filming. We have flown a director in from L.A. His name is Andre, and he is built like his governor, with long, flowing blond hair. He calls the actors to the set.

"Okay! Listen up!" he calls. "I need the extras to find seats in those desks. I want lawyer kid and death-row-murderer kid in these front two! Now, people!"

A mob of eight-year-olds stampedes onto the set and finds seats in the rows of desks. The two feature actors, a cute little black boy and a freckle-faced redhead, sit in the front-row seats.

"Okay! Great! Sara! Get the crack-whore girl into makeup! Death-row kid—"

"*Cut!*" I yell before I even realize what I'm doing. I know no one but the director is supposed to yell *cut*; I know the cameras aren't even rolling, but . . . yet again, I've lost control over my mouth.

"Yes?" Andre turns to me. "You have a problem?"

I am aware of all eyes on me. The majority of the crew has no idea who I am and think I'm just some disruptive crackpot who wandered in off the street. They are all slightly sneering at me as self-important TV people do.

"Umm . . ." I clear my throat. I've got to say this. "Can we not refer to the children as 'death-row kid' and 'crack-whore-girl'? I can't help but think this might be scarring to an eight-year-old's psyche."

Andre snorts a laugh. "They are actors," he says. "They are playing a part! If the part is of a crack-whore, then that is what they will be called, all right?"

"No, actually. You see, the kids aren't playing crack whores and death-row inmates—the adults are. The kids are playing *students*."

Andre is getting red-faced, and I'm sure his creative ego has had just about all it can take of me. "What do you want me to call them, Kerry? Student One and Student Two? Student Eight and Student Nine?"

"How about using their names?"

There are a few snickers and by the look in Andre's eyes, I know I have made an enemy for life. "Fine," he snaps. "What's your name, kid?"

"Thanks," Janet whispers. "That was bothering me, too."

"No problem," I whisper back. I am suddenly aware of Dave's eyes on me from across the set. He is staring at me, an amused smile playing on his lips. Uh-oh. I was being feisty again, wasn't I? I will never get him to fall out of love with me!

The rest of the shoot goes smoothly, and things are progressing ahead of schedule. Janet is so pleased that she even calls Sonja to tell her (which may score a few brownie points for me . . . and for Gavin, I guess). Andre is thrilled with the performances of the crack whore and Ms. Trailer Trash. There is only one fly in the ointment—Tanya and Dave are not getting along.

Tanya doesn't even show up on the third and final day of shooting. I can't say that I blame her. Dave has been flirting incessantly with this gorgeous Asian woman who plays crack-whore girl's—I mean Madison's—third-grade teacher. I suspect he has been doing this to throw Tanya off the scent of his feelings for me . . . but he's very convincing. They have even disappeared behind the makeup trailers on several occasions. If I didn't know better, I'd think he was really interested in her.

When we finally wrap on Friday afternoon, a group of us go to a nearby bar to celebrate a job well done. Dave is there without Tanya or his beautiful faux-girlfriend. I find an opportune moment when most of the other guests are doing tequila shots, and I ask him about it. I'm not sure why, but it seems I can't help myself.

"So . . . what happened to Tanya?" There is a hint of amusement in my voice.

"We broke up. She didn't feel like coming to the set anymore, so I told her she could work out of the office."

"That's too bad," I say as sincerely as possible.

"It's for the best. I think we both knew it was over."

"I hope your working relationship will be all right."

"We'll figure something out."

"I know you will . . . ," I say sympathetically. "So . . . I guess all the flirting you did with that Asian girl did the trick, eh?"

"Sorry?"

"Come on." I nudge him. "I saw what you were doing. You were totally flirting with crack-whore girl's teacher! Tanya must have noticed it, too."

"That may have had something to do with it." He takes a long pull on his beer.

"I have to say, Dave," I continue, my lips loosened by a couple of drinks, "that I really appreciate you throwing Tanya off with that actress. I really wouldn't want her to know that *I* am the reason you broke up with her."

Dave clears his throat. "Actually, Kerry . . . Shannon and I *are* dating."

"Sorry . . . what? Who?"

"Shannon . . . the actress . . . we're dating."

"Oh." I can feel my face turning crimson.

"Yeah, I guess I should have told you. I realized, a while ago, that my attraction to you was really just an excuse to get out of this thing with Tanya. You were just the closest available female, you know? And then when I met Shannon . . . well, I realized that she is what I'm looking for. She made me take the final step to end my relationship with Tanya."

"Well . . . that's great, then." I down the remains of my beer (the remains being seven eighths of the bottle). "I'm happy for you, Dave. I really am. I'd better go and check on Janet. . . ." I look over to see her licking salt off Andre's muscular chest. "See ya later."

I hate Dave.

Chapter 20

OKAY . . . SO, I HATE DAVE. HE IS COLD, INSENSITIVE, TWO-FACED, AND manipulative. He's not that good looking and I don't even respect his creative talent. So why is this bothering me so much? I should be happy that he is out of my hair and not alternately trying to kiss me or have me fired. But I can't help worrying about this. What if, by some crazy twist of fate, Dave was "the one" that Ramona predicted? Is my karma so bad that even the one the universe intended for me can easily be lured away by an attractive commercial actress?

I feel completely blue . . . not devastated as I did when I ended things with Sam, but blue nonetheless. I really am an idiot. And of course, my therapist picks this week to go on vacation. I wonder where she's going. Despite me spilling my most humiliating secrets to her biweekly, she tells me virtually nothing. Where would someone like her go on vacation? Probably to some back-to-basics retreat in the Cascades, where a bunch of women churn their own butter, make homemade jam, and sit around quilting. Although . . . you never know. They say it's the quiet ones that will surprise you.

Maybe she's at one of those weird medieval fairs dressed as a serving wench and doing the bidding of some muscular guy in chain mail whom she calls m'lord. Or maybe she's at a nudist colony, where— ewwww.

Okay, my therapist is on vacation, but I can cope on my own. With the help of deep breathing and *You Get What You Give*, I can handle this rejection. I've also purchased a Zen Kit to help me become one with the universe and spiritually free.

THE COMPLETE GUIDE TO ZEN IN A BOX, it says on the cover. It is this cute little kit I happened across in Safeway. (Please don't say I'm not going to find true Zen in Safeway. I've already had this conversation with myself.) Inside are some smooth polished stones, a couple of tea lights, some incense, and a small round mirror. There is also a red book with the Japanese symbol for Zen (I'm assuming, as I can't really read Japanese) on the cover. This is my "practical guide to gaining Zen wisdom."

I open the little red book and begin to read. It is really copy heavy (as we say in the ad biz). I think I will skip ahead to the section on finding enlightenment. Hmmm . . . okay . . . here we are:

Enlightenment or "satori" is the goal of all practitioners of the Zen school. But one must not actively seek enlightenment, but allow it to happen, through meditation, working, and living the "right" life. The harder one seeks to gain enlightenment, the further away from it they will be drawn. The mind and spirit must be occupied and focused simultaneously, neither seeking satori nor creating obstacles to prevent it.

Simple enough. I will just light these candles and the incense, and hold these smooth stones in my hands while I meditate. I will not actively seek enlightenment, just hope that it happens along and finds me. As I set up my meditation station, I notice the tiny round mirror included in the kit. A quick flip through the book does not provide any indication of the use of this object. I decide to place it in front of me as I sit in the lotus position and breathe deeply.

Uggh. I glance down at the mirror to a really unflattering view of my face. I look very jowly . . . a bit like a bloodhound, and every nose hair is explicitly visible. I turn the mirror facedown, thankful that no one has ever seen my face from that angle. I mean, how could they? A person would have to be lying down while I sat astride them—Oh, God! No wonder Sam broke up with me. He's probably seen me looking like a bloodhound at least fifty times!

Anyway . . . it is irrelevant now. All I can do is learn from my mistakes and never do it in the "girl on top" position again. Okay . . . I am twisted into lotus now . . . breathing deeply . . . Enlightenment, feel free to enter my mind . . . not that I really want you to or care either way . . . release the thoughts as they enter my brain . . . This incense smells nice. . . . I think . . . It might be giving me a headache, though. . . . Or maybe it is the pain from this rigid posture . . . The lotus position has turned my hips and inner thighs numb. . . . It is probably good to focus on the pain, thus allowing enlightenment to reach me while I am occupied with other things . . . like if I'll be able to walk after this. . . . I'm thirsty. . . . Now I have to pee. . . . Well, the book says enlightenment can come during any activity. . . .

Thank God! The phone!

I am so relieved to have a break from this bloody meditating that I don't even check the caller-ID box. Even a call from a telemarketer selling subscriptions to *Fisherman's Weekly* would provide a welcome respite.

"Hello?" I say cheerfully.

"Kerry? Hi. It's me, Sam."

"Uh . . . hello," I stammer, completely shocked to hear his deep, sexy voice.

"Am I catching you at a bad time?"

"Not really. I was just . . . cleaning."

"Well . . . you said I could call you sometime. Just to see how you're doing . . ."

"Of course. Right. I'm great, thanks. And you?"

"Good. Yeah . . . work's good . . . busy."

"Me, too. I just finished a TV shoot for Prism."

"Oh, yeah? How'd it go?"

"Really well, actually." I am suddenly so over this stupid Dave thing.

"And how's . . . uh . . . I don't even know his name." He sort of chuckles. "The guy you've been seeing?"

Long, awkward pause. "Oh, yes! He's great! Things are great."

"Yeah?" He sounds a bit disappointed.

"We broke up, actually."

"Really?" He sounds much more cheerful. "Well . . . how would you like to grab a drink sometime? Talk about old times?"

"Yeah." I shrug, trying to sound indifferent. "I suppose we could."

"How about now?" he says. "I could steal you away from your housework."

I know what I should say. I should say, "No thank you, Sam. The old times we had together aren't really worth talking about. Goodbye." Or, "Actually, Sam, I am still hopeful that what's-his-name and I will work things out so . . . it wouldn't be a good idea for us to get together." Or, "I've got the flu." Or, "My mom is here right now." Or, "I'm on house arrest." But I don't.

"Sure," I say, in a ridiculously seductive voice. "Where shall we meet?"

I show up at the bar fifteen minutes late. Sam is seated by a bank of windows with a 180-degree view of Elliott Bay. Okay . . . I tell myself as I approach . . . this is just a friendly catch-up drink. I'm not going to kiss him. I'm not going to sleep with him. And if I do, I definitely won't be on top. His face lights up when he sees me—like it never did when we were together.

"Hello," I say.

"Hi." He beams and stands to pull out my chair. "You look amazing."

"Thank you," I respond formally. "And you." I'm sure he does look amazing, but the truth is, I haven't had the courage to really look at him since I arrived. I'm afraid I'll melt into his arms the moment I lay eyes on him. Now that I don't have my imaginary boyfriend as an excuse, I'm not sure I have the strength of character to resist him. I preoccupy myself with the amazing view.

"Beautiful, isn't it?" I ask, staring out the rain-splattered glass.

"It is," he says huskily, and I can feel his eyes on me. I need him to back off.

"So . . . tell me what you've been up to," I say, forcing an upbeat tone.

"Let's get you a drink first. What are you having?"

"Glass of red, please. Merlot or Shiraz."

"I'll get it from the bar," he says, rising. "The waitress is a bit slow." When he returns, it is with a bottle of wine and two glasses.

"Uh, Sam . . . I just wanted a glass of wine," I say, annoyed. My therapist's past warnings on the dangers of mixing alcohol and Sam flit through my consciousness.

"Oh, come on." He smiles, his eyes twinkling. "We've got a lot of catching up to do."

"I'll have one glass," I say again. "I'm not about to sit here and drink a bottle of wine at four o'clock in the afternoon."

At five thirty, Sam says, "Should we get another bottle?"

"Well, I have plans tonight," I lie. "I don't think I should."

"Come on, Kerr." He puts his hand over mine, and I try not to shiver from the electric current between us. "Don't go yet. It's so great to see you."

"Well . . ." I begin to decline, but the truth is, I am really enjoying our conversation. "I guess I can stay for a bit longer. But I'd better order some food, or I'll be passed out in my chair by seven."

Sam laughs—really hard—at my little joke, and he summons the waitress to bring us menus and more wine.

As it grows dark, our waitress lights a candle on our table. We each enjoy a plate of seafood pasta while we sip wine and try not to stare into each other's eyes . . . at least I am trying not to. This suddenly feels way too much like a date. "What are we doing here, Sam?" I say softly. "We both know it's over between us."

"Is it, Kerry?"

"It is!" I insist. "We tried—really hard—to make it work. We're just not right together. There's too much history between us."

"But we are right together," Sam says, leaning in. "I didn't realize—until you were gone—how right we were together. I was an idiot to put my career before us. My priorities were out of whack. I made a lot of mistakes, Kerry, but I've learned from them. . . . God, I miss you so much."

"I miss you, too, but—"

"And I know *you* tried really hard before, but I didn't. Not like I would now . . . if you gave me another chance."

Oh, no. This is not good. Where is that stupid waitress? Why isn't she interrupting us with a dessert menu or something?

"Sam . . . I . . ."

"Take some time if you want," he says gently. "I'll wait."

"Okay." I tear my eyes away from his. "I'd better go."

Sam takes care of the bill and follows me outside. I hail a taxi, and he piles in beside me. I give the driver my address and then look at Sam.

"Right," he responds. "And the next stop will be Eastlake."

"I had such a great time tonight," he says, cuddling down beside me in the backseat.

"Yeah?" I say encouragingly.

"Since we've been apart, I've gone out with a couple of girls and . . . there's just no one who compares to you."

"Reeeeeeeeeeeally?" I feel myself softening toward him. "That's so sweet."

"It's true," he says. "You are one in a million . . . one in ten million." He kisses my mouth very lightly. I don't pull away.

The cab pulls up in front of my building in the nick of time: I was just about to straddle him and suck his lips off.

"Well," I say as I fish in my wallet for the fare. "Here we are."

"It's still early," Sam says. "Maybe I could come up for a coffee or something?"

I turn and look at him. Our eyes are locked in an intense gaze.

He reaches up and softly strokes my cheek. "You're beautiful," he whispers.

"So are you," I say through the lump in my throat.

"I had a great time tonight," he says tenderly. "A wonderful time."

"So did I," I croak.

"I'd really, *really* like to come up, Kerry."

There is a long pause as a jumble of thoughts and possibilities swirls through my head. "Sam? . . ."

"Yes?"

"I'm sorry but . . . no. Good night." I hop out of the cab and sprint into the lobby of my building so I don't have a chance to change my mind.

Chapter 21

" '*I AM WOMAN—HEAR ME ROAR!*' " I SING LOUDLY IN THE PRIVACY OF my car as I drive to the office from my weekly coffee date with Tiffany. " '*In numbers too big to ignore . . . da nana na nana na nana na naaaaaaaaaaa . . .*' " I don't know all the words, but that doesn't limit the power of my anthem. I am on a high after the events of last night. This is like one of my fantasies coming true: Sam begs me to come back, and I turn him down! " '*I am strong! I am invincible! I am womaaaaaaaaaaaaaaaan!*' "

I pull into my parking spot and lower the volume significantly as I exit my car and stroll leisurely to the office. (When the Transisters never really took off, I kind of lost confidence in my singing voice.) In the elevator, the song becomes just a murmur, barely audible to anyone else, but it is still fortifying me, congratulating me for my strength, my courage, my resolve.

Of course, the fact that I had not shaved my legs for four days or cleaned my apartment for two weeks had significant bearing on my decision not to invite Sam in. But he doesn't know that, does he?

And no one else needs to know it either. Besides, what really matters is that I did not sleep with him and start the cycle all over again.

I must admit, a small part of me is hoping my rejection will be a huge turn-on to him, spurring him to do something dramatic to win my affection. It would be a gesture so incredibly romantic that I would be able to say "How could I turn him down after that? It was obvious how much he really loved me!"

The elevator stops on four, and I get out. I haven't been in the office for almost two weeks. (After the shoot, we spent several days in an edit suite getting the spots ready for air.) There is a spring in my step as I walk to my office. I thought I might feel uncomfortable being back here after the whole Dave fiasco, but that is the furthest thing from my mind. " 'I am strong! Woo! I am—' "

"Oh, hello, Sonja," I say with a bright smile.

Sonja seems taken aback by my enthusiastic greeting. I decide to take it even further.

"And how are you on this fabulous Monday morning?"

"Well . . . ," she giggles rather nervously. "It's thirty-five degrees and raining . . . not exactly what I'd call fabulous!"

"Tut-tut-tut!" I say, waving my finger at her. "Glass half-empty, Sonja." Wow. I am really annoying when I am so happy. It's great.

"You're certainly in positive spirits," she says. "I hear the shoot went well?"

"Really well," I say. I decide to attribute my good mood to the success of the Prism shoot, thus ensuring that I look really into my job. "Have you seen the final spots? They look great, and we're all really pleased. The first one will be on air tomorrow."

"Great." She smiles. "Well . . . I'm sure you have a lot of work to catch up on, so I'll let you get to it."

"Thanks, Sonja. Have a great day!"

I boot up my computer and go directly to my e-mail in-box. Yikes, 212 e-mails! I scan through and look for the good ones (that is, ones not work related). There is a message from my brother, asking if I could please buy a gift for Dad because it is much cheaper to ship a parcel to London from the States than from Australia. He'll pay me back. There is one from Michelle, asking if I'd be interested in joining her at the women-in-communications brunch next week. There is one from Sandra. . . .

Sandra! Thank God! She has finally forgiven me. I hastily open the missive. It is addressed to Val, Michelle, and me.

Hello. I am writing to you all to give you an update on my current situation. No, I'm not pregnant. I have been having a very difficult time lately, and the fact that I don't have any friends to support me has not helped. On Sunday, I will be leaving for three weeks in the Dominican Republic. George and I felt that a little time away from all the pressures of life would do me good.

I also wanted to say that I am sorry I called the police on you and almost had you arrested. Perhaps it was an overreaction on my part; on the other hand, you were holding me there against my will. If you can all leave your judgments behind, I would be willing to discuss our (possible) continued friendship when I return.
Sincerely,
Sandra

Hmmm . . . She sounds a bit frosty and self-righteous, but at least she is taking the initiative and contacting us. I hit REPLY then realize she will already be in the Dominican, probably lying on a white sandy beach sipping a mai tai. I'll e-mail her in a week or two.

Scrolling down, I find most of my e-mails are from Dennis, and most of them have a red exclamation point beside them. I will leave those till last; I don't want anything ruining my mood. Here is one from Shooting Star.

Dear Shooting Star Mentors:
Believe it or not, Christmas is just around the corner! We'd like to invite all mentors and protégés to the annual Shooting Star Christmas party at the Point Defiance Zoo & Aquarium! We

hope you'll join us on November 18 for an evening of food, fun, festivities, and fish! This year promises to be just as much fun for protégés and mentors as it was last year. Please RSVP at your earliest convenience so we know how many will be attending.

Thanks for your time and commitment to helping a high- to medium-risk teen.
Theresa

Somehow I doubt this event will be Tiffany's cup of tea, but I hope I can convince her to attend.

Directly above this e-mail is one from an address I don't recognize: nick@artsmarts.com. It reads,

Hi Kerry,
It was great seeing you at the hockey game the other night. (Although, I've just been diagnosed as deaf in one ear from Tiffany's screaming.) Are you guys going to go to the Christmas party at the aquarium? We went last year and it was great. Anyway . . . I hope to see you there!
Nick

Ahhh, Nick! I reply.

Hi Nick,
It was great to see you too. Tiffany and I will definitely be at the Christmas party. I'll look for you. Have a great day.
Kerry

P.S. I hope your company has a good medical plan that covers hearing aids.

I hit SEND. Okay . . . I guess that's it for the fun stuff. I'd better deal with Dennis's e-mails before he shows up in my office to berate me. I'll just quickly call Val and ask her opinion on Sandra's e-mail.

When I finally hang up from that conversation, there is a voice message from Michelle wanting my opinion on the same topic. I discuss with Michelle, and a consensus is reached among the three of us. We will e-mail Sandra and tell her that we'd be very happy to meet with her, and while we don't agree with what she is doing with her life, we will listen and be supportive. But we will stand firm that the intervention was done with the best intentions and we have nothing to apologize for.

I look at my watch. Yikes! It's ten thirty! I'll just quickly phone home and check my voice messages—just in case there is one from Sam, pining away for me.

"You have—one—new message," the recorded voice says. Here we go! I am a-twitter to hear his voice.

"Hi, Kerry. It's just me, your mother calling. Darrel and I are going to have an open house on the twelfth of December. We'd really like you to pop by . . . and bring Sam if you two are back on again."

Oh. I'm somewhat disappointed, but at least my social calendar is filling up (even if it is just a party at my mom's house). I've just hung up when Trevor appears.

"Can we go for a latte?"

Oh, shit. I still haven't done any of the work I was supposed to catch up on. Dennis will kill me. But a boost of caffeine is what I need to tackle the projects ahead. And I'm dying to tell Trevor about my "sort of date" with Sam last night.

When we are seated in the café, I ask, "So . . . how's Captain von Trapp?"

"He's great, actually," Trevor says. "I decided that we can't have *everything* in common. That would be boring."

"True. And I really think if you gave *The Sound of Music* a chance . . ."

"Don't push it. We're going to have to agree to disagree on that one."

I am about to launch into my Sam story when Trevor leans in and whispers, "Your boyfriend's here."

"What?" I whirl my head in the direction he is indicating, expecting to see Sam. But no—it is Dave and Tanya, cloistered at a secluded table. They appear to be embroiled in a deep discussion.

"Oh, great," I mutter. "Keep your head down and talk quietly. Maybe they won't notice us."

"Okay," Trevor agrees. "Now what were you going to tell me?"

"Well . . . ," I begin excitedly. "Last night, I was practicing acquiring Zen wisdom, when the phone rang."

Trevor smiles quizzically. "You're trying to acquire Zen wisdom?"

"Well, I thought I'd give it a try, but I'm not sure it's for me. Anyway, the phone rang and interrupted my meditation."

"Were you really meditating? I've tried before, but never really got to that deep state of relaxation everyone talks about."

"I probably wasn't *actually* meditating. . . . I was more just . . . sitting really still. But anyway, the phone rang, and it was Sam!"

"No!"

"Yes! And then—"

But my story goes no further. There is a sudden eruption from the back corner of the restaurant. A chair is knocked over, and a female voice screams, "You make me sick! Consider this my resignation!" Trevor and I furtively peek over our booth just in time to see Tanya throwing a glass of water in Dave's face.

I can't help but snigger as I look at Dave's dripping countenance. Trevor and I exchange wickedly gleeful looks as Tanya stomps by us. But despite the fact that I have my hands over my face to stifle my laughter, she notices me. . . . And stops.

"You!" she screeches at me. "Here to watch all the fun?"

"Uh . . . sorry? What? I don't know what you're—"

"Don't give me that!" she roars. "You're enjoying this, aren't you?"

"I—uh—what? No!"

"You know what, Kerry? You deserve him." She glances over at wet Dave. "You are just as shallow and self-absorbed as he is. I hope you have a happy life together. I know you won't."

"Uh—Tanya—I, umm? What?"

"Good comeback, Kerry," Trevor whispers, amused.

But I'm speechless! Flabbergasted. What is she talking about? I look over at Dave, who's mopping his head with a napkin. My eyes narrow with hatred. I stand up and march over to him.

"What the hell was that?" I hiss at him through gritted teeth.

"Tanya resigned," he sniffs. "She's a little pissed off at me."

"She should be pissed off at *you!*" I growl. "Why is she pissed off at *me?*"

"Well . . . I didn't really see the point in telling her about Shannon, because she already thinks there's something going on between you and me."

"But there isn't!" I cry.

"I know that." He stands up and looks me in the eyes. "But I figured . . . why get her mad at Shannon, you know? Shannon's just an innocent bystander in all this."

"No, she's not!" I am really screaming now, and I can feel all eyes in the café on us. "She's your girlfriend! She's the reason you broke up with Tanya! *I'm* the innocent bystander here!"

"Come on, Kerry," he scoffs. "You loved the attention you were getting from me. You ate it up! Don't try to tell me you were innocent in all this."

"What? I—ulp—no!" I've lost the power of speech again. My face feels purple with rage.

"Anyway, Tanya is clearing out her office now. She'll be out of all our lives by the end of the day. There's no need to make such a big deal about this."

I am shaking uncontrollably. I have never ever been so angry! I want to throw hot coffee on him and scald him beyond recognition. I want to stab him with the butter knife lying beside his scone! I want to—I feel Trevor grabbing me gently but firmly by the shoulders and leading me back to our seat. "He's not worth it," he says. "Don't worry. He'll get his."

I sit and try to compose myself. I feel like I'm about to cry. "Trevor," I say, looking at him tearfully. "I don't think I can work there anymore."

He takes my hand. "I'd hate to see you go, but I can see your point."

"It's just too much weirdness."

"I know."

"After Christmas," I say. "I'm going to seriously start looking."

Chapter 22

WHY HASN'T HE CALLED? I DON'T UNDERSTAND IT. IT HAS BEEN TWENTY-three and a half days since my sort-of date with Sam, and he hasn't called once. That's sixteen workdays! Three weekends! Of course, the usual bouquet of roses turned up on day four, complete with bunny-rabbit-holding-heart-shaped-balloon card, but I've come to realize that this isn't necessarily the most heartfelt of gestures. Did I misread his sincerity? Maybe he didn't want to rekindle things with me after all. Was he really just after a roll in the hay with someone he thought was a sure thing (namely Kerry "slutty and easy with a few glasses of wine in her" Spence)?

Or . . . did he really want to get back together with me and when I turned him down I bruised his ego so badly that now he is afraid to call? In that case, should I call him? But what if the first scenario is the correct one and I call? Then I will seem really needy and pathetic and—Wait! What if he has been injured and is unable to call? What if his taxi was sideswiped by an SUV and he is lying semiconscious in the hospital? Maybe I'd better call?

Of course, I can't deny that this not-calling behavior fits Sam's past relationship profile to a T. It is just like him to profess his feelings, pour out his heart, and then not bother to pick up the phone or take me out for so much as a friggin' coffee. He's obviously so confident that I am crazy about him that he doesn't feel the need to even speak to me. Because why wouldn't I be? He's perfect—with his fancy car and his great job and his thick hair. I don't need more of his head games—I really don't. In fact, I'm tempted to call him up and read him the riot act. How dare he tell me I'm one in ten million and then not call me for twenty-three and a half days!

But a glance at my watch tells me that I won't have time right now. I've got to pick up Tiffany and get down to the Shooting Star Christmas party at the aquarium.

As anticipated, Tiffany wasn't exactly overjoyed at the prospect of eating Christmas cookies and drinking cocoa while wandering around looking at a bunch of fish. I appealed to her love of violence by mentioning that there may be a shark-feeding demonstration. "It's really bloody and gory," I ad-libbed.

"Okay," she relented. "I guess I can go."

We travel slowly through the Saturday afternoon traffic. Rain spatters the windshield, and the wipers slap back and forth methodically. I've learned from our weekly hour-long visits that conversation with Tiffany is initially painful, but if I persevere, she often becomes more chatty in the last ten minutes or so. It is a lot of work for a ten-minute reward, but when she does open up, we've had some great conversations. Besides, today we will have several hours together.

"So . . . ," I say, trying to fill the vacuum of silence. "How's school going?"

"Sucks."

"Really? That's too bad." More awkward silence. "What about English?" I ask hopefully. Tiffany had mentioned recently that they were reading *The Outsiders* and she was enjoying it.

"I failed my final paper," she says dully.

"Oh, no!" I am chagrined. "I thought you were enjoying *The Outsiders*?"

"The ending was sad and stupid, so I didn't feel like writing a paper on it."

"Oh . . . How will that affect your final grade?"

"I'll probably fail English." She shrugs.

Long, awkward silence.

"Uh . . . have you talked to your mom lately?"

"Yeah, I've talked to her. She's still a bitch."

Nervous giggle. "Oh, dear! I'm sure she's not all that bad."

"You haven't met her."

"True. I know how moms are, though. My mom and I have kind of a weird relationship."

Silence.

"How are things going, living with your aunt?"

"Lame," she says. "She's starting to get really bossy and act like she's my mother or something. I'm thinking of going to live with my dad."

"What?" I am taken aback. "In Canada?"

"Yeah."

It's been only a couple of months, and I have already failed her as a mentor. I can't believe she's going to leave town before I've even had a chance to help her. To turn her into Madeleine Albright or Janet Reno! (I know that wasn't expected of me, but I had secretly hoped that I would surpass all other mentors and turn a troubled teen into secretary of state or attorney general or whatever.) This is really going to look bad on my mentoring record. I can just see the look of disappointment on the school counselor's face. "We were so hopeful you'd have a positive impact," she'll say. "Oh, well. Can't win 'em all." And Theresa at Shooting Star will say, "Thanks for trying, Kerry, but I think you should leave mentoring to people who are hip and cutting edge despite their age."

"Are you sure that's such a great idea Tiffany?"

She shrugs. "I dunno. Since Rollie and I broke up, I don't really see any reason to stick around." Rollie is the twenty-year-old pot-head alcoholic she'd been dating just prior to us meeting.

"Well . . . have you talked to your dad?"

"He says I can come if I want."

"Where exactly does he live in Canada?"

"Calgary."

"Oh." I rack my brain to recall what I have heard about Calgary: mountains, snow, the Calgary Stampede (which is some big cowboy festival, I think). "Have you ever been to Calgary?" I ask.

"Once."

"It gets really cold there, you know."

Shrug.

"And a lot of the people dress in Western wear. I don't know how you feel about that, but personally I think that look should be reserved for rodeos and cowboy movies."

"Whatever," she says, looking out her window.

It dawns on me that bashing the weather and fashion sense of Calgary is probably not going to dissuade her from moving there. What would? What could I say that would make her stop and think? How can I keep her from leaving so I don't look like a complete and utter failure at yet another project?

And then it hits me. There, stuck in I-5 traffic with my fifteen-year-old protégée, I have something of an epiphany. I wouldn't say I'd acquired Zen wisdom, but this has to be pretty close.

I suddenly realize that Tiffany is not a *project;* she's a confused and frightened girl. And this isn't about me failing as a mentor at all. It isn't about *me,* period. I can't believe how selfish and self-absorbed I am. No wonder my karma is so crappy! Even when I'm trying to do something good and giving, it all comes back to how it affects me. It is more than a little disturbing that I am first having this revelation at thirty-one, but better late than never.

I turn and look at Tiffany. She is staring straight ahead, her expression blank. And suddenly I remember what it feels like to be fifteen and insecure, to have issues with your parents and no boyfriend. I can see through all the makeup, the faded jeans jacket and the love of wrestling and hockey fights.

"Tiffany . . . ," I say gently. She turns and looks at me. "I know you're going to do whatever you think is right, but I want you to know that . . . I'll miss you if you go."

"Thanks," she says, and smiles. It is the most genuine smile I've ever seen.

We enter the aquarium and find ourselves immersed in an eerie undersea reality. The lights are low, the undulating patterns of the water from the tanks reflect on our faces. We are amid a sea of people, milling about. The crowd is a mixture of somber business people, sullen teenagers, and other mentors, like me, with cheerful smiles pasted on their faces. Theresa, in a baggy black sweater covered in cat hair greets us warmly.

"Hey! Tiffany and Kerry! How's it going?"

"Good," I respond for both of us. "We're good."

"Cool. Let me get you some name tags," she says, writing our names with red marker on a couple of sticky tags. "Here you are."

"Thanks," I say as I place HELLO. MY NAME IS KERRY on my chest. Tiffany rolls her eyes but follows suit.

"Feel free to browse through the aquarium," Theresa continues. "You'll find food and beverages by the whale tank, courtesy of our corporate sponsor Raincoast, Inc." I recall that Raincoast is the large shipping firm that provided the hockey tickets. That would explain all the business people here.

"We'll all be gathering there for a couple of speeches later."

"Great." I look at Tiffany eagerly. She appears indifferent.

Theresa hands us a pink photocopied piece of paper. "Here are a few special events tonight that you might enjoy. We have some interactive exhibits with aquarium personnel. You can touch a real starfish and a sea cucumber!" she says, looking at Tiffany.

Tiffany looks at her like she'd just suggested waxing a fat man's back hair might be fun.

"And there will be a shark feeding at eight."

"Yessss!" Tiffany and I high-five. Theresa looks a bit bemused, but I don't care. We are really bonding.

"Shall we head to the snack table before the shark feeding?" I ask.

"Sure," Tiffany says brightly.

We meander through the walls of fish tanks, stopping periodically to look at unique sea creatures. Tiffany seems more open to the experience now that she has some blood and gore to look forward to. As we peer in at an octopus shooting its way fluidly through the water, we hear, "Hey, Tiffany!"

"Oh, hi, Brian," she replies—not quite enthusiastically, but at least not with open hostility. My eyes search for Brian's mentor, and I spot him making his way through the crowd toward us.

I smile, happy to see his familiar (and handsome) face. "Hi."

"Hi." Nick beams back, obviously pleased to see me, as well. "Are you guys having a good time?"

"We are," I say, again answering for Tiffany. "We were just heading to the snack table before the shark feeding."

"Oh, yeah! It's so right on!" Brian is effusive. "Last year we saw it, and it was so crazy!"

"Really?" Tiffany asks. Brian launches into a detailed description of the feeding frenzy, allowing Nick and me to chat.

"It's good to see you again." He smiles warmly.

"You, too."

"How are things at the advertising agency?"

"Oh, God." I moan and roll my eyes. "Terrible. I'm seriously thinking about looking for a new job after Christmas."

"That's too bad," he says. "Do you mean another job in advertising—or something different?"

"Well . . ." I pause thoughtfully. "I don't really know. I'd definitely be open to something new."

"Can we go eat now?" Tiffany interjects. Tiffany and Brian lead the way, with Brian stopping at sites of interest—piranhas, sting rays, electric eels (anything possibly lethal). Nick and I tag along behind.

"So Nick . . . you know that I have a lousy job in advertising. What do you do?"

"I'm the director of a program called Art Smarts. Have you heard of it?"

"Uh . . . no."

"We send artists into elementary schools to integrate art into the regular curriculum. We use creative projects to help students learn all subjects more effectively—from science to math to social studies. It's proven to have a very positive impact on learning."

"Wow," I say quietly. I am somewhat awed.

"Sorry," he laughs. "Sometimes I'm like a walking brochure."

"No . . . it sounds great." It really does. Nick is helping to shape young minds for the future. I make ads that scare people into thinking their children will develop crack addictions without a high-speed Internet connection. My life is so meaningless and empty.

"How long have you been with the arts program?" I ask when we reach the snack table.

"Four years," he says, pouring a glass of punch and offering it to me. "I started the program, actually."

"Did you?"

"Yeah. I was in sales before that."

"Eww!" I make a face. "Oh, sorry."

Nick laughs. "I know, I know! But it's not as bad as it sounds."

"Then why did you leave?"

"Well . . ." Nick takes a drink of his punch. "I was with one of the large beer companies, and my career was going really well, actually. But I just felt . . . like I wasn't doing any good in the world, you know? I mean, I have nothing against beer, but—I wanted to be helping people. I know it sounds corny."

"It doesn't," I say, staring at him with open admiration.

"And I'd always been really interested in art. I had initially wanted to get a fine arts degree, but everyone said it wasn't practical."

I nod agreement. I'd considered studying creative writing.

"And I love kids," he says, gesturing at our two protégés, who are filling their plates with sweets. "So I decided to combine the two. I hooked up with a couple of artist friends, and we came up with Art Smarts."

"I'm so impressed," I say, so impressed. "You just quit the corporate world and started your own charity? Do you realize how brave that is?"

"Well, I'd made some really good investments in the early nineties. When I cashed them out, I had some money to play with. My friends wanted me to go to Mexico with them, but I wanted to do something important with the money."

Suddenly, I can feel tears welling up. Damn it! How embarrassing. But something about meeting someone so selfless and caring and really trying to make a difference makes me feel emotional. "That's just . . . so . . . wonderful," I say, blinking frantically.

"It's okay." Nick squeezes my forearm. "I went to Mexico the next year."

"Kerry!" Tiffany calls through a mouthful of shortbread as I laugh and punch Nick playfully on the shoulder. "Check this out." I join Tiffany and Brian before the tank holding a dwarf crocodile.

When I return to my former spot, Nick has moved toward the whale tank and is talking to an older woman in a severe charcoal suit. His eyes dart up and meet mine, and I feel a dart of electricity between us—at least I think I do. Nick gestures for me to join them and then makes the introductions.

"Kerry, this is Sharon Talisman from Raincoast, Inc. Kerry works at Ferris and Shannon Advertising. She's just joined the mentoring program."

"Nice to meet you, Sharon." I shake her hand firmly.

"Ferris and Shannon, eh?" she says knowledgably. "I worked with Gerald Ferris back in the seventies. How is he?"

"Great . . . I think. He's retired so . . . how much better could he be?"

"Ha ha!" Sharon laughs loudly. "Well, nice meeting you, Kerry. And nice to see you, Nick. Duty calls!" And she heads up to the podium.

"Thank you for coming, everyone," she says into the microphone. As it turns out, Sharon Talisman is in charge of corporate sponsorship for Raincoast. She says a few words of gratitude for our commitment to helping high- to medium-risk teens and then introduces the director of Shooting Star. Meg Rosen is an athletic-looking, fortyish blonde who reiterates Sharon's points and then passes the mic to a mentor and protégé who want to share their rewarding experience with others.

After the speeches, we mill about until it is time to head to the shark feeding. I wander to the whale tank, irresistibly drawn to the black-and-white orcas. I always feel rather melancholy when I watch the beautiful giants float past, so dignified as they try to ignore the spectators gawking into their world. When I think that whales are nearly as intelligent as humans, and yet they're confined to these small concrete pools I—Oh, dear. Here I go. Think of something else! Think of something else! Don't start crying at the Shooting Star Christmas party. What is wrong with me? I must be premenstrual.

"I love whales." Suddenly, Nick is at my side.

"So do I," I say, looking up at him. God, he really is attractive— tall, with broad shoulders and those twinkly blue eyes. And that's not to mention that he is socially responsible, a wise investor, and a lover of whales.

"I'd rather see them in the wild, though. I find it kind of depressing to see them in these small concrete tanks. I've always wanted to go on one of those whale-watching expeditions in the Gulf Islands."

I bite my tongue to keep from offering to book us on the next tour. "That would be great, wouldn't it?" I say, in a tone that practically begs him to include me. Oops. I smile up at him and I feel another electrical moment between us. God, I hope he's feeling it, too.

"Let's go, you guys!" Brian calls to us. "We want to find a spot on the glass."

We are twenty minutes early, but Tiffany and Brian have secured a prime viewing spot. Tiffany is being so much nicer to Brian this meeting, it warms my heart. In fact, my heart is incredibly warm tonight—I don't know if it is my spiritual epiphany, the Christmas spirit, or hanging out with a nice guy like Nick—but I'm positively glowing with goodwill. And I feel on the verge of tears for some reason—must be the whales.

Nick and I talk easily while we wait for the feeding frenzy and are enjoying our conversation so much that we remain in our spots at the back, even as the event begins. We are like two proud parents watching our bloodthirsty children cheer as the sharks tear apart the fish tipped into the tank. Before I know it, the evening is over, and I find myself feeling disappointed.

"It was great to see you again, Nick," I say as Tiffany and I prepare to depart. "We'd better get going. I've got to drop Tiffany off in Auburn and then get back downtown to Queen Anne."

"You're in Queen Anne? I live in Belltown," Nick says. "Not too far from you."

"That's where my mom lives," I say. "On Battery."

"I'm just a couple of blocks from there."

Then before I know what I am saying, the words spill out of my mouth. "My mom's having an open house on the twelfth of December. Since you're in the neighborhood . . . maybe . . . you could drop by? It would keep me from dying of boredom . . . you know . . . if you want . . ."

He looks at me with an amused expression. For a brief moment, the magnitude of my stupidity almost overwhelms me! Did I really invite this guy I've just met to meet my hippie mother, her overly affectionate boy toy, and a wide range of family friends and relatives?

Then he says, "Sure. I'd love to meet your mother. Send me an e-mail with the details." And with a laugh and a squeeze of my shoulder, he leaves.

Mortifying Moment #7

"Oh, my God!" my friend Kelly shrieked, giving my hand a painful squeeze. "Can you fucking believe we're really here?"

"No!" I squealed back, squeezing her hand equally as hard. "I can't fucking believe it!"

"London! London fucking England," Kelly continued. "We are in fucking London, England!!" Kelly liked to swear a lot, which was apparently contagious.

"I know!" I replied, staring out the window of the speeding cab, soaking in my first glimpse of European scenery. Well . . . it was the first that I could remember. My parents had brought my brother and me here when I was two. "God! It's so fucking awesome."

"Even this taxi is cool," she said, gesturing widely with her arms to take in the spacious backseat of the vehicle. "A London fucking cab!"

Twenty minutes later, the London fucking cab pulled up in front of the Flying Mallard hostel in Earl's Court.

"That'll be twenty-two pounds girls," our rosy-cheeked, sweaty driver said.

"Twenty-two pounds?" We muttered to each other while fishing in our wallets. "That's like . . . sixty U.S. dollars, isn't it?"

"No, I think it's more like thirty . . . or is it forty?"

"Whatever it is," Kelly mumbled, hoisting her backpack from the sidewalk, where the driver had unceremoniously dumped it, "we'd better take the train back to the airport tomorrow."

Tomorrow, we would be returning to Heathrow airport, where we would go directly to the international arrivals gate, and pretend we had just deplaned. When my father came to pick us up, we would be jubilant but jet-lagged, elated but exhausted. It was all part of our plan.

You see, my dad had paid for my ticket to London—Kelly's, too. He had wanted my brother and me to come out for a visit, but Greg was in the midst of a (what he considered) very important soccer tournament. When I said I wasn't keen on traveling alone, he'd offered to pony up for a friend to accompany me. Kelly was a friend from college. We spent most weekends together drinking pints of beer, doing kamikaze shooters, and dancing into the wee hours at a variety of nightclubs. She was the perfect traveling companion.

The purpose of this trip was to visit family. I had not seen my dad for nearly a year and a half since he moved back to London. His Surrey house would be overflowing with aunts and uncles and cousins, none of whom I'd seen since I'd been potty-trained. I could hardly subject Kelly to all this without at least one night's respite.

So we checked into the Flying Mallard and deposited our luggage in the room we would share with six other girls. We each took a shower wearing flip-flops to avoid contracting any scary travelers' foot fungus, put on our cutest London-clubbing outfits, and headed to the nearest pub.

"Even the beer tastes different," I said, hoisting my heavy mug of lager.

"Tastes fucking great!" Kelly enthused, taking an enormous swallow.

"Excuse me?" It was a cute English bloke a couple of tables down. He was seated with an even cuter friend who was smoking a cigarette in that very cool British manner. "Where are you girls from?"

"Seattle," Kelly said.

"In the United States," I added.

"We know where Seattle is," the smoker said in his charming accent.

"Oh, do you now?" Kelly flirted. "How impressive!"

Within minutes, the two had joined us, and we were on our second pint of beer. Their names were Mick and Billy. They lived in Shepherds Bush. Mick had a job that had something to do with driving a lorry, and Billy was on some kind of maintenance crew, fixing up parks in the burrough. Wherever they lived, whatever they did, they were absolutely dreamy.

"Which one do you like?" Kelly whispered when Mick had gone to the "loo" and Billy was buying more drinks.

"I don't know," I giggled. "Which one do you like?"

"I think I like Mick, but I'm not sure he's into me," she said, lighting a cigarette. I followed suit. Neither of us smoked, but we did when we were out on the town in London.

"I think he's totally into you," I assured her.

"Really?" she asked skeptically, inhaling deeply. "I'm not sure—"

"Oh, yeah! It's really obvious."

"Well, I think Billy totally likes you."

"Really?" I blushed and giggled some more. "Do you think so?"

"Like, duh? You have this like . . . connection. I can totally feel it."

"Do we?" I tittered excitedly. "Can you?"

"Shhhh! Here they come."

Three pints later, Mick and Kelly had their own connection—at the mouth. They were making out as if they'd both just been released from prison, completely oblivious of our presence. Billy and I talked and laughed, trying to ignore the soft-porn scene carrying out just inches from us. I didn't mind, really. Billy was so funny, and so cute—thin and attractively unhealthy looking in his pale, English way. His hair flopped into his eyes, and his chin was covered in just the right amount of stubble. And maybe it was his accent, but everything he said sounded either incredibly intelligent or completely hilarious!

Finally Mick emerged, pulling Kelly off him like a leech. "Why don't we grab some cans and take this party back to my place?"

"Sounds good to me," Billy said, looking at me hungrily and dragging sexily on his unfiltered cigarette. I felt the bottom of my stomach drop with nervous excitement.

"Let's go." Kelly was already grabbing her coat.

"Can you excuse us for a second?" I said, grabbing Kelly by the collar and dragging her to the ladies' room.

"So?" I asked her, alone in the stark lighting of the bathroom. I closed one eye to improve my focus. The beer and the jet lag were making me feel dizzy.

"So what?" she said, going directly to the mirror and fluffing her hair.

"Well, should we go to Mick's place or what?" I said.

"Like, duh? Yeah, of course!" she said. "Why? What the fuck's the matter? Don't you like Billy?"

"I totally do. It's just that . . . I thought we wanted to go clubbing and stuff. You know, have the whole London experience?"

"I think these two can give us the London experience pretty good, don't you?" She elbowed me conspiratorially.

Soon we were in the back of another cab, where I rested my head *against Billy's tobacco-scented denim jacket while watching the scenery whiz past. Beside us, Kelly had one leg thrown over Mick and appeared to be eating the lower half of his face. Thankfully, within half an hour, we were inside Mick's dingy, cluttered, Shepherds Bush flat.*

"Drink anyone?" Mick passed out the cans that fizzed over as we opened them, having been jostled on the ride. We laughed and splashed each other with the foam. It was celebratory, a once-in-a-lifetime kind of night.

Almost immediately, Mick and Kelly fell into an armchair and reconvened their passionate kissing. It was now getting a little uncomfortable, having escalated to moaning, hair-clutching, and ass-grabbing. I wondered why Mick didn't take her off to his bedroom—she was obviously hot for him! But upon further visual inspection, I realized that we were in a one-room studio apartment. The dingy futon covered in questionable stains that Billy and I were seated on was actually Mick's bed. Eww! I stood up.

"Let's take a walk, shall we?" Billy said, reading my mind. He grabbed two cans and then escorted me outside. It was after midnight, and the streets were quiet. I thought I would have felt uneasy walking around a London neighborhood at such a late hour, but as Billy held my hand, I felt completely at ease. Something about him made me feel safe. I think it was his air of cool confidence—which was especially impressive, since he probably weighed several pounds less than I did.

We crossed the street and entered a park, Billy leading me knowledgeably to a secluded wrought-iron bench. We sat side by side, and he passed me a can of beer. "Cheers," he said, and we clinked the cans together. He held his drink up. "To meeting such a special girl . . . from so far away."

I smiled and blushed, taking a drink from my beer. God, he was so cool. I looked up at him. The streetlight in the distance shone behind him, giving him a halo effect. Our eyes met, and the moment suddenly felt incredibly special, magical, meant to be!

"Do you believe in fate?" I asked. It was a really nerdy thing to say, but my feelings had overwhelmed me. And I was drunk enough not to care if I sounded like a wiener.

"I do," he said, smiling down at me. "I think sometimes two people are intended to cross paths—even if it's only for a single night."

"That's what I think, too," I gushed. "I feel like I was meant to come here and to meet you and to sit in this park drinking beer with you!"

"You were meant to," he said huskily. He leaned in, and our lips met, softly, gently, tenderly.

Wow! Now I was really sure this moment was destiny. He was such a great kisser. Within seconds, we were swept away on a wave of passion. I grabbed his face and pressed my lips hard against his. I felt his arms wrap around me, his fingers creeping under my shirt, up my back to my bra clasp.

"Kerrrryyyyyy!" I heard my name called in the distance. Damn! It was Kelly. Were they finished already? "Kerrrrrrrrryyyyyy!"

"I guess she's ready to go," I said.

"Sounds like it," Billy said morosely, removing his hand from my shirt.

"I wish . . . I wish I could stay longer with you."

"Me, too." He gently tilted my chin so our eyes met. "But remember . . . we were meant to have this time together. If we're meant to see each other again, we will."

"I think we will," I said. "It's fated."

"Kerrrryyyy!" Kelly was sounding pissed off now.

"We'd better go," Billy said. He kissed me quickly then led me out of the park.

"DAD!" I CRIED, RUNNING INTO HIS ARMS. GOD, IT WAS SO GOOD TO SEE HIM after so long. I pressed my face into his tweedy jacket, inhaling the familiar scent of his pipe smoke and the greasy stuff he still used in his hair. Hopefully, the stale beer smell wasn't leaching from my pores, revealing our antics of the night before.

"How was your flight?" he asked as he led us to his car, a backpack in each hand.

"Long," I said. "I'm pretty jet-lagged."

"Yeah," Kelly said. "I'm really quite jet-lagged."

As we journeyed through the city, my dad pointed out sites of interest, and we both pretended we had never seen them before.

"So cool!" Kelly exclaimed. "I've never seen anything like it before in my life!" I shot her a look in the backseat, but she just winked at me. She was really overdoing it.

Eventually, we pulled up to my dad's new home, a quaint, two-story, redbrick structure.

"I hope you won't be too overwhelmed," my dad said as he lifted our luggage out of the boot. "But there are a lot of people who are so excited to see you."

"Umm . . . they're here now?" I had hoped to use my jet-lag excuse to sleep off the remains of my hangover.

"Not everyone. Only your auntie Rita, uncle Fred, and your cousins."

"Oh . . . okay," I said weakly. I vaguely recalled that Rita was my dad's middle sister. I'd seen pictures: grainy snapshots of their family in front of Stonehenge, to be precise. I think she had a couple of kids close to my age.

Before we'd reached the front steps, the door swung open, and there stood a pleasant-looking woman in her fifties wearing a formal Sunday suit. "There you are!" she rushed toward me in a cloud of perfume. She took me in a tight embrace then quickly released me. "Look at you!" she said, misting up. "You're such a beautiful young lady. We've missed so much."

"Thanks," I said awkwardly. "This is my friend Kelly."

"Hello, Kelly." Aunt Rita extended her hand briefly. "Fred!" she called to my uncle, who was somewhere in the depths of the house. "Kids! Your cousin Kerry is here!"

We managed to make it into the small foyer before being bombarded by the second wave of relatives. Uncle Fred, a fat, bald and jovial man hugged me briefly before joining his wife to marvel at how much growing I'd done over the past twenty years.

"And this is your cousin Gillian." My dad introduced me to a stout but pretty girl a little younger than me, with her mother's auburn hair and father's ruddy complexion.

"Hey," I said casually. We didn't embrace. "How's it going?"

"Good. Did you have a good trip?"

"Great." I smiled, recalling the special, destined moment of last night.

"Where is William?" Aunt Rita was flustered. "I thought he was with you?"

"Not with me," Uncle Fred replied. "William?" He boomed.

"William!" Aunt Rita cried. "William?"

God, I hoped William would appear soon and put a stop to their bellowing. My head was splitting.

"There you are!" Aunt Rita cried with delight. She and her husband parted ways to allow their son through.

"This is your cousin William," my aunt said proudly.

Ohgod. Ohgod. Ohgod. Ohgod. Ohgod. Ohgod. Ohgod.

"Oh, God!" Kelly vocalized my horror.

Despite the fact that he was clean shaven and his hair was combed neatly into a side part, there was no mistaking it: William . . . Will . . . Willy . . . Billy!

Yuck! I was speechless, vaguely nauseated! I couldn't believe that my fated, destined, meant-to-be romantic moment was with my cousin. My first cousin! I wanted to turn and run. I wanted to race to the airport, hop the next plane back to Seattle, where I would spend the next seven days brushing my teeth with Comet! Billy . . . er, Cousin William, was more composed.

"Yes . . . uh, nice to meet you . . . Kerry." He held out his hand.

Eww! Eww! Eww! I couldn't even look at him for fear that I'd visualize us making out again. And I'd been so into him. Thank god Kelly had called for me when she did, or who knew what could have happened? It was too revolting to contemplate. And now I had to shake the hand that had fumbled with my bra clasp! The blood-related hand that had fumbled with my bra clasp. I reached out and shook it quickly.

"I'm Kelly." Kelly stepped forward, smiling smugly at him, her hand extended.

He took it and politely said, "Good to meet you, as well, Kelly." He was really holding it together. Perhaps I was not the first relative he had accidentally almost got to second base with on a secluded park bench?

Kelly was smirking at me. Her words from the previous evening rang in my ears. "You have a connection," she'd said. "I can totally feel it." Of course we had a connection! Our parents were brother and sister, for Christ's sake! Jesus! Now that he was shaved, Billy actually vaguely resembled my brother Greg. I thought I might throw up.

"Isn't this wonderful?" Aunt Rita chortled. She scurried to the hall table and returned brandishing a camera. "Let's get some photos of the cousins together. William, come here and put your arm around Kerry. Aren't you two cute together? Gillian, you squeeze in there, too."

Chapter 23

MY THERAPIST IS BACK FROM HER VACATION. JUDGING BY HER PASTY complexion, if she was at a nudist colony, it wasn't anywhere sunny. She is reading my latest mortifying moment while I sit opposite her, suddenly feeling icky all over again. I watch her face to see if it contorts in disgust. Her expression is unreadable, but I can reasonably predict what she will say:

"So, is making out with blood relatives a habit of yours? Is no one off-limits to you?"

Or

"When visiting a new city, do you usually commemorate the occasion by getting disgustingly drunk and allowing yourself to be fondled by a total stranger? A stranger who just might turn out to be your father's sister's child?"

But instead she says, "I'm very pleased that you've continued with your journal in my absence. I'm sure this last entry was difficult to write, but I hope it made you see that it was nothing more than an unfortunate coincidence."

"Umm . . . yes . . . okay . . . thank you."

"Don't be too hard on yourself. In some cultures, marriages be-tween first cousins are actually desired."

"We only kissed for, like, five minutes!" I shriek. If she is trying to make me feel better, it's not working.

"Now, tell me what else has been going on with you while I was away?"

I am relieved for the shift in subject matter. "Well . . . ," I say, try-ing not to blatantly stare at her sensible (aka "hideous") pumps. Surely a woman of her education and means could wear some more stylish and attractive footwear? I clear my throat. "Yes, I do have some news to report. . . ." Then I gleefully recount my sort-of date with Sam and how I turned him down when he wanted to come home with me. (I do not mention my hairy legs or messy apart-ment.)

"Good for you," she says, smiling and nodding. "This is a very good sign that your self-esteem is getting back on track."

I was expecting something a little more enthusiastic than "good for you." She obviously doesn't realize how good looking he is. I will bring in a photograph next session, and then she will be more im-pressed.

In contrast, she seems very excited when I relay how I invited Nick to the open house at my mother's. "You must feel very comfort-able with him," she says.

"I guess I do." I shrug, blushing bright pink. "But you know . . . he lives, like, right around the corner from her, anyway. . . ."

"I'm encouraged to see that you still feel hopeful enough about your romantic future to take a chance like this."

But later, when I mention Nick's invitation to Trevor, he is flabbergasted—and not in a good way. He is sitting beside me in my office, pretending to discuss a piece of paper that we just pulled out of my recycling bin.

"You what!" he yelps.

"I, uh . . . invited him to my mom's open house."

"Are you joking?"

"No. He lives a couple of blocks away from her, so I just thought—"

"Kerry," he says, sounding exasperated with my stupidity. "Do you realize how weird this is?"

"He didn't seem to think it was so weird!" I snap.

"Okay. Tell me his reaction," Trevor says.

"He sort of laughed and said 'I'd love to meet your mother.' "

"See?" He flops back in his chair. "See? Can you imagine if he had invited you to meet *his* mother? Wouldn't that freak you out?"

"I don't know! I—" Trevor is making me feel insecure and full of doubt.

"Here's what you need to do," he says matter-of-factly. "Send him an e-mail and say: 'I don't know what I was thinking when I invited you to my mother's open house. Please don't feel obligated to attend. Why don't we grab a drink somewhere instead?' "

"Okay," I say weakly.

"Now," he says, speaking loudly and enunciating clearly. "You're really going to move the needle with this, Kerry. Way to push the envelope."

When Trevor leaves, I follow his advice. I send an e-mail disinviting Nick—or rather, giving him the option of avoiding spending an afternoon at my mom's condo, and suggesting a casual drink instead—because I would still really like to get together with him. I guess it was a little odd to invite him to meet my mom when we barely know each other. I mean, it's not like we're dating or anything but . . . I don't know. That night at the aquarium, I felt so comfortable with him that it didn't really seem like a big deal. But according to Trevor, it is definitely a big deal.

My phone rings. "Hello, this is Kerry."

"She's back," Michelle says directly. "She wants to meet with us."

"When?" I ask, matching her no-nonsense tone.

"Tonight. Six o'clock."

"Where?"

"Crocodile Café on Second."

"I'll be there," I say, then hang up. Oooh! That felt like a scene from a James Bond movie or something. Well, not quite international espionage, but we were discussing quite a dramatic event. The three of us have not been together with Sandra since the night she called the cops on us. Let's hope we don't have a repeat of that fiasco (but I will make sure I am looking my best, just in case.)

For the rest of the day, I am distracted and have difficulty focusing on work. My mind jumps from the impending meeting with Sandra to my e-mail disinvitation to Nick. These two factors, combined with my general lack of enthusiasm for my stupid job make getting anything done almost impossible. I can't stop checking my e-mail for a response from Nick, but find only work-related crap or my brother checking up on my Christmas shopping on his behalf.

At five thirty, as I am about to leave for my meeting with Sandra and the girls, my phone rings.

"Oh, good. You're still there," a male voice says.

"Yes. I was just leaving," I say formally.

"I'm glad I caught you. It's Nick Marra calling."

"Oh, Nick!" I say, a ridiculously large smile overtaking my face. "Sorry. I thought you were a media rep or someone."

"No!" he laughs. "I'm not selling anything. I just got your e-mail, and I wanted to call."

"Yeah, well . . ." I suddenly feel shy and self-conscious. I clear my throat. "I realized it was a bit weird of me to invite you to my mom's place when I've really just met you so I—"

"I'd love to come," he interrupts. "Unless my being there would make *you* uncomfortable?"

"Not at all!" I say in relief. "I just thought maybe you'd rather get together for a drink or something?"

"Well," he says. "If I have to choose, I guess I'd go for a nice quiet drink, just you and me. But I wouldn't want you to have to spend an afternoon alone with your parents' friends. I've done that before, and I don't advise it."

"How about we do both, then?" I say playfully.

"Sounds good," he replies in what sounds to me like a very sexy voice.

"I just didn't want you to feel awkward at my mom's," I continue. "I don't normally introduce guys to my mother on the first date!"

Date? Did I say *date*? Dammit! For all I know, Nick may think this is just a casual, pre-Christmas drink to discuss our experiences as Shooting Star mentors. Or our mutual love of whales. I can't believe I said *date*!

There is an awkward pause, and then Nick says, "No problem. I'm sure it'll be fun."

I mouth a silent thank-you to him for not mentioning the date comment. Talk about jumping the gun! "Well, that would be great, then," I say, and give him the address of my mom's condo.

"All right," he says. "I'll see you Saturday."

When I hang up, I realize I am grinning from ear to ear. I think I really like this guy! He is so good looking and kind and generous and . . . in an artistic field. And I met him at a work-related function. And he has sandyish hair. Yikes! If his name started with *D* I might think he was the one Ramona was talking about.

Just as I am about to turn off my computer, I hear the blip of an incoming e-mail. Though I am running late, something makes me check it.

Name: Sam Miller
Subject: Hi

I'm sorry it's been so long since you've heard from me. I'd like to explain, but I'm not sure I understand it myself. Just know that I haven't stopped thinking about you. I can't stop thinking about you. I miss you.
S.

I stare at the message on the screen. My heart is pounding, my chest feels tight, and I am sweating. I try to swallow through the lump of emotion in my throat. Why is he doing this to me? What is he playing at? Not a word from him for almost a month, and now this? A few seconds ago I was happy and hopeful and practically over him! Why is he resurfacing at this particular moment? It's like he has some sixth sense to tell him when I am finally moving on. Angry and confused, I stab the OFF button on my monitor.

When I arrive at the rustically upscale restaurant, I find Val and Michelle at a tall cedar table in the lounge, sipping martinis.

"She's not here yet?" I ask as I sit. "It's almost six thirty."

"Maybe she's chickened out?" Michelle says, biting into an olive.

"She hasn't chickened out," Val asserts. "She invited us."

"I don't know," I say as I order a drink. "If I were her, I wouldn't be too excited about—"

"There she is!" Val whispers excitedly, waving to the doorway.

We all turn and watch as Sandra moves toward us. Somehow, everything seems to slow down, and it is like Sandra is sashaying through the restaurant in slow-motion while "Love is a Many Splendored Thing" plays in the background. She looks amazing! Her skin is kissed by the sun, her honey hair has beach-blond highlights, and her brilliant smile radiates happiness and contentment. She is positively glowing! Oh, god. Does this mean she's pregnant?

"Hi!" she says, leaning down to kiss us each on the cheek. "How have you all been? I've missed you guys!" She is all sweetness and light.

"We've missed you, too," Val says.

"We have," I echo.

"Yeah," Michelle says grudgingly. She is leaning back in her chair, looking suspicious. Sandra is distracted by the waiter for a moment, and I kick Michelle's foot under the table. I shoot her a look that says, "Don't turn this into an antagonistic meeting," and she shoots one back that says, "Fuck off."

"I'm glad you all agreed to meet with me," Sandra says, smiling at us each in turn. "I know things have been a little crazy, but I want you to know that I still value our friendship."

"So do we!" Val says, reaching for Sandra's hand.

"We do," I chorus. Michelle is still silent and obviously not heeding my warning.

"I'm so glad!" Sandra says, and holds up her cocktail. "To great friendships!" she says. "To us!"

"Cheers!" we all say and drink. Michelle joins in, somewhat reluctantly.

"So . . . what have you all been up to?" Sandra asks. "It's been ages!"

"More important," Michelle says, her eyes narrowed, "what have you been up to?"

"Yeah! How was the Dominican Republic?" I ask breezily, trying to lighten the mood.

"Well," she says, looking directly at Michelle. "I have undergone some major changes since I've been away."

"Yes?" Michelle prompts.

"I may as well lay it all on the line." She takes a sip of her drink then places it on the table. "It's over between George and me."

"Really!" the three of us exclaim.

"I mean . . . ," I stammer. "Are you okay?"

"Uh . . . yeah." Val follows suit. "That must be hard."

"It was the right thing to do," Michelle says stoically.

"So, are you—?" I trail off, not sure if I should ask.

"I'm not pregnant."

"Phew!" we all say again.

"It's just that you're positively glowing," Val says. "You look amazing."

"Well . . ." Sandra's face lights up even more. "I met someone in the Dominican Republic."

"Great!"

"He's from San Francisco, but he lives in Punta Cana now. He owns a restaurant and bar on the beach."

"Wow!"

"Is he single?" Michelle asks.

"Yes," Sandra retorts.

"He's not, umm . . . like, uh . . . sixty, is he?" I had to ask.

"He's forty," she says. "And he is absolutely the most wonderful man I've ever met!"

"I'm so happy for you," Val says, leaning over to give her a hug.

"There's something else," Sandra says, when she's released. "I'm moving there."

"Where?" Michelle asks.

"The Dominican Republic! I've quit my job at the firm and filled out my immigration applications. John has offered me a job running his restaurant! I leave on the twenty-third. I'm going to spend Christmas on the beach with him!"

I can see by Michelle's face that she is about to say something negative. I stomp on the toe of her shoe to distract her.

"I think that sounds great!" I say, purposely ignoring the daggers flying at me from Michelle's eyes. "If you follow your heart, you can't go wrong!"

Chapter 24

"WHAT'S THE WORST THAT CAN HAPPEN? SO SHE LIVES IN THE DOMINI-can Republic for a while? It's not like she's moving to the West Bank!"

"She's following the same destructive patterns," Michelle says shrilly into the phone. "Who knows how this John guy is going to treat her? Are we just going to stand by and let her be crushed by some man again? What kind of friends are we?"

"Michelle," I say exasperatedly. "I agree that Sandra is sponta-neous and impulsive—"

"Try impetuous and irresponsible!"

"Whatever. But you need to take a chill pill, man."

There is a long pause then Michelle says, "Hello? Hello? Can you please put Kerry Spence back on the line? She's a thirty-one-year-old account manager. I seem to be speaking to a sixteen-year-old high school girl."

I laugh. "Sorry! I've been hanging out with Tiffany so much I'm starting to talk like her."

"Yes. You're very hip and cutting edge . . . dude."

"Anyway," I steer the conversation back to the subject at hand. "We *are* Sandra's friends, Michelle, and we're good friends. We're not supposed to try to change her. She may make mistakes, but—"

"Don't start spouting off about Dr. Rainbow Hashafasha again!"

"Hashwaaaaaaaaarma," I say, enunciating clearly. I really do think Michelle could benefit from picking up his book.

"You'll be singing a different tune when this John guy dumps her and she's a broken woman, miles from home with no one to talk to."

"I volunteer to fly to the Dominican Republic to console her," I say jokingly. Michelle does not laugh. "Anyway, I've got to go. My mom wants me to help her set up for the open house."

My mom is expecting close to fifty people to squeeze into her nine-hundred-square-foot condo over the course of the day. She has always loved to entertain. It was a big part of her role as a successful banker's wife.

"That was the only thing I enjoyed when I was married to Randall," she often says to whoever happens to be listening. "The social side of our life! He was as dull as dishwater, but he did have some interesting colleagues!"

This event promises to be far different from any soiree she would have held while married to my dad. This party will be primarily meat, dairy, and wheat-free. She will offer a wide assortment of herbal teas to drink. (Thank God she included a few bottles of liquor for my boozy Uncle Evan.) Her invited guests include

Her yoga instructor
Several "gals" from her pottery class
Several "folks" from her vegan cooking class
Some of Darrel's coworkers from Seattle Public Utilities
Various friends and relatives
Nick

My mom doesn't know I've invited Nick, per se, although I did mention that I'd asked a friend to join us. "It would be lovely to see one of the girls," she said distractedly while processing tofu in the blender to replace mayonnaise in her dips. I chose not to correct her.

Because, really . . . Nick *is* just a friend—a friend who makes me feel all shivery and giggly and fifteen when I talk to him—but still, just a friend. It's not like we've kissed or had any physical contact, really. I find myself smiling as I drive through the rainy December streets thinking about him. He e-mailed yesterday to confirm that he would definitely be there, but wouldn't arrive until about three. He was taking Brian Christmas shopping to get a gift for his mom.

For some reason, my mind switches tracks and Sam enters my thoughts. His e-mail the other day was so cryptic and strange. He's thinking about me? He's missing me? Then why didn't he pick up the phone and call me? Why didn't he ask me out on another date? My response the last time couldn't have been that discouraging? I did spend six hours with him and let him kiss me in the back of the taxi. I can't figure it out. I shake my head, trying to dislodge all thoughts of him. I was much happier daydreaming about Nick.

My mom answers the door wearing a flowing, tie-dyed purple robe and bare feet. She takes my coat and hangs it in the closet, then turns to take in my outfit. "You're looking sharp," she says, surveying my charcoal slacks and eggplant turtleneck.

"And you're looking very . . . bohemian."

"Well, thank you," she says cheerfully. "I've got an eclectic crowd coming today, so I don't think any dress would be inappropriate." She really is at her happiest when planning a party.

"Okay. Put me to work." I follow her into the kitchen, where Darrel is stirring a large copper pot of spiced apple cider. "How's it going, Darrel?"

"Excellent." He smiles. "We're going to have a great time today." He grabs my mom around the waist. "Thanks to this amazing woman! Martha Stewart's got nothing on her." (Wet sloppy kisses on neck while my mom titters like a schoolgirl.)

"You do have some wine here, don't you?" I ask, scanning the countertops.

"Of course." My mom breaks away from her boyfriend's fondling. "Are you wanting a drink already? It's only noon!"

"Oh, yeah," I say sheepishly. It would be "starting something" if I were to point out that being half-drunk makes it much easier to stomach Mom and Darrel's public displays of affection. "I was just wondering . . . for later."

"Don't worry," my mom says from inside the depths of the fridge. "We've got something for everyone."

By the time guests begin arriving at one, we are well prepared. The table has been spread with a wide variety of hors d'oeuvres. A line of red tape runs across the middle of the festive tablecloth to delineate the vegan dishes from those intended for the bloodthirsty carnivores.

I sit with my aunt and uncle (two alcohol-drinking, meat- and wheat-eaters like myself) and catch up on the progress of my more successful cousins.

"What do you hear from your brother? How's he doing in the land down under?" Aunt Ruth giggles.

"He's doing fabulously!" My mom makes a beeline across the room, her Spidey sense alerted to an opportunity to brag about her favorite offspring. "Greg is having the time of his life in Sydney! I tell you, if I could do it all over again. Don't you agree, Ruth?"

I slip away as they embark on a conversation about the supreme sacrifice of mothers, and steal into the kitchen to refill my wineglass. I hope my mother is not keeping track of my consumption. Grabbing a plate, I join the other guests mingling around the table and fill up on dishes from the non-vegan side of the tape.

"Nice to see you again," I say politely to one of Darrel's coworkers. I can't recall her name, but I remember her from last year's open house. She is at least three hundred pounds, so is a little hard to forget at a small gathering in a nine-hundred-square-foot condo. She is also eating from my side of the table.

The doorbell rings, and my mom's singsongy voice calls out, "I'll get it!" I glance at my watch. Nick won't be here for at least another hour.

"Namaste, Ted!" my mom says delightedly, and I catch a glimpse of her purple gown as she bows to her yoga instructor. "Please come in. Let me take your coat. The vegan food is at the far end of the table, and I have a wide assortment of herbal teas."

"Kerry." My uncle Evan approaches. "Getting enough to eat there?" He indicates my overflowing plate. "Stay away from that seaweed and tofu stuff. Wouldn't want you wasting away like your mother." He squeezes me into him. His breath reeks of scotch. Uncle Evan is the boozy uncle I mentioned before.

"Don't worry about me," I say. "What about you? Do you need anything?"

"I could use a refill on the scotch." He shakes his tumbler, and the ice cubes tinkle together.

"I'll get it for you." I take his glass.

"Ah, you've always been my favorite niece," he slurs. "What are you doing stuck here with us old fogies?"

"Oh, come on." I slap his arm playfully as I head to the kitchen. "You're not old! Anyway, I've got a friend joining me here later."

I pour him three fingers of amber liquid and return to the table. Uncle Evan seems to have moved. I scan the crowd for him when a deep voice behind me says,

"Hi, Kerry."

I turn to look and, "Oh, my God!" I jump, startled, and promptly spill Uncle Evan's drink all over my forearm. "What are you doing here?"

"What do you think?" Sam smiles at me fondly. "I'm here to see you."

"Well . . . how—how did you even know about this party? I mean—I didn't tell you about it!"

My mom's beaming face pops from behind him. "I invited him," she says. "We were chatting the other day, and I mentioned—"

"You were *chatting*?" I look from my mom to Sam in disbelief. "You two *chat*?"

"Now, don't get jealous," my mom titters. "He called to talk about *you*!"

"I had no idea. . . ." I am speechless, stupefied.

"I called your mom because I was thinking about you so much, but I didn't know if you wanted to talk to me. I told you'd I'd give you time to think and I didn't want to crowd you."

"I—uh—I—"

"Sam really poured his heart out to me," my mom says, putting her arm around him and giving him a squeeze. He squeezes her back and kisses the top of her head. "I knew you'd want to see him, Kerry—if you knew how he really felt."

"But—I—uh—" (As I mentioned, speechless and stupefied.)

"Kerry," Sam says, reaching for my hand. "These past few months apart have been horrible for me. The only good thing that's come from our splitting up is that I've realized that I don't ever, *ever* want to be apart from you again."

"See? See?" my mom says excitedly.

I notice that a crowd of guests is starting to mill around us, but Sam continues, apparently oblivious. "I want to make you see how important you are to me, Kerry—the most important thing in my life. Our relationship has been a roller-coaster ride, I admit it. But I'm tired of all the ups and downs, the highs and lows. I'm ready for some smooth sailing—some smooth sailing with you, Kerry."

"Well, Sam," I begin, but everyone bursts into applause. He pulls me into him and kisses me hard on the mouth; the cheers get louder. Before he releases me, I manage to hiss in his ear. "We need to talk about this in private."

"There'll be plenty of time for that," he whispers back. "But now . . . ," he says, in a booming voice. "There's something I need to ask you."

Jesus Christ! What is he doing? It is like slow motion as I watch Sam reach into his jacket pocket and retrieve a small black velvet box. He is lowering himself to one knee; my mom jumps up and down gleefully in the background.

"Kerry . . . will you make me the happiest man in the world and be my wife?" He flips open the box and an enormous emerald-cut diamond sparkles up at me.

"Uh—I—ummm—"

"They were meant to be together," I hear my mom tearfully telling Aunt Ruth. "They've been through a lot, but this is what she's always wanted."

I scan the faces of the onlookers. Their eyes encourage me, coaxing me to say yes to this madly romantic gesture. "Say yes," someone calls out and soon all the guests are chanting: "Yes, yes, yes, yes!" Okay . . . they're not actually chanting, but by the looks on their faces, they may as well be.

"I'd like to talk to Sam alone," I say hoarsely.

A moan of disappointment goes up from the crowd. Sam slowly gets to his feet and looks at me. I've never seen him so hurt. "I'm sorry," he says. "I guess I made a mistake. I thought . . . I don't know what I thought. . . ."

He snaps the little black box closed and turns toward the door. My mom shrieks "Kerry!" as if she's just realized I'm about to fall out a seventh-story window. I look at her, and her eyes implore me: Don't let him get away. You'll never get another opportunity like this.

And maybe she's right. Isn't this what I've wanted all along? A gesture so incredibly romantic that no one could blame me for going back to him? I mean, I know I used to want it. It's just that lately I've been so distracted that I forgot for a moment . . . Maybe *this* is my reward for becoming a better person? For volunteering and helping old ladies with their groceries? Perhaps my karma is so good now that Sam has become a changed man and wants to be with me forever?

"Sam?" I call to him. He turns back, his handsome JFK Jr. face full of pain. "I will," I say smiling at him. "My answer is yes."

He rushes back to me and takes me in his arms. The crowd of onlookers applauds wildly, someone even whistles through their fingers in the manner of hockey fans. Sam lifts me and spins me around with joy. I cling to him, trying to let his enthusiasm overtake me and wash away the doubt that is playing on my mind. When he stops turning and places my feet back on the floor, I am facing the doorway. And that's when I see him.

Nick. Oh, my God! It's Nick! He's standing at the door with a bouquet of flowers. In his expression there is a hint of confusion and disappointment masked by a pleasant smile.

"Congratulations," he says stepping forward. He thrusts the bouquet into my hands and kisses my cheek. "Sorry, but . . . I can't stay."

"Nick . . ." But I don't know what to say.

"Merry Christmas!" Then he departs.

"Who was that?" my mom asks distractedly. She turns to Sam. "Anyway . . . my soon to be son-in-law, let me introduce you to Darlene from my vegan cooking class."

Mortifying Moment #8

"Hello, is this Meredith Watt?"

"Yes." The voice at the other end of the line was distant and tinny. "Who's calling?"

"Aunt Meredith, it's your niece Kerry calling."

There was a long silence.

"Your brother Randall's daughter?"

"I know who you are, dear," she said in her strong British accent. "What is the reason for your call?"

Talk about getting to the point! Although, I was calling the U.K. from the U.S. so expediting this conversation would be prudent.

"Well," I cleared my throat. "It's about my wedding next summer. . . ." I trailed off.

"What about it, dear?"

"Ummm . . . well, we've had to cancel it."

"Oh, my," she said. "Whatever for?"

My brain scrambled to find the appropriate words. I had rehearsed my answer before I dialed, but somehow the words had deserted me. It was something about growing apart, pursuing our careers, not rushing into marriage when we weren't ready . . . These were all lies, of course, but the truth was not something I could share with Aunt Meredith.

"We were growing apart. We wanted to pursue our careers. We didn't want to rush into marriage when we weren't ready."

"Rush into marriage?" Aunt Meredith barked. "Haven't you been living with this young man for several years?"

"Just two, but—"

"I'll never understand you young people these days. You know each other two weeks and you move in together, but three years later you can't get married because it's rushing things!"

"Well, Aunt Meredith." My cheeks were burning. "I didn't move in with Hugh after two weeks. We actually dated for quite a while before we moved in together."

"But now you think you're rushing into marriage? In my day, you met a man, fell in love, and got married. And you stayed married! None of this living together, and separating and divorcing, and whatnot."

"Anyway," I said in an effort to cut the conversation short. I was on *the verge of tears and had to get off the phone. "I wanted to let you know as soon as possible so you didn't book your flight or anything like that."*

"Oh, don't worry, dear. You've always been a flighty one. I wasn't about to spend my hard-earned money on a plane ticket until I was sure it was going to happen."

I hung up, feeling slightly sick to my stomach. I looked at the list in front of me: twelve more phone calls to make. Notifying the paternal relatives was my responsibility (my dad was too busy to get in touch with everyone). My mom was kind enough to handle her family.

I hoped the next relatives on the list would be a little less judgmental and more sympathetic. I wondered what Hugh was telling his family? I'm sure he was using a similar excuse—probably attributing our breakup to the pressures of his career. Hugh was in the first year of his residency at Northwest Hospital. No one could fault a doctor for working too hard.

"Kerry just couldn't accept the fact that saving lives took up so much of my time," he'd say.

"How cold and shallow," they'd chorus, their voices full of sympathy. "Good thing you found out now, and not after you were married."

Only a few people knew the real reason we broke up. Make that two: Sandra and Val. I wished I could have told my mother the truth, because she was continually looking at me and shaking her head. "Why would she call off her marriage to a wonderful guy like Hugh? Why? Why? And a doctor, no less!" I could read her mind. "How could I have raised such a fickle and impractical daughter?"

I picked up the phone to dial the next aunt on the list then placed the receiver back in its cradle. My mind had been wrenched back to that fateful night—the beginning of the end.

It was a rainy Saturday evening, and we were meeting a pair of Hugh's oldest friends for drinks. They were in town for a few weeks over the summer. (Most of their year was spent in Mexico teaching scuba to tourists.) It had all started out so innocently. . . .

"I lived with Klaus and Lindsey for a year in Belize," Hugh said, smiling fondly. His handsome, preppy face glowed with remembrance. I had heard this story before . . . often. After his biology degree, Hugh had applied to medical school. When he wasn't accepted right away, he escaped to

Belize, planning to drop out of society for a while, and indulge his passion for diving. That was where he met Klaus and Lindsey.

"God, we had fun," he said, and I felt an uncomfortable twist in my stomach. It was painfully obvious that the year spent in Belize was the highlight of Hugh's life and now—well . . . was just now. "I've never felt so free, so uninhibited," he droned on. I gazed out the rain-spattered window of the taxi and tried to think of a comparable experience I could bring up.

"That's how I felt when I was in France," I said, hoping to give him a taste of his own medicine. "I felt more alive in France than I ever have."

"Yeah, but you were only there for two weeks!" He laughed. "Can you imagine if you had stayed a year?"

I can imagine. If I had spent a year living in France, my life now would seem like a big disappointment, too.

Ours was not a healthy relationship—I can see that now. We were competitive and resentful of each other. At least I was. Hugh probably didn't consider me worthy of competing with him. But everything he had ever done, all that he was going to be, made me feel inadequate. The incident with Klaus and Lindsey was really just the final straw. I should almost be thankful. I probably would have married him otherwise and been a divorcée with a couple of kids by now.

"Hugh!" They screamed as we entered the Spanish-style bar. I stood awkwardly, waiting to be acknowledged while they embraced and patted each other on the back. I took the opportunity to study them undetected. They were just what you would expect two diving instructors to look like: tanned, blond, fit, and gorgeous.

Hugh finally tore himself away from the love-in. "This is my fiancée, Kerry."

"Hi," I said rather awkwardly.

"Hi, Kerry," Klaus said warmly, taking my hand and kissing my cheek.

"It's so great to meet you," Lindsey echoed, also pecking my cheek.

"Nice to meet you, too," I said shyly. Maybe this wouldn't be so bad. They were friendly and lively and affectionate. But it was going to be so bad . . . worse than so bad.

We ordered a jug of sangria from our Latin waiter. "Remember that little restaurant we used to go to?" Hugh said. "They had the best sangria there—with chunks of cantaloupe in it."

"We went there last spring!" Lindsey squealed.

"God!" Hugh roared. "I'm so jealous!"

"Yeah, but remember the night you drank so much sangria that you were heaving everywhere?" Klaus jumped in. "And the next day you were so hungover that you couldn't dive and you missed the manta ray!"

Ha, ha, ha.

"You were with that local girl then—Conchita, was it?" Klaus continued. Lindsey elbowed him and shifted her eyes in my direction. "Oh, shit. Sorry."

"It was no big deal," Hugh laughed, shrugging it off. "It was a long time ago."

"No biggie," I forced myself to laugh along with them, although deep down I felt like throwing a temper tantrum and knocking all the dishes to the floor. I was sick of hearing about all the good times they had diving with manta rays and getting drunk with Conchita.

Lindsey changed the subject. "I can't believe you're getting married Hugh! You always said you were a free spirit and didn't need a piece of paper to tie you down!"

Hugh laughed. "That was before I met Kerry." He looked at me lovingly then, and I realized it was meant as a compliment. But inside I was seething. This was making me sound like a traditional fuddy-duddy who'd lassoed Hugh's free spirit and beat it into submission.

"Tell us about the wedding?" Lindsey smiled. I searched for a hint of mocking in her tone. There didn't seem to be any but maybe she was just really subtle?

"Well, it's a long way off," I responded. "Not until next summer so we haven't done much besides book the church and—"

"The church?" Klaus and Lindsey shrieked in unison.

"I don't believe it!" Klaus continued. "You are amazing, Kerry! You got him to marry you in a church!"

"Umm . . ." I blushed. "It's important to my dad's side of the family."

"I understand," Klaus said. "Nothing would make my mom happier

than for Lindsey and me to get married, but we're not going to let anyone define our relationship. Are we, hon?"

"Why mess with a good thing?" she said, staring into his eyes. Then they kissed very intimately, suddenly oblivious of our presence. When the waiter appeared with the next jug of sangria, I breathed a sigh of relief.

By the end of the night I had imbibed enough to numb myself to their constant reminiscence. To Hugh's credit, he did try to include me in the conversation where possible, but it wasn't easy: I didn't dive. I'd never been to Belize. I'd never stayed up all night on a deserted beach dropping acid and frolicking naked in the waves.

On the bright side, Klaus was very flirtatious with me, which I must admit I enjoyed. He was really good looking in an outdoorsy, Scandinavian sort of way. His behavior didn't seem to bother Lindsey and Hugh at all. I was hoping it would have had some effect on Hugh—maybe make him say to himself "Belize was fun, but now I have this beautiful fiancée that even my good friend Klaus can't keep away from!" But he seemed completely indifferent.

When Hugh had paid the bill, we all stumbled outside to grab taxis. "Come over for a nightcap," Lindsey pleaded, holding my coat sleeve. "Everything closes down so early here! In Mexico, we'd just be getting started."

I looked to Hugh. "It is only midnight," he said.

Klaus and Lindsey had rented a furnished condo in Capitol Hill for two months. We stumbled in noisily, and Hugh and I settled cozily on the tweedy couch. "Who wants wine?" Lindsey tripped into the room with a bottle and a corkscrew. Klaus followed with four glasses and a plastic baggie full of pot.

"Oh, gee," I said as they passed the joint around. "I think I'll pass." I was on the verge of nausea already and felt sure that smoking anything would put me over the edge. I hated to add to my fuddy-duddy image by refusing the joint, but I hated the thought of throwing up more.

By 3 AM I had hit the wall. The other three, unfortunately, were still giggling inanely and consuming more red wine. Hugh seemed oblivious of my exaggerated yawns and pointed looks. He was so wrapped up in being with Klaus and Lindsey again that he seemed oblivious of me, period.

Finally I excused myself and found the bathroom. I peed then splashed some cold water on my face, but it did little to revive me. I needed sleep. As much as I hated to put an end to his reunion, I was going to have to tell Hugh it was time to go. On the other hand, Hugh was still having a great time. Perhaps he could stay here while I went home to bed? But something about that didn't feel right. No, I wanted him to come home with me. I'm sure Klaus and Lindsey would roll their eyes and make cracks about "the old ball and chain" after we left. I wished I could be the kind of girlfriend who could sit up all night smoking pot and drinking with his open-minded friends, but I functioned much better on eight hours of sleep. Besides, I had an appointment with a potential caterer tomorrow. With a deep, fortifying breath, I returned to the living room.

"Sorry to be a drag you guys," I began, then stopped short. "Oh, my God!"

"Come on, Kerry," Klaus said, reaching his hand out to me. "Join us."

I averted my eyes. "Jeez . . . I—uh—ulp!" I said again.

"Come on, hon," Hugh said. "It's no big deal. Live a little."

"Uh—uh—Hugh, ummm . . ." I was in a state of shock. What did one say in this situation? My head was reeling, my stomach churning. What was the appropriate reaction when you stumbled upon three naked people embroiled in an orgy on the living room carpet? And what was the proper response when you found the man you were supposed to marry in nine months in the midst of a diving-instructor sandwich? "Uh . . . I just . . . I'll . . ." I stammered myself right out the door, sprinted down the street and flagged a taxi.

Hugh moved out the next day. We didn't even discuss trying to work it out. I think we both knew that the mental image of him, Klaus, and Lindsey writhing naked on the floor would cause insurmountable problems.

With a heavy sigh, I picked up the phone and dialed the next number on the list.

"Hello, Cousin Sarah? This is Kerry Spence calling from Seattle. . . . Ummm, yes . . . it's about my wedding. . . ."

Chapter 25

I CLOSE THE LILAC JOURNAL AND TUCK IT UNDER A SOFA CUSHION. FOR some inexplicable reason, I feel on the verge of tears. It certainly isn't because I miss Hugh or wish things had worked out between us. It's just that . . . well, I remember how trusting I was, how innocent and naïve before I stumbled upon that diving instructor–doctor sandwich. It really changed me forever.

It is ironic that I would choose this moment to write about the demise of my last engagement. I have been engaged for all of seventeen hours; my fiancé is mere feet away showering off the remnants of our sweaty night of passion. Perhaps *ironic* is not the right word for this timing; *disturbing* would be more appropriate.

More disturbing is the fact that I can't get Nick's face, the way it looked as he stood in the doorway of my mom's condo, out of my mind. It's irrational, I know. I mean, I barely knew him. We weren't even dating. But the thought that I will never know what could have happened between us makes me feel inexplicably morose. And the thought that I may have hurt and disappointed such a wonderful and kind man, makes me even . . . well . . . moroser, for lack of a better word.

The intercom rings and I shuffle in my slippers and housecoat to answer it.

"Hellooo, bride-to-be," she singsongs.

Great. My mom's here.

Within seconds she is at the door, laden with a bag of muffins and a heavy stack of bridal magazines.

"Were you up?" she asks, breezing inside.

"Yeah," I say. "I was just going to make coffee. Do you want some?"

"Oh! No caffeine for me! You may as well drink rat poison! I've found that starting the day with a good bowl of miso soup is more energizing and doesn't have all the harmful effects of coffee." She pauses for a moment. "Where's Sam?"

"In the shower."

"Well, why don't you run and freshen up a bit?" she whispers. "You don't want your new fiancé to see you looking so . . . well . . . I don't know—haggard?"

"Sam knows what I look like in the morning," I snap. "We used to live together, remember? And I'm really tired this morning, okay?"

"Oh, I don't doubt that!" My mom does the "nudge, nudge, wink, wink, say no more" action. Gross. I don't know why my mom has recently decided that we are girlfriends and can now talk openly about our sex lives.

"Anyway," she continues, seating herself in the living room. "I've brought some muffins for you and Sam and—" She pats the stack of glossy magazines. "—I've brought these so we can get planning!"

"We haven't even picked a date, Mother. I think it's a little soon to start making wedding plans."

"It's not too soon! Do you know how hard it is to get a church and a reception hall these days? You have to book a year in advance! Carol from my pottery class had booked eighteen months out for her daughter's wedding. It's much busier than when you were engaged to Hugh."

Sam enters the room looking just showered fresh, dressed in khakis and a long-sleeved polo shirt. "Gwen!" he says, obviously delighted to see my mom.

"How's my future son-in-law this fine morning?" She gets up so he can kiss her cheek. Jeez . . . maybe those two should just get married.

"I'm great," Sam says, moving behind me and wrapping his arms around me. "I couldn't be better." He buries his face in my neck and kisses me. It feels nice and he smells really good, but something about this intimate gesture in front of my mother makes me queasy.

"I've brought some bridal magazines so we can start making plans," my mom says. "Kerry thinks it's too soon, but I happen to know she's wrong."

"Well," Sam chuckles. "We haven't even set a date yet."

"If you want to get married anytime in the next year," my mom continues, "you have to start planning now."

"Well I'll leave those decisions to my future wife," Sam says, kissing me again.

"Do you have a calendar for next year?" my mom blathers on. "We can look at some possible weekends?"

"Honey," I say to Sam. "Didn't you mention that you had a lot of work to do?"

"On Sunday?" My mother's voice is shrill.

"Well . . . ," Sam says hesitantly. "We've got some potential investors in from Hong Kong, and they want a site tour."

"You should go," I say, turning him toward the door. "Don't worry about us."

"Are you sure?" he says seriously. "I won't go if you don't want me to."

"It's fine." I kiss him quickly on the lips.

"Take a muffin with you!" my mom calls.

She finally leaves at one to get to her two-o'clock Bikram yoga class. I have somehow managed to sit on the couch with her for three hours and put off making any decisions about the wedding. No matter what she asked or suggested, I remained noncommittal.

"When you were planning your wedding to Hugh, you wanted fuchsia bridesmaid's dresses. You don't *still* want that color do you?"

"Not really."

"And you'd planned to be married at Saint Matthew's United. I know that was really to please your father and since he's so distant these days, I think you should choose a venue that you and Sam are comfortable with."

"You're probably right."

"Shall we use the same guest list we put together when you were going to marry Hugh?"

"Maybe . . . for family, anyway."

"Fish or chicken?"

"How about both?"

The conversation went on in that manner until I finally said, "Look, Mom. I don't feel comfortable making any decisions about the wedding without discussing them with Sam first."

"You're probably right," my mom said, snapping the thick glossy magazine in her lap closed. "It's his wedding, too." She paused, looking at me seriously.

"What?"

"You're a very lucky girl, you know. He's a real catch."

"I know," I said somewhat defensively.

"He's so handsome and successful and loving."

"I'm aware of that, Mother," I said. I couldn't help but hear the words left unspoken: "And you're so unstable, in a dead-end career, and pear-shaped."

But by the mercy of God, she left before I could say something that might destroy our relationship forever. Thank goodness she isn't about to let the aging process begin again by missing a yoga class.

I flip listlessly through the magazines my mom left behind. All these thin gorgeous beaming models are so phony. They are obviously not real brides! Real brides have worry lines on their foreheads and stress induced acne. They feel nervous and slightly panicked, full of doubt and insecurity. At least that's how I'm feeling. I wish Sam were here. He seems so happy and excited. I need to talk to him to allay my concerns. On cue, the phone rings.

"Hey, babe," Sam says cheerily. "Is your mom still there?"

"No, she finally left. Thank God!"

He chuckles. "Well listen, hon, it looks like I'm going to be tied up here for quite a while. These investors seem pretty serious and they have a lot of questions."

"No problem," I say lightly. When we were together before, I would have resented being left alone on a Sunday. I would have fretted and worried, wondering if he really *needed* to be there, or would just *rather* be there than hanging out with me. But now I am his number-one priority. We are engaged. He wants to spend the rest of his life with me! What's one afternoon apart? "I'll see you for dinner, then?"

"Well . . . ," he says tentatively.

"What?"

"Robert wants us to take them out for dinner tonight. But if you don't want me to go, I can make an excuse."

"No . . . go ahead."

"You're sure? Because I meant what I said, Kerry. You're more important to me than anything else."

"I know, Sam," I say gently. "It's okay."

"I love you, Kerry. I'm so happy we're getting married."

"Me, too."

"I've got to run. I miss you and I love you."

"Love you, too," I say, before hanging up.

At work the next day I can't concentrate (not that that is anything new). I am relieved when Trevor invites me for a latte. It will save me from staring at the post-campaign analysis I am supposed to be writing for the Prism ads. So far I've written:

The Fall Prism post-campaign analysis indicates . . .

But all these research numbers are like the Russian alphabet to me. As soon as I look at them they seem to swim before my eyes and my mind starts wandering. Besides, why does Prism need a post-campaign analysis a month and a half into the campaign? Doesn't *post* mean "after"? This was Sonja's stupid idea.

"So how was your weekend?" Trevor asks when we are sipping our coffees.

"Interesting," I say.

"Really?"

"Yeah. I'm getting married."

"What?" Trevor lets out a high-pitched scream. "To who?"

"Whom."

"Shut up, you bitch! Are you really getting married?"

"Well, Sam proposed on Saturday."

"Sam? I thought you two were over."

"So did I, but apparently he's been pining away for me for weeks. He's been phoning my mom and everything."

"Wow." Trevor is silent for a few moments. "Wow," he says again. "Did he give you a ring?"

"Yeah. It's really beautiful."

"Where is it?"

"Oh . . . it's being sized," I say sheepishly. I don't know why I couldn't bring myself to wear the ring today.

"Are you happy?" Trevor asks, reading the troubled look on my face.

"Yeah . . . ," I say hesitantly.

"You don't sound very happy, Kerry."

"I think I'm in shock," I say with an awkward laugh. "Like you said, I thought Sam and I were over."

"And what about that Nick guy?" Trevor continues the inquisition. "You seemed really into him?"

"Nick?" A loud, forced laugh erupts from within me. "We were just friends! Barely even friends, actually . . . more acquaintances. I'll admit I thought he was cute and supernice and everything but . . . I barely knew him! Jeez!" For some stupid reason, my eyes feel on the verge of welling up.

"Well, if you're happy, I'm happy." Trevor leans over and kisses my cheek. "Congratulations."

"Thanks," I say mistily. "But can you do me a favor?"

"Oh!" he says clapping his hand to his chest. "Do you want me to be your maid of honor?"

"No! I mean, maybe, but that's not the favor."

"Okay."

"Can we just keep this between us for now? I'm not ready for everyone at work to know about it."

He eyes me suspiciously. "Are you sure you want to do this? You guys have a pretty rocky past."

"I'm sure," I say, patting his hand reassuringly. "He's changed."

At four o'clock I call Sam. "Tonight's the Prism Christmas cocktail party," I tell him with a heavy sigh. I am finding the thought of schmoozing clients more and more repulsive. "It starts at six, but I should be home by about ten."

"I'll catch up on some work and meet you at your place," Sam says. "Call me when you're leaving."

"Okay. See you in a bit."

"Kerry?"

"Yes?"

"I love you."

"I love you, too," I say, and hang up the phone. Gee, Sam is really sweet and loving now that we are engaged. I need to shake off this nagging feeling that the current state of our relationship is transitory. I will push all this doubt and insecurity into the farthest recesses of my mind. We're getting married, for God's sake! I should be filled with joy like Sam is. Like my mother is.

The Prism Christmas butt-smooch is being held at a martini bar in Pioneer Square. When I arrive, Sonja is already there holding court as if she owns the place. She is dressed in an attractive, winter-white pantsuit and looks positively regal. Gavin is standing beside her, ever the faithful court jester. As I head to the bar, I notice Dave lurking in a dark corner. Although he is a despicable human being, we do have one thing in common—we hate all this phony, schmoozy stuff.

With a martini in hand, I chat amiably with some of the Prism clients. They are all fairly nice people, but they seem obsessed with work. As hard as I try to steer the conversation toward Christmas or shopping or New Year's celebrations, it always seems to come back to their bloody jobs. It is sickening. I'm beginning to feel my brother has the right idea. Am I too old to be working at a bar all night and hanging out at the beach all day? Hmm . . . maybe not too old, but probably too fat in the rear-end area.

My reverie is interrupted by Dave. "How's it going?" he mumbles as he sidles up beside me.

"Great," I say through gritted teeth. "This is so much fun."

"I hear ya," he chuckles. "I hate this kind of thing. I'd rather be cleaning the fridge in the lunchroom."

"I'd rather be cleaning the toilet in the men's room."

He laughs again. "Oh, Kerry," he says with a sigh. "I'm glad we've been able to put the past behind us."

I raise my eyebrows. I am about to point out that it is a little hard to forget that he tried to have me fired, humiliated me in front of my coworkers on numerous occasions, and sexually harrassed me in a spooky darkened stairwell, when Sonja calls for everyone's attention.

She is standing on the small stage where a jazz band plays on weekend nights. *Ting ting ting.* She taps a spoon against her martini glass like she is at a wedding. "Excuse me everyone," she says. "I'd like to say a few, quick words. Don't worry! I won't keep you from your drinkie-poos too long!"

There is a smattering of polite laughter—except for Gavin, who looks like he's about to pee his pants from the hilarity of the word *drinkie-poos.* I must forcibly restrain myself from rolling my eyes. Dave nudges me and indicates my empty glass. "Sure." I nod. I could definitely use another drink.

Sonja launches into her speech. "It's been quite a year hasn't it?"

An affirmative murmur emanates from the crowd. Gavin says loudly "You can say that again, Sonja!"

If she actually says it again, I will throw my empty glass at her.

"Anyway," Sonja continues. "Two thousand three has not been without its challenges, but I think we've really come together as a team! And speaking on behalf of everyone at Ferris and Shannon, we feel privileged to be working with all of you at Prism, *the best damn clients in the world!*"

"Woo hoo! Yeah! Yeah!" Gavin hoots. Even Dave and I are pressured into clapping and cheering. It would be really obvious if we didn't.

"So I wish you all a wonderful holiday season and we look forward to starting 2004 with a bang!" she continues. Gavin leans in and whispers something to her. Sonja nods. "One more thing everyone, before we get back to the evening's festivities . . . I'd be remiss if I didn't take this opportunity to make an important announcement!"

Hmmm? What could it be? Let me guess—Gavin is being promoted. Or Sonja is being promoted. No—she's not likely to make an announcement about herself. Let's see . . . Janet is being promoted or—?

"Kerry? Kerry Spence? Could you come up here for a moment?"

No! No! Oh, my God! What is she going to do to me? What is she going to say? Surely even Sonja is not cruel enough to fire me in front of clients and coworkers at a Christmas party?

"Come on, Kerry," Gavin calls in a teasing tone. "Get up here."

I move numbly through the crowd, trying to keep the intense anguish I am experiencing from showing on my face. Soon, I am standing between Sonja and Gavin. This is too horrible for words. I swallow loudly, trying to dispel the huge lump of fear in my throat. "Don't start crying," I will myself. "No matter what she says, don't start crying."

"A little birdie told me a secret about you," Sonja says in her singsongy voice.

Uh-oh. Does she know I've been spending approximately six hours a day drinking lattes, sending personal e-mails, and talking on the phone? Who told her? Has Gavin been spying on me? I shoot him a look. He smiles back like the Cheshire cat.

"Everyone!" Sonja calls to the crowd. "Please join me in congratulating Kerry on her engagement!"

Everyone applauds, and Gavin kisses me (of all the weird moves). I blush a deep crimson but smile gracefully. Trevor is soooo dead! It was obviously he who leaked word to Gavin. "Thanks. Thanks," I say lamely. "That's very kind of you."

"Let's see the ring!" one of the drunker Prism gals calls out.

"It's . . . uh . . . being sized," I respond, blushing an even darker hue than before.

There is a moan of disappointment at there not being a big rock to ogle, and I take this opportunity to slip back into the anonymity of the crowd. I find a spot near the back of the room and heave a sigh of relief. I can feel normal color slowly returning to my face. Suddenly a blast of cold winter air hits me, and I turn in the direction of the icy gust. The exit door is banging shut behind Dave.

Chapter 26

AS ALWAYS, TREVOR HAD AN EXCUSE FOR HIS ACTIONS. AND AS ALWAYS, I forgave him.

"You were having a hard time coming to terms with the fact that you were actually engaged," he said, his handsome face pleading for forgiveness. "I thought that by getting it out in the open, it would make it more real for you. That way you'd be able to start dealing with it sooner."

I narrowed my eyes suspiciously. "So, this wasn't just about gossip too good to keep to yourself?"

"No!" He was aghast. "I did this for you, to help you." He grabbed my hands. "Besides, you know I'm great at keeping secrets."

Before I could respond, one of the VPs walked by my office, and we were forced to start murmuring "Yes, yes, totally shifting the paradigm."

I hate to admit it, but Trevor's plan has sort of worked. Now that everyone at the office knows I'm getting married it has forced me to deal with the eventuality of it. My coworkers (the female ones, anyway) are constantly barraging me with questions about receptions and bridesmaids and caterers and divorced parents at the wedding. . . . It is practically impossible to think of anything else. So I am wholeheartedly embarking on discussions about toasts, first-dance music, gifts for guests, wedding cakes, buffet versus à la carte . . .

"Gee, Carole, I think 'Angel' by Aerosmith would be a great song for our first dance. Very original."

"Portable cameras on all the tables is such a cute idea, Laurie! Thanks so much!"

"Well, Sue, I hadn't thought about burning CDs of all our favorite songs to hand out to guests, but it's an excellent idea." Not to mention illegal.

I have adopted the role of blushing bride—although, the blushing is more to cover up my awkwardness than from joy.

I am even wearing the engagement ring most of the time. It's a beautiful ring: a carat and a half, emerald-cut diamond in a platinum band. It's very beautiful and very big. It even looks good on my larger-than-average hands. But just because it's very big and sparkly doesn't mean that it's showy or ostentatious. So why do I feel so exposed when I wear it? Like everyone is staring at this huge, Ivana Trump kind of rock on my finger? It seems to scream, *Look at me! Look at me! I'm getting married!*

I am not a normal woman.

Part of me thinks I should discuss this with my therapist. She could help me work through these reservations. Although, would she really help me to get over my doubts? Or would she try to talk me out of this marriage? She knows more about my relationship with Sam than anyone. She will think I am a masochist to want to marry someone who has put me through so much anguish!

"Did you not learn anything from your diary of past encounters with men that may be contributing to your current negative and dysfunctional quasi-relationship?" she would say, voice calm but tinged with disappointment. "I do believe Sam was the main character in entry number two, was he not? Have you forgotten about him dumping you shortly after your wisdom teeth were removed? And what about Jasmine? Have you forgotten her, as well? May I suggest you commit yourself to a high-security facility for the mentally deranged, where you can work on developing a backbone?"

I just can't shake the feeling that my therapist will be extremely disappointed in me. I think she is very skeptical by nature. She will not believe that Sam has changed and become a kind and caring man who puts his fiancée first above all else. It is better not to risk bringing it up with her. I don't want any negative energy.

On the bright side, I'm not thinking about Nick anymore. Well . . . I'm not thinking about him much . . . not *very* much anyway. I was really upset and conflicted at first, but then, by dealing with my emotions in a straightforward and truthful manner, I got over it! I realized that it would be stupid to pine away for what might have been, when what might have been may well have been nothing at all! I mean, for all I know, Nick's interest in me may have been strictly platonic, just friendship, or even less. In fact, he probably just felt sorry for me, as it must have been terribly obvious that my life was meaningless, empty, and unfulfilling. Being so kind and caring and giving, Nick was probably powerless to refuse the invitation to my mother's vegan Christmas open house. Therefore, when he saw me accept Sam's proposal, he was probably relieved! By repeating this theory to myself every time he pops into my head, I'm starting to feel a little less morose about him.

Anyway, now I am throwing myself into Christmas. It has even afforded my mother a distraction from the impending wedding plans. She is frantically knitting Sam a vest made out of hemp yarn.

"I think the natural color will really look great on his olive skin tone. Or do you think I should have it dyed? There are a wide variety of vegetable dyes available that are nontoxic and not harmful to the environment. What do you think? Perhaps teal would look nice with his dark hair?"

"Stick with the natural color," I say, because Sam is slightly more likely to wear a beige hemp knitted vest than a teal one. Does she not realize he is a businessman who wears dark suits to work every day? I'm sure the wealthy investors from Hong Kong wouldn't expect their Northwest liaison to turn up at a meeting wearing a teal hemp vest! Or maybe they would? I suppose hemp vests would be considered more casual wear, anyway. But quite frankly, I'm not a big fan of men in vests—hemp, teal, or otherwise.

Today I am taking Tiffany out for a Christmas lunch. I also have a small gift for her—an Eminem CD. I'm not sure about her musical tastes but based on her love of violence I was able to narrow it down to Snoop Dogg, Eminem, or Marilyn Manson. I went with Eminem because I find his music to be the most catchy.

We are meeting at Rockin' Robin's, a young and hip burger joint—at least I thought it was a young and hip burger joint. Now that I'm here, it actually seems more juvenile and corny than young and hip. I'm seated in a cherry-red, vinyl booth perusing the menu that is shaped like a large record album. All the dishes have really cheesy names like Oinkers (pork ribs), Cheepers (chicken fingers), Rowdy Rockin' Moo Burgers, and on like that. This was definitely a bad choice. Tiffany is going to think it's really lame—especially this paper hat with a brim like a bird's beak and this red plastic bib that looks like a robin's red breast. What a stupid waste of marketing dollars! Who would ever wear this?

But when Tiffany hasn't arrived fifteen minutes later, I decide to try it on just to kill time. I peak at myself in the mirrored pillar across the aisle. I really do look quite a lot like a bird. Of course not a real live bird, but a bird mascot like the one for that baseball team . . . what is it?

"Kerry? Is that you?"

"Sonja! What are you doing here?" I jump in my seat.

"Nice to see you, too," she snorts.

"Oh, sorry, I'm just surprised to see you here . . . or anyone I know, for that matter."

"Obviously." She takes in my bird costume. "We're here with Richard's niece Emma. She's nine. We have a special day with *auntie and uncle* every quarter."

"That's nice." I smile as I try to yank the bird's beak from my head. Ouch! A staple attaching the elastic string to the hat is hopelessly caught in my hair. Extricating myself quickly is impossible! It's going to be a slow and painful process that will have to take place when Sonja leaves.

"And you?" Sonja smirks at my predicament. "What are you doing here?"

"Well, I mentor a fifteen-year-old girl through the Shooting Star program. We're having a Christmas lunch."

"Here?" Sonja laughs. "Don't you think this place is a bit juvenile for a teenager?"

"I do now."

"I think Emma will have outgrown it by next quarter!" Sonja laughs. "And listen. What about this fiancé of yours. Is he here?"

"Oh, no," I respond. "This lunch is just for Tiffany and me. He's got a lot of work to do, anyway."

"Well, I look forward to meeting him at the Christmas party," Sonja smiles. "I'd better get back." She waves to the table where her gray-haired attorney husband is sitting with a small blond girl in a bird hat. "See you at the office on Monday."

"You, too."

As she steps away from the table, she reveals Tiffany, who has been lurking behind her. "Nice hat," she says in her deadpan voice.

"It's stuck in my hair!" I say frantically. "Can you help me? Please! Get it off! Get it off!"

Tiffany calmly untangles my hair from the offending staple with a minimum of pain and breakage. I heave a sigh of relief when I pull the hat off. I can't believe I've just had a lengthy conversation with my supervisor who doesn't like me and will always hold me back while I'm dressed up as a bird. Excellent. I pull the bib off as well and crumple it up. Tiffany sits across from me.

"So . . . ," I say. "How's it going?"

"Not bad." She shrugs.

We look at our menus in relative silence for a while. As usual, Tiffany is initially uncommunicative, but I'm sure she'll warm up after some time. I make small talk, blabbering on about Christmas and shopping and what we're going to order. Then, my mouth once again having escaped my control, I find myself asking about Brian. It is a thinly veiled attempt to gain information about Nick, but maybe Tiffany won't pick up on it?

"Do you ever see Brian at school?"

"Sometimes." She shrugs. "Why?"

"Just wondering," I say nonchalantly although I feel my face getting hot. "You two had a good time at the aquarium."

"I guess." She sniffs. "Not as good a time as you had with his mentor." There is a twinkle in her eye.

"What?" I say, laughing self-consciously. "I mean, he's a nice guy but . . ."

"Yeah, he's nice. And hot."

"You think so? I never really thought about him that way."

"Oh, pleeeeeeeeeze!" Tiffany rolls her eyes. "You two were totally digging on each other."

"No we weren't! I mean, I don't think you'd call it *digging* . . . umm . . . I . . . we, uh . . . I'm going to have the Tasty Tijuana Moo burger."

Tiffany laughs, and I suddenly feel like I'm the high- to medium-risk teen and she is the older, wiser adult. "I'll have the Cajun Peeper burger platter."

Later, when we are diving into our monstrous hamburgers, I ask about her holiday plans. "So will you spend Christmas at your mom's?"

"I guess. If I can stand her."

"I hear ya," I echo. "My mom's been driving me crazy lately. She's always going on and on about . . ." I stop. I realize that I don't want to tell Tiffany I'm engaged. I'm not sure why, but I didn't wear the ring today either. "About stuff."

"Yeah? My aunt's not much better."

"That's too bad." I'm not sure what to say next so I bring out the gift-wrapped CD. "I got you a little something for Christmas."

"I got you something, too." She reaches into her purse.

"You did?" I am so touched. And thrilled! She actually likes me enough to get me a little something for Christmas! She hands me a small gift-wrapped box. "Should we open them now?" I ask. "Or wait?"

She smiles. "Now."

My heart thuds in my chest as she tears off the paper. What if she hates Eminem? What if she thinks he is a homophobic, misogynistic racist, like Moby does? Why didn't I get her a gift certificate so she could pick out her own CD? Why do I try so hard to have her think that I'm hip and cool enough to select music for a fifteen-year-old?

"Cool," she says to my relief. "I wanted this CD."

"You did? Are you sure because you can exchange it if you want?"

"No, I like it. Now open yours."

I tear off the paper and find a gift box of Ferrero Rocher chocolates. "I love these!" I enthuse. "Thank you so much."

"It's just a small thing," she says, playing with a cold french fry on her plate. "I don't have very much money."

"Really, Tiffany. These are my favorite!"

"Good." She smiles.

When we pull up in front of her aunt's apartment building she sits in the passenger seat for a long moment. "So . . . ," she says then trails off.

I get the definite sense she wants to tell me something. I give her an encouraging smile. "So?" I say to prompt her.

"Well . . . I . . . umm . . ."

"What is it, dear?" I say, sweetly—quite possibly too sweetly.

"I got suspended," she says flatly.

"Oh!" I am taken aback. "For . . . for what?"

"Smoking."

"Smoking?"

"Pot."

"Pot!"

"It was stupid," she says quickly. "Like, I wasn't even smoking it. I was just hanging out with some kids who were."

"Well . . . did you tell your principal that?" I say, making a great effort to keep my voice calm and even.

"No." Long pause. "I'd only had, like one toke. But they're out to get me because they think I hang with a bad crowd."

"It sounds like you do!" I want to cry. "Get new friends immediately!" But I recall that I'm not supposed to judge or scold. So what do I say here? What do I say? There is so much pressure! Okay. I can do this. I will provide guidance while still being hip despite my age. I clear my throat. "Sounds like a bad rap, dude, but smoking up is really not the best idea, especially around the school."

"I know," she says, staring at her feet.

"I guess you won't be doing that again, then?" I chuckle.

"Nope."

There is a long awkward silence. Finally I say, "Could I give you a call over the holidays? You know, to make sure you survived Christmas day with your mom? And to let you know that I did, too."

"Sure." She laughs. "You can call me."

"Okay. I will. Have a great holiday."

"You, too," she says as she grabs the door handle. I feel like I should give her a hug or something, but Shooting Star frowns on physical affection. You can't take any chances these days with people misconstruing an innocent Christmas hug between a protégée and mentor as some weird kind of lesbian child molestation, I guess.

Instead, I give her a "good buddy" kind of punch in the arm.

"Merry Christmas, Tiffany. I'll talk to you soon!"

"Yeah . . . Merry Christmas."

Chapter 27

BAH! I HATE CHRISTMAS. ALL THIS FESTIVE CRAP IS DRIVING ME INSANE. I've got three Christmas parties to go to this week, and thanks to all the Christmas lunches I've already been to, I can't fit into any of my Christmas outfits. And that's not to mention my mother's incessant phoning to request the measurement of Sam's back, from collar to waist, and the circumference of his head so she can make a matching hemp hat. It just gets better and better.

I am dreading all three parties. Tonight is a bon voyage get-together for Sandra, tomorrow is Sam's office party, and the following night is mine. I know it's the festive season and all, but I have a number of very legitimate reasons for my lack of enthusiasm.

Party Number 1: *Sandra's Bon Voyage*

✔ I really can't believe Sandra is leaving and will miss her terribly (recent problems aside).

✔ I will have to miss *The Bachelorette*.

Party Number 2: *Sam's Office Party*

✔ I've always found Sam's colleagues to be pompous dickheads who talk about nothing but money.

✔ Since the excuse Sam used when breaking up with me last time was his job, it is natural to harbor some resentment toward said job.

✔ Sam and I were "figuring things out" for nearly a year, during which time he could have brought any number of bimbos to office functions as dates. I'm terrified that everyone will be comparing me to his previous escorts. "This one has a much bigger butt than the last one," and "I preferred the tall thin blond girl who owned her own PR agency."

✔ Most of them know Jasmine.

✔ I will miss *Temptation Island: Australia.*

Party Number 3: *My Office Party*

✔ I hate everyone I work with (except Trevor and Shelley).

On the bright side, there are no good TV shows on Saturday nights.

Sam has been really sweet and supportive about Sandra's goodbye fete. "Do you want me to come?" he asks kindly. "For moral support?"

"That's okay," I say, patting his hand. "It's more of a girl thing."

"Okay. Have you told them about us yet?"

"Tonight," I respond, feeling my stomach churn uncomfortably. Next to my therapist, my girlfriends know the most about my past relationship with Sam. I am really nervous that they won't support my decision to marry him and will lock me away with only water and protein bars for sustenance. "I've been, uh . . . saving the news until I saw them in person."

When I am dressed in a short black skirt, tall boots and a tailored white shirt, I prepare to leave for the party. Sam whistles appreciatively from his makeshift office at the kitchen table as I pass.

"Look at you," he says, getting up from his laptop where he's been vigorously typing for over an hour. "You are gorgeous. I must be the luckiest guy in the world."

"You must be," I respond coyly, wrapping my arms around his neck. He kisses me but I pull away. "Watch the lipstick," I admonish. "I don't want to show up looking like some disheveled tramp who just made out with someone."

"Or a woman so madly in love with her fiancé that she can't resist him even when she's all dressed up for a party."

"I'm going to be late," I say giving him a last peck.

"All right," he says grudgingly, and releases me. He helps me into my coat and then hands me my gloves from the pocket.

"Hey?" he says, his brow furrowed. "Where's your ring?"

"What? I—uh—" I can feel my face turning beet red as I stammer out an explanation. "I t-took it off when I was putting my pantyhose on. I didn't want to get a run!" I scurry back into the bedroom and retrieve it from its velvet box. With the diamond sparkling on my finger, I return. "Phew! That was close!" I smile. "It wouldn't be right to announce our engagement to all my friends without the ring, now, would it? Thanks for reminding me!"

"No problem," Sam says, still looking mildly perplexed.

As I sit in the back of the cab, I finger the gigantic rock through the fabric of my glove. I really can't recall how it went from my finger to the tiny box on my dresser. Did I really take it off so I wouldn't snag my pantyhose? Or was I hoping that if I didn't wear the ring, I could just pretend everything was like it was before? Then I wouldn't have to risk being judged by Val, Michelle, and Sandra. God, life was so much simpler before Sam and I got engaged.

But that's crazy! How could I miss being single and alone and eating bowls of cream-cheese icing while watching *Law & Order* reruns every night? And then, as still frequently happens, thoughts of Nick and what might, possibly have been creep back into my head.

After the news of Tiffany's suspension, I had nearly phoned him. It would have been the perfect opportunity: I could have asked if I'd handled the mentoring situation correctly and apologized for agreeing to marry my old boyfriend right in front of him. I had the phone in hand, the phone book open to the Art Smarts office number . . . and then I chickened out. It would have been too awkward, too weird. Besides, like I said before, he's probably relieved that I'm out of his hair.

The cab arrives at Sandra's building, and I find the front door ajar. I climb the stairs and slip unnoticed into her apartment. Music is blaring, and I can hear the buzz of conversation and hum of activity emanating from the living room. I move through the spacious suite, bare now except for sporadic clusters of packing boxes. A large number of tea lights have been placed atop the myriad of boxes, giving the hollow room a warm and homey glow. I sigh despite myself. Sandra's life in Seattle has been packed away and will be put into storage. Soon, there will be no evidence that she was ever here.

"There you are!" Val spies me from the makeshift dance floor in the center of the living room. "Take your coat off and stay awhile."

"I'm a bit chilly," I say. "Great turnout."

"I know!" Val looks around. "I don't even know half these people. A lot of them are from her job."

"Kerry!" Sandra emerges from the kitchen with a large bowl of chips. She places them on one of the boxes and comes to embrace me.

"I can't believe you're leaving," I whisper into her hair, feeling the tears sting my eyes.

"Hey!" she says sternly, looking into my face. "Tonight is a celebration. No sad stuff! We're going to have a great time. Let me take your coat and gloves."

"I'm a bit chilly, actually," I say, huddling into my coat. "I'll just stay bundled up for a bit."

Michelle emerges through the crowd in the living room. "Take your coat off and come dance!" she calls. "We're playing eighties music."

Val hands me a glass of wine and I follow them to the dance floor.

"Her name is Rio, and she dances on the sand."

I probably look a little strange bopping around to Duran Duran while wearing my black, calf-length winter coat and black gloves, but I'm not ready to expose the ring. On the other hand, this look was actually rather popular in the 1980s. I will pretend I thought this was an '80s theme party! I launch into some shoulder-pumping choreography that I used to practice in front of the mirror in high school. I am a little rusty, but I'm sure everyone gets the idea. When I get a chance, I'll run to the bathroom and backcomb my bangs up in the air.

But four songs later, sweat is dripping from my forehead and I realize that if I don't remove my coat, I may suffer a heat-induced seizure. I should never have danced. I should have stood unobtrusively in a cool corner by the window. If only I wasn't such a sucker for the great tunes of the '80s.

I slip away to remove my coat and place it on the tall box serving as coat rack. Grabbing another glass of wine, I chat to a few acquaintances then rush back to the dance floor in time for "Rock the Casbah."

"Why are you wearing one glove?" Michelle calls.

"I'm Michael Jackson!" I say, attempting a moonwalk.

Michelle is looking at me suspiciously. "What's going on?" she calls over the Clash.

"Nothing! This is such a great song, eh?"

"Yeah. Why are you wearing that glove?"

"I told you! I'm Michael Jackson!" I grab my crotch.

But I'm not fooling Michelle. She grips me by the forearm and leads me to the kitchen. Sandra and Val, alerted to the excitement, follow us.

"Take it off, Kerry," Michelle demands.

"Why?" I sniff. "What's the big deal?"

"If it's not a big deal, then take it off!" Michelle is getting frustrated.

"Are you hiding something from us?" Sandra says gently.

With a heavy sigh, I peel off the black glove. My friends gasp in such shock that you'd think I was revealing a chicken claw for a hand!

"What is it?" Val says.

"A ring," I respond hoarsely, my throat constricted with fear. "An engagement ring."

"It's enormous!" Michelle whispers.

"You're engaged?" Sandra gasps.

"To who?" Val cries.

"Whom."

"Cut the shit, Kerry!" Michelle blurts. "Who gave you that engagement ring?"

"Sam."

There is a long silence where the drone of conversations and the Billy Squier playing in the background seem to fade to nothingness; all that is audible is the terrified beating of my heart.

"Sam?" Michelle finally breaks the silence.

"Yes," I croak.

Sandra suddenly springs to life. "Congratulations." She hugs me. "This is really exciting."

"Sandra! This is hardly cause for celebration . . . ," Michelle begins angrily, but Sandra cuts her off.

"Didn't you learn anything from the whole experience with George and me? You can't control what your friends do, and if you try to, you'll lose them."

"Well . . . ," Michelle says, but she trails off. To my surprise, her voice is shaky with emotion when she continues. "I just . . . I just don't want you to get hurt. I care about you . . . all of you."

Val squeezes Michelle's hand. "We know you do."

"She's following her heart." Sandra smiles at me. "Someone wise once told me that your heart will never steer you wrong."

"Thanks guys," I say, biting my lip to keep from bursting into tears.

"I'm happy for you," Val says, taking me into her arms. "I'm sure you know what you're doing."

"I do," I sniff. "He's changed. He promises."

We all look to Michelle for the expected retort, but instead, she is biting her lip in an effort to keep her emotions in check. "You guys are right," she says hoarsely. "I can't risk losing another friend. Come here."

The four of us embrace, and the lump of emotion lodged in my throat bubbles forth in a torrent of tears. I'm racked with sobs as I cling to my three best friends, crying because I love them so much, because Sandra is leaving, because Michelle let us see her vulnerable side, because I'm relieved they didn't judge me . . . I can't put a name on all the emotions I'm feeling. We stay like that for a long time, until someone puts "Billy Jean" on.

"Come on, Michael," Michelle says, breaking away and wiping the tears from her cheeks. "Let's dance."

Mortifying Moment #9

"Welcome, class!" The instructor, Helen, greeted us enthusiastically. She was a fiftyish woman with long, bushy brown hair and a voluptuous figure squeezed into a pink velour track suit. The seven women comprising the class mumbled hello awkwardly from our cross-legged positions on rattan mats. We were squeezed into a tiny studio apartment furnished sparely with a dingy floral sofa, two bean-bag chairs and a multitude of ferns. Behind us, what looked like the headboard of a wrought-iron bed was propped against the wall.

"I'd like to start out by quoting Freud, if I may." Helen beamed at us. " 'The only abnormal sex is no sex.' So let's take all those sexual inhibitions and throw them out the window!"

Following Helen's lead, we all mimed extracting our inhibitions (mostly from the head region but some from the chest and abdomen), crumpling them into a ball and hurling them out the window.

"This particular class is devoted to freeing your inner dominatrix."

I shot Val a look—a mixture of shock, horror, and outrage. Our attendance at this seminar had been her idea (she was in a promising new relationship), but the brochure she'd shown us had been titled Deepening Intimacy. The content had focused on connecting emotionally with your partner and heightening sexual excitement through shared growth and mutual understanding. I hadn't read anything about freeing my inner dominatrix! I wasn't even sure I had one!

Val smiled sheepishly, instantly revealing that she was well aware of the curriculum, and that her boyfriend Stuart was in for an exciting evening. I turned to Michelle, who smiled and raised her eyebrows in anticipation. I was not surprised that she was eager to unleash her inner whip-wielding, leather-wearing mistress on Thomas, the attorney she'd been dating.

I, on the other hand, was instantly uncomfortable. My unease was due in part to my own long-ingrained inhibitions (despite their mimed removal) and concern about the reaction of my current boyfriend. I'd been seeing Kevin, the VP of a market research firm for five months. He was witty, intelligent and attractive—in his conservative, market-researcher sort of way. He had great taste in restaurants, was a connoisseur of wines, and could engage me in conversations—in turns thought-provoking and hilarious—for hours on end. But physically, we'd been taking it slow.

We'd waited three months to become intimate, and when we had, it had been very . . . nice, but definitely tame. I was fairly sure that Kevin was a rule-follower, a low-risk taker, a fan of the tried-and-true formula. I wasn't sure how he was going to take to his relatively new lover coming at him with whips and batons and who knew what else!

Helen, apparently, was reading my mind. "Some of you may feel shocked and uncomfortable at first," she continued. "But I can assure you that the reaction of your partner will be so intensely positive that you'll wonder why you didn't try this a long time ago!" Val and Michelle exchanged gleeful looks and then both included me hopefully. I managed a weak smile. Everyone else seemed really enthusiastic. Since I was here, I may as well give it a try.

The Freeing Your Inner Dominatrix course was broken into three sections. First, Helen instructed us on creating the perfect setting: multiple candles, gauzy scarves draped from bedposts and over lampshades, seductive background music—anything from Enya to Nine Inch Nails would work—whatever helped you connect with the "naughty lady deep within."

Next, Helen displayed the tools of the trade. For us novices, these included feathers, fringed leather whips, fur-lined handcuffs, silk blindfolds, et cetera. Michelle smiled at me encouragingly. I smiled back. This wasn't nearly as kinky as I'd expected, and I found I was actually enjoying myself. It helped that Helen's assistant, a middle-aged Asian man clad in a yellow kimono-style robe and black satin pants, served us a continual stream of champagne.

Finally, it was time for the demonstration. Helen removed the pink track suit to reveal a horrifying studded leather G-string and bustier, to which she added thigh-high leather boots, and a small black mask that obscured only her eyes.

Then, the champagne-serving assistant dropped his kimono and satin pants, revealing tight white briefs and the fit body of an eighteen-year-old Olympic gymnast. There were several gasps to accompany my own as well as a smattering of nervous giggles, but our instructors were oblivious.

"Lie down!" Helen barked, and her partner eagerly prostrated himself facedown on a rattan mat. He obediently extended his arms which she cuffed to two posts of the headboard structure. "Now!" she snapped, as she strode around his body, her butt cheeks jiggling ferociously with each step. "You belong to me! You will obey my every command for without me, you are worthless. You will call me Mistress Raven Claw, and I shall call you Slave Dog!" To emphasize her point, she smacked Slave Dog's bare back with a menacing device that resembled a riding crop.

Most of the audience shifted uncomfortably as he moaned, "Yes, Mistress Raven Claw," in a voice both obsequious and turned on.

"Shut up!" she yelled, startling us all as she whacked his back and buttocks again. "You will not speak unless I speak your name . . . Slave Dog!"

Long pause.

"I said Slave Dog!" Smack with whip.

"Yes, Mistress Raven Claw!" he wailed.

"Anyway," Helen addressed us in a completely normal voice despite her outfit and recent actions. "It's a good idea to give yourselves dominant and submissive pseudonyms as we have. That way, what happens in the bedroom doesn't infringe on your regular lives." She turned her attentions back to Slave Dog, her voice morphing back into dominatrix mode. "Slave Dog! I want you to lick my toes."

"Yes, Mistress Raven Claw."

All seven audience members recoiled in disgust and several of us covered our eyes in terror.

"This is just an example of the type of demands you can make on your slave," Helen said cheerily. "Most of you won't be ready for ultimate submission yet, but I wanted to show you how satisfying this type of sexual encounter can ultimately be." She lowered her voice conspiratorially. "Trust me, ladies . . . there is not a man alive who won't be turned on by some level of S and M. Often, the more powerful they are in the corporate world, the more submissive they'd like to be in the bedroom. Ron here is CFO of a multinational company. We've been in a dominant–submissive relationship for nine years now, and we're both extremely fulfilled."

"Yes," Ron agreed, lifting his head to nod enthusiastically.

"Shut up!" she screeched. "Slave Dog is not obeying orders and will be severely punished when the audience leaves!"

With that, we were dismissed.

When we were on the street in the fading afternoon light, Michelle said, "So?"

"So?" Val and I giggled.

"Let's go down to Carl's Adult Emporium and get the stuff we need."

"I'm game!" Val said.

"Okay," I acquiesced. "But we'd better hurry before the champagne wears off."

An hour and a half later we emerged, burdened down with S&M paraphernalia.

"I don't know . . . ," I said, peeking in the bag that held my three-hundred-dollar leather teddy, a leather crop, and a pair of handcuffs. The alcohol buzz had worn off, and I could feel doubt creeping over me. Not to mention remorse for the amount of money I'd just spent.

The girls pounced on my skepticism.

"Remember what Helen said?"

"The more conservative men are, the more they're into this kind of thing!"

"Kevin will love it!"

"He'll go crazy!"

"I thought she said 'the more powerful they are,' " I countered.

"Powerful and conservative!" Michelle insisted.

"And Kevin is both, right?" Val added.

"He's the perfect candidate. You'll drive him wild!" Michelle affirmed. "I can't wait to try this out on Thomas!"

"And Stuart!"

"Besides . . . you've bought all the stuff," Michelle added practically. "You have to do it now."

"I will!" I said, a sudden surge of courage washing over me. "I'm going to rock his world!"

Later that night, Kevin buzzed me in the front doors of his squat, brick apartment complex. I struggled with my three large shopping bags through the upscale lobby to the elevator. When he opened the door to his chic suite, I stumbled inside. "Don't worry," I laughed nervously. "I'm not moving in. I just have . . . a little surprise for you." I forced a seductive tone.

"Oh, really?" Kevin replied sexily, removing his wire-rimmed glasses and kissing me.

I played with the buttons of his perfectly pressed white shirt. "I think you're really going to like it."

He kissed me again. "I'm sure I will. And I have a surprise for you, as well."

"Oh?"

"A 1982 bottle of French cabernet sauvignon! It's from the Bergerac region, which, in my opinion, grows superior grapes. The specialty wine shop near the office got it in today. I just had to rush right down and pick it up!"

The girls were right. Kevin was sure to love what I had in store for him.

I sent Kevin to the kitchen to open the wine, with instructions to join me in the bedroom when summoned. I busied myself creating the perfect setting, draping gauzy scarves (and some not so gauzy as my gauzy supply was limited) over the bedside lamp, the bedposts, the mirror, and side tables. Next, I tore into a bag containing forty tea lights, scattering them on every available surface, and in a vaguely satanic pattern on the floor around the bed. I popped a Lenny Kravitz CD into the player and hoped he would do his job bringing out the naughty lady hidden inside me.

Okay . . . there was no putting it off. It was time to free my inner dominatrix. But first I needed some liquid courage. I scurried to the kitchen where Kevin was sniffing the wine cork, a look of ecstasy on his face.

"Are you ready?" he asked.

"Not yet." I took the proffered wineglass and downed it in large, noisy gulps. "Bring me a refill," I instructed and then rushed back to the bedroom to squeeze into my leather underwear.

When the multitude of candles were lit, I tentatively called, "Kevin?"

"Ready?" He responded from the kitchen.

"Ummm . . . yes . . . I mean . . . Get in here! Now!" I said forcefully, smacking my hand with the whip for practice.

He stopped in the doorway, his eyes behind his glasses wide, his mouth dropped open in shock.

I suddenly felt incredibly foolish in my leather corset, French-cut panties, and fishnet stockings. I wobbled momentarily in my stiletto heels, the whip falling limply to my side.

"Wow," Kevin said, his voice thick with desire.

"Strip!" I barked, instantly warming to the role now that Kevin's enthusiasm was so obvious. He handed me the wineglasses and began to hurriedly undress.

"Now," I ordered, downing my wine and most of Kevin's before placing the glasses on the dresser. "Face down on the bed!" I proceeded to cuff Kevin's wrists to the bedposts and then smacked him lightly on the buttocks with my whip. "You are my slave and you belong to me!" I continued in my most commanding voice. "You will call me—" Shit! I'd completely forgotten to make up a dominatrix name. "—You will call me—Mistress—Wolf—Fang. And I will call you—Toad Boy."

"Toad Boy?"

"Shut up!" I screeched, smacking his back. "You will not speak unless spoken to."

"Sorry, Mistress Wolf Fang."

"Very good . . . Toad Boy." I patted his head awkwardly. "Now, my worthless slave . . . ," I continued, circling the bed precariously on my four-inch heels. I had to admit I was really enjoying playing Mistress Wolf Fang. It was a heady feeling—being so completely in control and having Kevin at my mercy. I was drunk with power—and 1982 Cabernet.

"Uh . . . Kerry?"

"No!" I yelled, tapping his leg smartly with the whip. "My name is Mistress Wolf Fang, and you are not to—"

"Kerry! The scarf on the lamp! It's too close to the candle!"

I turned in the direction that Kevin was frantically jerking his head, but it was too late. The thin fabric burst into flame.

"Oh, no! Oh, no! I'll get water!" I called, tottering to the master bathroom. Unfortunately, I stumbled in my stilettos, knocking over several tea lights. Now, another scarf began to curl, menacingly signaling its proximity to the flame.

"Holy shit!" Kevin began to panic. "Uncuff me! Uncuff me!"

"Okay! Okay!" I froze between the bathroom and the bed, momentarily stunned and motionless. The keys! Where were the handcuff keys?

"Hurry! Hurry! For Christ's sake, Kerry!" The pitch of Kevin's voice rose with the flames.

"The keys are in my purse!" I called, rushing as fast as my heels would allow to the front room.

I rummaged through my bag. "For the love of God!" Kevin shrieked from the bedroom. He actually sounded like he was crying! "Help me! Pleeeeeeeeeeze! Help me!"

When I returned, the reason for Kevin's panic became evident. The flames were licking at one side of the bed clothes as I released him. Who knew gauzy scarves were so darned flammable? They should come with a warning for smokers.

Kevin grabbed my wrist and dragged me from what was now verging on an inferno.

"Do you have a fire extinguisher?" I asked hopefully.

"It's too late for that," he cried, grabbing his cell phone and a pillow from the couch to cover his privates. "We've got to get out of here!"

As we made our way down the hall we banged on the doors of the other tenants to alert them to the danger. "Fire!" I screamed, my fists aching from the pounding. "Fire!"

Kevin screamed into his cell phone. "My entire bedroom's on fire! Seven hundred Robertson Drive, Apartment two-oh-four! Please! Hurry!"

We were outside the lobby when the fire truck wailed up and the firemen burst through the doors and ran up the stairs. We waited, with about forty other tenants, shivering in the chill night air, for them to return with a prognosis. It felt like hours, days, weeks . . . In our haste, Kevin and I hadn't had time to grab coats or clothes to cover our near—or in his case, complete—nakedness. The scratchy blankets the firemen had provided did a poor job of shielding us from the cold—and the judgmental stares of the other apartment dwellers, an uncanny number of whom were women over sixty-five. Finally, the firemen emerged.

"The fire's out!" the burly, mustachioed chief bellowed. "You can all return to your apartments now—except the tenants in two-oh-four. We'll need to speak with them," he said ominously.

"The naked guy and the pervert in the leather!" one of the old ladies called out helpfully. Then they shuffled past us, each muttering "sickos" or "weirdos" or another variation on the sexually deviant theme.

Chapter 28

THAT WAS THE END OF THAT RELATIONSHIP, OF COURSE. WHEN I'D FI-
nally screwed up the courage to call Kevin and apologize, he said he
was too busy looking for a new apartment to speak with me. I offered
helpfully to pay for the damage to his bedroom, but he said it was
more the humiliation he'd suffered in front of his neighbors than the
cost of home renos that was causing him to move. We didn't speak
again after that.

I tuck the journal away in the junk drawer and head to the bathroom. Despite having just relived the horrific demise of yet another
relationship, I am feeling upbeat. The success of the previous night
has somewhat lessened my apprehension about Sam's office party. If
I can face my girlfriends with such a positive and heartwarming outcome, maybe I have nothing to fear from his coworkers? Who are
they to judge our relationship? They don't even know us—well, they
don't know me. Given the fact that Sam has spent an average of
twelve hours a day working with them for the last four years, I guess
they know him quite well.

But with my girlfriend's supportive (or at least nonjudgmental) words ringing in my ears, I prepare for Sam's party. I painstakingly apply my makeup, blow out my hair, squeeze into control-top panty-hose and a formfitting black dress. There. I take in my reflection in the full-length mirror. I look poised, sophisticated . . . glamorous, even. I am the perfect match for Sam. I am every bit as attractive, charming, and successful as he is. No one will be shocked that he is engaged to such a big fat lump, because I am not one. I am . . . well, probably not *quite* as attractive or successful as Sam is . . . or as charming, for that matter. But I can be funny! Probably even funnier than he is. Everyone at Kazzerkoff Developments will adore me. The men will make comments like, "Miller, you lucky dog, you!" and "Does she have any sisters?" The women will probably just stare at me, seething with jealously. In their heads they'll say, "She's got it all. She's attractive, confident, and happily engaged. And to the best-looking guy in our office, too!" No one will say "What is gorgeous Sam doing with her?" No one! It will be wonderful.

"IT WAS AWFUL!" I WAIL AS WE RACE HOME DOWN THE I-90.

"Tell me what happened!" Sam demands, his driving speed mounting with his frustration.

"Are you blind?" I shriek. "Didn't you see how they were treating me?"

"I'm sorry, I didn't. That's why I'm asking you what happened!"

"Just forget it," I say, sulking back into my seat. "If you didn't notice, then I'm not going to tell you."

"That's just great!" he growls. "You make us leave the party because you're having such an awful time, and now you won't even tell me why. Nice."

"It wasn't one specific thing, Sam!" I yell. "It was the prevailing attitude of all those stuck-up jerks you work with. They were all looking down their noses at me, like I'm one of your disposable dates whom they'll never see again."

"They don't think that, Kerry!"

"They do! No one even knew we were engaged. And when they noticed the ring, they were all like, 'What a beautiful ring. Where'd you get it?' Gasp. 'From Sam? You're kidding! We had no idea! I wouldn't have thought Sam would ever settle down.' "

"That's my fault," Sam says, his voice lowering slightly. "I don't share my personal life with my coworkers. They didn't know I was engaged. They were surprised, that's all."

"And who is this Caroline person?" I continue, ignoring him. "Why haven't you ever mentioned her before?"

"She's our new administrative coordinator," he says, flustered. "I didn't mention her because I didn't think you'd be interested."

"Oh, right!" I bark. "Why *would* I be interested? Why would I care that my fiancé is working closely with a former swimsuit model with silicone D-cups!"

"She was a runway model, not just a swimsuit model."

"Oh! Now you're defending her! Is something going on between you two?"

"Kerry, stop it! You're being paranoid."

"Oh, really? Like I was paranoid when you cheated on me with Jasmine?"

"I can't believe you're bringing that up!" he bellows. "We said we'd put the past behind us!"

He's right; we did say that. And I thought I had. But suddenly, it feels like only yesterday that I was lying on the couch, my cheeks swollen to the size of Caroline's breasts while Sam told me he was leaving but it had nothing to do with the sexy consultant he'd been working with. I feel emotionally unglued, mentally unhinged! What is wrong with me? Of course, the eight or so glasses of champagne are not exactly helping things. I burst into tears.

"I'm sorry." Tears of self-pity pour down my cheeks. "But tonight I felt like . . . like . . . everyone was in shock that you were engaged to someone as fat and stupid as me!"

"You're drunk," he says, annoyed. "That's crazy."

"Oh! So now I'm fat, stupid, drunk, and crazy! Thanks Sam. You're really making me feel a lot better."

"Calm down," he says. "You're being hysterical."

"Great! Now I'm fat, stupid, drunk, crazy, and—"

"*Don't!*" he roars. He pulls the car off onto a side street and slams it into park. He turns to me. "I'm sorry to yell, but you have to stop this. I can't stand all this self-deprecation."

"But—but—it's how I feel," I sob. "What's wrong with me? What's wrong with us?"

"There's nothing wrong with us!" Sam says, gripping me by the shoulders. "There's nothing wrong with *you*."

"I know there's not!" I shriek, pulling away. "That's the problem. Why do I feel this way? I'm thirty-one years old, and you've turned me into an insecure teenager!"

"*I've* turned you into an insecure teenager?"

"I don't mean that you've actually done anything consciously. . . . I just mean that you . . . this relationship . . . It makes me feel . . ." I trail off.

Sam turns away from me and puts the car into gear. Without a word, he pulls it back onto the street, heading toward home.

"I'm sorry," I say, suddenly gripped with panic. "You're right. I'm being hysterical."

"You can't help how you feel, Kerry," he says impassively.

"It's the stress of Christmas and the engagement," I babble. "My mother's been phoning me every five minutes to talk about bridesmaid's dresses or get the measurement of another one of your body parts. It's wearing on me. I'm just not feeling myself. And I know I drank too much tonight. I'm not thinking straight."

He is silent and hostile, so I follow suit. The rest of the ride home is quiet but for the sound of tires on wet pavement, and the rhythmic slapping of windshield wipers. When we pull up in front of my building, he doesn't turn the car off.

"Aren't you coming in?" I ask frostily.

"I think it would be better if we spent the night apart," he says, looking straight ahead. "To give us some time to collect our thoughts."

"Fine," I say angrily as I undo my seat belt. "Collect away!" I jump out and slam the door behind me. As I stomp up the walk to my building, I realize that "collect away" was an inane retort and not at all indicative of the feelings I was trying to relay. But it's too late now. I dig angrily for my keys, which seem to have disappeared into the furthest recesses of my purse. I can't believe Sam doesn't want to talk about the events of this evening! Everyone knows you're not supposed to go to bed mad! I am so immersed in my thoughts and the search for my keys that I don't realize I've reached the front steps until I trip on the bottom one. My purse and its contents fly from my grip and go skittering across the doorstep.

"Shit!!!" I yell, stomping my feet like a two year old who's dropped her ice cream cone. This really tops it off! "Shit! Shit! Shit!" I look over my shoulder to see if Sam is witnessing my childish tantrum but he is long gone. Very nice. Now I will have to crawl through the muck and hedges to retrieve my belongings all on my own. With tears rolling down my cheeks, I search blindly for my lipstick, my keys, my Palm, my phone. After what feels like an hour I've retrieved most items—at least I've got my keys. I'll come back and search in the morning when it's light. Tomorrow is another day.

Tomorrow

9:12 AM

After a fitful sleep, I am not feeling any more secure or hopeful. I lie diagonally across my spacious bed and ponder the events of the previous evening. Were Sam's coworkers really looking down their noses at me, or was that just a reflection of my own insecurity? Was he sticking up for the bikini model/administrative coordinator or just stating a fact? Am I a screwed-up basket case, or do I just feel like one when in a relationship with Sam?

10:22 AM

I crawl out of bed and trudge to the shower. I will not let my neuroses overwhelm me. I now have many tools in my repertoire to combat these feelings of low self-esteem and lunacy.

11:15 AM

I am seated comfortably on the couch with *You Get What You Give* in my lap. I flick through the pages, searching for the appropriate section. But it seems Dr. Rainbow Hashwarma never had any problems with the opposite sex—or at least none that have any relevance to my current situation. The wise doctor does discuss the challenges of relationships between individuals with different religious beliefs, value systems, and socioeconomic backgrounds. And there is a section on increasing sexual intimacy by becoming a more giving lover, but absolutely nothing on having a boyfriend who is extraordinarily handsome and successful and makes you feel like a big fat frump! Thanks a lot.

11:47 AM

The journal of mortifying moments is now open on my lap. The vanilla candle is burning on the end table. I have a cup of herbal tea before me (it is a little early for wine) and a ballpoint pen in hand. I will write down the events of last night in order to examine them, analyze the dynamics of my relationship with Sam, and ultimately heal this dull ache in my chest. Okay . . . here I go. . . .

But I can't! I simply can't! My hand refuses to form the letters that will spell out the disaster of the previous evening. It refuses to create the words that will solidify the dysfunction in my relationship with Sam. I just cannot write this down and give Sam a recurring role in the journal of mortifying moments. He's the man I'm going to marry, for God's sake! Even Hugh is only in there once!

12:12 PM

Fine. I will meditate. I will breathe deeply . . . clear my mind . . . But meditating doesn't seem to be working either. Every time I try to clear my mind, I end up conjuring an image of Sam's handsome face, followed by Caroline in a tiny bikini, and Jasmine in a hard hat and negligee. (I don't actually know what she looks like, but I've created a mental picture of her much like the princess in *Aladdin*.) I squint my eyes and grip the smooth Zen stones, hoping to chase away these negative vibrations. But soon they return, this time in the form of my grandmother's cottage-cheese butt—or is it mine?!

12:25 PM

I do three sun salutations, triangle pose, pigeon posture, and a shoulder stand. I think I may have dislocated a vertebra (if that is possible).

12:36 PM

That's it! I'm going to phone him. We are two mature individuals who are planning to get married, for God's sake! Surely we can talk through this one little issue? It's only our first fight since we've been back together.

"Hi. You've reached Sam Miller of Kazzerkoff Developments. Please leave a message and—"

I hang up. That's strange. I've rarely known Sam to not answer his phone. He must be on the other line with someone else—someone taller and thinner with a smaller ass and bigger boobs! Stop! My imagination is running amok. I'm sure he's on a business call—or maybe he's trying to phone *me*? I must stay off the phone then, to ensure I don't miss him. But what if he saw it was me calling and is trying to avoid speaking to me?

12:39 PM

After several minutes of this manic internal dialogue I decide that the mature thing to do would be to leave a message. I dial his cell phone again.

"Hi. You've reached Sam Miller of Kazzerkoff Developments. Please leave a message, and I'll return your call as soon as possible."

I hang up. No, I'm not going to leave a message. Why should I be the one to apologize? It would be setting a bad precedent. If I leave a message today, then every time we have a fight in the future, the onus will be on me to admit it is my fault. He's not infallible in this! And besides, he drove off, leaving me to rummage through a hedge in the dark! I could have died of hypothermia! Or been attacked by a passing rapist!

12:41 PM

After another cup of herbal tea and some toast, I am feeling much more positive. Sam will call me and we will laugh about our silly tiff and all will be well. Tonight, he will escort me to my Christmas party and all the women will drool over him. "Look at Kerry," they will all be thinking. "She's so attractive, confident, and happily engaged." It's all going to be fine.

Chapter 29

Later

5:30 PM

Apparently, it is not fine! I still have not heard a word from him. The Christmas party starts at seven. What the hell is going on? Why is he doing this to me? Surely he can't be *that* angry about last night, can he? I mean, I admit I was a bit wobbly, but I can't believe that he'd never speak to me again over it?

I am pacing the apartment with a glass of red wine in hand. My hair and makeup are done; my underwear and pantyhose are on; my dress is pressed and hanging on a hook on the back of my bedroom door. I take a long slurp of merlot in an attempt to calm my nerves. I look at my watch again. To get there on time I will need to leave in twenty minutes. What should I do?

Every possible scenario to explain Sam's absence has played through my mind (including the one where he is sideswiped by an SUV). But something in my gut tells me that he is actually fine and healthy, and that this is some kind of punishment for my behavior the night before. Maybe it's all over between us and he just hasn't bothered to tell me? Has he called the wedding off? If so, who would he contact? I rack my brain to think of who might have heard from him. Of course! I pick up the phone and dial.

"Heyyyyyy, Mom," I say casually. "Howzit going?"

"Oh, hello. I'm surprised to be hearing from you. Don't you have a 'do' to go to tonight?"

Glug glug glug. "Ummm, yes, but I just wanted to call to say 'Hey, Mom.' "

"Well . . . hey . . ."

"How's your day going? Anything interesting happen?"

"Not really."

"Have you talked to anyone?" Pour, refill. *glug glug glug.*

"Wellllll . . ."

"Yes?"

"Just Ruth . . . and Debbie from Vegan Cooking Two."

"Oh. Okay. I'd better get going."

"Is everything all right, dear?"

"Uh . . . yeah. I'd better go."

"Is Sam there?"

"Not yet."

"Well don't worry. I'm sure he'll arrive in time. He's very reliable."

"Thanks, Mom," I say, my chin quivering with emotion. "Bye."

As soon as I hang up, the phone rings. *Thank God!*

"Hello?" I say anxiously.

"Joseph wants to know what gorgeous Sam is wearing tonight," Trevor says exasperatedly. "He thinks I'm too flamboyant because I'm wearing a black see-through shirt and trousers. He wants to wear a suit, but I think that's too stuffy, so we wanted to know what Sam is wearing, because I'm sure it will be perfect."

"Umm . . . well . . ." Uh-oh. Here I go. "I—I—I don't know!" I burst into tears.

"Kerry, what's wrong?"

Between sobs and loud nose blows, I manage to stammer out the situation.

"You'll come with us," Trevor says forcefully.

"I don't think I want to go," I snivel. "Everyone will think I'm pathetic, showing up without my fiancé."

"You have to go," he says, dismissing my protestations. "You're the only person I really like at the office! Fix your makeup, throw on your sexiest party dress, and we'll pick you up in fifteen minutes."

I am feeling a lot better as our taxi cruises through the illuminated streets en route to the hotel. I am sandwiched between Trevor and Joseph, a handsome older gentleman who seems very down-to-earth and warm. It is obvious he is mad about Trevor, and personally, I am looking forward to discussing *South Pacific* in detail over dinner. Trevor is at his light and funny best, trying to distract me from the trauma I've endured over the past twenty-four hours.

"You are so gorgeous!" he raves, taking in my strapless chocolate-brown dress and strappy heels. "How will Dave ever control himself?"

"Oh, no!" I say, enjoying the attention. "I will have to enlist you two as bodyguards to keep him away from me!"

"It'll cost ya," Trevor responds. "What do you think, Joseph? A bottle of champagne, and we're hers for the evening?"

Joseph plays along. "Sounds about right."

"Consider it done," I say, squeezing Trevor's hand. "Thanks, pal." I feel my eyes welling up.

"None of that!" he admonishes sternly. "Tonight is a night for celebration, not moping over a bratty boyfriend who can't even pick up the phone to call and apologize for being an inconsiderate jerk!"

"Hear, hear!" I say jubilantly. The fact that I've already imbibed over half a bottle of wine has made getting into the festive spirit much easier.

But when we pull up in front of the venue for the evening I feel my stomach lurch uncomfortably. How is this going to look when I show up sans the new fiancé I've been blabbering on about? Sonja's words from that afternoon at Rockin' Robin's provide a haunting soundtrack: *"I look forward to meeting your fiancé at the Christmas party."* (I dismiss the part of the memory where I am dressed as a bird.)

Trevor and Joseph each take my hand and we march confidently into the grand lobby of the Heritage Hotel. The Ferris & Shannon party is in the Orca Room on the second floor. In the vintage brass elevator, I take deep breaths to keep calm and centered: I am attractive, confident and possibly still engaged. And if not, I am attractive, confident and have two handsome gay dates.

But for all my inner poise, I visibly wilt upon entering the Orca Room. Is it my imagination or did all four hundred guests just turn to look at me?

"Take a picture—it'll last longer!" Trevor calls, verifying my worst suspicions. He whispers to me, "It's just because we're the three best-looking people here."

"Sure," I say as we move toward the bar. But it's almost like I can read their thoughts as I pass by. There's Carole from accounting thinking, "Hmm . . . where's her fiancé? Only last week she was gushing on about writing her own vows and china patterns." And Sue from the studio is wondering, "Where is he? She was going on and on about the seating arrangements for his family just the other day." And Sonja is thinking—Oh, shit. Sonja.

"Well, hello." She slithers toward us in her fitted black pantsuit. "I don't believe we've met?" She addresses Joseph.

"This is my partner, Joseph Everett," Trevor says debonairly. "Joseph, this is one of our directors, Sonja Fletcher."

"Pleased to meet you, Sonja." Joseph takes her hand and sort of bows to it. As much as I like him, I'm annoyed at this obsequious gesture.

"And you, Joseph," Sonja says with a self-satisfied smile. "Kerry!" She turns to me. "Where's your mysterious fiancé? We've all been looking forward to meeting him."

"Have you?" I say, stalling for time. "Well . . . you see, Sonja . . ." Trevor sticks a martini in my hand, and I immediately take a long sip.

"You haven't met Sam?" Trevor comes to my aid. "Well, I have to tell you he is absolutely stunning. I'd say a cross between Patrick Dempsey and JFK Jr. He's an executive with Kazzerkoff Developments, don't you know? It was just our luck that he was tied up with a work engagement tonight so Joseph and I have the pleasure of escorting Kerry."

"Ummm . . . yes," I echo. "Tied up with a work engagement." I dunk my lips back into the martini.

"What a shame," she says somewhat skeptically. "Well, we'll meet him another time perhaps? Enjoy yourselves." And she slinks back to her table.

With that ugliness out of the way, the rest of the evening is not too bad. As planned, Shelley and her husband have saved us an inconspicuous table at the back of the spacious ballroom where we can mock our coworkers' outfits, spouses, and dancing styles undetected.

"Look at Dave and his latest conquest," Shelley whispers as he and Shannon take to the dance floor.

"Poor thing," Trevor says. "So pretty and yet so dumb."

"I'd hate to be in her shoes," I say, perhaps a little too fervently. Dave and his beautiful actress are swaying seductively to some sickeningly romantic song by Celine Dion.

But after three martinis, I am hardly noticing Dave or the empty place at the table intended for Sam. In fact, I've almost tricked myself into believing that all is well in our relationship and he actually *is* tied up at a work function. As long as I don't venture outside my safety zone in this back corner, I will be fine. I even manage to restrain myself from rushing to the dance floor when "I Ran" by A Flock of Seagulls begins to play. But unfortunately, there is no escaping the fact that my bladder is going to burst if I don't go to the ladies' room soon.

I skulk along the outside wall and manage to exit the Orca Room basically unnoticed. The bathroom is across the foyer and down the hall. I scurry as quickly as my high heels will allow, rushing so as not to be seen by any nosy coworkers or leave a puddle of pee on the floor. I made it! Alone in the elegant ladies' room I use the toilet then face myself in the vanity mirror above the row of sinks. I wash my hands and take in my reflection. I actually look quite good—my slightly red eyes are the only evidence of my emotionally distraught day. And really, the bloodshot look could just as easily be caused by my martini consumption. No one need know that I've spent the afternoon crying—they will just think I am an alcoholic!

I carefully apply more lipstick, fluff my hair, and prepare to re-join the party. I am feeling even stronger now than when I left the room. In fact, I may march right across the dance floor to my back corner table. What's the big deal? My fiancé is tied up at a work thingy, and so I came with my two handsome gay dates! I've got nothing to feel ashamed of! With a flourish I pull open the ladies' room door, stride confidently into the hall, and walk smack-dab into Dave.

"Ahhhhhhh!" I scream, sort of running on the spot and flapping my hands in hysterics. "Ahhhhhhhhh!"

"Calm down, will you?" He hushes me, annoyed by my reaction. "I need to talk to you."

"Well . . . ," I say, collecting myself. "I don't really think we have anything to talk about."

"I think we do." He grabs my arm and escorts me to a secluded seating area down the hall and around the corner. I really dislike Dave, but in my current inebriated and weakened state, I must admit his forcefulness is kind of sexy.

"What do you want, Dave?" I say, when we are seated on the bro-cade settee. I am enunciating carefully so as not to slur.

"Look," he says. "I know you've had a tough year, but this wasn't necessary."

"Sorry?" I am sincerely confused.

"Kerry . . . ," he says with exasperation. "Are you going to make me spell it out?"

"Maybe you'd better."

"Fine . . ." He takes a swig from the beer in his hand. "You didn't have to do all this."

"All what?"

"Come on, Kerry—this whole fiancé thing. If you wanted to be with me, why didn't you just say something? You didn't have to *pretend* to be engaged to make me jealous and realize I want you."

"*What?*" I stand up in shock and outrage, but my three-inch heels and the three martinis cause me to fall back to my seat. "What did you say, Dave?" I ask more calmly.

"Come on," he says, putting his hand on my knee. "Everyone's talking about it. How you made up a fiancé so you wouldn't look so lonely and pathetic? Sending yourself roses, wearing that big fake ring and everything? But I realized that this wasn't about what everyone else thought; this was about me. You were doing this because of Shannon and me. You thought that if I felt I couldn't have you, that it would make me want you more. And you were right, Kerry. I can see now that Shannon isn't right for me. You and I have so much more in common."

"Oh my God," I say in a small voice.

"You won, babe," he says, tilting my chin to look at him. "I *do* want you."

"Oh, my God!" I say in horror.

And then I bolt. *Bolt* might be a stronger verb than necessary to describe me tottering down the hallway in my high heels and fitted dress, but I am moving as fast as I can. I run directly to the elevator and frantically stab the down arrow. I vaguely recall that I left my wrap at the table with Trevor and Joseph, but I'm sure they'll bring it home for me. And frankly, I don't care if I freeze to death in thirty-degree weather in a strapless dress. My life is not worth living!

"Kerry! Stop!" Dave calls angrily just as I step into the elevator.

The doors close, and I lean against the back wall, closing my eyes. I can feel the tears forming behind my eyelids, threatening to seep out and ruin my makeup. I can't believe they were all whispering about me and laughing at me. I admit I did go on and on about the details of my impending wedding, but that was an attempt to get myself excited about the prospect and to cover my own doubts! I can't believe they thought I was making it all up!

When the doors open seconds later, I make a beeline for the row of taxis outside the front door. That's when I hear my name called again.

"Kerry!"

Damn that Dave! He must have taken the stairs and beaten me down here!

"Kerry! Wait!"

But slowly I realize that it is not Dave's voice calling me. I stop and turn around.

"Sam," I say hoarsely.

"What's going on?" he asks, approaching me. His face is a mixture of concern and annoyance.

"I—I'm going home!" I burst into tears. "You—you—you didn't—you didn't . . ."

"Calm down," he says gently, taking me in his arms and holding me against his black sports coat. "It's okay," he whispers, stroking my hair. "I'm here now. It's okay."

But it's not really okay. I'm very drunk. My makeup is ruined, and much of it is smeared over the front of Sam's jacket. Suddenly, I don't even want to talk about why he didn't call me today or even if we're still engaged. I just want to get out of here, and away from everyone I work with. I want to curl up in my bed and pretend this day never happened. I look up at him. "Can you please take me home?"

"What about your coat?" he asks, taking in my skimpy dress.

I shake my head and begin walking toward the front doors. I feel him slip his blazer over my bare shoulders before he puts his arm around me and leads me to his car.

Chapter 30

WHEN I WAKE UP MY HEAD IS THROBBING AND MY MOUTH IS PARCHED.
"Ohhhhh, gawwwwwwwwwd . . . ," I moan in agony, rolling over
and preparing to go back to sleep. That's when I notice a naked Sam
lying beside me. Surely his nakedness would indicate that we are still
engaged? Or at the very least still seeing each other?

"Hey," he says, smiling at me sleepily. "You okay?"

"Yeah . . ."

"We need to talk."

"I know we do." I sit up and my brain sloshes painfully inside my
skull. "I feel awful."

"You drank way too much," he says.

"I know. Actually . . . can you excuse me for a second?" I run to
the bathroom and barf last night's martinis and wine into the toilet.
This is not good. I feel absolutely hideous, and a glance in the mirror
confirms that I look it, too. I slip into the shower and feel the beads of
hot water tapping away at the pain in my head. Perhaps if I stay in

here long enough I'll be able to wash away the shame and humiliation that are creeping back into my consciousness?

About fifteen minutes later, Sam enters the bathroom and pees
into the toilet beside me with only the transparent shower curtain
between us. We must definitely still be engaged. "Are you ever coming out of there?" He peeks his head into the shower.

"I'm almost done," I say. But I stall another ten minutes until the
water begins to cool and I have no excuse but to emerge. Wrapped in
my robe with a towel twisted around my head, I find him in the
kitchen making coffee.

"Do you want some toast?" he asks.

"Not right now," I respond, my stomach churning at the mention of food.

"I'm going to make some."

"Okay. Make sure you unplug the coffeemaker."

"Right. Do you want some juice?"

"I don't have any juice."

"Oh . . . water?"

"Yes, please."

When we've exhausted the breakfast banter, we sit across from
each other at the tiny kitchen table. "Shall I start?" he asks.

"Okay." I stare at my water glass, running my fingers along the
cool, wet surface.

"Why didn't you call me yesterday?"

"Why didn't *you* call *me?*"

"I did," he says. "I called you on your cell several times, but you
didn't answer. I even left messages."

"Well I didn't hear it ring, and I had it with me all day. Besides, I
was home. You could have called me here!"

"I thought you'd be out Christmas shopping!" he says angrily.
"Look, Kerry, I was pissed off about the way you acted at my office
party. I decided I'd spend the day at the site because we've got a lot to
do before the Christmas break. But at least I took the initiative and
called you."

"I called you, too, but you didn't answer."

"I was on-site! There's construction and equipment running. I can't hear my phone. Why didn't you leave a message?"

"Because . . . well . . ."

"*Well* what?"

"Your toast popped."

"It can wait," he grumbles. "I want to know what you were playing at."

"I wasn't playing at anything," I tell him. "I was upset and I couldn't believe you didn't call. And then when you didn't show up to take me to my Christmas party . . ."

"I didn't think you wanted me there!" he cries. "I assumed you were really angry when you didn't call me back. And then finally I decided that we were acting like children and that I wanted to see you, but I didn't even know where the party was! I called every hotel in the goddamn city until I found the one that was hosting it!"

"Well!" I say indignantly. "When I hadn't heard from you by five thirty, I assumed it was all over between us. I mean, it was humiliating showing up at my Christmas party without you! Everyone was like, Where's your mysterious fiancé? Or should we say *fictitious* fiancé? I couldn't believe you'd do that to me if you still cared about me!"

"Jesus, Kerry," he mutters, standing and going to the toaster. "All this stupidity could have been avoided if you had just checked your messages."

"I told you, my cell phone didn't even ring!" I stomp into the hallway and grab my purse off the floor. I return to the table and rummage through it for my phone. "As you'll see," I say as I dig frantically. "I don't have any . . . Uh . . . What the—?"

"What's wrong?"

"My phone's not here."

"Have you checked your coat?"

As I head to the closet, it dawns on me. The other night when I dropped my purse on the doorstep and its contents rolled into the hedge, I'd thought I'd picked up most of my belongings, but in my distraught state I must have missed it! Barefoot, and in my robe and towel, I explode out of the apartment and scurry down the stairs.

"Kerry?" Sam calls behind me. "What are you doing?"

It is raining again, but I am oblivious as I jump off the steps into the soggy grass below. I crouch down, peering into the thick hedge that borders the building. My towel-turban catches on a thorny bush, and as I pull away, it falls from my head. I'm sure my wet hair has been molded into some kind of frightening hair sculpture, but I don't care, because that's when I see it. Nestled against the building is a compact, black-and-gray object. It's my phone!

I reach in and retrieve it, ignoring the brambles scratching at my sleeve and wrist. Despite being in the cold and damp for thirty-six hours, it appears to be working. The small display screen reads 4 NEW MESSAGES.

I look up and Sam has joined me on the steps. He is looking down at me, but I can't read his expression. One thing is for certain—it's not a look that says, look at her cute hair sculpture.

"Uh—my ph-phone," I stammer. "It was in the hedge all this time."

"Come inside," he says coolly. "You'll catch a cold if you stay out here."

THE LETTER ARRIVES ON CHRISTMAS EVE—AN INNOCUOUS GREEN ENVE-lope that would somehow change everything. I sift through the last mail delivery before the holidays, opening a card from my dentist's office, one from the Shooting Star program and another from my dad. Inside is a sweet note and a money order for two hundred pounds. That's quite a lot of money when converted—must be six hundred dollars! Or is it three hundred? Either way, it will probably cover the cost of the Christmas gifts I had to buy on behalf of my brother, who will never pay me back.

It is in the last envelope, postmarked with an address I don't rec-ognize in Calgary, Alberta, Canada. As I open the Christmas card, a letter flutters to the floor. I pick it up and begin to read.

*   *   *

Dear Kerry,

I am writing to tell you that I have moved to Calgary. I wanted to call you before I left, but I didn't get a chance to. Sorry.

I left just after I got suspended. My mom went mental about it, and even my aunt was starting to rag on me all the time. I knew I couldn't live with either of them anymore. I talked to my mom about going to Canada and she totally freaked at first. She said I was running away from my problems and that they would follow me wherever I went. But I told her I just needed a fresh start and things would be better in Calgary. Eventually she came around and even drove me to the bus station.

My dad has been cool so far. He has a girlfriend named Donna who's really nice. She doesn't live with us but she's here a lot. Dad converted his den into a room for me. I even have a computer I can use! (If you want to e-mail me, my address is chix_kickazz@hotmail.com) There is a school a couple blocks away where I will go in the New Year.

Anyway, I hope you don't think I am terrible for leaving and not facing up to things, but sometimes I think it's best just to wipe the slate clean, you know? I will miss hanging out with you. It was fun but let's keep in touch anyway. I hope you have a very Merry Christmas (and that your mom doesn't drive you too nuts). Hope to hear from you soon.

Your friend,

Tiffany

PS) You're right. It's pretty cold here.

PPS) Have only seen a couple of "cowboys" so far.

When I finish reading, I have a huge lump of emotion in my throat. I can't believe she's really gone. I'd had a feeling that she had more to tell me that day after our Christmas lunch—had she known then that she was leaving? I place the card on the mantel and refold the letter. I sigh heavily. Now that Tiffany is gone, I suddenly realize how much sanity she brought to my life. I don't know if I proved any use to her as a mentor, but she really put things into perspective for me. Sometimes you do just have to wipe the slate clean.

Sam's laptop is still set up on the kitchen table from when he was working late last night. I will send Tiffany a quick e-mail to let her know I received her card and letter.

From: Sam Miller
To: Tiffany Cranston
Subject: It's me, Kerry!

Dear Tiffany,

I got your letter and card today. Thanks so much. I am really going to miss you but I wish you all the best in Calgary. I'm glad to hear things are going well with your dad. When you come back to Seattle for a visit, we can do something fun (I will e-mail if I hear WWF or RAW are coming to town).

Tiffany, I don't think you're running away from your problems at all. I think you are a very smart girl and you know when it's time to cut your losses and start fresh. I've actually learned a lot from you (I think it was supposed to be the other way around!).

Anyway—I'm not on my computer, but my home e-mail address is ksinseattle@hotmail.com. Please e-mail back soon!

All the best to you! Merry Christmas!

Your friend,

Kerry

Chapter 31

I SURVIVED CHRISTMAS . . . BARELY. SAM'S PRESENCE AT MY MOM'S condo helped somewhat. She was less inclined to stick her tongue in Darrel's ear when there was another male present to fawn over. The three of them seemed to have a great time. Sam put on a good show of adoring the hemp hat and vest, and wore them all Christmas day. He pitched in preparing the Tofurkey and a variety of salads, laughing and joking with mom and Darrel while sipping nonalcoholic spiced apple cider. And now, as I have so often over the holiday, I find myself alone in the front room, pretending to read *Natural Living* magazine while I contemplate the events of the past few months.

Since Tiffany's letter, I've become increasingly reflective. I can see how her mother thought Tiffany should have stayed and faced her problems, but on the other hand, wiping the slate clean and starting over makes a lot of sense, too. That course of action is really very appealing to me. Of course, I'm not a teenager with no responsibilities who can just drop everything and leave town, but I can't help but admire Tiffany for taking that step. Sometimes, things are beyond fixing and are better left behind.

"Hey . . ." Sam sits on the arm of the sofa beside me, interrupting my reverie. "Spiced apple cider?" He holds a steaming mug out to me.

"Thanks." I smile up at him then take a sip. Ugh. Hot apple juice has never been my thing.

"Are you okay?" Sam asks quietly.

"Yeah, I'm just not a real fan of apple cider."

"That's not what I mean."

"Oh. Well . . . I've just been thinking. Can we take a walk?"

We stroll down the street to Elliott Bay Park. The day is cool and crisp, and we are bundled up appropriately, one of us in a plethora of hemp yarn. The icy spray of the ocean mists us lightly, the salt air clearing our heads after so many days cooped up in my mom's condo without meat or wheat or white sugar.

"So?" Sam finally says, filling the long silence between us. "What's going on, Kerry? You've been quiet the entire holiday."

I am tempted to launch into an excuse about spending Christmas with my mom and Darrel causing me anxiety attacks, but I know the time has come. I look up at him, and my eyes fill with tears.

"What?" he says, his handsome face full of concern. "Tell me."

"Sam . . . I . . . I don't think this is working anymore."

"Sorry?"

I take him by his mittened hand and lead him to a picnic bench along the path. When we're seated, I speak again. "I just . . . I don't feel that . . . I'm sorry, Sam."

"What are you talking about?" He is quietly angry.

"Well . . . ," I begin, but my voice trails off. I really should have rehearsed what I was going to say, but I hadn't realized this would happen so soon. How do I explain? Should I divulge the fact that I've been seeing a therapist for over a year, largely due to the effect our relationship has had on me? And do I really want to reveal that I've been keeping a diary of all my negative relationship experiences in which he plays a supporting, but pivotal role?

I can't help but feel like the journal of mortifying moments was integral in bringing me to this decision. By rereading all my journal entries, my therapist and I were able to discern a pattern to my past disasters. The majority of them were just flukes, coincidences, bad choices, or bad luck. If the objective of this diary was to absolve myself of blame, then in most cases, it worked like a charm. I now realize that I couldn't help it if an eleven-year-old foreigner was too frightened to neck with me behind the kissing bush. And I could hardly stop my nose from bleeding if it wanted to, could I? As for making out with a thief and my cousin—I'd say those were a combination of bad luck and bad choices. If gauzy scarves were treated with some kind of flame retardant, that mortifying moment would never have happened! As for the tape on the forehead—well, that was just plain forgetfulness.

There were only three entries that I actually had to accept responsibility for: the disastrous attempt at devirgining in high school, Hugh's diving instructor orgy, and Sam's unceremonious dumping of me. And here's where the real pattern emerged. In every relationship, I had been trying desperately to be someone that I wasn't.

In high school, I had wanted to be the girlfriend of the cool guy, the future NBA star (which, of course, never came to fruition). God, I don't think Brent and I ever had a meaningful conversation, and yet I wasted a year of my young life with him! The demise of that relationship was inevitable.

And in retrospect, I knew Hugh wasn't the right guy for me, I knew that relationship wasn't working. But at the time I thought, "He's a doctor—a brilliant, handsome saver of lives who will one day be very wealthy." So instead of being strong enough to end it, I tried to change myself to better suit him. I molded myself into the perfect "doctor's girlfriend," planning an extravagant white wedding. I even wore pearls for a while! I shouldn't have been surprised that Hugh cheated on me. I wasn't being true to myself, so how could I expect him to be?

With Sam . . . well, all this time I'd been thinking that there must be something wrong with *me*. I'm so lucky to be with him, so . . . why am I not happy? Sam is perfect! He's successful and charming! He drives a Mercedes! He's a cross between Patrick Dempsey and JFK Jr., for heaven's sake! What girl wouldn't want to be with him?

Of course, I had come to the conclusion that all our problems must be my fault (a theory I'm sure my mother would wholeheartedly support, but I'm not about to ask her). So, I'd been trying to morph myself into "the fiancée of an extraordinarily good-looking, ridiculously successful property developer." Unfortunately, the transformation was accompanied by overwhelming jealousy, debilitating insecurity, and warped body image.

So that's what I learned: If you are not being true to yourself in a relationship, then it is not meant to be. And at the risk of sounding like Dr. Rainbow Hashwarma, if a relationship is not meant to be, it will end itself. And in my case anyway, relationships end themselves in really horrific and humiliating scenarios. It's better to beat them to the punch.

Unfortunately, articulating all this to Sam would be a little more difficult.

"Well . . . I've learned a lot about myself over the past year."

"Okay?"

"I've learned that I really, really need to be true to myself and with you . . . I'm different."

"Different how?" His voice is cold; his anger contained just under the surface.

"Look," I say with a heavy sigh. "I know I'm far from perfect: I can be clumsy, I have consistently poor judgment, I cry too easily and eat too much icing without the cake. . . ."

He is looking at me like I left "I'm a babbling idiot" off the list.

"But that's who I am, Sam," I continue. "And despite all my flaws, I think I'm a pretty good person. But when I'm in a relationship with you, I try to be something that I'm not. I try to be poised and perfect and beautiful."

"But you are, Kerry!"

"I'm not!" I say, and I can feel small tears spilling from my eyes. "And that's okay with me. But I'm not sure it's okay with you. I don't think you love the real me; you love the act I've been putting on for you. I'm not sure you even know the real me. And I want to be in a relationship where I feel like the real me is enough."

"Well." He stands up angrily. "If I don't even know you, then whose fault is that? I'm not the one who's been putting on an act, Kerry. How am I supposed to know the real you if you hide her away from me?"

"I know!" I say, standing to join him. "I know. And I've tried, twice, to be more genuine with you, but . . . I think this is one of those problems that's just beyond fixing."

"What are you saying?"

"I'm saying I need to be in a relationship where I can feel good about being myself." I twist the ring off my finger and offer it to him. "I'm sorry, Sam. It's over." The diamond catches a sliver of sunshine peeking through the cloud cover, and I marvel, for one last time, at its beauty.

"Keep it," he says quietly, staring out at the horizon. "What am I going to do with it?"

"I can't keep it, Sam." I slip the ring into his coat pocket and do up the zipper. We turn and walk silently back toward my mother's neighborhood.

When we reach Sam's car parked a block from the condo, I am suddenly filled with panic. For the entire walk, I've been embroiled in a rigorous internal battle. Yes, I've learned a lot in therapy and by keeping my journal of mortifying moments, but come on! I can't become this strong, "do the right thing" kind of woman just like that, can I? Am I being too hasty? Am I letting the best guy ever to walk the face of the planet get away from me? Am I? Am I?

Sam unlocks the driver's side door with a small *be-bleep*. He opens it, but before getting in, he turns to me. His face is cold and impassive, but I can see the pain in his eyes. "I'm sorry things didn't work out, Kerry," he says coldly. "I thought . . . I thought we were right together."

"I'm sorry, too, Sam," I say, biting my lip to keep from sobbing. My doubts suddenly overwhelm me, and I'm terrified by the finality of what I've just done. "But you know . . . ," I blurt. "If you wanted to continue to see each other casually . . . you know, like once in a while . . ." Sam looks at me like I'm making some kind of retaliatory joke.

"I don't think so," he says. Then he hops in his car and with a squeal of tires, disappears. They are the last words he will ever speak to me.

But the worst is yet to come. I still have to tell my mother.

"What?" she gasps, her mouth gaping open in shock. "Just like that, you ended it? After all you went through to finally get him, you just ended it? Just like that? Just now?"

"I don't expect you to understand," I begin.

"You're right. I don't understand. For years you wanted him to make a commitment to you, and then when he does, you end it. I just hope you don't wind up regretting this decision for the rest of your life."

"But, Mom!" I say in the voice of a whining teenager. "I . . . I wasn't being . . . I wasn't being . . . true . . ." And then, all the pent-up emotion bursts forth, and I dissolve into tears.

"Oh . . . Come here," she says almost grudgingly, but when she wraps her arms around me, they are tender and comforting. "It's okay . . . ," she murmurs consolingly. "You'll be okay. . . . We'll be okay."

Chapter 32

As hard as it was to end my relationship with Sam, I can feel that the slate of my life is cleaner already. But there is one more major step I need to take. And this one will be much less painful.

On the first day back to work after the holidays, I march into Sonja's office and hand her my letter of resignation.

"Kerry, I'm shocked!" she says, her face paling under her impeccable makeup. "I hope this doesn't have anything to do with the Christmas party."

"Well, not really . . ."

"Because I'll admit that it was childish of the staff to speculate on the validity of your engagement and the existence of your fiancé. I really have no explanation for their behavior other than alcohol consumption and group contagion . . . but that's all been cleared up now, hasn't it?"

"It has?" I ask with mild interest.

"Well, of course! Dave put that rumor to rest when he returned from witnessing your reunion with Sam in the lobby. And then he had a terrible fight with his girlfriend over his feelings for you, and she left angry. He had a complete meltdown, even throwing a table over. Trust me, Kerry," she says, fixing me with her steady gaze. "*You* have nothing to be embarrassed about."

"I know I don't, Sonja," I say with a smile. "It's really not about the Christmas party. I think I have developed an ethical issue with the whole concept of advertising."

"Oh, really?" she snorts. "Well, far be it from me to try to influence your ethics, but I hope you realize that without advertising, the booming economy of the western world would come to a screeching halt!"

"Well, be that as it may, I'd still rather not be a part of it."

"Well, then," she says curtly, standing behind her desk. "I suggest you make today your last day in the office. I'm sure Gavin will have no problem assuming your responsibilities. I'll notify your clients this afternoon."

The next morning, I wake up with a mild hangover after the good-bye drinks Trevor and Shelley had organized for me. I roll over languidly to look at the clock. It is 9:17—long past the time my alarm would have gone off if I still had a job to go to. I breathe a sigh of relief. I've done it. The slate of my life is clean. I can now start fresh. I have no boyfriend and no job. . . . I am free! Free to . . .

Oh, God! I sit bolt upright. I have no boyfriend and no job! Why am I so impulsive? So irresponsible? I have no other prospects, no opportunities lined up, and no one to love me! But the panic attack is temporary. As I head to the shower, I somehow know it was the right thing to do.

I give myself two days to unwind. I get my hair cut. I meet Val for coffee. I actually go to a real yoga class (not at my mother's yoga studio as I haven't quite brought myself to tell her I'm unemployed as well as unengaged). Then, it is time to get serious about the next chapter of my life.

But first, I have to visit the Shooting Star offices to discuss Tiffany's relocation. I'm feeling a bit choked up as I sit with Theresa and Meg, the athletic-looking program director I'd seen speak at the aquarium.

"We're still in touch by e-mail," I say, biting my lip to keep from falling apart. "But I miss her."

"Well I think you made great progress with Tiffany," Theresa says kindly. "We e-mailed her an evaluation form, and she raved about the mentoring program—and especially about you."

"Really?" I say. Uh-oh. The tears began to spill over.

Meg pats my hand reassuringly and says, "Do you think you'd like to help another high- to medium-risk teen?"

"Well, I would . . . ," I reply hesitantly. "But it's probably not the best time to take on a new protégée. You see, I've recently undergone some major life changes."

"Really?"

"Yeah. I've just resigned from my job at Ferris and Shannon Advertising."

"Oh?" Theresa and Meg exchange quick looks of concern.

"My role as a mentor actually helped inspire me to move on," I continue. "I decided that I want to do something that contributes to society—that has a positive impact on someone's life. I just felt that advertising was so . . . soulless."

"Well . . . ," Meg says with the flicker of a smile. "I've got something you might be interested in."

I wait excitedly while Meg returns to her office to make a call. I can hardly allow myself to believe that she might have a job opportunity for me to pursue so soon. But you never know! Dr. Rainbow Hashwarma says that when you're making the right choices in your life, things will just click into place.

"Here." Meg returns and hands me a slip of paper. "I've got you an interview for tomorrow morning."

I look down at the small white note in my hand. It reads:

Sharon Talisman
Director, Corporate Sponsorship & Charitable Giving
Raincoast, Inc.
9:00 AM

"Thank you," I say excitedly, taking Meg's hand and pumping it up and down like a complete Jerry Lewis. "Thank you so much."

"KERRY?" MY CO-WORKER LESLIE POPS HER HEAD INTO MY OFFICE. "I'M heading down to Starbucks to get a coffee. Do you want anything?"

I swivel in my padded chair. "Thanks, Les, but I'm fine. I'm getting ready for the budget meeting at ten."

"Okay. I'll see you at lunch, then?"

"Sounds good!" I turn back to my computer, add a couple of items to the agenda I've been working on, and press PRINT. There: finished with twenty minutes to spare. As I have done often over the past two months, I take this opportunity to gaze at the stunning view of Puget Sound that my new office affords, and reflect on the transformation my life has undergone.

As you can likely deduce, I got the job. My new title is Manager, Corporate Sponsorship and Charitable Giving for Raincoast Shipping Incorporated. Although Sharon Talisman only vaguely recalled meeting me at the Christmas party with Nick, she hired me within the week. I've got a comfortable office, a comfortable salary, and more important, I actually *care* about what I'm doing. It's such a refreshing change!

With several minutes until the budget meeting, I check my e-mail for any personal missives. (I haven't changed completely!) Ah, there's one from Trevor. I open it with the eagerness of a child at Christmas. Trevor has kept me in the loop *and* in stitches over the continued antics at the advertising agency.

Name: Trevor Anderson
Subject: NewsFlash!!

Kerry!! Ohmigawd!!! So much has happened since we last e-mailed. Dave is leaving the agency! He's getting married to Shannon and moving to Hong Kong! Can you believe it? The poor girl—she seemed sweet but obviously not the brightest bulb on the Christmas tree. I mean, who would be dumb enough to marry someone with his track record? Anyway, the good news is, he's leaving! (Maybe you'd consider coming back now? LOL)

Gavin was just promoted to supervisor and he is sitting in your old office. Isn't that creepy? I think his infatuation with the bitch-devil from hell is starting to fade a bit. I took him for lunch and he went on and on about the recent lecture Sonja had given him on managing his timelines or budgets or something . . . I wasn't really listening. You know, Gavin's really filled out lately and is looking a lot cuter.

Anyway, Kerr-Bear, can we have dinner soon? Joseph's been working late all week and I'm just not sure if things are progressing the way I want them to. Love to talk to you about it over shrimp and pesto pizza at Veronique's.

Kisses,

Trevor

I e-mail back.

Trevor,

Thanks for the scoop. Glad to hear Dave is gone. And Gavin . . . well . . . he will always be an unattractive little wiener, no matter how much he "fills out," okay?

Would love to talk over pizza—just tell me when. You know I am just a Law & Order–loving spinster with no social life now.

Kisses back,

Kerry

And it's true. The schedule of my life has been increasingly dictated by whether *Law & Order CI, SVU,* or the original is on (I'm willing to skip *SVU,* can tape the original, but can't miss *Criminal Intent*—big crush on Vincent D'Onofrio). It's a pathetic existence for someone in the prime of life, but for now, I think it's wiser to spend my nights with Jack, Lenny and the cute black guy that is his latest partner.

With a small sigh, I gather my documents and head to the boardroom. Of course, I still have doubts about whether breaking up with Sam was the right thing to do, but I feel quite sure . . . fairly sure. And besides, my life isn't *just* work and TV dramas. Michelle and I are flying to Punta Cana in April to visit Sandra.

"Hi, everyone." I smile brightly as I enter the boardroom. It is still a joy not to worry about being sneered at, ignored, or insulted by my coworkers.

"Hi, Kerry," my boss, Sharon Talisman says. "As soon as Graham from accounting gets here, we'll get down to business."

Sharon is presenting the marketing budget for the year and the portion that is allocated toward corporate sponsorships and charitable donations. My role in the meeting is to present a list of potential recipients that represent Raincoast's commitment to supporting youth in the community. Of course, the Shooting Star program is on my list.

I make my presentation confidently, eager to be given the go-ahead to start allocating funds and working out sponsor partnerships. Sharon peruses the list, nodding in agreement. "This looks great, Kerry, but I'd like you to add another organization."

"Okay."

"It's a program called Art Smarts. It's run by this brilliant young exec named Dominic Marra. I think he's really going to take it places and we should get in on the ground floor."

"Art Smarts?" I say, more to myself than to the boardroom.

"That's right." Sharon pencils in the name at the bottom of her list. "I'll e-mail you Nick's number so you can discuss the program in more detail."

"Nick Marra from Art Smarts?" I mumble, my cheeks suddenly turning pink.

"Oh, do you know him from Shooting Star?"

"His name is really Dominic?"

"Yes."

"But . . . that starts with *D?*"

"Yes, it does," Sharon says with a bemused smile. "That's very good. Now . . . can you tell me what *Kerry* starts with?"

There are chuckles around the table.

"Sorry!" I say, realizing how odd I must sound. "It's just that I . . . umm . . . I assumed that Nick was short for Nicholas, which starts with *N* and not *D.*" Jeez, this is hardly helping! I clear my throat. "If you'll e-mail me Nick's number, I'd love to give him a call."

I would most definitely love to give him a call.

Mortifying Moment #10

I rehearsed every possible scenario before making the phone call.

Me: Yes, hello, Nick? It's Kerry Spence calling.

Nick: Who?

Me: Kerry Spence . . . I met you through the Shooting Star program, invited you to my mother's house shortly thereafter, where I proceeded to get engaged right in front of you?

Nick: Oh, right. Click (as he hangs up in disgust).

Or more likely . . .

Me: Hello, Nick? This is Kerry Sp—

Nick: Click (as he hangs up in disgust).

Perhaps it would be best not to identify myself right off the bat?

Me: Hello, Mr. Dominic Marra? I'm calling from Raincoast Incorporated's Charitable Giving program. My name is . . . Mary Pents. . . . *[I would mumble this so that when we met in person, I could be all like, "What? Mary Pents? I said Kerry Spence! You must have misheard me!"]* We're interested in making a significant donation to Art Smarts, and I'd like to meet with you to discuss.

Then hopefully, when we did meet in person, the promise of a monetary gift to his organization would be enough to keep him from running screaming at the sight of me.

Or . . . I could disguise myself. Wear a curly wig and glasses. I could continue to pass myself off as Mary Pents until Nick began to fall in love with me. I could envision it already.

"I love you, Mary," he'd say.

"Kerry," I'd correct him, whipping off the wig and glasses (hopefully not exposing flattened-down wig hair).

Of course he'd be shocked at first, but eventually he'd be thrilled. He would realize he was in love with the same, wonderful person but with much better hair and contact lenses! It sounded far-fetched to be sure, but a similar trick had worked in Yentl *hadn't it?*

Hopefully, I dialed the number.

"Hi. You've reached Nick Marra with the Art Smarts program. Please leave a message and I'll get back to you." Beep . . .

Damn! I'd rehearsed every scenario except the voice-mail one! But perhaps leaving a message would be easier? I cleared my throat. Unfortunately, I think it sounded rather phlegmy.

"Yes, hello, Nick?" I began formally. "I'm calling from Raincoast Incorporated's Charitable Giving program. Sharon Talisman suggested I call you to discuss the possibility of us contributing to your organization. If you could please call me back . . ." I recited my number. "My name is . . . uh . . . Mary," *I mumbled. "Umm . . .* Pents *. . . I mean . . . well . . ." I paused then, for what felt like a good twenty minutes. Finally, "It's actually Kerry Spence calling," I blurted. "I know the last time I saw you was . . . well . . . uncomfortable . . ."*

And then the words came tumbling forth. "Okay, I know it must have been downright horrible, but I'm working with Sharon now, and she asked me to call you and I was really happy to have another chance to talk to you because . . . well . . . you're such an amazing guy, and I really like you— I mean I know I barely know you, but what I do know of you I really like . . ." Stop! Stop talking! I willed my mouth but to no avail. "I mean, I'm sure I've totally blown it and you'd never want to see me again, but I wanted you to know that I'm not getting married. You probably don't even care, but the engagement was a huge mistake. I felt pressured . . . by my mom and, and society, and . . . I don't know . . . my biological clock, I guess." D'oh! Good one! Now there was absolutely no chance he'd ever want to see me again.

I sighed heavily. "Anyway . . . all that aside, Sharon and I really believe in your program and all you're doing for youth in the community. We'd like to give you our support so . . . I hope you can bring yourself to call me back . . . for the sake of the children."

And then, like an idiot, I hung up. Instead of trying to find a way to delete the ridiculously embarrassing recording, I dropped the receiver like it was scorching my hand. "For the sake of the children." My God!

It was quite possibly the worst voice message ever left for anyone . . . ever. In addition to being personally humiliating, it was also completely unprofessional. Nick could quite easily complain to Sharon Talisman about my conduct and probably have me fired. But something told me he wouldn't do that. And who knew? Maybe he'd appreciate my honesty? I'd been really open about my feelings and maybe he'd respect—even admire me for it? Maybe to someone as kind and true as Nick was, the message wouldn't seem weird at all? I needed a second opinion.

"You said, 'Call me back for the sake of the children?' " Trevor let out a high-pitched scream of a laugh. "That's hilarious!"

"It's not that funny," I retorted. "We're talking about a children's charity, so—"

"It is that funny!" Trevor squealed, his voice quaking with hysterical laughter. "F-for the sake of the ch-children! Classic!"

"I've got to go." I hung up and called Val.

"You mentioned your biological clock?"

"Just briefly."

"Sorry, hon, but that's like showing up for your first date with a catalog of china patterns."

"I've got to go." There was no need to ask Michelle's opinion. I already knew what it would be.

They were right. I had blown it with Nick—twice. There was no chance that he'd ever call me back. I just hoped that he'd get in touch with Sharon to sort out our contribution—you know . . . for the, uh . . . sake of the children.

Two weeks later, my office phone rang. "Hello? Kerry Spence speaking," I answered mundanely. It had taken thirteen days, but I had finally stopped affecting a cheerful, professional yet slightly sexy tone . . . just in case.

"Kerry? It's Meg Rosen calling."

"Meg!" I said, genuinely pleased to hear from her. I really liked Meg. She was a little too fit and active to be someone I hung out with on a regu-

lar basis, but she was a very nice lady and I owed her a lot. "How are you? How are things at Shooting Star?"

"Good. We're all good," she said hurriedly. "Look Kerry, I'm calling because I need a huge favor."

"What is it? I'll help if I can."

"We have a fund-raiser appreciation dinner tonight at the Chinook Club."

"Nice." The Chinook Club was a very exclusive and chic-chic venue.

"It should be, but we have a problem. One of our mentors was supposed to speak tonight about his experiences with Shooting Star, but he's been out of the country, and his flight home was delayed. I know it's short notice, but I was hoping you could fill in?"

"Well . . . sure. Umm . . . How long of a speech are we talking about?"

"Don't worry. It can be very brief and casual. It's an intimate gathering, not more than fifty or sixty guests. Most are private or corporate donors; some are representatives from government funding agencies. We'll open the floor up to questions and make it as interactive as possible. You'd really only need to prepare a three- or four-minute speech."

"I'll do it!" I said, happy to help out. "What time tonight?"

"Well . . . the dinner starts at six. We'd like you to speak at seven."

"But it's five thirty already!"

"I know. I'm sorry. And don't worry about what you're wearing. It's a black-tie affair but business attire is absolutely fine for a guest speaker. When I introduce you, I can explain that you came straight from the office."

"Okay. I'll be there as soon as I can."

It was not until I hung up the phone that I looked down at my business attire and screeched, "Damn it! It's casual Friday!"

"Are you okay?" My friend and coworker Leslie popped her head into my office with a bemused expression.

"Not really," I said. "I have to give a speech at the Chinook Club in just over an hour, and look at me!"

"Ohhh," she said, feeling my pain. "You have that big coffee stain on your jeans."

"What?" Sure enough, I did. "Shit! What am I going to do? I can't get up in front of a bunch of rich philanthropists and corporate bigwigs looking like this! Do you think I can make it home to Queen Anne and over to Mercer Island in an hour and a half?"

"No . . . but I have a great idea!" Leslie said gleefully.

"What? What?"

"I live two blocks from here! You can borrow something of mine!"

"Really? Oh, my God!" I jumped up and hugged her. "You are such a lifesaver!"

"It's no problem." Leslie laughed. "We're about the same size."

"You're thinner," I said, almost automatically.

Leslie suddenly gasped. "I've got the perfect dress! It's absolutely gorgeous and will look fabulous on you."

"Let's go!" I said excitedly, grabbing my briefcase.

Leslie's apartment was slightly smaller than mine, which I would previously have thought impossible. I sat in the living room on her overstuffed couch while she rummaged in her bedroom closet looking for the perfect dress. "I haven't even worn it!" she called. "I fell in love with it in the store and had to have it, but I haven't had an occasion to wear it."

"Are you sure you want to lend it to me?" I called back. "You know I sometimes spill things. . . ."

Leslie emerged, clutching a garment bag. "I'd be honored for you to wear it," she said sweetly. "It's for such a good cause, and you'll look beautiful in it."

"Thank you so much," I said sincerely, watching in anticipation as she gingerly removed the dress from its covering.

"Voila!" she said, holding the gown up by the hanger.

Oh, God!! Oh God!! Noooooooooooooooooo!!

"Isn't it gorgeous?" she asked eagerly.

"It's so . . ." My brain scrambled for the words. Eighties? Alexis Carrington? Soap opera-ish? Finally, I settled for, " . . . fancy."

"It'll be perfect for the Chinook Club!" Leslie said, caressing the fuchsia satin. "Oops. The sleeves got a little flattened down in the garment bag. I'll just fluff them up for you."

"Thanks," I said weakly. "Let's get them nice and puffy."

"And I have some dangly rhinestone earrings that will be perfect with it."

I made one last ditch effort to save myself. "I don't know, Les," I said. "You haven't even worn it and it's so, so beautiful—I wouldn't feel right. Maybe I could just borrow a black skirt or something?"

Leslie's eyes actually misted up when she looked at me. "I want you to wear it, Kerry. What's the point of having such a gorgeous dress if it's just going to hang in the back of my closet forever? Please wear it?"

"Of course I will," I said bravely. "Thank you so much."

I ARRIVED AT THE CHINOOK CLUB TEN MINUTES BEFORE SEVEN. THERESA MET me at the entrance, looking every bit as awkward in her royal blue gown as I felt in my Dynasty outfit.

"Kerry! I'm so glad you made it. You really saved us!"

"My pleasure," I said glumly, my rhinestone danglers slapping against my cheeks as I spoke.

"There's a podium set up at the front of the dining room where you'll be speaking. Meg's already inside. She'll introduce you in a few minutes then you can go right to the microphone. Also, for Tiffany's privacy, please don't use her real name when speaking—just refer to her as your protégée."

"No problem."

"I'm sure you'll be fantastic." She squeezed my hand. "And you look . . . great . . . really . . . fancy."

"Thanks."

Theresa escorted me to a side entrance where we waited, peeking through a crack in the door, for my cue to enter. I tried to get a glimpse of the other guests from this vantage point. It was difficult in the low lighting, but I was fairly sure that there was at least one diner in an outfit similar to mine. Of course, she appeared to be in her sixties with a platinum blond bouffant hairdo complete with tiara, but at least I wouldn't be the sole fashion faux pas tonight.

Meg strode to the microphone dressed in an annoyingly sophisticated, black crepe de chine sheath. *"Good evening, everyone, and thank you for coming."*

Okay . . . I inhaled deeply. What is really important is what I have to say, not how I look. No one will even notice my outfit as they will be so enthralled by my account of mentoring a high- to medium-risk teen. With all the money they're donating to the program, they'll be absolutely thrilled to hear about a really successful mentoring relationship.

"And now, I'd like to introduce one of our mentors to give you a first-hand account of the Shooting Star experience. It was so kind of her to agree to speak tonight on such incredibly short notice. We had a speaker cancel due to a plane delay, so I called Kerry at her office, less than two hours ago. She so kindly agreed to fill in and share with us her experiences with her protégée. So here she is, straight from the office . . . Kerry Spence."

There was a smattering of applause as I entered the room in a burst of puffy sleeves and fuchsia satin. Meg gaped at me momentarily in what looked like horror, but quickly composed herself, ushering me to the podium.

"Thanks, Meg," I said graciously, forcing myself to stare straight ahead so as not to be distracted by the pouf of sleeves in my peripheral vision. The lights directly overhead obscured the audience, and I was able to concentrate fully on the short speech I'd prepared.

"I'm honored to be able to talk to you tonight about Shooting Star," I began confidently. "I became involved with the program last year, and I can honestly say that the experience was life altering for me." I then proceeded to relay how much my relationship with Tiffany brought to my life, how it helped me put my own problems and issues into perspective, and how her bravery was such an inspiration to me. "Thank you so much for your commitment to supporting high- to medium-risk teens in our community," I concluded. "I'd be happy to answer any questions you might have."

Thankfully, the applause that followed was a bit more than a smattering, signifying that despite my dress, the speech was well received.

"I have a question!" a man in the audience called out. He stood up and through the bright lights I took in his graying hair, tall, fit frame and dignified deportment. "I enjoyed your speech Ms. Spence, and I'm very glad you found your mentoring experience so rewarding."

"Thank you." I smiled.

"But frankly, I'm more interested in how the mentoring relationship benefited your protégée than yourself. After all, we're providing funds to help youth, not full-grown women." There were a few chuckles from the crowd.

"Of—of course," I stammered, taken aback by his mildly confrontational tone. "My protégée spoke very highly of her experience in a recent survey. And I feel confident that the friendship and connection I feel toward her is reciprocated."

"But what about some tangibles," the man continued in a condescending tone. "Did she improve academically during your relationship?"

"Well, she's a bright girl, but she didn't really like school very much," I said honestly. "Although, she did enjoy reading The Outsiders in English class . . . except for the ending, which I have to agree is really sad and she thought really stupid. So . . . she didn't want to write a paper about it and . . . umm . . . as a result, I think she may have failed that class."

"Interesting," the pompous ass continued. "And what about disciplinary issues? Was there any improvement on that front?"

"Oh, yes!" I said quickly. "She didn't have any disciplinary issues until . . . until the very end, when . . . when . . ." I realized it was too late to stop mid sentence. My eyes searched frantically for Meg for support or an indication on how to handle this, but I couldn't find her anywhere. I'd probably embarrassed her so much she'd left.

"When—?" the pretentious dickhead prompted.

"When . . ." I cleared my throat. "When she was suspended for . . . drugs."

"Drugs?" a female voice in the audience gasped.

"Just pot," I said quickly.

"Just pot?" the snotty pants remarked, prompting a chorus of titters to arise. "Is that the attitude you took with an impressionable teenager toward illegal narcotics?"

"No!" I said defensively. "I just didn't want you thinking she was shooting up or something."

Now it seemed like every guest in attendance was gasping in horror and whispering to their neighbor about how they must pull their funding immediately! The situation was terrible, absolutely terrible. But I didn't know what to say to remedy it. I was afraid to open my mouth for fear of making things worse!

"I have a question," another male voice called out.

"Sure," I said weakly without looking in the direction of the speaker. "Fire away."

"I'm also involved with Shooting Star," the man continued. "And it's my understanding that the program isn't intended to turn troubled teenagers into high achievers with excellent grades and perfect behavior. Nor is it to judge or scold them for their actions. A lot of these kids have far bigger worries than English papers or grades or even suspensions. They're dealing with serious family issues, abuse issues, learning disabilities, bullying!"

That's when I squinted through the lights in my eyes to identify the speaker. He was tall, with broad shoulders and brown hair; on second thought, his hair was more sandyish. Yes, definitely on the sandy side! It was Nick! Despite being on display in a horrendous dress in front of an antagonistic crowd, a broad smile spread across my face.

"So would you agree, Ms. Spence," he continued forcefully, "that Shooting Star is more about helping these kids survive their teenage years, and keeping them physically, emotionally, and psychologically safe, than trying to turn them into . . . I don't know—?"

"Secretary of state or attorney general or whatever?" I finished hopefully.

"Exactly." He smiled at me.

"Yes, I would certainly agree with that," I said, shooting a look at the arrogant jerk who had returned to his seat. The crowd was silent for a long moment until someone began to clap. Before long, the others joined in, and I could feel my heart swell with the goodwill that had returned to the room.

"Thank you very much, everyone," I said when the applause had died down. I smiled brightly out into the crowd in the general direction of Nick. It was difficult to see him now that he had returned to his seat, but it was

almost as if I could sense his presence, could feel him out there smiling back at me. He really was an incredible guy—so kind, giving, and true. And the way he had so gallantly come to my rescue—well, that was just downright hot! I suddenly felt hopeful again. Maybe . . . just maybe he didn't think I was such a terrible person after all? Of course, it was entirely possible that he had merely been trying to protect Shooting Star's funding, but wasn't there also a chance that he had come to my aid because, despite everything . . . he kind of . . . liked me? Could he maybe, kind of see that I was also a kind, giving, and true person—or at least trying damned hard to be one? If there was the slimmest chance that this was the case, there was something I had to do. Because even if Nick could see the good person within me, he was probably wondering what the hell was going on with the one on the outside!

"I'd like to make one final, special thank-you if I may—"

I could see a few encouraging smiles in the crowd and heard someone say, "Of course."

"I'd like to thank my friend Leslie . . . for lending me—actually, I should say insisting *that I borrow this dress for tonight's event."*

There was an awkward silence. It was probably only a few seconds, but standing under the hot lights encased in fuchsia satin, it felt like ten minutes. And then I heard it—a booming, jovial laughter coming from the back of the room. It was Nick. He was laughing—and not in a "she's such an idiot" kind of way! Eventually, the rest of the crowd joined in, and the room was filled with sounds of their laughter. For once, I felt pretty confident that it was the "with me" kind.

Read on for a special treat—
a sneak peek at Robyn Harding's new novel

The Secret Desires
of a
Soccer Mom

Available Summer 2006
from Ballantine Books

Chapter 1

WE WERE LOADING COFFEE CUPS INTO THE DISHWASHER, WHEN MY FRIEND Karen made a startling confession.

"I have something to tell you," she said.

"Okay." I continued tipping the dregs of cold coffee into the sink and plunking the empty cups into the top tray. It was a Wednesday, the day the five of us got together for coffee and conversation. This week, it had been my turn to host. When the others left to pick up various children from pre-school, run errands, or go to the gym, Karen had volunteered to stay behind and help me clean up. Although . . . she wasn't really helping anymore. Now, she was just standing there, leaning against the blue tiles of my kitchen island, with a strange look on her face.

"Don't judge me, okay?"

"Okay." This time I stopped what I was doing and looked at my friend. Her cheeks were pink under her late summer tan and she seemed to be trying to maintain a somber expression while on the verge of hysterical giggles.

"Umm . . ." She cleared her throat. "I've been seeing someone."

I was silent for a few moments, choosing my words carefully. "Well, that's nothing to feel ashamed of. I've often thought I should get some therapy to deal with my parent's divorce. I know I was twenty-seven when they split up, but that doesn't mean that it didn't still hurt."

"I'm not seeing a shrink, Paige."

"Oh . . ." It took me a second. "Oh!"

"You promised not to judge me!"

"I won't. I'm not! It's just that . . ."

"What?"

"I'm just shocked, that's all. I thought that you and Doug were so happy."

"We were happy. But when I met—*this* person," Karen said, blushing again and forcing away the delighted smile that was threatening to curl her lips. "I realized that my relationship with Doug just wasn't enough for me. I know it sounds terrible."

"Well . . . ," I said.

"If you're going to look down on me for this, then I won't say any more." Karen moved to retrieve her coat off the back of a kitchen chair.

"No, don't go," I soothed, realizing that I had offended her. "Let's have some more cake and talk." I cut two enormous slabs of Sarah Lee apple-cinnamon coffee cake and led her to the breakfast nook. When we were seated at the pine kitchen table in the sunny alcove, I took a moment to study my friend. The sun streaming in through the bank of windows picked up the highlights in her chestnut hair and gave her complexion a golden glow. With her sparkling blue eyes and flush of delighted embarrassment, she looked almost impossibly girlish and pretty—far younger than her thirty-six years. Extramarital sex obviously agreed with her.

"Okay . . . ," I said gently. "Tell me how this happened." Of course, I was trying to be a supportive and nonjudgmental friend, but a small part of me was positively gleeful! This was the most exciting news I'd heard in years. Our Denver suburb was very quiet.

"Well . . . ," she began, daintily picking at the drizzled icing with her fork tines. "Like I said, Doug and I were happy. We have the big house, the nice cars, the time share in Playa del Carmen . . . I was content, complacent even. But sexually—"

I choked on my mouthful of cake. "I'm fine," I mumbled. "Go on."

"Sexually, I wasn't fulfilled. You know we've been trying to get pregnant for almost two years now, thanks to Doug's low-mobility sperm. That's really taken the fun out of it—the schedules, the ovulation predictor, the cold packs in Doug's shorts . . ."

I managed to refrain from choking again, but I was sure I'd never look at Karen's C.F.O. husband the same way again.

"Sex should be spontaneous! Passionate! Sex should make you feel like you are the most beautiful, sensual creature on the planet, like you could conquer the world."

I was nodding along here, but it had been a very long time since sex had made me feel anything but . . . *good.* If it had ever made me feel like a world conqueror, I couldn't remember it.

"And that's how I feel when I make love with Javier. It's mind-blowing! I've never had this kind of sex with Doug."

"Javier?"

"He's Spaaaanish!" She said this like she was saying "He's covered in chocolate."

"Where did you meet him?"

"At my art class. I know it's wrong, Paige, but I swear, he's completely irresistible!" Cue the pink cheeks and girlish giggles.

"Spanish *and* an artist," I said. "That does sound pretty irresistible."

"He's not an artist. He's the model."

"Oh! Wow!"

"Yeah, I know," she practically squealed. "He's also a barista—to make ends meet. He doesn't care about status and he doesn't want to get caught up in the rat race. It's a different culture, a different attitude."

"Well, I, personally, love coffee," I said gamely.

"He is just so beautiful, inside and out—and not in that plastic, Hollywood kind of way. His face has so much character. That's why he's so great to draw. And his body is unbelievable! And his eyes! Oh God, Paige, his eyes—they smoulder."

"Smoulder, eh?" I didn't know what else to say.

"Smoulder," she said, flopping back in her chair with a positively postcoital sigh.

I cleared my throat. "He sounds amazing, but . . ."

"And it's not just his looks. He really gets me, you know? Like, he can see who I am—the real me—deep down inside. There's a bit of a language barrier, of course, but it's almost like we transcend words."

"Umm . . . okay. But what does this mean for you and Doug?"

She sat forward and stabbed a forkful of cake. "I don't know. When this all started, I thought it would be a fling. It was just passion, just lust in the beginning. But now . . . we have so much more." She stuffed the cake into her mouth.

"Do you still love Doug?"

"Of course I do," she mumbled through her apple-cinnamon confection, "but isn't it possible to love someone, and yet not feel a real emotional connection to him?"

I thought about my own marriage for a second. Paul and I had celebrated our twelfth anniversary last month, but would I say we had a real emotional connection? We certainly did have one when we were first together, but over the last ten years, things had changed. His life revolved around his job in software sales and mine had been focused on our two kids. But I still loved him. He was my husband, the father of my children . . . "I suppose it's possible," I said.

"And now I just want to be with Javier all the time! Honestly, Paige, I can't get enough of him—physically, emotionally, spiritually. I don't know how much longer I can keep up this façade with Doug."

"But, Karen," I said solemnly, "you and Doug have a life together. You and Javier just have great sex."

"Ha!" A humorless laugh erupted from within her. "Doug and

I have *things* together, possessions. That's not a life, Paige. Javier taught me that. Seriously . . ." She looked at me intently. "I'm beginning to think there was a reason I couldn't get pregnant. If I had a baby with Doug, I'd be tied to him forever."

"True," I murmured. My own fruitful marriage suddenly felt like a life sentence in Sing Sing.

Karen suddenly looked at her watch. "I've got to go." She jumped up. "I've got a bikini wax at noon." I followed her down the hall and into the front foyer, a large open space with an Italian tiled floor and a high, coved ceiling. This "grand entryway," as the architect had called it, was a common feature in the area's newer homes. Undoubtedly, it was intended to give the impression of a Georgian Manor or something, but the piles of kids' shoes, sporting equipment, and school books tended to detract from its grandeur. I waited patiently while Karen slipped into her chocolate leather blazer, zipping up her matching stiletto boots.

"Thanks for coffee," she said, taking my hands in hers. "And thanks for listening. Really, I was bursting to talk to someone and you're the only person I felt safe telling my secret to."

I have to admit I was somewhat surprised by this. Not that I couldn't keep a secret. I could. I felt fairly confident that I would take this information to my grave—even though it was the juiciest thing to happen in Aberdeen Mists for about eight years. But although Karen and I were very close, I wouldn't really have considered us confidantes. In fact, I would have thought she'd had a more open and sharing kind of relationship with some of the other women in our clique. So why had she chosen me?

Karen was probably closest to Carly. She lived two houses away from me and six houses from Karen. She was a more recent member of our social circle, having moved to the neighborhood just two years earlier. Carly had arrived, a beaming newlywed, eager to start a family and immerse herself in suburban bliss. Shortly after relocating, her husband, Brian, left her for a middle-aged insurance adjuster with two young sons and an enormous pair of fake boobs.

Carly had been devastated. All she had ever wanted was to have a family. We had all rallied around our new neighbor in her time of crisis, and since then, she'd become an inextricable part of our social network. But I often wondered why she didn't move back to the city after Brian's cruel desertion. In Aberdeen Mists, she was literally surrounded by smiling familial units. It was like an alcoholic working in a bar, or a Jenny Craig devotee living above a bakery! If it were me, I'd have moved to Washington Park, or another trendy area full of restaurants and nightclubs and single men. I would have gone out dancing, done tequila shots, and made out with men much too young for me. But Carly stayed put, and thanks to time (and an ongoing prescription for Xanax), she began to heal.

Carly and Karen had a friendship unique to them: They were virtually the only women in the neighborhood who did not have children. This afforded them more free time to bond over drinks, to go out to movies, to go to the gym . . . Of course, Carly was busy with her home-based accounting practice, and Karen was busy having mind-blowing sex with a Spanish model/barista, but they still spent more time together than the rest of us.

I suppose it made sense that Karen had not confessed her affair to Carly. Given the adulterous demise of Carly's marriage, she may not have been as open-minded and understanding as I was. Carly was kind-hearted and generous to a fault, but Karen's admission may have hit a little too close to home. Carly always assured us that she was healing, moving on, and putting Brian—and what might have been—behind her. But I often thought her smile seemed stretched a bit too tight and her fawning over our children was a little forced.

Our friend Jane, on the other hand, would have been in no position to judge Karen's fling. Her marriage to Daniel, a fifty-eight-year-old oil company executive, was the product of just such an affair. Jane had been Daniel's secretary several years ago when they "accidentally" fell in love. She no longer worked for him, of course. Now, she devoted her time to their two young daughters—and to her looks. Jane definitely qualified as a yummy-mummy. Thanks to regular salon visits she had a lustrous mane of long, honey-colored hair;

frequent facials (and I suspected, a little Botox) had given her a glowing and youthful complexion; thrice-weekly Pilates classes had resulted in a body like Cameron Diaz; and a very talented plastic surgeon had provided her the perky breasts of an eighteen-year-old cheerleader. I had to admit, I really envied those boobs. They were just so . . . *perfect*. Mine were positively decimated by the breastfeeding. Not that I was particularly voluptuous before, but now they hung off my chest like two popped balloons.

As much as I coveted them, I knew I couldn't afford a boob job: It was evident that my ten-year-old daughter, Chloe, would be needing braces in a couple of years. I also harbored a deep-seeded fear that if I ever did have my breasts done, I would have a reaction to the anesthetic and die on the operating table. On the slim chance that I did survive the procedure, one of the implants would be sure to burst, leaking toxic chemicals into my bloodstream, eventually killing me. While I would have truly loved a pair like Jane's, I could already hear my post–breast implant eulogy:

Paige was a loving wife and mother. Unfortunately, she was also an incredibly vain woman, whose quest for larger breasts has left her young children motherless, and her husband, a widower.

Perfect breasts aside, Jane was a very compassionate woman and a good listener. And she could have provided much wiser counsel on the whole affair situation than a novice like me. On the other hand, Jane's cheating streak appeared to be in the past. She and Daniel were extremely committed to one another—weirdly so. Due to the adulterous beginnings of their relationship, they had serious trust issues which manifested themselves in multiple phone calls back and forth each day, numerous "date nights," extravagant gifts, and couples holidays, all in an effort to prove they were still in love with each other and not screwing any of the staff. No, when I thought about it, it was probably better that Karen had confided in me.

The other member of our Tuesday coffee clatch was Trudy. There was no way that Karen would have divulged her secret to her! Trudy was quite possibly the sweetest, kindest person I knew. She was also the most virtuous . . . really, almost . . . *pious.* She was the type of woman who, after dropping a grocery bag full of canned goods on her bare foot, would say, "sugar," or possibly "fudge"—but only if her toe was actually broken. Before she had children she had been a nursery school teacher.

Trudy's marriage was something she kept private. Her husband, Ken, was director of marketing for a telecommunications company. With his nonstop travel and frequent eighteen-hour work days, he made my husband, Paul, look like a slacker. But unlike me, her spouse's long hours and commitment to his job never seemed to bother her. I'd asked her about it once, and she'd responded with a cheery, "Well . . . sometimes it's hard, but I just thank my lucky stars that I've married a man who can provide for our family and allow me to stay home to be with the children. It's really a gift you know."

"Yes, it is," I had responded weakly. Only moments before, I'd intercepted my son, Spencer, writing the word "poo" on Jane's daughter's forehead with my lipstick.

So though we knew little about Trudy's marriage, it was likely as perfect as the rest of her perfect life. Probably a little bland, I would have to surmise, but solid. Trudy and Ken seemed like the "missionary-position-every-second-Friday" kind of couple. If Karen had confessed the sordid details of her extramarital sex romps to Trudy, she may have spontaneously combusted.

I guess it did make sense for Karen to open up to me. I smiled at my friend and gave her hands a squeeze. "You're secret is safe with me." Then I mimed locking my lips and throwing away the key. Corny, I know, but I couldn't help it. I spent a large majority of my time hanging out with a six-year-old boy.

THAT AFTERNOON, I DROVE TO PICK UP MY KIDS FROM SCHOOL WITH KAREN'S confession replaying in my head. I knew that what she was doing was wrong, and I pitied poor, clueless Doug. But I couldn't deny the fact that my friend seemed so full of life, of joy, of . . . *joi de vivre!* And her skin looked fantastic.

It was the sex, I knew it was. Karen was experiencing the passion and intensity of a new relationship, while I was experiencing the same old thing I'd been experiencing for the past fourteen years. Not that there was anything wrong with the way Paul and I *experienced* together. We both knew the routine to follow to ensure the desired results. It was nice . . . *good* even. But it wasn't exactly improving my complexion anymore.

I pulled the massive SUV into a parking spot bordering Rosedale Elementary's playing field, and turned off the ignition. The digital clock on the dashboard indicated that I was seven minutes early. Since it was only Spencer's second week of school, I didn't want to risk turning up late. I could practically hear him telling his future therapist how he had abandonment issues because his mother wasn't there to pick him up one afternoon during first grade. It was a beautiful September afternoon and the sun, filtered just enough by the yellowing oak leaves, warmed my face through the windshield. As I rested my head against the leather seat, my mind slipped back to Karen's admission.

It was a real dilemma. Despite her denials, Karen and Doug *did* have a life together. They'd been married for six years. They had a beautiful home. They were a part of the community. Doug was a good husband, offering her stability, security, and companionship—and that's not to mention the time share and the BMW. It wouldn't be easy to walk away from all that. Okay, maybe he was a little dull in the sack, but was that really his fault? Any man could crack under all that baby-making pressure.

And if she were to choose Javier, what kind of life would they have? They'd end up renting a dingy, one-bedroom apartment in East Colfax, scraping to get by on his barista wages and occasional modeling gigs. Karen would have to get a job. She'd left her event-planning career behind years ago; there was no way she could pick up where she left off now. She'd be forced to waitress at some late-night diner or a sleazy bar. They'd have to eat canned ravioli and ramen noodles for most meals. There would be no evenings out, no holidays, no meat that didn't come from a can . . . They would have nothing . . . nothing but each other and mind-blowing sex. I heaved a heavy sigh. It was a very tough choice.

Suddenly, the SUV lurched like it had been charged by a rhinoceros. I jumped in my seat, startled, until I heard the familiar giggling of my son and his friend Nigel, who had just propelled their slight bodies into the passenger door.

"Bye, poo hair!" Spencer called, opening the door to the back seat.

"Bye, snot eyes!" Nigel called back, as he was hurriedly corralled by his Filipino nanny.

"See you tomorrow, booger breath!"

"Okay, pee face!"

"Okay . . . ummm . . . diarrhea brain!" Spencer screamed out the window.

"Spencer, that's enough," I said gently, but firmly. I was glad he had a new school chum, but their entire friendship seemed to revolve around assigning rude adjectives to body parts. "Those words are not appropriate."

"What words?" he asked, climbing into his booster seat and buckling his seatbelt.

"You know which words—*bodily functions*, okay?"

"Okay.

"So, how was your day?"

"Good. Can we go now?"

"As soon as your sister gets here." At that moment, I spied my eldest child, standing in the school yard, ensconced in a gaggle of squealing and giggling girls. At ten years old, Chloe was at least four inches taller than her friends, and looked gawky, coltish, even spindly. She also had enormous front teeth that would be demanding orthodontia in a year or two, and an unflattering, center-part hairstyle, that worked with neither her fine hair nor her narrow face. Lately, when I looked at my daughter, the term "awkward stage" came to mind. "There she is," I said to Spencer. "She'll be here in a sec."

"I really need to go home," he responded, his blue eyes wide. "I'm starving and dying of thirst and I have to go pee sooooo bad."

"How bad?"

"Bad."

"Can you wait until we get home or do you want to go back in the school?"

"Umm . . . wait! . . . I think."

"Okay. She'll be here in a minute." But Chloe appeared to be in no hurry to join us, laughing, shrieking, and throwing pine cones at a group of nearby boys. To be fair, she didn't realize her brother was about to pee on the seats of our $40,000 SUV, but my patience was wearing thin. I tooted the horn briefly to catch her attention. Chloe's eyes darted nervously in our direction, but she angled her body away from us and continued her antics with her friends.

"I need to peeeeeeeeeeeeeeeee," Spencer moaned.

"Let's go back in the school." I undid my seatbelt.

"No. I want to pee at home in my home toilet."

"What's the difference? Just go to the bathroom here."

"It smells in there and sometimes the toilets flood and there's wet paper towels stuck on the ceiling."

"Fine. Cross your legs and I'll get you home as fast as I can." I leaned on the horn once, following up with three staccato bursts. This time, Chloe didn't even turn around.

"I think the pee's coming!" Spencer shrieked.

"Hang on!" I cried. Hopping out of the car, I called to my daughter. "Chloe! Come on! We have to go!" It was obvious that she was pretending not to hear me. Despite being only ten, Chloe liked to give the impression that she had no family, and lived alone in a small apartment, supporting herself as a cocktail waitress in the evenings.

From inside the car, I heard, "Oh no! Oh no!"

"CHLOE ATWELL! NOW!" I bellowed. It had the desired effect. Not only did Chloe turn, but I now had the attention of approximately two hundred Rosedale students. Suddenly, I heard a car door open, followed by a sound like running water. I turned to see my son, standing on the sidewalk, relieving himself on the chain-link fence. The entire schoolyard erupted into laughter and horrified squeals. Chloe's face registered her mortification. She stalked silently to the car.

When we got home, I called Paul.

"Hey, babe. What's up?" I could hear his fingers tapping away at the keyboard as he spoke.

"Chloe wants to change schools."

"Why?"

"Her brother peed in front of the entire student population."

"What?" Paul chuckled, and then called, "Hey, Mike! I'm gonna need the costings for the Wellington project ASAP. Conference call at five thirty! . . . Sorry, Paige."

"That's okay."

"So . . . yeah . . . ," he said, distractedly. "The kids had a good day?" (tap, tap, tap on keyboard)

"Not particularly," I muttered. God, was he even listening to me?

"Good . . . good . . ." (tap, tap, tap)

Obviously, he wasn't. I heaved a sigh of exasperation. "I thought I'd get pizza tonight. It might cheer Chloe up. Is that good for you?"

"Mike! Call Monayim in San Diego! He should have half of those numbers ready to go." Paul turned his attention back to me. "Sorry, hon, but I've gotta run. We're having some problems with the Wellington pilot install. The server was dead out of the box and the blah blah blah isn't interfacing with the blabbidy blah blah."

I'd never understood Paul's computer jargon. "Okay. So . . . pizza tonight? Or I could pick up chicken?"

"Don't count on me for dinner. I'm not sure if we can get the blah blah in time for the blabbidy blab blah . . ."

I hung up, feeling annoyed with my husband for his obvious distraction. Sometimes, it didn't feel fair. I'd forfeited a promising career in public relations to stay home and raise babies, while Paul continued to thrive out in the business world. It was my choice, I knew that. But at times, I really envied him his dynamic and exciting job—especially when I was stuck at home with a surly, adolescent girl and her exhibitionist little brother.

I decided a glass of red wine and a little quiet time was in order. With Chloe pouting and blaring Avril Lavigne in her room, and Spencer happily playing Bionicles on the family-room floor, I moved to the front of the house. Opening the French doors, I entered the formal living room. Intended to host reserved gatherings or sophisticated cocktail parties, this room sat largely unused. A thin layer of dust coated the antique furniture, handed down from Paul's maternal grandmother. I always felt slightly uneasy in here, like a stranger in my own formal living room. But on the other hand, it provided a wonderful escape from the rest of my frenzied household.

Taking a sip of syrah, I wandered to the front window. Through the sheer curtain, I could see that it was getting dark. My neighbors' lights shone like beacons: A lone kitchen light signified that a wife was busily preparing dinner for her husband; a darkened house with only the porch light on meant that a couple would be arriving home from work, sooner or later; a home ablaze with electricity meant a houseful, all going about the chaotic business of being a family.

Pulling back the sheer fabric, I peered into the street. At the end of the block, I could just see Karen and Doug's house. It was completely dark. Obviously, Doug was still at work, and Karen was probably off having multiple orgasms with Javier. Suddenly, I was overcome by an intense feeling of loneliness. Dropping the curtain, I moved to the center of the room, where I flicked on the standing lamp, then perched awkwardly on Grandmother Maple's chintz sofa. I took a deep breath and tried to quell the malaise taking over me. It was strange: This feeling of emptiness seemed completely unprovoked. Paul worked late often; I was used to spending evenings alone with the children. What was so different about tonight?

After another sip of wine I was back at the window. Karen's house was still dark, but as I stared, I thought I sensed movement inside. Maybe she and Javier were in there right now? Would she be so brazen? Could they be doing it, at this very moment, in a myriad of exciting positions, in Karen and Doug's own bedroom? Or the living room? Or kitchen? Maybe that added to the excitement—the fact that Doug could walk in at any moment. If I kept watching, I might see Doug's BMW pull up out front and Javier would scurry out the back window half naked. Or completely naked! I stared at the darkened house for another few minutes, before realizing that my imagination had run away with me.

"Enough," I said to the empty, austere room, shaking off my melancholy mood. I had absolutely no reason to feel down. I had a good life! I was happy! It was only natural to pine, just a little, for those early days of passion, romance, and multiple sex positions. After twelve years of marriage, it was perfectly normal to fantasize, occasionally, about raking your fingernails down some muscular stud's back, or riding him like a young thoroughbred. But those days were over for me, replaced by comfort, security, a house in the suburbs, and an SUV. It wasn't like I was *jealous* of Karen's affair. God no! And I certainly wasn't *obsessed* with her love life. I mean, of course I was interested: I was her sole confessional, after all. But I hadn't turned into some voyeuristic sex maniac, peeking out the window at my friend's love nest. I was curious, that's all. Besides, I had many other things to occupy my mind. Like my children, who needed me to order pizza for them. I walked back to the kitchen to call Domino's.

PHOTO: © GARRY SARRE

ROBYN HARDING was born in Vancouver, British Columbia. In her indecisive youth she studied English literature, journalism, and marketing before embarking on a seven-year career in the advertising industry. She is married and has two young children. *The Journal of Mortifying Moments* is her first novel.